This book ~~~~ to

Roy Harris

RAF Sgt and Retired Police Officer

1930—2010

my loving husband for 45 years

For Tracey

Best Wishes

Tabbie

TABBIE BROWNE   ABOUT THE AUTHOR

Tabbie Browne seems to have been writing all her life in one way or another. She didn't have the fear of compositions, later known as essays, at school and would err on the side of writing too much rather than too little.

Although she likes to communicate with people, she has learnt that it sometimes better to sit back and observe the way they act.

She also believes in listening to your vibrations, if you don't get a good feeling when you are with someone, there is probably a good reason for it.

So she follows her instincts much more now, being older and wiser and having found out the hard way that looking for the good in everyone doesn't always pay off.

ISBN: 978-1-84944-155-1

British Library Cataloguing in Publication Data.
A catalogue record for this book is available from the British Library.

Published by UKUnpublished.

UKUnpublished
.CO.UK

www.ukunpublished.co.uk
info@ukunpublished.co.uk

THE UNFORGIVABLE ERROR

By

TABBIE BROWNE

PART ONE - SHANE

CHAPTER 1

"For goodness sake child, will you stop that infernal scratching." This was not a request, but a demand nurtured by days of watching Shane constantly scouring his arm.

Jane grabbed her son, a bit rougher than she intended, and dragged him over to the window. The nine year old protested at first, but reasoned that if his mother could actually see something, she may realise that this awful irritation may not be 'all in the mind' as she had suggested. Holding his left hand firmly, she pushed up the sleeve of his shirt.

"There! What did I tell you? There is no rash. There are no spots. Nothing."

"But Mum, it's driving me mad, and it's getting worse." The lad, although he liked to appear a tough guy to his friends, stood there almost in tears from the frustration of this unseen affliction.

Faced with this unexpected reaction, Jane softened and drew him near to her.

"OK. Tell you what. Why don't we pop along and let Dr. Mann have a look, just to be on the safe side?"

Shane sniffed and nodded, a little relieved that he was being listened to at last. As he pulled down his sleeve he thought, "Doctor's not that bad, and anything would be better than this."

Tony Bryant turned off the Chipping Norton road and drove the mile downhill to Ascott under Wychwood. The tiny hamlet nestled almost hidden in the valley and saw little passing traffic. To leave the village in the opposite direction meant climbing another mile up to meet the Charlbury road. The only other exit was to leave the village by the country lane leading to Shipton, a pretty little route skirted by farmer's fields, and hedgerows full of wild flowers.

Although he had lived here all his life, Tony still admired the beauty of this area. Crossing the little stone bridge over the River Evenlode, he always remembered the many times he and Jane had stood there during their courting days. Feeling rather weary, he was relieved to be turning into the drive at the side of the cottage.

His wife met him at the door. "Don't put the car away, I want to take Shane to the doctor."

"Why, what's the trouble?" Tony collected his briefcase from the front seat and handed her the keys.

"Oh, probably nothing, but that itching won't seem to go away, so I'm just having him checked out to be on the safe side." As her husband kissed her lightly, she said "Your dinner's all ready, help yourself, won't be long, I want to get there in good time, be first in the queue."

Shane joined her and with a quick, "Hello Dad, Bye Dad", they were gone.

Dr.Mann did not run an appointment system as he didn't consider it necessary. Everything ran pretty well, thanks to his efficient secretary and the two part time receptionists. There had never been a problem, so why spoil a good thing for the sake of keeping up with what every one else was doing.

There was only one patient in front of Shane, who told them, whether they wanted to know or not, that he wouldn't be long as he only wanted another sick note. He was about to go into graphic detail about his boils when, thankfully he was called into the surgery.

"I'm glad I haven't got boils," sniggered the lad.

"Shh" Jane felt she should not encourage him, but had to smile in agreement.

The first patient re-appeared in the waiting room. "There! Told you I wouldn't be long. He's good he is." This man could hold a conversation with himself, which saved anyone else having to contribute. Before he had reached the door he imparted "Hey, he's got one of them trainee blokes with 'im."

The receptionist indicated for Jane and her son to go in.

"Hello. Do sit down." Dr.Mann was of the old school, and it showed. Before Jane could speak he continued "This is Dr. Martin, he's doing some research work locally and is joining me for a few days. Do you have any objection to his presence?"

"No, that's fine," Jane cast a quick glance at the boy who seemed more interested in a glass paperweight on the desk. "It's nothing really, but I thought I should bring him."

"Ah" the doctor looked at his notes, "Shane, isn't it?"

Surprised at suddenly being addressed personally, he replied, "Yes, sir."

"And suppose you tell me what's bothering you young man."

Jane opened her mouth to speak, but Dr.Mann smiled and said, "In a moment, let's see what he has to say first." From some people, a mother's back would have risen, but this man had such a way with him, you had to conform.

The doctor raised his eyebrows slightly, indicating Shane to begin.

"Well, it's just - um - I keep scratching, and it won't stop, the itching I mean, but we can't see anything, can we Mum?"

Jane shook her head.

"Well, let's have a little look." The doctor hesitated slightly; aware it could be a touch embarrassing depending on where the site was located, but he had noticed the boy worrying his left arm while they had been talking, and knew that would be a start.

With the arm now exposed, both men took it in turns to examine the surface. The older man turned to his colleague.

"Well?"

Dr.Martin said softly "Do you mind if I have a really close look Shane?"

"No. But you can't see anything can you?"

The young man smiled. "Well something's causing it isn't it? And we must find out what it is. Can't have you going around scraping your skin off." His levity made the youngster laugh and he and his mother happily followed Dr Martin into another room, unaware of the glance exchanged by the two medical men.

"Just pop onto the couch will you Shane? That's excellent." He carefully manoeuvred a chair for Jane to sit on, which he knew would shield her view whilst he was examining the boy.

Opening his bag he took out an instrument, and pulled the overhead angle light into position.

"What's that? I've never seen one of those. What does it do?"

"Now. Which question do you want me to answer first?"

The boy smiled. He liked this doctor. "Doesn't matter."

"All right. What is it? Well, the name is so long, you couldn't spell it and I can hardly say it, so shall we pass on that one?"

Shane nodded, grinning broadly.

"What does it do? Ah, well it helps me to see what is going on inside your body. Now, as the bottom piece of glass presses down on your arm, I look

through this magnifying glass above it, and look under the surface of your skin." As he spoke he drew the light nearer. "And it doesn't even hurt does it?"
"No. It's cool."

Dr.Martin switched off the light and turned to Jane. "He says it's cool." She smiled "One of these modern sayings. Did you find anything Doctor?"
"I just want a word with Dr.Mann while Shane gets dressed. Take your time."

As he left the room, the boy said, "He doesn't know does he Mum, he's got to ask Dr.Mann. That other man said he was a trainee."
Jane felt she should reassure him, so replied, "Well, we've all got to learn sometime, and I expect they let him just look at the simple things, so that must mean you haven't got anything serious doesn't it." Her rambling was more to boost her own spirits, and had she overheard the conversation in the surgery, she would not have felt so relaxed.

Dr.Paul Martin, far from being a trainee, was studying a lethal outbreak of an unknown disease which was attacking people at random, from all walks of life. Up to now, research had found no common factor which could have provided the scientists with a preventative medicine or vaccine. Due to the severity of the virus, a handful of doctors from one of the Oxford Universities were visiting local G.P.s to make them aware of the deadly condition, so that it could not be overlooked, or fobbed off as imagination.

It was also being kept fairly secret, for there were always the hypochondriacs who must have anything going and could fill the surgeries with fake symptoms, possibly overshadowing the few genuine cases.

Of the fifty or so patients diagnosed to date, all but five had died, and most of them within fourteen days of the first signs, which was why it was imperative to recognise them as early as possible. Unfortunately, most had ignored, or put up with the initial stages and only consulted the doctor when it was too late. Some busy folk hadn't even sought medical advice, pushed the problem to one side and appeared to have died suddenly.

"Well?" Dr Mann knew he didn't have to ask the question, for the younger man's face held the answer. "Oh No. Isn't there any hope for him?"
Dr.Martin barely whispered "None that I can see." He sat down as Jane and her son joined them.

Out of courtesy Paul let his superior start the conversation.
"Now then Shane, Mrs. Bryant, Dr.Martin here is very interested in your arm. He would like to do some tests if that's all right, Doctor, would you like to explain."

"Yes thank you." Knowing what he had to say would be a shock, he decided to break the news gently a little at a time. If he could get the child to the special unit set aside for these cases, more facts could be fed to the parents then.

"We'd like Shane to go to one of our hospitals, tonight."

"What?" Jane felt something kick her in the pit of her stomach. "But I thought you said it was nothing to worry about."

He tilted his head to one side. "No, I didn't actually."

Jane studied his face. "No" she almost whispered, "you didn't."

"Is your husband at home? I'd think he ought to come too."

"Yes, but, Oh Doctor, what's the matter?" What had started out, as a simple quick check appeared to be turning into a nightmare.

"I think Shane has a nasty irritation that could be caused by a virus. That's what's been annoying him recently, the last week you said Shane?"

"Yes it started Saturday when I was playing football with my mate."

Being Tuesday, he was already on the fourth day. The prospect was not good.

Dr.Martin looked at Jane. "We need to have a good look, and we can't do it here." He chose his words very carefully, especially not saying the usual "if we are going to be able to help him" kind of jargon which he knew would raise false hopes only to be dashed shortly putting the parents on an emotional roller coaster. They were going to have to cope with enough heartache, without him making it worse.

CHAPTER 2

Tony finished his dinner, and knowing he wouldn't have to go out again reached for the bottle of whisky. He made his drink, put it on the side table and settled back into the armchair. As he switched on the television the phone rang.

"Oh no. Who's that?" He had planned on a quiet night, away from telephones, stupid individuals asking stupid questions, just him and his family. Was it too much to ask?

"Tony," Jane's voice sounded strange. "I'm at the doctor's, they want Shane to go to hospital, now, straight away."

"What?" Tony eyed the whisky and soda, glad that he hadn't yet touched it. He was suddenly very much alert and asked for all the details.

"Right. You stay put. I don't want you driving back to fetch me, I'll get Jack next door to nip me up, then I'll drive to Oxford."

"Oh Tony, what do you think it is?"

"We'll know more when they've had a chance to look at him properly. What's happening now?"

"Well Dr.Martin is phoning to arrange it, so that they expect us, but he says he wants us there as soon as possible."

Tony wanted to be sure of all the facts. "And we can take him?"

"Yes, but Dr. Martin is following in his car, so that he's there with us."

"O.K. sweetheart, try not to worry. See you in ten minutes."

Like his wife, Tony felt a strange intuitive feeling of dread in his middle region. Something must be terribly wrong. No one sent a child to hospital at that time in the evening, and to a special one at that. Why not to the usual one?

These and many more questions burned in his brain as he sat beside Jack on the way to meet his wife. But he must not show any concern in front of his one and only son. He must be brave. Thanking his neighbour for his kindness, he made his way into the waiting room. Immediately he took stock of the situation. Shane was flicking through some boys' comics appearing quite unconcerned, whilst the pain was there on his wife's face.

He sat beside her and held her hand tightly. Almost immediately Dr. Martin joined them and they exchanged brief introductions.

"Please follow me," the doctor instructed. It was obvious he was very keen to get away without further delay. "When we get to the hospital, stay close behind me, I will clear it for you to enter."

The parents looked a little apprehensive at this, so he quickly covered himself by saying "Security you know, we have to be very careful these days."

"Oh, yes of course." They seemed satisfied.

The journey seemed to take forever. Both parents attempted small talk, but Shane seemed unperturbed by the whole business. If anything, he was relieved that somebody realised he had got a very bad itch.

He scratched his arm again, but this time it hurt. Instinctively, he stifled a cry, knowing his mother would only start fussing about it and decided to tell the nice doctor when they arrived. After all, that's what they were going for.

"He's turning into those gates." Jane pointed to the car in front.

"Yes, I see him." Tony was concentrating on the leading driver, but couldn't help noticing the looks being cast by the security guard.

"You'd think it was a prison." Jane whispered. "I thought he said it was a hospital."

"Some research at the University," Tony tried to make it sound better without much conviction.

They were beckoned forward, and followed the doctor's car through the grounds until they reached the rear of the building. They all parked near a door, more like a tradesman's entrance than the expected foyer.

"There's a camera, and another one." Shane sounded as though he was enjoying this.

"What a strange set up, "Jane whispered, "I don't like it much."

"Shh. I'm sure he knows what he's doing." Tony watched as Dr.Martin got out, locked his car and approached them.

"If you could just hang on here a second."

As he made his way to the innocent looking door, it opened and a person appeared dressed in a white overall, white boots, cap and gloves. A mask covered the face so that no skin area was exposed. There was a short exchange between the two and Paul returned to the car.

"Could I just have Shane for now, they can get him ready and we can follow?"

"But I want to be with him all the time." As Jane tried to get out of the car she noticed about six other white clad persons had surrounded their vehicle.

"What's going on?" Tony was also getting agitated.

Paul gave a signal to the awaiting escort who stood back, then indicated for the family to join him. "Of course, I'm sorry, it's not a problem."
Immediately Shane was clear of the car, a trolley appeared and he was placed on it with a clear tent covering his whole body.

"What are you doing?" Jane didn't like the way events were taking their course, and almost wished she had never agreed to bring her son here.

Paul's soft voice calmed her a little as he explained. "It's quite a way, let the lad have a ride, he's enjoying it, look."
Tony cut in " But why the - whatever it is, that plastic thing?"

"Oh don't worry about that, it's probably the only one they had available." He extended his arm, "If you've locked your car, shall we follow?"

The time it took for Tony to check the doors was all it needed for the party to disappear with their new patient. As the door shut behind them, Jane became hysterical, running forward hammering on it shouting to be let in. Dr.Martin held up his hand. "Don't worry. It's an automatic closing device. One of them must have forgotten to hold it open for us. We can get in."

The door was locked long enough for Shane to be cleared from view, then a security guard re-opened it, apologising, but all very carefully planned. Not knowing the layout, the two parents had no option but to follow the young doctor trusting they would shortly be re-united with their son.

"Where are they now?" Professor Solomons peered over his half spectacles at Paul who was donning a surgical looking garb and scrubbing his hands.
"In Room X41."
"Good. And you haven't touched them?"
"No, I examined the lad at the local G.P.'s, with the special gloves, but that's it."
"Hmm. Can't be too careful, until we know."

The professor, similarly clad accompanied Paul to Room X41. This was kept for people, usually families who had been in close contact with infected patients, and was decontaminated after each use.

They entered a side room which kept them apart from the occupants, but with a panel by which they could communicate. Jane immediately threw herself at the window screaming at them to let her see her son, Whilst Tony, although very upset, tried to restrain her hoping they would soon learn what this was all about.

Dr.Martin eventually calmed them enough, with promises of a full explanation.

"We believe your son has something very serious. Although we don't think it is contagious, we have to take all precautions possible, until we know more."

Tony was grim faced. "Is that why we are here?"

The professor nodded.

"And where is Shane?" Jane was feeling weak and dizzy from the shock.

"He is being well looked after in a private room, so that we can do the necessary tests, to see if he has the virus." Dr. Martin gave time for this to sink in, knowing there was much the parents would want to know. Then he continued "At the moment, he has all the signs and I have to warn you, if the tests prove positive---" his voice trailed hoping they would form their own conclusion.

It was Tony who spoke. "You don't mean, not fatal." The two medical men looked at each other that said it all.

"NO." As the cry left Jane's lips she collapsed into a huddle crying into her hands.

It was the usual sorry scene as the men left the side room, giving the parents time to come to terms with the inevitable. Even after the previous patients, the job didn't become any easier.

"This is the youngest yet Paul."

"Yes I know. Seems so unfair. He hasn't had his life yet."

"Well, can't put it off, we'd better go and see what they've found already." And both men made their way along the basement to the secure intensive study area.

CHAPTER 3

Although still not admitted, those powers in the know are aware of several alien life forms inhabiting the earth at this present time. Whilst some prefer to push the facts away, filed under ' Unexplained', others have proof which, for years they have been forced to keep secret. As the facts are slowly leaking out across the globe, people make up their own minds, but who can challenge someone so fiercely adamant of their own experiences.

One species having been co-habiting for the last 50-60 years originated from this very planet many centuries ago, even before the ancient Egyptians. They were extremely advanced and conquered space travel, leaving what they thought was an extinct area, in search of better things.

They returned at different historical periods, leaving their knowledge to advance the races, earthly man often taking the credit for inventions or discoveries.

Being well versed in the after life they tried to teach the truth of everlasting existence to the masses. Unfortunately there were those who misinterpreted the facts and believed that the mortal body carried the soul on, hence the elaborate burials with riches for the journey.

On one of the return visits, the earth angels were accompanied by another species whom it was thought could also contribute their knowledge and advancement. Unfortunately these demons wrought havoc across the world, and instead of the good work already done, they delighted in spreading evil. From that time, the two forces continued to oppose one another, either using the good or bad contacts already in existence, or setting up their own forces to outwit the other.

"I cannot believe you did that." An earth angel screamed at one of the demon leaders. She had just learned of the virus planted in the living beings, the virus which now threatened to cut short the earthly passage of young Shane. The demon, also not inhabiting a physical body at present was self-satisfied.

"What's the difference? I shall take great pleasure in seeing this one over."

"You will leave him for us to take through his passing. You will not intervene."

Angel Ana knew the fate if the others got to the child. He would not rest for the necessary time, or be allowed to return to earth in peaceful surroundings. Instead he would suffer mental torture, searching for his loved ones, and witnessing all the suffering and distress the world endured.

"Oh I will treat him as my own, he will get my undivided attention" was the reply Demon Raz threw back as she left.

"My arm is really hurting now." Shane looked up at the nearest person. He thought it was a doctor; it was hard to tell with the mask and everything. A kindly voice answered.

"I know Shane. You're being very brave. Try to relax. We've given you an injection."

"Where's my Mum and Dad? I want to see them."

"Soon. We are just trying to find out what's hurting you." The doctor knew the reason only too well. All the reactions were identical to the previous cases, the itching, and the painful area, which was now beginning to erupt in red whorls.

They had hidden the arm from view so as not to distress the lad by the sight of it. It wasn't going to be pleasant. The other five patients were in the same secure area, in various stages of the disease. The most advanced, a gentleman in his late 70's was not expected to last the night. Paul thought of him and realised what this poor little chap in front of him would have to endure. All his training took a back seat as he wished he could put the boy out of his misery now and not let him suffer the terrible fate. If he were an animal - but he wasn't. But this was inhuman, both to the boy and to the parents. They would be shielded from some of it, but they would know he must be suffering.

He spoke softly. "Shane, its Dr. Martin. We are going to look after you while you are poorly." The soothing voice calmed the boy until he was feeling quite drowsy.

The doctor left, stripped in the anteroom and sealed his clothes in a bag for immediate incineration. Putting on a fresh lot he made his way to Room X41 and the awaiting parents.

The specially designed X rooms were fully self contained with en suite bathroom, sleeping area and a small kitchen where the occupants could make fresh drinks. Food was supplied through a small two-door hatch, but most of the previous relatives had little or no appetite.

The virus still appeared to be non-contagious, but in view of its severe toll, the researchers were taking no chances with possible carriers, thus the apparent extreme measures.

As news of the condition was still closely guarded, no personal phone calls were allowed by residents, however, one of the staff had already confirmed that the Bryants had no more family at home, and there were no pets in need of attention. It was regarded as totally unnecessary to inform neighbours or other family members of the child's exact whereabouts, sufficient to know that he was in hospital. The fact that people would worry seemed insignificant compared with the true facts.

Although the parents had only been in the building a couple of hours, Jane was showing all the effects of a mother's distress, and Tony, although trying to be strong for her, was also looking drawn and pale.

"What's the news Doctor?" The father was first at the communication window.

"I want to be with him." Jane sobbed without rising from her chair.

Dr.Martin gave a faint sympathetic smile. "Let me explain, as kindly as possible". He indicated for Tony to sit beside his wife before he continued.

"At this stage, we can take you to see him, but you will have to just look at him through a window, we can't let you get near, do you understand?"

"NO." Jane was on her feet now with her face as close to the screen as she could manage. "Tell me, is he receiving medical attention? Are there doctors and nurses with him?"

"Of course, he won't be left alone."

"Well then, "Jan spoke quietly but very determined now."What about their risk. If they can take it so can I."

Tony joined her slipping his arm around her. "What she is saying Doctor is that we would rather run the risk of infection, and be able to touch him, be with him, than stare at him like an exhibit."

Paul smiled at them both. "Everyone has the same reaction, but we have to warn you, not only for your safety but that of others."

Tony looked from Jane to the doctor. "Meaning?"

"If we let you do as you ask, and it is possible, it does mean you are then in high risk, and........." he paused to make sure they understood fully, "we can't guarantee when you would be released, - afterwards - if you understand what I am saying."

Tony's voice shook, "You mean, when he has died........." his voice trailed off as the realisation of the truth hit him, and he hugged his wife as the tears ran.

Paul gave them a moment to compose themselves then said, "Somebody will be down shortly with some things we'd like you to wear. Put everything on if you would."

The parents nodded, encouraged by the prospect of being reunited with Shane after what seemed an eternity.

The doctor left, knowing these people had enough to come to terms with for the time being, but aware that it wouldn't be long before they would be barred from watching the final moments of this terrible thing. Then, they would have to pull on all the strength they could, for they were going to need it.

Raz was hovering, like a vulture waiting to pounce on her next victim. She had been involved with a few of the previous casualties, but this was going to be hers. As with creatures in the wild, if one demon captured a supply of nourishment, it wasn't long before the message went out, and there were flocks of others eager to snatch the spoils. She had done it herself, quite successfully in fact, so she was wise to all the tricks. Also there were the angels who were determined to thwart this growing malice, and who were becoming as cunning and devious as the demon race.

Ana appeared over Shane's bed and gently stroked his face, but was immediately attacked by Raz who flew at her to remove her from the boy's soul. She must protect that at all costs until his passing, for if Ana, or one of the others of her kind took possession of it, she could loose forever, that which she had so carefully planned.

"Leave him," she screamed. "He is not yours."

The tussle, which ensued, was unobserved by the medics, and even the patient himself, but was none the less extremely severe and disrupted the spiritual atmosphere like ripples on a pool. The two enemies rose up and away from the area, only parting when Ana was sure the evil power was far enough away to leave the child in peace.

As they departed, the parents entered the room accompanied by a doctor. Tony froze as he saw the sight before him, but Jane rushed to the bed and clasped her son's right hand, vainly attempting to kiss it through her mask. Shane lay semi drugged but with a pained expression on his little face, his left arm hidden from view by a small screen with an aperture just large enough to take the limb.

"Mum, Dad, is that you?" The voice was so weak and the speech barely audible.

"Sh, yes we're both here darling."

His mouth moved so Jane bent closer to hear him whisper, "I love you both." Tony joined her and stroked his son's good arm. "Be brave little soldier" was all he could utter before his voice broke.

Professor Solomons put his hand on their shoulders and said gently "We'll perhaps let him have a little rest now, he's had something to make him more comfortable." It was obviously a request to leave but there was a tone of command about it, and there was much these two brave people had to be prepared for judging by the speed this case was taking.

The truth was, that the professor had seen the development of the arm behind the screen, and knew he had to get the family out as quickly as possible, but knowing full well that this would most likely be the last contact they would ever have with their son to the point of never seeing him again.

Organising an escort to take them back to their quarters, the man returned to the room and the unpleasant task in hand.

Before Ana's arrival, Raz had secured enough time to agitate the virus, thus quickening the process to bring home her prey. The arm that in the earlier part of the evening had simply itched, was now covered in pulsating lumps until the limb was almost twice its normal size, the skin threatening to burst open.

The screen was removed, as the lad appeared too drugged to be aware of the horrible eruption, which was now spreading across his chest and down his body. Within minutes it had encompassed the whole surface area, pulsating like a foreign life form taking over everything in its path.

"This is rapid." One of the medics said in a hushed tone. "They've never been this speedy."

"Do you think his age has anything to do with it?" another asked.

All shook their heads, baffled by this deadly virus which appeared unstoppable.

The scream that came from Shane's lips almost froze them to the spot. Raz had returned. She was trying to wrench the soul away before death had released it, but it was still too firmly rooted and not ready to depart. Also, she was fighting the laws of eternal existence by planting the virus, thus terminating physical life before the given time, which meant that the soul of Shane Bryant was not ready to move on, and should not have been for many more earth years.

CHAPTER 4

As with the different signs in astrology, earth angels, demons and other non-physical forms are centred around their own particular area, namely earth, air, wind, fire, gases, water and ice. Some are concentrated within the earth itself, and some only cover the space areas.

Many spirits in human form on this planet, or in another life form elsewhere in the universe, often give little thought to their sign, whilst others live by them, letting them govern their decisions and way of life.

Nature's animals exist on the same piece of rotating rock in space, happily living alongside one other by sharing the various elements and times of feeding. Likewise the unseen forces have their own territory and time for occupying it. Although it is unusual for a force from one category to be in conflict with one from a different state, in cases of violent unrest it can happen with disastrous results.

Spirits from one state, e.g. water are responsible for overseeing the passing of souls from that source, so if someone drowned they would be carried over by a water spirit, whereas one perishing in a blaze would be carried over by a fire spirit regardless of the sign of the person in transit.

Both Ana and Raz were of the air sector which is how they became connected in opposing situations. Their times of occupation were more or less identical which meant that if Ana was not due to be in presence, nor should Raz. But there were ways round it, as both knew and were prepared to use.

To cover production in a factory, the shift system is used, but if one person was away on their particular tour of duty, somebody else could come in and operate that machine. The same applies to spiritual presence. If there is a gap it can be filled provided it has been confirmed that the using spirit is occupied elsewhere. If an opportunist fills a place without checking the vacancy, they will be ousted immediately on the return of the rightful inhabitant.

But a desperate force will slot into any available space it finds, regardless of protocol, and run the risk of being taken to task by the hierarchy.

It was time for Ana, Raz and all like forces to exit their allotted air space time, and a new wave to enter. But, as with a new shift reporting for duty, details were passed on to the incoming spirits for them to continue the vigilance of tasks in hand. This was essential for all types whatever the governing sign, for all could be sure that the slightest negligence on one part could open the gateway for the ever waiting opposition.

Ana quickly passed Shane's progress on to Kyn as he took her space, but simultaneously Raz was passing the same to her replacement, Fica, a sadistic little madam who would stop at nothing to gain power over all in her path. Raz was secretly disappointed the way the rota had fallen, as she knew this vixen would try to obtain the boy's soul for her own, and by the time she herself returned for her next stint, all could be lost.

For once she was secretly glad the opposing forces would give this upstart a good run and may even succeed in holding her at bay until she, Raz, could take what was hers.

Little did she know there was another force to deal with.

Kyn watched the tormented little boy bravely still fighting the virus, which threatened not only his mortal existence, but also his everlasting being. The angel was conscious of another force at his side, and expecting it to be one of the demon variety, was surprised to encounter one of the elementals normally confined to the inner reaches of the earth.

"Out of your domain aren't you?" Kyn ventured. The aura was kind and he didn't want to cause any unrest in the atmosphere.

"Not necessarily." The answer was followed by a pause.
Thinking he would not learn more unless he asked, Kyn ventured gently "Are you here for him?"

"To assist."

"But he is to be taken by the air sentinels; you are from deep earth are you not?"

"And you wonder why I am involved?"

This was not an easy exchange and although Kyn was desperate for many answers, he sensed he could not push this spirit so he tried another approach.

"I am Kyn of the air, and I am here to guard our little friend until his passing, but there are others who would have him."

"We are aware of the situation Kyn of the air. I, Eeron of the deep earth am here because you are on the limits of our boundary, in fact, strictly speaking. You are in the earth, not the air sector."

"But he is in air."

"There is air present. But he has been placed in the basement area, which is in the earth."

This was a shock for Kyn, who had not reasoned this until now. He wished Ana was in presence; she would have the answer being much more experienced in the marginal areas.

"I observe that you know I am right, but do not fear, we are happy for you to oversee, especially in the circumstances, and we will add our force to save the boy from that which threatens."

"You mean you will oppose another sign?"

"Only when necessary and we feel it may be."

Eeron looked at Shane and said, "It is not quite time, I will return."

Alone, Kyn was beginning to realise the seriousness of this passing. There would be nothing easy or natural about it, but a brutal battle, from which there could only be one victor.

In the privacy of room X41 the two sad parents sat huddled together, united in shock of the past few hours, and the grief, which was already closing over them.

"I - I - only took him to the doctor's as a safety measure," Jane could hardly speak but had to pour out her thoughts, vainly trying for an answer to it all.

"I know pet," Tony tried to comfort her, but also feeling the weight of the stress, knew it offered little in the way of consolation.

"Tony, I must be with him, I'm his mother. If he's going to – to - I want to be there." A little while ago she would have been screaming hysterically, but now the weakness, along with a sedative given earlier by Dr.Martin were calming her almost into a submissive state.

The medics took this precaution now as standard procedure, having witnessed the violent reaction of previous relatives. Tony reached out and pressed the button indicating they wanted attention. Soon Professor Solomons appeared in the anteroom.

"How can I help?" he asked softly.

Tony leaned on the window near the communicator. "Please, doctor, my wife wants to be with our son. Is that too much?"

The learned man stroked his chin and bent towards the microphone. "Believe me, Shane wouldn't know you were there, and it would be terribly distressing for both of you."

"But why? What's happening?"

"Mr.Bryant, Tony, this is a very, very aggressive virus. We've had to relieve him of the effects to make it bearable, I'm sure you would want that."

"Well of course, we don't want him to suffer any more than he has to.

Professor Solomons was joined by Paul Martin who gave him a meaningful glance. The older man smiled at the parents and said "It won't be long. Please be brave, we appreciate it is difficult." They both left the ante-chamber to return to the patient.

"I don't know which way is up, I don't know anything any more," Jane sobbed uncontrollably, "I want to be with him, I want my baby."

Tony could not be brave any longer, no matter what the doctor had said.

"I want him too. I want to touch him, hold him. While he is alive. Not when he is dead."

Jane sniffed. "They will let us see him then won't they?"

Tony hadn't given this a thought until now. "God they'd better. Well, of course they will. They've got to haven't they, I mean it's our right."

"I want to share his last moments," Jane began crying again, "I want to tell him I love him, that I didn't mean to tell him off for scratching."

"He knows we love him." Tony stared into space.

Little had the father guessed the path the evening would take as he settled back for a quiet night with his beloved wife and son.

As the professor and young doctor rejoined the team round Shane's bed, they couldn't help appreciate the diligence of the workers. Even to their experienced eyes and with their experiments in the laboratories, nothing could have prepared them for the task in hand.

One of the crew was taking a few minutes in the secure anteroom to re-charge his inner batteries for the remainder of the gruesome job.

Shane was unrecognisable as the energetic little boy wheeled into the room. His whole body had erupted, one part after another, the giant lumps pulsating independently as though a thousand evil spirits were celebrating the take over. No area was unaffected. His front, back, head, every inch of him lay there like something from a horror movie. As each section burst open, a creamy greenish pus shot across the room at speed, covering anything in its path.

Attempts had been made to cover the next expected explosion but to no avail, for it took the dressings with it. The staff were well protected from contact by their specially designed suits, but they could not be saved from the dreadful sight evolving before them, an encounter they could never forget.

"Don't try to clean up at this stage," the professor ordered, "it's pointless, it will be taken care of shortly."

The tragedy of this awful scene was that Shane was still alive. The tubes and various trappings had been removed, as to keep him 'ticking over' artificially seemed sadistic at this moment. But he held on as if by an unseen force.

"Give up lad. Let go." Even Paul was touched deeply by the tenacity of one so young, little knowing the struggle Kyn was having inches from him.

Raz was gloating. She had returned early, moving a lesser demon to another position.

"I have come to take what is mine, and there is nothing you can do. Fancy them letting a mere minion like you stay in charge."

Kyn ignored her taunts, but secretly knew she had greater power than most.

They both looked towards Shane awaiting the moment of release. It was obvious it would be the first one in at the precise moment who would take his spirit.

"You and yours will never be forgiven for creating such a terrible thing." Kyn thought he would divert her attention. "You must put a stop to it now, before there are any more."

"I must. I must. Who is giving the orders angel?"

He had her. With her attention directed at him in anger, she was not concentrating solely on the bed. Kyn dived at the boy's spirit to take him but it was not the exact moment of release. Quick as a flash Raz, realising he could not conduct him over, seized her opponent and they rose locked in mental combat above the group.

The struggle was short lived but long enough. As they returned to the body, both were aware of the emptiness, the spirit of Shane had gone.

CHAPTER 5

This part was always difficult. Professor Solomons, a father himself, knew the automatic reaction of a parent who had been refused the viewing of their child, and so the Bryants were only acting as expected. It had been bad enough when they were prevented from seeing Shane alive, but they fully expected the right to visit him now he was at peace.

"It is for your own good, and it can do nothing for him, and would only distress you deeply. Better you remember your son as he was when you brought him in."

"But surely, he can't be that bad?" Tony felt he must plead on Jane's behalf.

The professor said slowly, "I'm afraid so. You must take my word. We can't allow it."

"Allow." The mother's feeble word floated across the room. "You can't allow."

"I'm sorry. I'll leave you for a moment, but due to the severity of the case, we will have to run a few tests on you both.

"What, now?" Tony couldn't believe what he was hearing. "We've just lost our son, we are not allowed to see his body, and you want us to succumb to your TESTS!" The last word was screamed at the glass with such a venom the pane almost shuddered.

Jane, barely able to stand, joined her husband, pointing her finger accusingly at the professor, "If you are so clever," she fought for breath" why couldn't you save his life?"

Tony put his arm round her and helped her to the bed, where they sat silent, numb, trying to piece it all together and praying that it was just a bad dream from which they would soon awake.

If the sad people could have seen the room where Shane died, they may have eventually understood the professor's concern. The area had been set up for this particular kind of emergency but was still running on a trial basis. In the case of a major outbreak, much larger premises would be required; also the professor had to justify the need and running costs to the university.

The treatment room TR4 which was now being cleared, was one of six identical chambers all with a chute leading directly into an incinerator for the immediate disposal of necessary material. Opposite each room was a laboratory dedicated to the study of each individual patient, namely LAB1 examined the samples from TR1 and so on. These rooms were also used for autopsies thus keeping anything fatal away from the usual mortuary staff in the main hospital wing. As with the TRs, the labs were connected to an incinerator.

Further on there were two operating theatres along with their usual anterooms for anaesthetics etc, although to date they had not been needed.

The holders of the university purse had deemed it an extravagance to have six labs when they felt one would have sufficed, thus cutting the costs considerably. The professor reminded them, in no uncertain terms, that a price could not be placed upon a life or the subsequent reason for an infectious death. One day it might be theirs. And so he got his separate labs happy in the knowledge that anything that needed to be contained, would be.

It was in LAB4 that the remains of Shane Bryant now lay for examination.

Ana had been summoned to return to the scene, and having gained all the facts from Kyn, decided to leave him there and begin the hunt for Shane's spirit. Raz was still hovering in the hopes that whoever had released the boy would return him to his body for him to leave it at will, because a spirit snatched cannot travel until it has mentally released itself from its physical trappings. If she did not get to him soon, it would be too late to take possession of his spirit, as it would already be free. That is, provided a godly force had helped him, but if an evil kind had intervened, she would feel equally cheated.

As expected the patient in his 70's had also died in the early hours of the morning, and had been transferred from TR6 to LAB6 for examination. The onlookers could not help but compare the two males, one nearing the end of his life, one just beginning but both dead, struck by the same hideous virus whose source was eluding this selected group of very clever scientists.

Being the first time two deaths had occurred within such a short time it was decided to compare notes throughout the autopsies to try and glean a comparison. Previously, due to the haste of the examinations, one corpse had already been despatched before another became available. Of course there were extensive notes, but that wasn't quite the same as having the actual samples there in front of you.

To contain any possible spread of infection when the remains were dissected, the research scientists would discuss the proceedings by means of an internal communication system. This meant anyone could talk to anyone in the unit, and a conference could be set up with as many joining in as wished.

Professor Solomons was having a light refreshment before starting the elderly gentleman's post mortem, joined by Dr.Martin who was due to undertake the one on Shane.

"We've just got to find a link man." The professor sipped his tea.

"You think this might just give us a lead?" Paul wasn't looking forward to the task before him, but his enquiring mind cleared any personal thoughts from his head.

"We know it's not confined to either sex. We thought it was only hitting the over 50's, then came a speight of 20-30 year olds, but now this little fellow. What next? Babies?"

"Just a minute" Paul was suddenly excited. "Listen to what you are saying. The cases are getting younger." he drew his chair closer to the table. "We know all are unrelated people. It doesn't seem to manifest itself in close relatives, friends etc."

"Random selection." The older man nodded. "So what are you getting at?"

"I wish I could be certain, but there has to be a pattern. Is it food related?"

"Seems unlikely to me," Solomons disregarded the possibility. "Most families have more than one person who eats the same food, so if that were the case, when one dropped so would another."

"I hope something comes from the two we have to examine." The young doctor got up to leave followed by the professor.

"I agree. And we can't put it off any longer. Time is the essence as usual."

It was nearing seven o'clock in the morning. About twelve hours since the family had arrived at this place, but during which time so much had happened to shatter their seemingly ordinary lives.

A nurse arrived at X41. She had left this and room X61 until last, knowing the occupants of both would hardly be hungry, having lost loved ones that night. She offered the tray through the double door hatch, wishing she could ease the pain of these poor people. The parents staring back at her bore little resemblance to the two, which had arrived the previous evening. Quietly she said into the communicator "Is there anything I can do?"
The father shook his head.

"I'll just leave this, in case you want something. Try and eat a little if you can."

She left, knowing her words were in vain and wondering how long she could take this tomb like existence which housed nothing but death and sorrow.

Jack Cox put out his hand, switched off the alarm and got out of bed.
"Is it that time already?" His wife yawned. "I've been awake most of the night wondering about young Shane. I didn't hear them come home did you?"
"No I didn't." Jack made his way to the bathroom.
Anne swung her feet out of bed and staggered to the window which overlooked the back of their neighbour's garden. She called out "They must have had a taxi."
As her husband returned to the room he said "How do you make that out?"
She thought for a moment then said "Well, the car's not there, and don't forget we were up late hoping to find out what the panic was, and they hadn't come back then."
Jack cut in "Bet he's put it away then."
His wife shook her head. "No I'd have heard the garage door, it makes a squeak. Jane was going to get Tony to oil it."
After a few minutes thought Anne went on "It can only mean he's been kept in, and they've stayed with him."
"Must be serious." Even her husband was beginning to sense something wrong. "Tell you what," he decided, "I'll just check before I go to work, I'll soon see if they are there."
"And if they aren't I'll ring the hospital," she announced.
"Do you know which one?" Jack looked questioningly.
"Oh. It must be the main one. You said they were going to Oxford?"
"That's what the man said."
"Well I'll ring there then. Poor little soul."
She busied about in the kitchen her mind elsewhere, determined to find out what was going on.

Shane's spirit was free. He had been seen through his passing, at just the right moment by Eeron of the deep earth, and been released to travel on. While Kyn and Raz had been in conflict, the guardian had been standing by. He was therefore able to take the spirit who was passing on the edge of his territory, but unable then to hand him over to the air angels once he was in possession as the deep earth spirits are confined to their space area. He felt he was doing his best by releasing the child to progress through his pre-ordained path to everlasting happiness, as he had not been snatched before his time. All should be well. But this was the greatest mistake Eeron could have made.

It can be understood, that not many human souls perish within the confines of the rock on which they live. Most of the creatures never seeing the light of day are worms, insects and other various life forms, but for man to die below ground is not such a common event. Therefore the knowledge of such a passing is limited among the deep earth sector, whereas the air and water spirits are very experienced in such matters.

Had Kyn been more alert, or Ana been in presence, they would have fought to take possession knowing they could then follow on with the boy's spirit, never leaving him to wander or become lost, and even worse, return to earth, due to his not being able to accept the wrongful shortening of his life.

Dr.Martin was in position in LAB4 when the professor called him on the intercom.

"Have you started yet Paul?"

"Was just about to. Did you want something before I get going?"

A pause. "Well, I was just thinking, no offence but due to the speed at which the lad was taken, I was wondering................"

Paul laughed, "If I'd mind you muscling in on this one.'Instead of' do you mean or 'as well'?"

The professor sounded relieved, "Oh more as an onlooker, but I thought we could discuss anything as you progress through it."

"Sounds like a wonderful idea. Would appreciate your observations."

Within seconds the two men were equipped ready to start the gruesome job in hand.

The video recorder was switched on, and Paul began the usual preliminary introductions, deceased name, age, etc. as he began to pull back the white cloth covering the lad's remains. As he did so, both men gave an involuntary gasp as they almost recoiled at the horror of what lay before them. Little was left of anything which could be easily identified, except the size of the skeleton, most of which was clearly visible.

Almost in a whisper, Solomons said "It's as if it's eaten him."

Paul was equally hushed. "I know, and after he died." Then turning to the professor he said, "And the parents wanted to see him."

"I know. Unthinkable isn't it?"

Paul held up the scalpel. "Bit redundant don't you think?"

Solomons had moved to the feet, when he suddenly bent forward. "Quick, move the mag-light down here."

Paul quickly swung the illuminated magnifier until it was just over the boy's right foot. "What do you see?"

"Don't know, take a look for yourself." Paul bent over and peered at the spot.

"Can't see - wait a minute, what's that mark?"

Solomons was agitated. "That's the one. What do you reckon?"

"It's moving!" The young man almost screamed.

"Good, I thought it was an old man's eyes playing tricks."

It didn't take long for the two men to make the decision to contain this foreign body. Almost without communication, the professor had grabbed a sample dish while Paul cut the remaining piece of flesh from the bone and it was secured in the lidded pot.

"I'd give anything to see a slide of it under the microscope." Paul knew this was not practicable, but the alternative would suffice. They placed the receptacle in a sealed unit where it could be manoeuvred by arms controlled from outside. The fixed powerful microscope directed down from the ceiling of the unit was now switched on.

Both men had their eyes fixed on the monitor as Paul moved the dish slowly around.

"Can't see anything yet?" He whispered as he scanned the sample, but then

"Wait." He homed in on one particular piece.

"Can you bring it up more than that?" Solomons had seen it too, but in a few moments he would wish it was something he had never faced.

The nurse smiled at Jane and Tony. "We know how much you want to see your son."

She waited for the facts to get through. This was nothing new to her; she'd done it a few times now. As the parents both looked up she went on "You know you can't get near him, but we have worked out an alternative for you." As the two eager faces joined her at the window she said "Would seeing him at peace on a screen help?"

Tony's face lit up. "Anything." Then putting his arm round his wife said "It's something." Even her distraught features lightened a little. "When?"

The nurse indicated for them to sit down.

"As you know everything has to be recorded, and we have the tape of your last visit when Shane spoke to you. You could see that first."

"But that's not him." Jane's face fell.

"No, but then we can switch to the camera where he is lying at rest, you will see he is in no pain any more."

This seemed to restore the hope and the nurse asked, if they were ready, to switch on the monitor in their room. She inserted the tape in the machine in the anteroom and dimmed the lights.

The two bereaved clutched each other as they watched their last visit, Jane trying to kiss her son, Tony fighting to hold back the tears. The picture faded for a moment, then a new shot emerged of Shane lying on a bed covered with a white cloth up to his head. His eyes were closed, he was beautiful. A doctor appeared on the screen dressed in the familiar protective clothing, and laid a white rose on the boy's chest. Giving a little bow he left the picture.

As the shot faded, the nurse said quietly, "I hope that helped, I'll leave you for a while." There was no reply from the two huddled figures sobbing into each other's arms.

The charade had been cleverly staged with precise accuracy. Knowing the demands the parents would make, the scientists took all steps possible to prevent anyone delving into their domain. Therefore, as soon as the Bryants had visited the boy, he was heavily sedated, and the recording made. As he was unaware of what was going on, he knew nothing of the plastic rose being put on his chest, or the tableau he was helping to produce.

This piece of trickery was stored for future requirements but not offered to the family immediately. Timing was the important thing in the handling of 'outsiders' as they were called. Bad enough they had to be allowed into the place, but as long as they only see what they were supposed to see and nothing more, everything should be controlled.

So as Tony and Jane grieved, slightly comforted by the sight of their son at peace, all they had been fed was a length of videotape.

CHAPTER 6

Anne Cox didn't have long to wait for her husband to appear from next door.

"Nothing." He called. "Nobody there at all, the curtains are still drawn back. They can't have come home."

"You go to work then, I'll do some phoning." As she went back into the small cottage her mind was trying to sort out the strange happenings. She had always got on well with Jane, and although they didn't go out much socially, they often shared a neighbourly cup of coffee, and were always there for each other if there was a problem.

"So why didn't she just phone and let us know. It's not like her." Anne spoke aloud as if to reassure herself but reasoned that, being the thoughtful person she was, Jane wouldn't have wanted to trouble them if it was very late at night.

"But she must have known I'd worry." she thought as she thumbed through the telephone book to find the number of the hospital. Within minutes she was trying to explain the facts to the switchboard operator who really only wanted to know which extension Anne wanted so that she could put her through and get on with the next caller.

"I don't know. All I know is that the child was brought in yesterday evening and he hasn't come home yet."

"I'll put you through to admissions."

Before Anne even had chance to say "Thank you" the line went dead for a moment with some violin strains playing until the department answered.

After talking with several different members of staff, she felt she was going round in circles. Nobody knew anything of the case, there was no patient called Shane Bryant, in fact no children had been admitted the previous evening, so she had no option but to put the phone down feeling very deflated.

"The Doctor." she decided. He would know because he had sent Shane in, and hadn't Tony told Jack something about another doctor going as well? She struggled to remember everything that her husband had repeated on his return.

"What was his name? Oh I wish I'd thought of this when I phoned the hospital." She was talking aloud again, as if hearing the logic would make it all clearer. Glancing at her watch, she realised there would be nobody at the surgery until 8.30am. She would ring then.

Shane was at his front door, alone. He was frightened now. What a bad dream, all about hospitals and a lot of pain, but then being lifted away from the discomfort and floating, floating through the night and then into the beautiful blue light. That had been fun, but now he needed the reality of being with somebody he knew, he wanted his parents to explain he had only had a nightmare.

"Mum. Dad." As he called out he realised he was making no sound. He tried to hammer on the door but he could not feel any contact with the wood. Terror began to take over now as he tried to run to the back of the building but he only rolled helplessly over and over.

Now he was inside his home, trying to walk but finding he was floating just above the ground.

"I'm still dreaming," he thought," I wish I could wake up." He tried pinching himself but felt no pain, his right hand merging with his left arm. As he looked he saw the hideous sight his bodily limb had become before the virus had spread through the rest of his body.

Normally he would have donned an image of his perfect self, but due to the circumstances and speed of his passing, part of the effect had travelled with him. He was lucky that the whole sight was not transferred, for at the moment of death his body had erupted to become the specimen the two scientists examined prior to the loss of flesh.

He was realising that something was not normal, that this was not a dream, because no dream, good or bad usually went on this long or was so clear. There was his father's untouched drink, the television, his comics, everything as he knew it. As the panic subsided a little, he began to retrace his movements since he last stood in this room.

Being newly passed over with no knowledge of the other side, the boy could only follow the route previously taken in body by travelling along its physical path. Also he was not fully in the 'at peace' stage, which meant he was vulnerable to any force that happened to find him wandering, and there were plenty who scoured the atmosphere seeking just such a catch.

He was unaware of the frantic search going on for his spirit, both from Ana and her good air spirits, but also from Raz who must have this picking for herself. Trying to beat them all was Fica the air demon who looked on the possible triumph, as a leap ahead in her lust for power.

As Shane floated up the hill leading from the village, he realised he could move quicker than when in his body, and after a few attempts, managed to keep fairly stable whilst increasing the speed. It was therefore only a few moments before he reached Charlbury, and the doctor's surgery. Placing himself with the building behind him, he took the road leading to Oxford, but as he approached the outskirts of the city, he realised he had no idea of the hospital's whereabouts. He knew it wasn't the main one, and he remembered the young doctor talking about a university but that was no help in a city full of little else. If only there was someone who could help him find his parents. He had an instinct that then everything would be alright, but he had still not realised the fact that he was no longer of the physical form, he was dead. The one thing he was too aware of was that he was alone.

"Are you alright old chap?" Professor Solomons had looked away from the monitor for a moment and glanced at the ashen face of his colleague.
Dr.Martin gulped. "Think so." He pulled his mask down, then after a deep breath went on "This isn't the same is it?"
"In no way resembles any of the others. Look at it." The older man returned his attention to the pulsating purple mass and shook his head.
Paul Martin said, almost as if the thing could hear him "It feels bad."
"I know. I didn't like to mention it, but there's an evil power almost emitting from it. Does that make sense?"
"Didn't like to say it myself, but that's exactly it. I'm glad you're here Professor."
Solomons looked back to the sample dish. "The frightening thing is that you'd miss it if you just saw that, but up there........."

As his voice trailed, the force coming from the virus increased although there was no physical change in the minute specimen. It hadn't grown, or changed colour, it was still almost undetectable to the naked eye, but the vibration it was sending towards the two men was beginning to make the thick glass tremble to such an extent, they both moved back involuntarily.
"Look." Dr.Martin pointed at the screen. The faint outline of facial features was appearing in the mass.
"Is the video picking this up?" Solomons moved back and tried to aim the camera at the unit, but seizing the opportunity of the two being separate, the force drew the younger man to the glass sucking him to the surface until his face was flattened, the skin drained of all natural colour. He struggled to push

himself away with his hands, but whatever was holding him was much greater in power until finally, he had to succumb, unable to fight it.

From the inside of the unit, Fica was using the doctors as a distraction from the boy's remains. She knew they would soon dispose of the skeleton and she wanted to delay that as long as she could. Like an instinct, she felt that the boy, although released from his body by Eeron, would feel lost without a proper guide and want to return to the area of his body, even though he would not re-enter it.

That is when she would take him. Let the others wander space vainly searching for him, expecting him to be floating aimlessly searching for his parents. "This is where he will be." she thought smugly.

The nurse entered the anteroom to X41 and noticed a slight change in the Bryants. Although still distressed, they seemed to have been eased by the video, so perhaps the medics knew what they were doing.

"When can we take him, you know, to make the arrangements?" Tony couldn't yet bring himself to say the funeral. It didn't seem real.

The nurse smiled. "This is going to be a bit hard for you, but please try and understand what I am going to say."

"Why hard?" Jane's voice was still weak.

"Because of the seriousness of the virus, I'm afraid we can't let you take his body, as it is."

Tony was on his feet. "What do you mean, we can't take him, and what in hell is 'as it is'. The child is dead for God's sake."

The nurse was very calm. "Mr. Bryant." she waited for him to sit beside his wife who was now apparently staring into space, unseeing and unhearing anymore. When they appeared ready she continued. "We have to cremate the patients immediately, it is the law, but you will be given his ashes in a lovely little casket which........." she was not allowed to finish.

Jane had got to her feet and was slowly, almost in a trance, making her way to the door. At first she began knocking on it, very quietly, but slowly the knocks became bangs, until she was hammering with every ounce of strength left in her, and crying for them to let her see him.

"Mrs. Bryant," the nurse had lost control of the situation, "Jane, please, that won't do you any good." But the mother continued the relentless hammering until her husband sank onto the chair his hands cupping both his ears, trying to shut out the frantic calling. He was sobbing, not only for Jane but also for himself now. The pain of seeing his son, of loosing him, and now having to witness the mental torment of his beloved Jane, knowing he did not have the answer.

The nurse quietly left the anteroom, and as she was making her way back to the office, also brushed away a tear.

Anne Cox picked up the telephone, paused, and replaced the receiver. She felt an urge to call the police, but what could she say? That her neighbours had disappeared? She had gained no satisfaction from the doctor's receptionist, who was obviously trained to ward off unwanted callers, politely explaining that Doctor was in surgery at present and couldn't be disturbed. Also as she wasn't a relative, he would not be able to discuss the case with her.

Frustration mixed with apprehension was taking over her every thought. But she had to do something practical. There was something very wrong, she knew it, but she had to convince someone who could help. Maybe the police could make the doctor say where Shane had been taken. These and other thoughts raced through her brain as she paced the room, the increasing feeling of dread gnawing at her stomach. She would have been amazed to know that a few moments earlier, the little lad about whom she was so worried, had been only yards away, now in spirit, trying in vain to understand his new state.

Eeron of the deep earth was attempting to explain to his superior forces the unusual passing of his earthly charge.

"If only you could have held him a moment longer, at least we would be sure of his spiritual safety." The elder, although deeply saddened at this mishap, realised there was little Eeron could have done, restricted by the bounds of their territory.

"I realise the truth of it," he answered" but the guilt - that is something that is mine. I was the one in place."

"Other work awaits, you must put it from your present thought" he was commanded, and although he knew he must obey, he was sure that the weight of his action would always be with him, taunting him, reminding him. To Eeron of the deep earth this would be the unforgivable error of all time.

CHAPTER 7

"SHANE." The boy looked ahead as the figure calling his name approached from the building in front of him, the one that housed his parents and his own skeleton. Delight surged through his being.

"Mum, is that you?"

Within seconds, the familiar form of his mother was embracing him in her arms. It took a moment for the lad to realise he could feel again. First the tender stroking of his hair then the firm hold on his body. The only thing missing was the scent. To Shane his Mum always smelt of one particular perfume, or soap or powder, he wasn't sure which; they were all just scents to a young lad, but his Mum had a favourite and usually smelled of that one. He didn't know which it was. Didn't matter really, but it was a reassuring smell, one of security and love.

"I've been looking all over for you." The voice was familiar, but in his relief to find something tangible, Shane didn't realise the slight difference in terminology. His mother would have said she had been looking 'everywhere', and although he didn't know exactly what it was, it was enough to plant a tiny seed of doubt in this newly released spirit. He would have to learn fast but it would be the hard way, and something most people thankfully would never experience.

"Come on, let's go find Dad." The vision was already trying to lead him away but Shane purposely stayed where he was.

"Where is he?"

Fica had been pleased with her resemblance to Jane, but had not reckoned on the non co-operation of the child. The self-assured demon had not fully done her homework, but had charged into the situation as was her wont. Raz, taking on such a role, would have studied not only the mother's way of addressing her son, but the facets of a young boy's stubbornness and habit of always wanting a suitable answer to his questions. But Fica wasn't going to let this prize slip from her grasp, not now.

"At the hospital of course." Her vision smiled at the boy who was reasoning that being with someone else might not be so bad.

Having located Shane, the demon had no further use for the occupants of LAB4, including the remains of the body. There would be no need now for him to try to return to his physical form, as she would take control, whether he liked it or not. But she hadn't reckoned with the many forces opposing.

Professor Solomons' hand was rooted to the camera, as he watched in horror while Paul Martin's body slowly slid down the glass and finished in an apparently lifeless heap on the floor. The young man's white face looked as though it had never seen a drop of blood, his mouth distorted from the pressure and several teeth broken.

As if suddenly unlocked from his position, the professor dashed to Paul's side fearing the worst, but gasped with relief as the young doctor took a slight breath. But he was so cold. The air in LAB4 had dropped to below freezing whilst Fica had been in presence, but as soon as she sensed the approach of her victim and had left the laboratory, the temperature was slowly rising again.

Relief filled Solomons as he felt the slight warmth returning to the room, because, due to the nature of the work carried out there, there was nothing in the way of blankets or warm clothing with which the patient could be covered. The whole unit was kept at a steady temperature, but was not equipped to combat the chilling power it had just experienced in this one place.

Using the only warmth available, his own body, the older man wrapped himself around Paul until he slowly came round. His eyes widened in horror as he stared up into the professor's worried face.

"What - what - was that?" The words were barely audible.

"Don't try to speak now. We must get you out of here." Caution dictated that until the remains of the body were despatched down the chute, nobody else could be permitted to enter. Hard as it seemed, Paul would have to be strong enough to walk out himself. They both knew this.

As the blood began to flow back into the battered face, some began to ooze from the damaged teeth, causing more concern for Solomons.

"Stay back." He ordered rather sharply. "Let me get this" he indicated to the skeleton, "out of the way, and pull your mask back on."

There wasn't much to move. The professor pulled a body bag onto the skimpy frame, wheeled it over to the hatch, and with a short heart felt blessing, sent what was left to the incinerator.

Whether it was partly the paranormal events or the hideous ending of a young life, or a combination of both didn't matter, but as the two experienced men scrubbed before leaving, neither tried to hide the tears.

Ana had returned. She took a quick appraisal of the treatment room, the laboratory and the incinerator. Although time was of the essence, she allowed a few seconds to view the parents making a thought note to send a helper to be with them and inject the kindness and caring that was significant of the earth angels.

Kyn had contacted her with the news that Fica had left the building and was entrapping the new spirit, time for them to swap places and let Ana's experience fight this lesser fiend. They both knew that Fica would not want Raz around yet, not until she had taken command. If Ana could have contacted the arch demon, she would have been tempted to do so, if only to watch the fury between the two like powers, however, she would handle the situation as delicately as possible for the boy's sake and try to release him in the meantime.

The more experienced spiritual forces are able to take a sweep of a larger area in much less time than the lower forms. Here Ana had an advantage, and quickly located the boy and his temporary keeper. Calling on her standby air angels, they all surged forward, Ana grasping the boy as the others attacked Fica. This demon had much to learn. Only the draw of power drove her to think she could achieve the impossible alone. She wanted all the glory for herself, whereas an elder would have secured back up forces, as Ana did.

The fury emitting from the overcome air demon almost rattled the atmosphere, but the little army of angel soldiers continued to aggravate her, leaving Ana enough time to depart to another zone. The fracas had attracted Raz who was now present, her fury directed not only at the angels, but more at this little upstart who had jeopardised the whole operation. Within seconds the two air demons had gone, leaving Ana's followers in the calm that now reigned. As they left to return to other tasks, helpers Voni and Ciru remained and soon descended to room X41 to carry out the task set by their area leader.

"But why won't you listen?" Anne Cox's voice had raised at least two octaves as she spoke to the constable on the end of the telephone. He didn't seem the least concerned that her neighbours had rushed their little boy to a hospital, somewhere and hadn't returned.

"Madam" the voice waited for a break in her outburst." Now don't you think that if there had been anything to worry about, they would have let you know? Telephoned or something?"

"But they haven't. Don't you see? That's what's so strange about it. They would have, by now. It was last night, well evening really and now it's getting on for lunch time and if you don't see something wrong with it - well" she was running out of words and patience, " I don't know that's all."

"So what are you asking me to do? I mean we haven't had any reports of any accidents, and you say the hospital doesn't know anything. What makes you so sure he even went to hospital?"

"Oh forget it. I'm sorry to have troubled you. I just hope for your sake nothing's happened." She slammed the receiver down with such despair it almost jumped off the housing. A coffee had gone cold at her side. She felt the cup and as she took it to the kitchen, she started to cry with frustrated sadness.

Having no children herself, she had often looked at little Shane and wished "If only we'd had one like him. A girl would have been nice too." But it was not to be, so Anne had accepted it eventually. It was on occasions like this that the natural mother instinct flew to the fore.

"I bet that copper hasn't any kids, or he would have been different." She quickly wiped her face and pulled herself together wondering if she should have another go at the doctor. He must have known where Shane had been taken.

Without knowing why she did it, she felt herself drawn back into the small lounge and almost as if by force she sat on the sofa, her eyes half closed. Gently, as a breeze wafting across her mind she heard a sweet voice almost like the tinkling strains of a melody.

"We want you to help us look after Shane." She nodded her head.

"Your protection will guard him. It will be for only a short time. We need the safety."

Again she nodded. There would be many times when she looked back to this moment, she would wonder why she accepted everything, never questioning, just agreeing.

"You are one of our kind, although you don't realise it, we need to hide the spirit of the young passing in your body. You will protect him at all costs. Do you feel strong enough?"

"Anything. But what ..?"

"All will be explained, but time is short. There will be forces trying to trace him, please be on your guard. We will leave him with you now."

As if waking from a doze, Anne shook herself and thought she must have been dreaming. She hadn't seen anyone, only heard, but did she hear? Trying to understand what was happening, she didn't realise that she no longer wanted to locate the hospital or her neighbours. Also she had no indication of the terror that lay ahead.

Raz should have been on her allotted earth location time, but suspecting that Ana had whisked the boy's spirit to another plane to rest, she quickly put another air demon in her place, leaving her free to find her target. Believing this to be the reaction, Ana had purposely put Shane in familiar surroundings leaving a helper to guide him peacefully through his transition, which up to now had been beset with turmoil.

The practice of placing a new passing into a physical body as a passenger was only used in extreme cases, but afforded a greater protection than leaving him to float about aimlessly. Although Anne had no conscious knowledge of it, helpers had often used her for such tasks, as her gentle but caring self provided a safe haven for short periods.

To satisfy her fury with the lesser demon, Raz had despatched Fica to a task far away from the earth area. She knew she could be of no help in locating the boy and she certainly didn't want her around when he was found. But distrust for her underling was to the fore, so she sent a message to several of her trusty equal powers to watch the movements of the wayward power seeker. Pausing over the hospital building, she quickly ascertained that all the primary players in this game had left, and as she confirmed that the urn containing the newest pile of ashes was labelled 'Shane Bryant' she knew he could not try to re-enter his remains.

In some cases a lost soul will try to stay near their last known earthly connection, but when the end was so horrific, it followed that someone in the unrested state would not want to dwell on the trauma and therefore would seek refuge in happier vibrations.

So, he would not be here, but where? His home seemed the obvious answer. This was a lost child she was dealing with, and he would want to feel safe. It was easy for such a demon as Raz to acquire earthly whereabouts immediately, and within seconds she was hovering near the Bryant home.

There were many spirits 'living' in the village, as they had done in life, unable to break the ties, but some were just passing through on their way to a fresh task, and there were the residents, guardians or guides to those still in body. Ignoring the earth angels, she soon found one of her kind busily stirring up trouble between neighbours and enquired as to whether it knew of any new arrivals. Another was by the river, enticing two little girls further into the water.

Fortunately, or unfortunately, depending which side you are on, when some of these evil entities are engrossed on perpetrating aggravation, they are so intent on the success of their meddling, they hardly notice other activities unless it directly affects or threatens them.

The arch demon soon realised she would get little help from these minions, so decided to quickly scan the whole village herself, disregarding the unwanted spirits in the hope of finding the one she sought. She soon realised he was not here, and time was not on her side, so without wasting another second she departed to higher planes to spread the word amongst her own kind, that the new passing must be retrieved at all costs.

CHAPTER 8

Air angel helpers Voni and Ciru were well experienced in comforting bereaved parents, but had never lost the compassion essential in such cases.

"Must we wait for them to sleep?" Ciru was eager to start the calming reassuring process but knew Tony and Jane were both fighting to stay awake, knowing that when they woke up, their little boy would not be there, and they would have to start all over again trying to accept the horrible events.

"I don't think it will be long, they're exhausted and the nurse has given them a sedative. It's nearly time."

Soon the regular breathing of the mother and father was welcomed as a signal, and the two companions drew the ideals (spirits or souls) away from the scene and placed them in a cool green wooded area with the soft lapping of a little stream. The regular guides had been left to guard the physical bodies until the ideals were returned safely. It was essential that every precaution be taken, for the slightest slip could mean letting in the most unwanted forces.

Voni had her arm around Jane who gave herself a little shake. "Am I dreaming?"

"You could call it that." She didn't elaborate, leaving it for the mother to make the moves. Ciru, in male form was supporting Tony who looked equally bemused.

"Let's all sit over there," the air angel pointed to a seat surrounded by blossoms.

"I must be dreaming, this is beautiful."

Jane looked almost relaxed for a moment, but as her facial vision clouded with the thoughts of her son, Voni said quickly "We are here to help you."

Ciru joined in, "We know all you have been through, but we can reassure you that Shane is not suffering, he is almost at rest."

"How do you know, and who are you?" Tony was looking from one to the other.

Voni briefly explained their purpose, keeping the facts to the illness that had taken their child. She had to handle the next part very carefully without revealing the full peril.

"Please be assured that your son is safely adapting to his new, pain free state, but of course, we always have to be careful with people newly passing."

As worry appeared on the parents' faces, Voni continued, "Think of it as an astronaut returned to earth, there is always a danger, but it's always alright isn't it?"

The next question was expected. "Is it possible," Jane hesitated "could we meet him?"

Ciru leaned across "Soon probably. But we must let him have the right period of rest, for his sake." It was essential to play for time knowing Shane's location. In normal circumstances, a family member or a close friend meets the departed to assure them they are in a better place and happy. But when a spirit is 'in placement' it is impossible, or the secret area would be revealed.

After a few more moments, the two angels knew they had given the pair enough to build their strength for the time being, and slowly returned them to the charge of the guardians who thankfully had nothing untoward to report. Bidding them farewell, but warning them to be extra vigilant Voni and Ciru left for other similar tasks.

Shane was in a semi sleep state which gave him an almost drugged feeling. He knew he was being protected for a short time, and that it was for his own good, and although he still wanted desperately to be reunited with his parents, Ana had calmed him enough to accept his present surroundings. He was vaguely aware of Mrs. Cox moving around her home but was not mentally (in the spirit sense) alert to be active enough to draw attention from any wandering sentinel Raz may have placed in the area. So, for the time being he was reasonably safe.

Paul Martin had recovered slightly from his ordeal. As he sat huddled in a chair in the professor's office, sipping the hot drink, his hand was still visibly trembling and his face was drawn and ashen.

"How are you feeling now?" Solomons' features also showed the strain of the ordeal in LAB4.

"I'll be OK." The young man tried to sound unconcerned, but the professor was not convinced.

"In the circumstances," he watched Paul's reaction "I think it best if I see the parents alone."

"But, is that fair, I mean we both......" he wasn't allowed to finish the sentence.

"Look Paul, if they see you looking like that, well, is it going to be much comfort to them?" He waited.

"No I suppose not."

"Finish your tea, I'll go and get it over with." Getting to his feet he quickly checked his appearance in a mirror, and with a reassuring pat on Paul's shoulder he left for the unenviable task ahead.

Raz weighed up the situation. The battle in progress was being waged between her, the air arch demon, and Ana the air angel of the highest order, who had at her command, an endless army of air spirits, not only connected to the earth area, but reaching far into the outer galaxies and ready to assist at her request. The demon had many such entities of her own kind, some with their own score to settle for previous encounters, but some such as Fica who just wanted to boost their own standing. Fica. The thought of this usurper snapped Raz's concentration into top gear. Maybe she should direct her waves in her direction, for she knew the young demon would want to snatch the child back having once lost him from her grasp.

She hovered just above the earth, wondering what Ana would be plotting. The fact that the angel had left the area rekindled the thought that she had hidden the boy in a far off safe place. But this evil one was too experienced to fall into such a well planned trap and knew she must not disregard the obvious.

It was now Wednesday evening and Jack Cox returned from work to find a very contented wife busily setting the table for dinner.

"Heard anything? You look very contented, change from this morning I must say."

Anne smiled back, "Take your shoes off, dinners nearly ready."

Jack, knowing her as he did, assumed that everything was alright or she would be running round frantically by now.

"So how's the lad?" he called over his shoulder toward the kitchen. Anne came in with a pie straight from the oven. "Made your favourite."

"Anne." Her husband felt uneasy and the name came out sharper than he intended. He had quite expected her to greet him with news of the boy, or the parents being home and who said what before he even got inside the door.

"Yes dear." She carried on dishing out the meal.

"Anne, what's happened, is everything all right?" He tried to stay calm.

"Well I don't know really. Jane and Tony aren't back yet but I think everything's going to be all right.

"You don't know do you?"

"Like I said, nobody has rung yet, and you know what they say about no news?"

It was the man's turn to feel worried. He couldn't understand how his wife could appear so unconcerned, when this morning she was the one who was going to get to the bottom of it all.

Little did he guess what she was unconsciously hiding, guarding against the approaching terror.

"I think I've been dreaming." Jane raised her head and looked at Tony as he emerged from the small bathroom.

"I know I did" he rubbed the back of his neck with a towel. "We were in a beautiful place, and somebody - I don't know who it was, they told us Shane was out of pain."

"I can't remember much," Jane tried to think but it wouldn't come "I know it was nice."

The good work done by Voni and Ciru was very evident, for the two parents now had an air of acceptance about them, noticed immediately by Professor Solomons as he entered the room. This was the first time he had not used the adjoining ante room; also he was in normal medical outfit used in the area, but without the masks and extra protective garments.

After the usual greeting, he sat down opposite the Bryants.

"I think it has been explained to you that, due to the severity of the illness, we had to cremate your son's body. But you can now take his ashes and give him a proper service and burial. All the required papers are signed and everything is in order."

"It all seems so final doesn't it?" Tony, although he felt much stronger, knew that until the funeral arrangements had been made, they couldn't begin to rebuild their lives.

"When can we go?" Jane just wanted to get out of this false environment.

The professor smiled. "Very soon now. Umm - I think it was also mentioned that, and this is again because of the terrible virus involved, that we just needed to be certain that neither of you had any trace of it in your systems." He paused, knowing that timing was most important. "We would like to do a blood test and a couple of other small tests, just to be sure you understand."

As they cast each other wary glances he continued "After all you have been through, the last thing you need now is for one of you to contract the same thing because we didn't bother to check you out. You'd never forgive us would you?"

He had chosen his words carefully, ending with a question to which he knew they must agree.

"When?" Tony shifted in his seat. "When could you do these tests? Only we really need to get out of here as soon as we can."

"Of course," Solomons smiled warmly. "I'll arrange it straight away, then, "he paused for effect, "you will be free to go."

"How will we get home?" the thought only just occurred to Jane. "Tony isn't in a fit state to drive."

Again a reassuring smile, "Don't worry, we will provide you with transport."

When he had left Tony look puzzled. "I don't understand it"

"What's that?" Jane had started to tidy round in a mental attempt to show they were leaving soon. Her husband scratched his head.

"He wasn't wearing all the space walk stuff, and he came in here."

"So?"

"So, why do we still have to have the tests?"

"Well he told us, we'd never forgive ourselves if...... " her voice trailed off.

"Exactly." Tony exclaimed. "If they really thought we were at risk, they wouldn't put themselves in such a vulnerable position by touching us. No. There's something I still don't like."

Immediately the atmosphere in the room took on a distrusting air, and Jane stopped fussing with the table and sat with her husband staring ahead, wondering when it would finally end, and how.

The River Evenlode skirted the village of Ascott and the little bridge at the foot of the hill provided a pretty place to pause when taking an evening stroll. Due to its tranquillity, many water angels used this as a regular resting place following arduous tasks. As may be expected, the water demons too found it an ideal place to cast their mischievous or deadlier plans. Here, people would come with their minds relaxed and open, perfect targets.

Raz's recent visit had not gone unnoticed by one of the water angels, Ohley, who had protected the little girls from the malevolent being attempting to lead them into deeper water. Knowing the capabilities of this demon, she knew something important must be brewing, or the force would not have come herself but sent one of her underlings.

Quickly, she contacted her next link Lonar, a water angel with much experience in the ungodly practices used in their element. He was equal in power to Ana of the air and could call upon an army of helpers should the need arise. Also he could spread a message in their own sphere in a fragment of the time it would take beings such as her.

As he received the requirement, he was overseeing a tragic boating accident in the Solent, a stretch of water near the Isle of Wight on the south coast. The necessary helpers were already at work, and Lonar knew he could leave a trusty aide in charge in his absence. Having gleaned the gist of the problem from Ohley by ideal thought conference, he knew he must be in situ without delay to absorb the vibration pattern left in the water by the passing demon.

As a wind can ripple the surface of water, so can an entity, good or bad, leave a 'footprint' for a space of time, the length depending on the period of visitation. Lonar knew that the lesser beings disturbed the flow, but it was always quickly restored to its natural state by the little army of angels protecting the place and the visitors. However, one such as Raz, a known evil species would cause greater waves simply by being there. There was no time to loose.

Ana had been very busy. The news of Shane's demise had spread throughout the air angel sector of the earth and to the far reaches of the galaxy, so that all would be on the alert for the slightest indication of trouble. She estimated that with all the publicity, as she called it, no-one could move without one of her kind being aware of it. As on earth, news casting is not selective, and Ana's tactics were soon being debated in the upper realms of the demon field. Although this was not an isolated case, for many poor souls pass over in turmoil, what made this so despicable was the fact that the whole thing had been engineered with the object of snatching a young soul at the precise time of transition. Had this been successful, the far-reaching effects would have been unthinkable, for if an experiment works, it will be repeated and expanded. How long before all young spirits would be condemned to eternal hell by the demons, not only of the air but all other elements?

The scheme had another purpose. Knowing she would be under close scrutiny, for only she knew of the true location of the boy, she tried to attract the attention as far away from the little village as possible. Although the clever Raz suspected her motives, she dare not relax her coverage of her opponent's movements, as the slightest slip from each side could have meant defeat.

The guardian spirit in regular attendance with Anne Cox had been instantly instructed to 'switch off' his thoughts of the boy and concentrate on his usual tasks of protection, this would suffice for a short while. He watched as Anne finished clearing the kitchen after the meal and then sat in the easy chair to watch the television.

Jack eyed her from his chair. "What do you think is going on?"
After a minute with her eyes fixed on the screen she said "In what way?"
It had been a tiring day and her husband wasn't in the mood for games. He knew she was being evasive, and he wanted to know why.
"Oh for goodness sake Anne. Have you switched your brain off or something? The lad of course. What do you think I'm talking about?" His fierceness made her sit up. Someone was asking delving questions and her defences went up.
"We'll be told when there's something to tell."
"So you've not been round then?"
"What's the point? They're not there."

Jack snorted. This was getting him no-where. "Well, I'm concerned if you're not. Something's not right, and I just can't understand your sudden lack of interest."

The two guardians were aware that the aggravation was attracting playful beings eager to jump on the fight and fuel it into a full blown row. Jack's guardian was always very alert and quickly dispersed them with instruction that it was only a friendly tiff, and they could find better to occupy them elsewhere.
"That could have been dangerous" the angel passed the thought to his companion.
"Loose it" was the sharp order, for to dwell could have attracted stronger unwanted powers

But one of the jokers had remained long enough to spot the shadow of a resting soul in placement, and although the identity was not self evident, it raised the doubt as to why one should be placed so near the Bryant home at such a time. To an ordinary passing demon this would not have been too important, but to the satisfied entity now hovering at a safe distance, it was of the utmost bearing, for this was none other than the revenging Fica.

CHAPTER 9

"Where is she, and why did you let her out of your watch?" Raz's fury echoed across space as she admonished the workers she had carefully placed to monitor Fica's movements. But the rebel had easily outsmarted all of her keepers, and returned to the earth area she felt housed the location of the child. The tactics had not gone unnoticed by Ana's band of sentinels, among them Kyn who felt this situation provided him with a chance to redeem himself. Like Eeron of the deep earth, this caring angel believed it was partly due to his negligence that the boy was now at risk.

It didn't take him long to track Fica's route, and with Ana's sanction remained at a safe distance to observe the activity. He therefore realised simultaneously where his senior had placed Shane, and knowing Fica would try to keep this information to herself, he felt he had a slight edge. If she had wanted to relay this snippet, it would have jeopardised her final glory, and there was no way she would put that at risk, so she would try and retrieve the prize alone.

Kyn left the village in order to attract the least attention. He knew the boy could not easily be relocated and returned to consult with Ana as to the next move. They quite rightly guessed that the young demon would not travel far from her objective, but knew that time would not be on her side, for Raz would soon learn of her disobedience and be on hand, both to scold and seize the boy for her own ends.

"He will have to be moved." Ana decided as soon as Kyn reported the safe haven had been discovered. "To leave him there will only attract danger, both to him and to his protecting body." She thanked Kyn who was gratified when she asked him to assist her in the undertaking.

"Where will he go?" he asked.

"You'll see," was all she would offer, but added "he has another forty eight hours at least to rest, and in the circumstances of the trauma, that could double, so our problem is by no means over."

Kyn was satisfied at the reply and realised the caution surrounding the operation but pleased to be included in the arrangements.

As Shane rested in his bodily cocoon, his conscious ideal rose to take in his whereabouts, then sank again to the oblivion of calm, his entire being grateful for the escape albeit a temporary one. He was very slowly becoming accustomed to the fact that he no longer had the use of his own physical body, but that seemed unimportant at the moment and he drifted back into what could be described as a deep peaceful sleep.

Paul Martin gathered together his possessions, stuffed them into a holdall and, now dressed in his normal attire prepared to leave the complex. He bore little resemblance to the good looking lively young doctor that had arrived the previous day, the effect of the evil attack evident by the broken teeth and the bruising to his face. Solomons had decided Paul should get out for a while and clear his mind of the horror. There were enough staff to cope with patients and relatives in the limited space available, and he hoped the virus would not spread to an epidemic level, as there were no facilities at their disposal to manage such a terrible possibility.

Leaving the building by the door leading to the car park, he received a curious glance from the security guard.

"I shouldn't like to see the other one." The man offered with more jollity than Paul could stand, and gave, for him, a rather curt "Really," in reply.

He sat for a moment in his car, wondering what his next move should be. The professor had been right when he told him to take a break, and if the roles had been reversed he would have offered the same advice. But he felt he was running away, leaving his responsibilities behind the closed door. He thought of the parents. Keeping his distance had seemed reasonable, but couldn't he have lied? Couldn't he have said he had taken a fall? In their state they probably wouldn't have noticed anyway. He felt sorry for them, knowing they wouldn't be released until the necessary drug had been administered, clouding their memory enough that anything repeated would seem like the ramblings of distressed parents. It wasn't a practice he particularly liked, but it was inevitable so he accepted it.

As he started the car engine, the thought crossed his mind to give Dr Mann a ring and let him know of the boys' death, just for the record, but he knew that there was a strict protocol laid down and in his present state he could invoke more questions than he felt capable of dealing with. So, very wearily he turned the vehicle out of the gate and headed off to his little house on the outskirts of the city.

Anne had woken suddenly. The clock showed a luminous 3.20am and all seemed still apart from her husbands' rhythmic gently snoring. As she gathered her wits she wondered if her neighbours had returned home and the familiar noise of the door had aroused her. It was Thursday morning and yet they seemed to have been gone for ages with still no word, although she still took the fact in her stride. Also it didn't strike her has peculiar for them to be returning at this hour.

After lying still for a few moments, she realised that whatever had woken her was not outside, but in the house. Quietly she nudged Jack.

"Hmm - what?" he responded sleepily.

"I think there's someone downstairs." She kept her voice to a whisper but he was full awake instantly.

"Listen" she breathed.

They both sat perfectly still.

"Can't hear anything," Jack started to get out of bed "but I'll go and have a look, just to be on the safe side." As Anne made to join him he warned "No, you stay here."

"Be careful."

"I will" and he picked up an old cricket bat kept behind the bedroom door for such occasions.

He was soon at the top of the stairs, treading gingerly to avoid any creaking floorboards, then started the curved flight leading directing into the lounge.

As soon as he was out of sight, Anne sensed a presence in the bedroom. The air had gone very chilled, and she thought she felt an icy arm slip round her shoulders. Without thinking she jumped away from where she felt the power to be but seemed to move nearer to it whichever way she tried. The overwhelming protective feeling took over giving her a tremendous weapon against the fear which now threatened to swallow her. With one hand on the dressing table to steady her she automatically reached out with the other commanding to power to leave her alone.

Nothing could have prepared her for what happened next. A sadistic laugh filled the room deafening her. She tried to call out for Jack but knew he must have heard the ungodly noise and would come back upstairs straight away but no Jack appeared. She was fighting this unknown power alone not knowing who or what it was, but instinctively aware of what it wanted. Before she had time to wonder as to her next move the thing had attacked her full on, talons clutching and ripping at her breasts, stomach, even reaching through as though it would rip out every organ in her body. The pain was so intense, that even with the poor woman's endeavour she was forced to collapse to the floor, most of her inside appearing to be hanging through the gaping hole.

She would realise later that she was perfectly intact, but such was the power over a mortal's mind that made the evil Fica think she could outwit her hierarchy.

Jack, on reaching the foot of the stairs could remember nothing until he came to in the armchair near the window, with no recollection of how long he had been there. Bewildered he dashed back upstairs to find his wife stretched out on the floor. All thoughts of an intruder had vanished as he hit the light switch to take stock of the situation.

As he tried to cradle her head she looked at him with frozen terror on her face. "Something attacked me," she whispered weakly.

"What was it?"

"I don't know, I didn't see."

Jack eased her to a sitting position. "There's something very strange going on here."

Anne looked drained of every scrap of energy. "Didn't you hear anything?"

"I can't remember anything let alone hear, not since I went downstairs. It's a blank." His wife's shivering made him reach for her dressing gown, and as his hand passed the clock he turned back. "I don't believe this."

"What?"

"What time did you wake up?" He pulled the gown around her shoulders.

"About quarter past three."

"It's now five past five."

"Can't be." She tried to get to her feet.

"Look, let's both go downstairs and make a hot drink. We both need it."

As they reached the lounge and went into the little kitchen Anne was certain of one thing which made her feel even more deflated. Whatever she had been protecting was no longer within her. It had been snatched from her by vicious means. An overwhelming sense of failure clutched at her and she broke down, but Jack merely thought it was the effect of the experience and thankfully didn't pry. They sat sipping their tea in silence, many questions leaped all over their conscious minds, but there were no answers.

Shane stirred, his ideal knew he had been moved under frantic conditions, but he was calm again and fell once more into his peaceful oblivion.

Fica's fury was festering to a degree that was dangerous, not only to her foes but to herself, for it would cloud her reasoning and judgement, and force her to make rash moves purely from anger and malice than from well timed planning.

The intervention of her snatch by Ana, Kyn and their followers had put her back to such an extent, she now had to start all over again to locate the boy. Also, she was sure that news must have filtered through to Raz of the failure, making the arch demon even more determined to see her fall.

The message was brief. Dr Mann's receptionist had put the Thursday morning mail in a neat pile on his desk. The top item which was merely a standard memo from the hospital was headed 'Department of Virology' and consisted of a few lines of essential data for record purposes.
Name: Shane Bryant, followed by address, date of birth and family doctor's name.
Date of death, Wednesday's date had been inserted.
Cause of death. Ac.vir inf. had been scribbled and was almost illegible.
The signature appeared to be that of a Prof.Solomons.

Dr.Mann sat staring at the message for some minutes before flicking through the rest of his mail. Satisfied there was nothing requiring his immediate attention, he returned to the form. From the information Paul Martin had given him, he knew that the strain of virus wending its way through the population was deadly, and he was equally aware of the secrecy surrounding it, but such a curt way of informing him seemed mercenary with such a young patient.

He read the form again as if to glean anything further, but the thing puzzling him the most was the fact that the young doctor had not contacted him directly. He had examined the boy in his presence only two days before, and it seemed a natural process for him to want to follow it through. A simple phone call would have been nice. Suddenly he sat bolt upright in his chair. What if Paul couldn't ring because he too had contracted the fatal disease by working so close to the patients?

Flicking through his book of contact telephone numbers he stabbed his finger on Dr.Martin's entry. The number was the hospital who told him that Dr.Martin was on leave at present, and sorry they didn't know for how long, and again sorry but they could not give out staff's personal telephone numbers.

He replaced the receiver, the uneasy feeling growing in his stomach, hoping that Paul would contact him, if he could.

Ana and Kyn had moved quickly after securing Shane's resting form leaving their air angel army to distract Fica for as long as possible. Again they had managed to outwit the fiend but knew the net would be closing. If only they could protect the spirit until he had rested sufficiently.

Another temporary position had been found nearby, but it would be impossible to leave the child there for too long although Ana was aware that they could not keep moving him around or it would greatly extend his resting period and they wanted to get that finalised as soon as they could, leaving him less at risk. Previous experience nudged Ana to beware Raz's apparent lack of interest for she was aware of the clever devious means used by this cunning one. It wouldn't be the first time a lesser angel had been lulled into a careless move thereby paving the way for the arch demon to seize a wandering soul.

Although not in presence directly, Raz had without doubt placed trusties to report every slightest move. Ana felt a sense of delight as she imagined the reaction when the news of Fica's fumbling reached her, not only for the obvious reason but, by their own hand it would cause a momentary distraction, time enough for Ana to secrete Shane in a more permanent position.

Although not shown to her lower powers, Raz's fury was partly directed towards herself. Feeling sure Ana would move the boy as far away from his life source as possible, to make detection longer and more difficult, she had kept herself at a space position where she could oversee all possible movement reported back to her. She would then be free to move into the designated area immediately and pounce. Due to Ana's careful placing, none of the sentinels had been able to locate the child, therefore Raz had received no warning and concentrated the search elsewhere. The fact that the Fica creature had achieved the sighting without her knowledge did nothing for the demon's self esteem or standing, and she knew the young one would use this as a weapon against her.

The arch air demon summoned the meddler to her holding zone. Most would have arrived in an instant, not wishing to invoke further wrath, but this one was so cocky, so sure of herself that she took her time and appeared when she was ready, fully aware of the animosity that would be directed towards her.

To her surprise, Raz greeted her warmly, congratulating her on finding the target, a feat not expected from one so inexperienced. The next statement came as such a surprise it toppled the young demon's arrogance. But she was up against the expert.

"I did wonder if you would be able to pull it off." Raz paused, knowing the effect this would have. Sensing the expected bewilderment she continued slowly and precisely. "You found him quicker than I estimated. Well done."

"You knew all along?" Fica, being so full of herself failed to see the curtain of deceit that was being drawn across her being.

"Why, of course. But I was a little surprised you didn't report it back quicker. You usually like to be first."

Fica's thought was in top gear, sifting and sorting the facts. "So who told you first?" She would make her own enquiries and find out if it was true. But Raz was ahead of her.

"No-one."

"Then ......,"

"How did I know you had found him?" Raz finished the sentence with satisfaction. Her standing restored she revelled in the next moments.

"My dear young child, I have known all along where the boy had been placed, it's an old trick, but one only recognised by such as I. The lookouts placed in the village were far too inexperienced to spot the tactic."

Fica's form took on an ugly look. "You hand picked them. You didn't want them to trace him did you?"

"No. Whilst I knew of his whereabouts, but held off, I knew there would be no pressure to have him moved."

The impulsive youngster fumed "But why not take him when you could?"

Again a pause from the elder. "When will you learn? It is not always wise to dash in. That has been proved by your actions." Each short sentence was now snapped with clarity. Raz no longer appeared so welcoming and friendly, gathering strength by her manoeuvring out of a tricky situation, thus releasing herself from any blackmailing tactics the young power might be storing up for the future. That idea had been well and truly shattered as the evil goddess tore into Fica with such venom, that the junior left the presence fully aware of her own failings. It wouldn't take her long to regain the vengefulness upon which she thrived, however for the time being, better to remain at a safe distance and let the atmosphere cool a little.

Paul Martin turned over in bed. It was dark. At first he panicked, and wondering how long he had been asleep, stretched out his hand and reached for the light.

"Ten o'clock," he murmured, then as the realisation hit him, he jumped up "Ten o'clock, at night."

For a moment he sat on the edge of the bed gathering his thoughts. He vaguely remembered wearily climbing into bed some time this morning, but he had been without sleep so long, his body had caught up with the shortage.

His mouth felt dry, so he pulled on a dressing gown and slowly went downstairs to make a cup of tea. He didn't know why, perhaps it was sheer tiredness, but he felt peculiar. There was no other way to describe it, he wasn't ill as far as he knew, but something was not as it should be. His hand froze on the kettle. Supposing he had contracted the virus, and on leaving the secure unit had brought the strain out of the hospital and into the community. Remembering with vivid horror the speed at which the boy's body had been devoured, he knew that if there was the slightest possibility he had the virus, he must do something about it and fast.

He made the tea and took it into the small sitting room. With the cup in one hand, he dialled Professor Solomons' direct line in the unit. After a few rings, one of the special nurses answered.

"Hello Doctor, it's Steve" he said as soon as he recognised Paul's voice, "Sorry, the Prof's in Lab 3 at the moment. Can I take a message?"

"Not another one gone?" Paul felt weak.

"'Fraid so. That lady who was always smiling."

"I know. Look, get him to ring me when he's free could you. Quite important."

"Will do Doctor. Writing it on his pad as we speak."

They said the usual goodbyes, and Paul sipped his tea as he took a medical view of his condition.

Did he have the itching described initially by all the patients up to now? No. Not even the slightest irritation. He stripped to the waist and examined himself in the mirror. His fine body bore no unusual mark. He took a quick peep inside his pyjama trousers and as all seemed fine, he gave a little shrug and replaced the items. Physically he seemed perfectly fit, all right, very tired, but who wouldn't be?

He sat down again and ran his fingers through his hair. "I don't feel ill," he decided, " I just feel different, strange, but not unpleasant." A slight laugh crept into his voice as he said aloud "If you were a woman, I'd ask if you were pregnant."

The smile that had flickered around the corners of his mouth faded as quickly as he realised that this was exactly how he felt, or imagined it was how you would feel. Vague recollections of a dream flicked through his mind. He had been in a beautiful place, a garden, and someone had been holding him close. Something had filled his being with love, and he knew he had to protect it at all costs, and at the same moment he felt a wonderful peace. Nothing was clear or lasting, just flashes of an experience which was being dangled in front of his consciousness, so he wasn't sure of how real it was.

At this moment he knew he hadn't caught the virus, but what he had was something much more important.

CHAPTER 10

Shane was aware of a change in his surroundings following the upheaval of his move. It was now over forty-eight hours since his passing and he should have been well into a deep resting period with another twenty-four hours to go. Although he was being kept fairly safe, the circumstances would no doubt extend his sleeping time by any amount necessary for him to be ready to pass onto the next stage.

With his youthful outlook, for he was still a young spirit regardless of his previous bodily form, Shane began to feel restless, much as a child who is told they must take a nap now, but has far too much energy to use before succumbing to sleep. His main intention was to find out his present location. In earthly terms, he was bored.

The sentinel placed close by, but not in obvious attendance was aware of his agitation and tried to send back a message to Ana by a roundabout route. This would take longer but not draw immediate attention from unwanted sources, thereby affording valuable seconds.

As Shane began to realise where he was, the horror of his transition began to flood his thought, the very thing the air angels had been trying to avoid. Newly released souls do not always act as their protectors would wish, many exercising the free will they used in the physical form, for why should they react any differently? They were in effect, the same people, whether resting, in active ideal work, or living a normal earth or other planetary life.

Living with the Bryants, the boy had been fairly obedient, but nevertheless bore all the characteristics of a lad starting out in the world. There was still much to learn about this place and he wasn't ready to leave it for a 'ghostly existence'. He wanted to stay. Due to the intervention of the evil ones, his life had been snatched before its allotted span, so whatever the air angels attempted on his behalf, the fact was that Shane would be earthbound for many years.

Ana consulted with her higher powers as to whether they could work in conjunction with another element, for instance the water forces, and place Shane out of the air sector for a limited period. She was reminded that firstly, the situation was not extreme enough for such measures, and secondly, the other elements had equally evil fiends at work who would delight in picking him for their uses. Being wise enough to accept the guidance she returned to where the boy had been positioned to assure herself of his present safety.

The guardian met her, agitating the air with ripples of panic.

"He's gone, by himself."

"Where, do we know?" Even with the impending complication Ana always managed to spread a calmness.

"Not far, he's wandering round the hospital unit, but he won't stay in one place."

"Who's with him?"

"Voni's following, she should be helping the most recently bereaved, but Ciru says he can manage."

"That's good." Ana mentally comforted the helper, knowing Voni had much more experience in tracking, "You stay with Ciru now."

Kyn arrived, and together the two archangels left to join Voni, arriving just as the boy was taking off at speed towards Dr. Martin's home.

"He's going back," Kyn announced, "I wonder why?"

Ana wasn't so elated. "Not for long, I think he's just getting his bearings."

Kyn asked "Won't all this energy set him back?"

"Very much so." Ana didn't hide the worry this time. "He's refusing to rest, we're now fighting him as well."

"We're not alone," Voni indicated to their right, "they've picked up on it."

"Not surprising," Ana watched Raz and her followers approaching at speed, then turning to Kyn ordered "you snatch him this time, we'll impede."

But Raz was prepared for the usual tactics and halted her team at a safe distance, keeping the child in view. She knew where he was, but was aware that she must time her attack to achieve success.

Before Ana could check him, Kyn had already sprung into action, and although not planned, it couldn't have been better timed, for Raz did not anticipate an angel other than Ana seizing the boy. It was over in an instant and by the time the demon realised what was happening, the boy had disappeared.

Her anger rose expectedly, but Ana held her back long enough to portray

"We do not have him."

"What?" The air vibrated. "You took him."

"No. We just made sure that you did not get him. He has gone his own way. He is free."

Raz pulled back a little, weighing up the situation. "We both know he cannot be free, he hasn't had time."

Ana hoped this ruse would work and she kept the air calm around her as she delivered the punch "He has chosen. Even we cannot hold him any longer. We have both lost him."

It seemed to work but Raz wanted proof.

"So where is your servant?" She scanned the skies, then loaded with sarcasm asked "Dare he not show himself? Is he too ashamed?" This was immediately followed with "Or is he with the boy right now?"

"No, I'm here," Kyn appeared taking quick stock of the situation turned to Ana and said "I'm so sorry, he was far too slippery, nothing can hold him."

As Ana acknowledged the angel, she was aware of Raz retreating, and felt relief surge through her spirit. They had won this little battle, but only for now.

Friday morning was crisp and the little village of Ascott was becoming covered in the autumn leaves being blown from the trees with some force. The weather was fluctuating between rain and some very warm sunny periods.

Anne Cox peeped out of the bedroom window. She still looked pale from her recent frightening experience and had refused to see the doctor against Jack's protest. It had been her intention to have a word with the local vicar, but due to cut backs they no longer had their own in the village, and had to share one with Leafield, a neighbouring hamlet. This made any urgent consultation virtually impossible, with parishioners having to make appointments if they had any trouble.

Jack joined her, "Wonder what today will bring." He looked out across the fields leading up the hill.

"Don't know." Anne sounded almost detached.

Her husband tried to lighten the tone. "It's the autumn sale tomorrow, we're going don't forget. That'll be nice."

"I don't feel much like meeting people, not at the moment." She sat back on the bed toying with the ribbons on her nightdress.

Jack was about to mention their neighbours, but decided against it, knowing it may only add to her distress, although he couldn't help thinking how strange it was that they had still received no word.

"Better get ready for work, fancy a cup of tea?" he went into the bathroom.

"I'll do it, I've got to get your breakfast anyway." She reached for her dressing gown and pulled it round her.

"If you feel OK." Jack was still worried about her and didn't really like to leave her alone.

"I'll be fine," she called as she disappeared downstairs.

The feeling of emptiness still held her, as though something had been ripped from her, but it sounded so silly. Who would believe her? Even the doctor would only give her some pills and say it was her nerves. Well perhaps it was. But she was still haunted by the evil presence that had invaded their home, and although it was no longer there, she knew she would always live under the threat of it returning.

Dr.Solomons smiled at Tony and Jane. "Good news. You go home today."
The Bryants looked weak but brightened at the prospect.
"You mean that?" Jane asked.
"Certainly." The professor sat down. "I can't tell you how sorry we all are."
They nodded in reply, there were no words. After a moment he went on, "As we told you, we will just have to give you an injection, it's an anti-virus jab, just to give you as much protection as possible."

Again a nod from both parents. He indicated for the nurse to bring in the needles and she quickly administered the drug that would wipe their minds clear of most of the facts, and people would assume they were too distraught to talk about their son's death. It didn't take long to work and they soon felt very hazy about the recent events. They knew Shane had died but couldn't be sure about any of the details. The doctors would say they were doing it out of kindness, but in truth they dare not let the facts escape, and this would ensure that no-one outside of the secure unit would learn of the horror.

Shane's ashes, or what they believed were his remains, were brought to them in a white casket bearing his name, and within the hour the sad pair and their cargo were taken home by one of the plain clothed security staff.

Neither of them remembered much of the journey, and they entered their little home almost in a trance. Tony carried the casket up to Shane's room and laid it carefully on the bed. He stood for a moment sharing the private moment with his son, and started as he heard a movement behind him.

"I told the man to go." Jane's voice was little more than a whisper. "I said we'd be all right now." As she finished the words, her voice shook and as her husband took her in his arms they both shed tears away from the prying eyes of the hospital unit. After a few moments she reached out towards the little white box but Tony held her back.

"Let's leave him to rest. Come on." He guided her downstairs, knowing she would try to cling to the last remaining scrap of their boy and this would only upset her more. It would be a relief to have the funeral over and try to come to terms with their loss. For whatever had gone on over the last few days one thing was certain, they no longer had a living child.

They tried to force down a slice of toast and a cup of tea but most of the scant meal was still on the table when a gentle tap on the door made them jump.

"I'll go." Tony was half way to the door before Jane even turned her head.

"It's Anne," he said as he returned with their neighbour.

Jane forced a smile. "Sit down Anne, good of you to pop round."

It only took seconds for the visitor to realise there was something drastically wrong, and as she reached out her hand Jane started sobbing, "He's dead, my baby's dead." As she put her arms round the distraught woman, she looked to Tony for some answers, but he turned away to hide his own grief.

"When?"

Jane shook her head. "We're not sure."

Alarm bells started to go off in Anne's head. She wasn't sure why, but with the recent events she instinctively knew there had to be a connection. Patiently, she didn't pressurise her friend but waited until she felt able to talk.

"We don't know much, but he had a virus, and it killed him."

Tony joined them now, trusting his voice not to crack. "When did we leave here?"

Anne looked puzzled. "Why, Tuesday evening, when you went to the doctors. We haven't heard anything since."

"What's today?" Tony was hesitant.

"Friday, nearly dinner time." It was obvious the grief had played tricks with the pair, and, as the doctors had anticipated, if a close neighbour would accept it, so would the rest of the village.

But this neighbour had been through her own ordeal which made her need to ask questions, not of the couple in front of her, but of someone with the answers, a priest.

Making sure she could be of no further help and realising that the poor people just wanted to be on their own, she made her way back to her home. It was imperative that she find out when the local vicar would visit to give comfort and arrange the funeral, for that was when he could council her on her own problem.

Shane wanted his friends. He wanted to play football and all the things young lads do, but it was with a frightening longing as he tried desperately to place himself in familiar surroundings. What had started out to be nothing but a bad dream was now stark reality that he had changed, he no longer had his body and what was worse was that he had no base, nowhere stable to set down and take stock. He vaguely remembered someone comforting him and sending him off to sleep, then being moved in a hurry, and something about Dr. Martin. He was nice, the boy had felt safe with him but then he had been moved quickly again.

The mental effects of his death were becoming vivid, and as his attention was drawn to his left arm, still hideous in ethereal appearance, he felt an anger well up inside him. No longer was he tired. Rest was unimportant now. Slowly the innocent boyish looks disappeared to be replaced with a sadistic snarl, worn on the face of the small form which now sought revenge on whoever had made him like this.

Within seconds he was at his home. This is where he would start to seek out the source of his horror, his living hell. He saw his parents huddled together talking to a man dressed all in black and recoiled as he realised the purpose of his visit. They were arranging his funeral. He knew they could have had no part in this and seeing them so drained and overcome with grief he did not want to remain any longer. Instead of becoming upset, the anger grew inside him and he quickly moved himself to the road outside the cottage. Where next?

His attention was drawn to the neighbouring cottage. Mr and Mrs. Cox seemed alright, but were they? A new feeling now engulfed him, one of distrust. Someone had to take the blame and it had to be somebody he'd been in contact with. Better check it out.

Jack had just come in for his evening meal and was washing his hands before sitting at the table. Shane noticed how pale Anne looked. Without stopping to consider the possibility of her being upset at his death, he toyed with the thought that she may have had something to do with his illness and now she felt guilty. That was it.

He moved to her side as she carried a hot dish to the table. Without knowing how he did it, he directed all the venom and malicious thought he could muster, sending it to envelope her being. Suddenly her hands trembled and she almost dropped the meal onto the pad. All was safe but she jumped back trembling. Jack joined her. "What's up?"

She pointed speechless to the table. "I- I -I". The words froze, her mouth hung open.

Her husband looked bewildered from her to the dish, then slowly put his arm around her. "It's the shock of the lad, that's all." He tried to comfort her but she still shook.

"It was here again." She managed to get out in a rush.

"What was?" Jack didn't really want to hear the answer but knew he must make his wife speak out or she would be in need of serious help if this went on. Anne was sobbing now. "Evil I'm telling you, whatever attacked me upstairs was back and it's going to get me."

Jack sat her down on one of the dining chairs. "And where is it now?"

She looked about her. "I think it's gone, for now."

"Good." Jack was convinced that whatever may have disrupted their night had nothing to do with how his wife was reacting now. It must just be a reaction. He had felt nothing in the room, so she must be overwrought. Carefully he suggested she see the doctor but she withdrew and vigorously rejected the thought.

Shane watched all this with mild amusement feeling no shame or sorrow at what he had just invoked. But he mused on the fact that something had been there recently that had produced a devastating change in the woman. However, that was not his concern, and this pair could be ticked off his list as they seemed to have no part to play in his present condition.

He quite liked this new feeling of aggression, it made him strong, powerful and with a new energy never before experienced. Maybe this was better than boy's games.

As he approached the seventy two hour deadline since his death, which marked the end of the allotted resting period for his ideal, he should have been peacefully passing on to his new state with the help of the air angels who had so carefully guarded him. Instead, he was becoming a wandering soul growing in confidence by the minute and ready to take on any force that opposed him. He was turning evil.

CHAPTER 11

"But I thought he was safe" Kyn was insistent, "I placed him with a guardian in the area, but knew I had to get back or Raz would have followed."

Ana was very sombre. "Your intentions were perfect Kyn, and it would have worked. But how were we to know he would become vagrant in such a short time?"

For a moment neither exchanged thoughts. Then Ana imparted "The other problem is, "she paused for a moment "we thought we had fooled Raz, but in fact she knows the truth."

Kyn was crushed. "I seem to have done it again."

"Don't forget" Ana reminded him "that we are up against the top powers of the air sector."

"I know, but it doesn't help." He was not going to be lifted very easily.

Ana waited a minute before saying "There is the other problem." She didn't elaborate as she wanted Kyn to participate fully.

"You mean..." he thought long enough to grasp her direction "Shane?"

"He's the most difficult part of it now. In fact, I'm not sure we can do much now he has slipped away."

Kyn was horrified "You don't mean give up, we can't."

"Oh I don't intend to. It will just make it all the harder. We are virtually fighting him, or rather his free will."

"I was wondering," Kyn started then stopped.

"Go on."

"What is his own element, is he also of the air?"

"I'm ahead of you. It was one of the first things I checked when I sought help from other sources. Yes he's an air sign, so he will have to remain in our boundaries."

"For what it's worth, that's a small comfort." Kyn tried to boost his spirit a little.

"Yes, and we must wait for any report coming in and act immediately, for you can be sure that he will be spotted."

Ana didn't add the inevitable, that Shane may draw attention from other areas equally ready to pounce.

The Rev. Desmond Conway read through his notes and prepared to drive the few miles to Ascott. Now in his early forties and having grown up in the area, he felt he knew most people in the surrounding villages. He had arranged to meet the Bryants first, feeling their need was greater than the visit requested on a rather garbled message left by their neighbour.

It was dark as he pulled up outside the cottage. The night air was rather chilly and he was pleased that Tony opened the door without delay and welcomed him inside. After the usual expressions of condolence the vicar started to enquire gently into the events leading up to the death.

With his experience he knew that the couple would be either very withdrawn or want to talk endlessly, pouring out their grief in memories of the one they had lost. But there was something different yet vaguely familiar about this situation.

As they spoke it dawned on him. This was the third case recently where the bereaved seemed to be trying to tell him something, or rather trying to remember what had happened but it wouldn't come. Not a case of they didn't want to, they couldn't. Making a mental note to look into the other similar events on his return to the vicarage, he confirmed that the funeral would be held in the village church the following Tuesday, and the lad's ashes would be buried over Jane's grandma. Satisfied that they were fully aware of the details, he left for the visit next door with some feeling of intrigue.

The temperature seemed to have dropped even further as Desmond stepped carefully over the large flagstones leading to the Cox's abode.

"Oh Good Evening vicar, what brings you here?" Jack's welcome was warm but somewhat bemused.

"I asked him to come." Anne immediately appeared at her husband's side. "Won't you come in please?"

"Thank you," he replied, but in an attempt to put them at ease added "a bit parky outside."

"Yes, it is, please sit down." Anne motioned to an armchair by the fire. She sat in the chair opposite toying with the edge of a cushion.

Rev. Conway sensed a great strain in this household but imagined it must have something to do with the lad's death. However, he hoped to glean the purpose of his visit easily and wondered if the lady would open up more if her husband was not in the room.

As if on cue, Jack offered "Cup of tea or coffee vicar?"

"That would be most welcome, thank you. Black coffee, no sugar."

As the man disappeared into the kitchen Desmond smiled sympathetically at Anne. "What's troubling you?"

She cast a glance in the direction of the kitchen, leaned forward slightly and said "Something's wrong, there's a bad force around here."

"In what way? Have you felt it or seen it?"

This wasn't quite what he had expected. He was used to the run of the mill problems but anything verging on the boundary of evil spirits didn't crop up that often in the little villages, although enough ghost stories were passed down through the families.

Slowly Anne related the events of the night earlier in the week, pausing in horror as she relived the experience. Jack had purposely taken his time with the drinks to let her finish but now he joined them.

"Here you are," he put the coffee on a small table, "I have to admit I'm glad she's told you." Then giving his wife her tea murmured "You should have said you'd called him."

"Anyway, the important thing is I'm here now, and glad to help in whatever way possible." Desmond sensed a tension in the atmosphere and was keen to keep everything calm.

Jack slipped a comforting arm around his wife's shoulders as he sat on the arm of her chair. Looking at the vicar he said "It wasn't imagination, I experienced it too, well not with Anne exactly."

Desmond smiled. "I'd like to hear your side also, if that's OK?"

"Certainly, but, well, there isn't much, but I felt I had been drawn away, so that we were separated on purpose. Does that make sense?"

"You can only say what you experienced, whether or not it appears to make sense at this stage." They appeared to be relaxing, so he took a drink of his coffee. After a moment he said "Tell me all you can remember."

The husband looked at his wife, almost for reassurance, then related his side of the events. It was now the clergyman's face took on a more serious expression for he knew that as both of these good people had gone through the ordeal it could not have been imagination. Something unpleasant was at work, and he needed the guidance of one more experienced in these things.

Eager to get as much information at the onset he coaxed, "Is there any more?" He still felt Anne was hiding something.

"Well," she started, "there was that feeling with the dish."

"That's right," Jack joined in but directed his comments to Desmond. "I'm ashamed to admit I thought she was upset, you know with ..." he nodded his head in the direction of next door. "But now I think she was right."

Relief flooded Anne's face, and as she looked up at her husband the first trace of a smile appeared. Willingly now she explained how something had been trying to make her drop the hot food as if it wanted to hurt her.

"And it felt the same as the other night?" Desmond must find out all he could before he could speak to higher authority for he would need all the answers.

"I think so." Anne thought for a moment. "I can't see why it shouldn't have been."

"What are you getting at vicar?" Jack was beginning to sense there was more to this than the holy man was telling them.

"Just being sure. I want to talk to one of my colleagues if that's all right with you?" He looked from one to the other. They both nodded.

"So you believe me." Anne look even more relieved. "See Jack, it wasn't a doctor I needed."

As Desmond got up to leave he paused. "One thing, sorry I probably didn't grasp it first time." Of course he didn't, she hadn't told him, but he was trying to catch her while the defences were down. "What was it again that you felt they were trying to get from you?"

As her lower lip trembled she whispered "I felt I was protecting something, but they took it away." The smile was now replaced with extreme sadness and Desmond couldn't help draw comparison between this woman and the bereaved mother next door.

As he left the little household his mind raced as he drove back to Leafield, turning the facts over and over in his mind.

Raz was smarting at the loss of her carefully engineered prize and still blamed Fica's bungling, something for which the meddler would pay eventually. Time was unimportant as long as the balance was kept.   The arch demon still didn't trust Ana, and although by a quirk of fate she had learned the truth, couldn't quite bring herself to believe it totally. She wanted proof. If the lad had gone free, none of them would ever control him, but if this was another clever ruse, there was still time to grab him.

The golden opportunity was too good to miss. Why not let the would-be usurper do the dirty work? She summoned her forces to bring Fica to her and within moments the two again faced each other.

"I have a special task which I can only give to someone I can trust to complete it." She was giving out the usual flattery, and as usual the young demon was lapping it up, blind to the trick which was about to be perpetrated.

"There are a few floaters around need reigning in." She made it all sound very casual, listing wayward spirits coming out of rest. Almost as an afterthought she said "Oh yes, I've let that new one go, what was his name now? He was too must trouble for what he was worth. Take him if you want."

"You mean Shane?" It was obvious the news of his wandering hadn't reached Fica and Raz was self-gratified.

"That's the one, you'll have to find him though. He's of no interest to me."

As the evil servant departed on her new quest with the capture of the boy's spirit foremost, Raz congratulated herself in the knowledge this little fiend would never oust her. Not only was she too full of her own importance but she would never stop and weigh up all the consequences of her mindless actions. Had she been that way inclined, she would have seen straight through her superior's plan. Instead she was hurtling headlong into the next disaster as she sought to seize the boy for her own trophy.

"That'll keep her busy for a while, as well as answer my question." Raz always liked to get the most out of her underlings, and this one was going to play right into her hands.

"The rest of the list? They can wait." thought Fica as she headed towards the village planning her moves. She had already decided that the success of this mission would put her in good standing amongst her kind, but also give her the chance to practice her arts. There were many ruses she had seen more experienced demons perform and was determined to excel, not only in perfecting others tricks but a few of her own invention. Shane would be a perfect guinea pig, if she could find him.

"Is that you Graham? Sorry to ring you so late, but I think I've got something not too savoury going on." Desmond had an understanding with his old friend, that if something occurred which was in the realms of possession or unwanted presences of any kind, he could contact him night or day.

The Rev. Graham Sanders had known the local priest for many years when he covered the neighbouring villages, but had recently moved to Gloucestershire, the next county, after the death of his beloved wife. His only son, also a man of the cloth was living down south and only visited a couple of times a year although they kept in close contact.

"What can I do for you my friend?" Graham never sounded put out and was always willing to listen.

"Not sure. Have you got a minute?"

"Of course. Tell me all about it." He settled back in his chair giving his full attention to what the younger man had to say. Slowly, Desmond recounted all he had just learned from the Cox's.

"This is more your area Graham, what do you make of it?"

"Hmm. Dispensing with the fact that they could have imagined it, because I don't think for one minute they did, and by the way, you were right to let me know straight away, there is definitely something hanging around there."

Desmond was relieved. "Well I thought there must be. I didn't feel anything while I was there."

"Well, you wouldn't you see, if it is only intermittent. You may have even kept it away by you simply being there. Depends how strong it is, and what it wants."

With only the scant facts, and not having visited the site, Graham could only guess at this stage what he thought the problem could be, however he was eager to give his colleague as much help as possible.

"You've had so many dealings with this sort of thing, do you think it's the same entity?" Desmond knew he would get an honest reply.

"Maybe not, the two instances have definite differences."

Desmond gave a little laugh, "That's your trained instinct. I knew you'd be able to help. You will won't you?"

"Of course, if I can. Now tell me more about the sad passing of the next door neighbour." Graham reached for a notebook. Skipping over the partly written sermon, he found a clean page.

"Why? Do you think it's got something to do with him?" Desmond sounded puzzled.

"Never discount anything. I don't feel it's him directly, but his age and passing could attract. You know what I mean."

"Oh, I see." The younger vicar related as much as he could from the scant information he had drawn from the parents, adding the similarity to the other cases where the memory appeared distorted.

"And have they, the other ones, told you of anything unusual?" Graham scribbled as he spoke.

"Not as yet. Should I ask them? Not directly of course."

"No, I know what you are saying." Graham paused. "May be a good idea to just drop in to see if they are coping. Another thing."

"Yes?"

"I know you said the parents were – how shall we say – hazy."

"That's right."

"But they hadn't had any feeling of anything evil in presence?"

Desmond didn't have to think. "Nothing, and I feel they would have, don't you?" Without waiting for a reply he went on "The Cox's, the neighbours who had the experiences, they were so frightened by it, I feel if any of the others including the Bryants had had the same, they would have said something."

"You'd think so, but it doesn't always follow, and people put a lot down to grief as you know."

Desmond nodded to himself as he replied "That's very true."

"Look," Graham put the notepad on the table, "it's difficult with it not being continual, the thing or things only come and go at the moment."

"So what are you saying?"

"Don't worry, I'm not fobbing you off. I'd like to come and have a feel of the place."

This cheered the younger man. "Could you arrange it? Get someone to cover for a day or so? You could stay at the vicarage, anyway it would be great to see you again."

"Leave it with me for now, and in the meantime keep an eye on the Cox's. Make sure they can get hold of you quickly, and get them to tell you every little detail if anything happens again."

"Graham, you are a marvel. Good night."

"Good night my friend." As he replaced the receiver the Rev. Sanders smiled to himself. There would be no need for him to travel to Oxfordshire to obtain the information he needed, but his physical presence would give comfort and reassurance to those affected.

He switched off the table lamp. "There's work ahead for you tonight," he told himself as he made his way to his bed.

CHAPTER 12

Dr.Martin had not returned to work since the frightening episode in the lab. Much against his will, he followed the advice of his leader and tried to clear his mind of the horror before continuing the unpleasant task of watching the poor victims under their care.

He was due to return the following morning, and after familiarising himself with the current patients would take charge on Sunday to allow the Professor to have a day with his family. The two men had kept in touch and Paul was aware there would be little for him to do, as there were only two remaining patients in the unit, the rest having passed away and no others being admitted.

This should have been good news, heralding the end of the virus, but he knew there had been an outbreak down south, and another in East Anglia. It had been suggested the patients be transferred to the Oxford unit, but on weighing up all the consequences, the people had been treated in isolation in their own areas, mainly in an attempt to confine the spread of the unknown disease.

"Might as well have an early night," the young doctor thought as he switched off the television. "Charge my inner batteries up for the morning." Although he appeared flippant, it was with a certain degree of apprehension that he looked forward to working in the unit again. How would he cope? Could he visit that room? Shaking himself he said aloud, "You'll just have to, won't you?"

Shane had been here before, he didn't know when, but the place was familiar. He watched the doctor enter the bedroom and start to get undressed. In life he had liked this person, but now he regarded him as an enemy. If the man had been such a clever doctor, why hadn't he saved him? Why had he let him go through this torment? Why had he let him look so horrible? A quick glance at his pulsating arm invoked a sinister sneer across the boyish face.

As Paul put his shirt on the bed, Shane pushed it off, pulling back amused at the reaction. The man picked up the article, looked at it and put it further on the bed. As his attention was turned to taking off his trousers, the shirt slipped over the other side of the bed. If he could have seen the image in front of him, he would hardly have recognised the young boy in his care less than a week ago. But he felt the hair rise on the back of his neck as he used all his force to walk round the bed the where the shirt lay.

He was not normally a nervous individual, but the recent experience flashed before his mind and he feared he was about to undergo a similar ordeal. Whatever it was, must have followed him. Something was with him, something evil.

He never knew what made him make the next move, but instinctively he rushed to the chest of drawers snatched open the top one and pulled out a bible given to him by his mother. He threw it onto the bed shouting "Whatever you are, get out of here and leave me alone."

Shane was not ready for such an outburst and rushed past Paul leaving a cold gush of air in his wake. The doctor shivered at first, but knew the entity had left, for the room was now calm. Still shaking he went back downstairs for a stiff drink and it took all his effort to re-climb the stairs, but he knew he had to overcome the fear of sleeping in the room now, or he would never be able to do so again.

Anger now filled the boy's ideal, and he so hated Dr. Martin for opposing him that he vowed to return when he had mastered his current state a little more. He felt the power surging within him, being fuelled by his growing contempt for all about him, but at the same time he felt lost, and, seeking something familiar, he again returned to the village.

It was approaching midnight, most people already in their beds. He wanted to visit his parents, but at the same time it grieved him to see them upset, unable to communicate with him. His sadness was immediately replaced by the anger threatening to consume his soul and with this foremost he viewed his bed with the casket lying just below the pillow. The reminder of events flooded his being and with all the force he could muster he brought the image of his horrible arm down through the sturdy lid smashing the timber as if it were merely balsa wood. Screaming he threw the ashes all over the room until only a fine dust was all that remained. As the fury reached its height he left at speed flying over the fields and river in the torment that raged.

As he slowed, he found himself near the small school in the centre of the village. Positioning himself by the porch, any good that remained in him came to the fore and had he still been in bodily form, would have reached the hearts of any passer by. For the little lad sat hugging his knees sobbing as though all the sadness of the world rested upon his shoulders.

After a few moments, he felt a kindly arm slip around him and his first instinct was to cuddle up to the source of the comfort, but he pulled away and faced the being who seemed to mingle with the stonework.

"Come, come now lad, there's no need to be so defensive. I'm here to help you." The thought was soothing and inviting with no suggestion of pressure.

"Who are you?" Shane was still very wary, but the loneliness was not something he cared for very much.

"Shall we say a friend?" The being seemed to be that of an older man.

"I don't know you. You're not one of my friends, you're too old." Shane made as if to leave but stopped. At least this was company of a sort.

"Suit yourself." The man floated across the playground and was disappearing across the small green.

"Wait." Shane followed quickly. "You're like me aren't you?"

"And what would that be?" The being had his back to the boy and it suddenly occurred to him that he hadn't seen his face or anything recognisable.

"I mean," the boy didn't know quite how to express it, but his thought reached out "you're dead too."

"Not really."

"But you must be." Sensing the thing, whoever it was, was playing with him, he felt the anger returning and was in no mood to get involved in guessing games. "Go away, leave me alone."

"Very well, if that's what you want." The man floated over the small field and on towards the tiny railway station. Realising there was still no pressure on him, Shane followed.

"Wait."

The image in front of him slowed but seemed to be fading from him. He called again "Please, don't go, stay and talk to me."

"Communicate would be a better description young man." For a moment the figure hovered, then turning he said "For a while, I don't have long. Come." He indicated for the lad to return to the school.

The spirit guided Shane to the infant's schoolroom. "Let's sit, we can talk better." Although he knew the exercise was unnecessary for they could have communicated anywhere, stationary, travelling, even at a distance, the man knew he must provide the newly passed over with something familiar. He had to let the boy do things he was used to, anything to let him feel secure for that was the only way he could gain the knowledge he had come to seek.

After a moment Shane asked "If you're not dead, how can you talk to me?"

The man smiled, his face now fully visible. "We all have spirit forms, but you know that from going to church and Sunday school." He smiled again waiting for a reaction.

Shane thought before saying "Isn't that only after you die? I've got one now haven't I, but I don't remember having one before."

"It isn't easy to understand, and don't worry, there's a lot of grown ups who will never grasp it, or want to," he added sadly, "but that's why I do the job I do in earthly form, sorry Shane, while I have a body, while I'm alive."

Shane almost jumped for joy as he slowly recognised the kindly man and the familiar plain white collar.

"I know you. You used to live near here." But his face clouded slightly as he said "Why didn't I know you straight away. I couldn't make you out until now."

The memory of the trick played by Fica when she tried to impersonate his mother flashed before him and he draw back.

"How can I trust you?"

The reply was not what he expected. "You can't."

Now the boy was lost for words, but Graham, now fully recognisable continued.

"Tell me why you are so cautious Shane, it's a very good thing by the way."

Feeling he could believe in the figure of the priest, the boy said "I thought someone was my mother, only it wasn't."

"You have had a rough time, haven't you?"

Not wishing to dwell on the event, and questions still flooding his thoughts Shane reverted to an earlier question. "You still haven't told me how you can do both."

"Both?"

"You know, you're a ghost like me, but you're still alive, is that what you said?"

Graham laughed now, pleased to have stilled the anger he had witnessed as he followed the boy. "You may not remember but you still had this ideal, as we call it, your other self if that's easier for you, when you were in body, sorry, when you were still alive."

"Oh. So aren't I a ghost?"

"Isn't spirit a nicer way of putting it?"

Shane was silent. "I don't like it. It's no fun. And anyway, if my friends have got these souls, why can't I play with them?" The sadness and loneliness was creeping back and Graham knew he must work fast and give the lad some hope."

"You can, not just now, but if you do as I say, it will happen quicker, and you'll be happier. How does that sound?"

"I don't know."

Graham knew he must get back to his body quickly. His light line, the beam connecting him to his mortal flesh was pulling him urgently. "Look I have to go, come with me, at least for now."

But the decision took too long to make, and in an instant Shane was alone again.

Fica was uncontrollable. Considering she had been sent on a special mission, she now assumed even greater delusions of power, ordered all those below her and equal to her to do her bidding. Many times she thought she had succeeded in taking to task those on a higher level, little knowing they were only carrying out Raz's orders, enabling the rebel to play into her mistress's hands. She was, in fact perpetrating her own tremendous downfall, and the higher she climbed, could only result in the inevitable greater fall.

News of her arrival at the village reached Raz immediately through the usual message channels and watchers were set up to report any activity. Most clever air demons had an instinct for being observed, making them difficult to track, but this one was oblivious to the movements of puerile underlings with nothing better to do than snoop into things that did not concern them. Any little demon getting too close would feel the breeze of her patronising tones as they were instructed to mind their own business. In such event, the tactic was to replace one that was detected with another watcher, and so allay any suspicion. Raz was well aware that Fica would have her attention on the matter in hand, and all these little diversions would be fobbed off as tiresome, but once again the arch demon was well versed on the personal attitude of her servants, hence her choice of pawn in this game.

Fica had seen from a distance the meeting of the priest's ideal with her target, and even she was not stupid enough to try and intervene during the communication. She was aware of the light line connecting the man to his earthly form, and gloated as she realised that here was a perfect way of achieving her goal through him. If he proved to be as easy to manipulate as the young doctor there would be no problem, but not only was this one older, in body, he was greatly experienced in the world of the ideal. Little known to the conniving fiend, he was way above her station. In the realms of the air angels, he was equal to Kyn, and about to achieve Ana's level, although to the little communities in which he preached, he was no more than a very understanding village parson.

Expecting the lad to remain in his familiar surroundings, Fica followed the trail of the light line and got a position on the vicar's earthly placing. He had been drawn back by the telephone ringing at the side of his bed. She hovered long enough to ascertain that the man was required immediately to visit one of the elderly parishioners who was about to 'leave the world', as her family put it.

Satisfied he would be busy for a while, the air demon returned to Ascott and positioned her presence near the boy. Gradually she drew closer to him and quietly sent the thought "Deserted you, did he?"

Shane was still sitting in the schoolroom pondering the visit. This being a church school bearing a cross on the old small pointed tower, Fica was not happy entering the place and realised she would have more power if she could only get the boy outside. Earlier Graham had carefully encouraged Shane to enter the building for the same reason, knowing it would afford some protection for now. He would have preferred to get the boy into the church, but knew that would mean getting him to move a greater distance, although the church was only a few yards away.

"Who's that?" Shane's attention was drawn to the caller.

"Oh just an old friend. You won't remember me." She hovered around a horse chestnut tree in the middle of the little green. Curious, Shane slowly floated from the building searching for the source of the thoughts.

"Where are you?" He was leaving the playground and stopped at the edge of the grass. Silence.

"Says he was your friend I expect, yes he's done that to me before now." Even in the world of the spiritual ideals, the lies flow on command especially in one this treacherous.

There was something vaguely familiar about this presence that stopped Shane where he was. "I know you." He wasn't absolutely sure whom he was challenging but wanted to give the impression of certainty, another thing he had learnt recently.

"Come here." The thought seemed to come from the other side of the tree, obscuring any image. Again caution rose.

"No, you come here if you need to speak to me." It came as a surprise to the boy that he had suddenly become so tactical. Had the vicar's visit done this?

Fica was not used to insubordination from anyone, least a young person, newly passed who had to date caused so much trouble. She wondered if this was why Raz had rejected him. Always ready for a challenge, this demon was not going to give in so easily. She would prove he could be controlled, and by her.

In an instant she was confronting the boy who was remembering for the second time how she had tricked him. All the good work Graham had achieved only minutes ago was undone as the peacefulness left, and Shane was filled with anger and hatred directed at this female form.

Even the evil one was not prepared for the action that followed. Shane appeared to grow in stature, and thrusting his left arm towards her advanced causing her to feel pushed back by his power. Slowly the impression of his pulsating limb spread across his body, as it had done in life, but this time at tremendous speed so that he became transformed into a horrible mass through which his features could still be seen, staring, snarling at her.

As she tried to regain control, parts of the mass detached themselves and flew in her direction until all that was left was the sight of the skeleton previously despatched to the incinerator.

"You did this." He screamed until the disturbed air reached the next village.

"You made me like this, so now you can have it." But the words were not of his doing. Kyn had seized the opportunity to take over the form on Fica's approach hoping he could retrieve the boy and take him on to peace. He knew Ana would not be happy with the way he had reacted, but the impulsive move had taken the evil one so much by surprise and horror, she had departed the area for now.

As Kyn tried to coax Shane back to his normal state, it was his turn for a surprise.

"You are all the same." The words were the boy's now. "You are all fighting each other. No one cares for me. I hate this. I hate you. I want to be alive again."

The mournful cry echoed the night sky. There was no doubt now as to Shane's whereabouts, even a non-attentive spirit couldn't have missed the vibrations. Reaction varied from the sadness felt by the angels from different elements to the sadistic pleasure reaped from the evil parallels.

But one fact evolved from the confrontation. The seventy-two hours since his death had passed and no-one had captured the boy's ideal to secure its safety or otherwise. Not only was he now wandering in his present unsettled earth bound state, it was apparent that he was making it impossible, by his own doing to be approached by any force good or bad.

Raz now had the answer to her question.

CHAPTER 13

The Rev. Sanders made a cup of strong coffee. It was 6am on Saturday and he felt drained, mainly with frustration from not achieving a better and more lasting result with the boy, than the abrupt awakening to visit Mrs. Vinor during her last moments on earth.

"If only I could have had a few more minutes," he thought as he sipped his drink. These things couldn't be settled in the time he had been allowed. He needed to extract the anger and replace it with the calmness needed if the child was to have a chance of a peaceful existence.

Another thought concerned him. Kyn said that this spirit was young in the realms of earthly visits, this being only his second on this planet. What would this experience do to him in his future lives? Also if this span had been prematurely shortened, he would not be due to return for some time. Having met Shane, Graham was also aware of the strong possibility of the boy being earth bound, maybe until the end of his pre-allotted time, or until he could be put into a delayed rest state.

All these notions churned around in his head for some time then suddenly he felt a chill down his back. With his experience he knew instantly the heralding of an evil force and strengthened his aura with pure thought to protect himself. As quickly as it had come, the feeling vanished but Graham was too wily to dismiss the experience as imagination. It was obvious that he had been tracked by some interested party, and being so soon after his audience with the boy, it followed that the scout had traced his light line and hence his earthly position.

This fact did not concern him greatly, as most of his battles had been fought on upper levels, but this was common knowledge to the hierarchy of all elements which could only mean one of two things. Firstly, this was something more than just an ordinary passing gone wrong and held a more sinister weight. Secondly, a young demon cadet was trying to earn his or her stripes by interfering in something above their station. But knowing he was attracting attention of whatever kind always put him on his guard.

He waited for the clock to show 7am, then picked up the telephone and rang Desmond's number.

"Hello, no I was awake anyway, want to make an early start today." The vicar's tone was light although the concern was just under the surface. "I didn't expect to hear from you just yet. Are you coming over?"

"Soon, hopefully. In the meantime there's something you could do for me." Desmond was only too eager to help. "Of course, what is it?"

"I'd like you to keep a close watch on the two families in Ascott. You know, pop in frequently, just to see how they are, you know the thing."

"Any particular reason? You sound very serious Graham."

The older man didn't want to give too much away at this point but warned "In these circumstances we have to use all the protection we can, and your constant visiting puts another little brick in the wall."

Desmond didn't want to push his friend but felt the need to confirm his suspicions.

"So you do think there is something to worry about?"

"There's something needs sorting out," was all Graham would offer but added "you were right to call me at this stage." Eager not to divulge any more he changed the subject. "So, are you ready for the bazaar?"

"Oh yes, it's just the usual autumn sale at the village hall, but we raise a few funds for the church and it's good to see the parishioners working together."

"We can do with as many good feelings floating around as possible Desmond. I'll talk to you tomorrow."

"Oh that's fine, and I'll let you know how much we make." He laughed for a moment, but the serious tone returned as he added "also very convenient to make those visits today."

As they made their farewells Graham thought "More essential than convenient." He knew the vicar was far from experienced in the upper reaches of the spiritual zones, but he was a positive man spreading good vibrations on the middle levels and as support was needed all through the spheres, some of these up and coming pure forces proved quite an asset. Desmond was one of those that emitted warmth and kindness naturally, spreading his light to all who came in contact with him. It was obvious that through his devotion he would learn quickly, and when once ascended to the higher realms, would be a force to be reckoned with.

However, for now the Rev. Conway was more aware of his work on the physical plain and how he could enrich people's daily lives and prepare them for the spiritual peace in which he believed but had little proof. He would have been amazed at some of the work he had achieved during his sleep state, awaking with no knowledge of the part he had played. Graham had used him regularly, knowing that one day Desmond would have full recall of his experiences and use them to guide others.

"I'll make a list" he spoke aloud and took a notepad and pen from his desk. He had offered to collect as many things as possible from the parishioners in Leafield, and take them down to Ascott in time for setting up the hall. This was a popular practice of Desmond's making and it worked very well. When one village held an event, the locals from the other village supported it, be it a fund raising effort or a musical evening.

Following the 'collection run' he would leave earlier than planned and call upon the two families before delivering his treasures. It would seem natural to just pop in and enquire how they were. He could then report back to Graham quickly if anything seemed amiss. And with his mind thus occupied he started to write an orderly rota for the morning.

"I thought I'd find you up here." The sadness in Tony Bryant's voice could not be masked as he joined his wife in Shane's room. Jane sat motionless at the side of the bed staring at the little box still in tact as it had been left the previous night. Shane's wrath had achieved no physical change to the container or his remains but he was not in any state to realise this.

"I can't help it." The mother's voice still held the anguish she had experienced at the hospital and Tony slowly slipped his arms around her shoulders but at the same time trying to choke back his own tears.

"I know......" was all he was able to whisper before his emotions released and they both unashamedly let flow the grief which was cutting away at their bodies like a thousand knives.

"I c-c-can't let him go, I want him here." Jane finally managed to utter, but Tony knew he was now facing the toughest job of all. Very gently he turned her to face him, caressing her face waiting for the reaction which had to come.

"It isn't him in there Jane, not as we knew him. We have to let him rest."

"But it's all we've got of him, and there's another thing." She was trembling now. Tony looked questioningly at her knowing she would have to speak at her own

pace. She was growing paler by the minute as she said in a voice barely audible

"I told him off, I shouldn't have, if only I'd known, he must have thought I didn't love him, but I did Tony, I did, I did." She fell into his arms flopped liked a rag doll, her energy spent. He knew he couldn't leave her here and until the funeral had taken place she wasn't going to change for the better but would get weaker by the day.

Carefully he raised her up and said gently, "Enough for now love, come and have a cup of tea downstairs, it is for the best, just now." He knew he had to get her to at least drink, food was probably out of the question, but he would try to coax her with something or she would soon be too weak to wash and dress or do any of the regular daily needs which would normally come as second nature.

They had only been in the kitchen a few minutes, when there was a gentle tap at the front door. Tony made sure Jane was safely seated at the table but with a little apprehension went to unlock the door wondering who could be calling so early as it was only a little after 8am.

"Hello," the voice was gentle and kind, "I thought I'd just come and see if you needed anything, er – I was in the area and….."

"I seem to know you but the name escapes me." Something was telling Tony he should recognise this man but his mind was churning.

"I'm Doctor Martin."

As a slight memory flicked through his brain Tony opened the door wide for the man to enter. "That's very kind, um - please come in." Paul Martin couldn't help but notice the man's trembling lip as he directed him into the kitchen. He was also aware that Tony hadn't appeared to notice the bruising still very noticeable on his own face

"Look love, it's a doctor."

Jane's reaction even in her weak state was not what her husband expected. She turned and looked at the young doctor.

"What do you want?" Her eyes were staring at him." I don't know who you are, but I feel you had something to do with our sons'……." Her voice trailed off as she couldn't bear to say the word death.

"It's alright Doctor," Tony cut in "we don't blame you, it's just so hard to cope with, to understand, and I'm worried about Jane, her health you see."

"That's partly why I am here. I have spoken to Dr. Mann and he agreed I could come and see you as I was so involved at the time, but you are under his care and he will see you have all the support you need from now on. I have brought something to help you over the week end and Dr Mann will see you early next week." He gave Tony a small bottle containing a few pills nodding towards Jane. "They should help, do you need anything for yourself?"

"No, I will be all right thank you, I want to keep as clear a head as possible, if you know what I mean." Again he looked at his wife. "It's just that we can't seem to remember all that's happened, as though it was a dream, it just doesn't seem to be real and we want to wake up and.." he paused for a moment then said "but it isn't going to is it?"

Paul placed a gentle hand on his shoulder "It does happen like that after something as traumatic as you have experienced, but you do have to look after yourself too." Tony took the bottle then said, "You must think me very rude, I didn't offer you a cup of tea."

"Don't worry, I have to go now. I've left a card with a number to ring if you can't cope or need someone urgently. Good Bye Jane." There was no response.

"Thank you Doctor," Tony answered for both of them as he saw the young man out.

"Who is he?" Jane asked without looking up as Tony returned.

"Not sure, but he seemed to know us all right. It's funny, I feel I should have recognised him but it's all a blur. Perhaps it'll come back." He perched on the arm of her chair and slipped his arm round an unresponsive form.

As Paul Martin drove away he should have been glad that he could report to Prof. Solomons that the drug they were using was working and neither parents seemed to remember any of the horrific facts although they knew something awful had taken place and their precious son was dead. But somehow he felt that however kind this might be to them, they were still being cheated of the facts essential as it may be. He directed the car towards Oxford almost dreading to return to the hospital and the sights of further outbreaks that may await him.

CHAPTER 14

Shane was feeling very strange. The encounter with the vicar had somehow had a lasting effect on him and the thought that someone was on his side rose to the surface but was soon dashed by the negative feeling towards the next encounter. But then who was it that had tried to help by seemingly defending him? He wanted to distrust everyone but he knew he couldn't go on forever in this nightmare. At some time he would have to believe in someone, but who? He realised it was morning as he was aware of the light but seemed to have drifted into a half sleep state as he floated back and forth over the village until he felt a sudden urge drawing him towards the river.

As he approached the little bridge he was aware of a small group of lads on the far bank. They watched him for a moment then the biggest stood up and beckoned him over. He felt comfort in the fact that they were all about his own age and slowly moved over the bridge keeping a safe distance from them. His wits were returning and he could make out four boys, the one who was still waving him to come nearer, two having a friendly scrap and a little lad sitting quietly watching them.

"Hello, I'm Mikey, who are you?" the lad sat down again so as not to appear intimidating.

"Um – Shane." His eyes focused on the other three as he edged his way closer. Mikey followed his line of view and said with a laugh "Oh don't mind them, they're always doing that. Hey, Bobby, Jimmy, stop it we have company." The two looked towards Shane and said "Hello Shane" and promptly carried on scrapping.

Shane was beginning to feel a bit easier as, for the first time he didn't feel threatened and sat down near Mikey his attention drawn towards the small boy. Again Mikey explained "Oh that's little Billy, we have to watch out for him" at which Billy beamed a warm smile in Shane's direction.

"Wait a minute." Shane started to move back, "you can see me, hear me?"

"Understand you, or rather communicate with you would be a better description." Mikey was now using words not fitting of a lad of his age. He beckoned Shane back to sit down as he said "If you are asking if we are the same as you, the answer is 'Yes'".

"You mean, you died too?"

He was answered by a nod and a smile.

"What, all of you, together I mean?"

"No," Mikey paused to let the realisation sink in, "I was killed in a road accident, Bobby and Jimmy here were - I'm sad to say murdered, and little Billy was ill and died very young. So yes we are all like you but we've had longer to get used to it. I guess you are still in the 'shock stage' as I call it. Am I making sense?"

Shane nodded and realising this was the best he had felt since Tuesday night he started to relax.

"Uhhh – why do you have your arm like that?" Little Billy was standing now pointed at Shane's left arm.

"Shh Billy, that's rude" Bobby cut in.

"But look at it, why doesn't he change it?" Billy wouldn't take his gaze off the arm, drawing everyone's attention to it.

Any thought of distrust forgotten, Shane said quite defiantly "You don't think I like it do you, this is how I was left."

"Then do something about it." Jimmy spoke for the first time. "Look at all of us, you don't think we were left like this. We look how we want to look. You can do the same."

This was a new angle for Shane to cope with, he wasn't being told he was being advised and for his own good too. Nobody seemed to be enticing him or lecturing him they were just a bunch of lads sharing their knowledge.

"But how would I do it?"

"In your mind." Mikey was quite near him now. "Just think, very hard, concentrate, how you want it to look." While Shane's attention was taken on the task, the others exchanged thoughts that time was running out and they had to move quickly as attention would be drawn to their activities.

Graham had been very careful in his selection of experienced air angels for this task. They had taken on the forms of people that Shane would trust, his own age group and far from being young spirits they were very experienced in the ways of the demons and their tricks. But this four had tricks of their own, for far from little Billy being just a young slip of a thing, he was very adept at taking any form which had often fooled even the most cunning evil force. Graham had Ana's agreement that he would be used for this delicate operation and it was he who was now in control of the plan. He had successfully caught Shane off guard about his arm and was now ready to act.

As expected the so called scrap between the two lads was a ruse to attract slight attention to the area and it didn't take long for Fica to home in on the ripples but timing was the main factor. Although she couldn't be certain Shane was there, she couldn't let any possible sighting go unchecked. Shane had been manoeuvred to a position near Billy while Mikey and the other two were almost circling them when Fica appeared over the bridge. They had not been entirely sure from which direction she would appear but had just received a thought wave from Ana as to her route so the first encounter she had was with the three causing a vortex in front of her. Billy had grown until he enveloped Shane, cloaking him from Fica's searching powers. On cue, the water angels which had agreed to lend their help at the precise moment, caused a wave in the river which rose and hit the bridge with force. All this distraction confused the self opinionated demon, so that by the time she had regained her control there was no sign of Billy. She frantically scanned the area.

"What have you done with him?" her venom was directed at the three.

"Done with who?" Mikey used the bad grammar to keep the image of a young lad as all were aware that if they dropped their masquerade now this demon would know they had been used for a special purpose.

"She means Billy." Bobby said to Jimmy. "He's always going off on his own somewhere."

Fica felt defeated but wanted to squeeze every last ounce of information out of these lads.

"Where do you think he has gone, and was he alone?"

It was imperative at this point not to appear to cocky or clever so they just shrugged and Mikey added an indifferent "Dunno." before the two others turned their attention to having another scrap, ignoring Fica completely.

"Fools" she spat at them before departing.

After a few moments the three resumed their own forms and left the area communicating that they thought this had been a success except for one thing. They were not sure as to whether or not Billy had successfully taken Shane with him or if the lad had departed of his own will.

Graham stirred in his chair. He had been asleep just long enough to get the message from Ana that the operation appeared to have worked but until Billy confirmed that he had Shane the whereabouts of the two remained a mystery.

Rev Desmond Conway had ticked off most of the jobs on his list and had deposited the donated items at the village hall so he could now turn his attention to the two families. In a way he wished that Graham could have joined him but there were times when too many people could be rather intimidating, and he would have pleasure in relating all the facts later.

He mulled over which couple to visit first, both having advantages but decided on the Bryants as theirs was the most severe situation. Soon, he was knocking on the front door and it seemed ages before Tony's head appeared through the partly opened space. Unlike the earlier visit, Tony recognised the vicar immediately.

"Please, come in." The words were hardly audible as he stepped aside, Desmond following him into the sitting room. He wasn't prepared for the sight that met him. Jane sat propped in an easy chair, untouched food at her side.

"Sit down vicar," Tony indicated to the chair opposite.

"Thank you Tony. Hello Jane." His words were soft and soothing but fell on deaf ears. As he looked up Tony started to speak but turned suddenly and fled from the room. One look at Jane told Desmond that she wouldn't know if he was there or not so he quietly followed Tony to the kitchen where he found the poor man draped over the kitchen unit, his head in his hands sobbing uncontrollably.

He stood beside him for a few moments then gently laid his hand upon the distraught man's shoulder.

"You have two burdens to carry," he whispered "your own grief which you cannot let escape and that of your wife, who I can see is not doing well, is she?" Tony raised himself slightly and shook his head.

"I don't know what to do."

Desmond helped him to a chair and said "It doesn't help much but we are there for you, at times like this. I'm not pretending it is easy, or will be easy, but you do have someone to lean on, and we all need it at some time."

Tony sniffed and said "I know, I shouldn't be like this but..." his voice trailed off again.

Desmond sat with him for a while then persuaded him to have a cup of tea. They returned to Jane who had not moved and Desmond whispered "Has the doctor been?"

"One came, I think it was earlier and left some pills for her."

"And what about you, have you got any for yourself?"

Tony began shaking again, "I can't. I don't want to be drugged, I have to look after her" and he nodded in the direction of his wife.

Desmond realised there was little he could do to help this sad pair at present but made a note to ask for more medical help as that was what was needed. He also noted that there seemed to be nothing more in this home than the terrible grief being suffered by these good people, but Desmond would have realised that this alone can attract unwelcome entities who gloat on this for the sheer pleasure of it.

The few steps to next door took only seconds and he was soon talking to Anne and Jack in a totally different atmosphere. They asked after their neighbours and said that after the last visit they felt as though they were intruding by going round but were very worried about them as they didn't know too much of what had actually happened to Shane, apart from the fact that he had died in hospital very suddenly. The true fact was of course, that nobody did, even the parents, thanks to the drugs they had been given. Desmond confirmed that they were probably best left for now, give them time to cope with the forthcoming funeral etc.

He let the conversation roll on naturally until he slowly turned it round to their recent experiences. To his surprise they each gave each other a glance and Jack offered "Well, I have to tell you vicar, it seemed very strange at the time, we did have a couple of things going on but it seems to have gone now, doesn't it Anne?"

"Yes, like Jack says, I was pretty scared, but now there is nothing." She paused then said "Funny though, it was only when they were away next door, but now they are back, it isn't, does that sound strange?" She didn't want to dwell on the feeling of peace she had when she was carrying Shane's ideal for protection, not that she realised she was a haven even now.

"Well, I'm very glad to hear that." Desmond was rather relieved and thought how pleased Graham would be when he heard the news. He got up to leave and as an afterthought said "If it's all right with you, I'll pop in again when I'm visiting your neighbours, if that's OK."

"Of course" they answered in unison to which Anne added "Any time vicar, you are always welcome."

They said their goodbyes and as Desmond left he couldn't help but compare the two households and wished he had some way of alleviating the pain of the parents, but that was too great a task at present.

Later that evening, Graham arrived at the vicarage for an in depth talk with Desmond. The two had agreed they needed a face to face meeting urgently due to recent events. After a light supper they settled down with a drink and commented briefly about the autumn sale which had done very well and was enjoyed by all.

The elder was keen to get to the subject of the visits and the younger man related in detail all he had observed. They both agreed that something on the medical side was needed soon as regards the Bryants as these two couldn't hope for any solace until Jane was more responsive and that needed more than spiritual care. Desmond eagerly recounted the conversation with the Cox's but was surprised at the reaction he got.

"Then where has it gone?" Graham thumped the arm of the chair.

"Um – what exactly do you mean?" Desmond was keen to know what the man was thinking.

Graham thought for a moment then said "You know, from your last visit, that something had been in that house and had scared the living daylights out of them and, don't forget the fact that the lady felt something had been taken away from her."

"No, but isn't it good that the place seems clear now, for their sakes I mean."

"I'm not forgetting that point and yes, for them it is, and it won't be back because what they want isn't there now"

Desmond took a gulp of his drink and said "Now you are loosing me."

After a slight pause Graham smiled and explained "This might be a bit over your head but the lady was right when she noticed it only happened when the Bryants were at the hospital or to be precise, after Shane died, whatever time that was." He went on "Cast your mind away from the bodily for the moment."

"You mean concentrate on just the spiritual - Oh my........." his mouth was left open as the realisation hit him. "You mean that was Shane's spirit, but why would it be bad, that doesn't make sense."

Graham held up his hand to stop the flow of words. "No, No, not Shane but a force that had something to do with his passing, an evil force probably after his ideal. I have come across it before. And what gives me the clue is that the lady, what's her name, Anne that's it, was probably used as a host for a short period."

Again Desmond sat with his mouth open. "There's more to this than I could ever imagine. Graham smiled "Give it time." Graham decided it was time to fill Desmond in on the recent meeting with Shane and the attempt to move him on out of the way of the demons and finished by telling him of the earlier enactment by the river.

"So," Desmond looked satisfied "Shane is safe, at least for now. Where will he be placed?"

"Not so fast." Graham looked sombre. "We think and I emphasise think, that Billy was clever enough to remove him from the clutches of the evil ones but..." he looked Desmond in the eye "we have not had confirmation, so at this time nobody apart from Billy knows and to keep the whereabouts unknown, Billy will not be able to communicate."

Silence filled the room as Desmond tried to assimilate the facts as they churned around his mind.

"You see," Graham broke into his thoughts "this is not a new thing, it has been going on for eternity, good against evil, each one trying to overcome the other, and it will go on."

As the two clergymen sat in thought the one unanswered question remained. Where was Shane?

End of Part One

PART 2 GEMINI

CHAPTER 1

A sad lonely figure, stood head bowed in front of a small grave in the village churchyard. A miniature rose tree had been planted in front of the little headstone bearing Shane's name. More than ten years had passed since his ashes had been buried in a special corner near the church. The clergy wanted to afford as much protection as possible to his remains, although his spirit had long fled. It was a useless gesture and they knew it, but the Reverend Graham Sanders felt that every precaution should be taken and local vicar Rev. Desmond Conway was only too eager to abide by his suggestion as he was learning that time was nothing in the different dimension in which Shane was obviously now existing.

Tony stepped back, a lump in his throat even after all this time and was just about to go when a voice cut into the silence.
"Oh, I think it's lovely what you do, coming here I mean."
He turned slowly and for the first time noticed he had been watched by one of the local elderly ladies. Not feeling in the mood for a long conversation – he never did when visiting his son – he just nodded in her direction and hoped she would have the decency to leave. But she wasn't put off that easily.
"You come a lot don't you, well I mean, it's understandable but not everybody would do it you know."
Tony felt that unless he put a stop to the flow it would go on for ever so he cut in "I like to be quiet and have my thoughts to myself when I come here. I'm sure you understand. Good day Mrs. Preston."
She opened her mouth to reply but he lowered his head and almost ran to the churchyard gates looking neither right nor left.

Nora Preston finally closed her mouth feeling somewhat let down that she hadn't been able to get a tasty morsel to share with her cronies, but she wouldn't give up as she felt there was more to learn from this man, especially as to his wife's whereabouts.

It was no secret that Jane was in a nursing home but nobody knew exactly where. The poor woman had never got over the death of her beloved Shane even with the constant support of her husband. The events leading up to it couldn't be blamed as the drugs had wiped all knowledge of the details, but she never came to terms with the speed of it. One moment she was taking him to the doctor with a minor irritation, and the next, he had gone.

She had been so drugged at the funeral she was almost carried there but didn't seem to be taking in what was going on. The doctors recommended a period of rest, partly to give Tony a break but mainly to observe her actual mental state. She was therefore admitted to a mental hospital where she had remained, never recovering enough for even a visit to her home. People had been told she was in a nursing home the other side of Oxford but as no visitors were allowed, no other details had been given to anyone which after a while made people suspicious. Many soon forgot her when events in their own lives took over and not many asked after her which was somewhat of a relief to Tony.

Jack and Anne had left the village which meant he had new neighbours, but he saw little of them as they were at work all week and had their own interests at the week end. Most of the locals had remained the same, babies had been born, older people had died as is the pattern of things; not many new people had come in as houses were only available when a lone occupant died or the odd family moved. No new houses had been built as the farmers didn't want to part with the land so the village had not grown in size. Tony had returned to his work after Shane's death and they had been very understanding, letting him ease his way back in gradually. Working in the offices of a grocery and provisions company meant he didn't have to deal with the general public, just the workmates in his section for which he was very grateful. Now approaching fifty, he didn't relish the idea of change and was glad to float along in his present state.

He had coped with two major upsets. Apart from Shane, he watched his wife become a stranger, disappearing into her own inner world, not seeming to recognize him. He felt that he was no longer a husband, and not even a carer, he was nothing. He couldn't have looked after her in the state she was in, but that somehow didn't make him feel any better.

In any small community there are the characters, and Ascott had its own. There was old Tom who would sit in the corner of the pub every evening and for a free pint would recount tales his father and grandfather had told him. Sometimes he would sing one of the old songs and many thought what a pity it was they weren't recorded as they would die with him. But he was a wily old chap and could 'smell' a recording device if it got near him.

But the main ones in this particular hamlet were Nosey Nora's brood. Nothing was safe from their prying eyes and ears. Nora of course deemed herself to be at the head with a little more breeding than the rest. If fact she was no better than anyone else but had tried to loose some of the local dialect which didn't always work, especially when she got excited about the latest snippet and her 'put on' accent dropped. She was a widow, as were Janet Mercer and Dulcie Woods, all retired. The remaining little soul was Miss Fay Anders, now in her eighties who told everyone that didn't already know that she had been named after a film star. On her own she wouldn't have been too bad but loneliness had drawn her into the flock and it gave Nora someone else to preside over.

As opposed to Nora whose frame was best described as buxom, Fay was nothing but skin and bone and only about five feet tall. The other two ladies were ordinary build, similar hair style, and whose main topic of conversation was what they would be having for tea.

There were not many activities in the local villages as most people got into their cars and went off to a nearby town or Oxford for their entertainment, but there was the odd church sale or little concert given by the school children. Some volunteers had tried a new idea of opening up the village hall for a couple of mornings a week as a 'Coffee Break' where anyone, but mostly directed at the elderly could go and have a cup of tea or coffee and a biscuit or piece of cake. It had proved quite successful and provided the ladies with a perfect venue for their exchange of information, none of them being too keen to have the others in their own home and they were all too old now to be standing on street corners with the latest gossip.

Rev.Desmond Conway, now getting on for sixty often tried to pop in and keep in touch with things. Sadly his friend Graham had been 'called home' as he put it but he knew from what he had learned from him that Graham's work here was finished and he had higher levels to reach. He also believed that his friend would watch over him and be there if needed and that was a certainty not a possibility, for Desmond had been taught well and now knew that he mustn't drop his guard for an instant as there were more entities ready to claim a vacant space that people could ever imagine. Little did he realize how important this would be in the near future.

Ana of the air spirits kept a watchful eye on the area surrounding Ascott knowing Shane was not in the space, but ever vigilant. The minor happenings could easily be handled by the lesser spirits who would alert her immediately anything unusual was in presence. Raz meanwhile appeared to have lost all interest in the boy's wandering spirit and put her attentions to other parts of the world where there was great unrest with fighting and killing taking over. But Ana didn't trust her as she knew this would always be a score to settle between them. Fica too had not been in presence for some time, possible bored with the lack of action and had moved to pastures new. But Ana knew that it would only take something to ripple the air enough to draw them all back so while everything was reasonably calm she was satisfied that nothing untoward was going on.

"Have you seen them yet?" Nora's question was more of a demand. She wanted answers.

"Only once." Dulcie sipped her tea and looked round the hall to make sure they were not being watched.

"When?" Nora was getting impatient.

"Yesterday, I were walkin' Joe's dog for 'im, 'ees bin bad with 'is leg and so I......"

"Never mind about Joe's leg, what did you see?"
Janet cut in, much to Nora's annoyance "What's 'he done to his leg then?"

"Forget Joe's leg," Nora was now going a bit red with frustration "tell me what they are like."

"Who?" Dulcie now had her face half buried in a slice of chocolate cake.

"For goodness sake woman, the people who have moved into Bell's house at the top end of the village."

"Oh" Janet piped up again "'Av they moved in now then?"

"Give me strength." Nora looked as though she would explode. Did these idiots do it on purpose, but no, they wouldn't have the brains to do that. "Are we likely to know what they – the new people – are like?" and she brought her fist down on the table with such a force the cups rattled in their saucers.

Dulcie took a deep breath for effect and said "I aint seen the parents but I 'ave seen the girls. Twins. I only got a quick look, they don't 'ang around."

"Is that it?" Nora looked most disappointed as she was hoping for a full description. Then suddenly she brightened. "Ah."

"Ah what?" Dulcie and Janet chorused.

Nora inclined her head to the latest arrival in the room. Ben the local postman dumped his empty sack two tables away from them and went over to the hatch.

"Usual Ben?" Sally the volunteer grabbed a tea bag, leaned forward and whispered "D'you want a mug?"

"Ooh Ah, that'd be champion, and a bit o' cake."

"You sit down Ben, I'll bring 'em over." She was a friendly young woman and appreciated he would be glad of a sit down.

Nora had watched all this and waited for Ben to be seated before she came in for the kill.

"You all right Ben? Bit of a long trek for you, now there's somebody in Bell's old place?"

"Ah, I got my bike though, that 'elps."

Not what Nora wanted. Did one have to drag every last bit of information out of people?

"They have moved in I take it?"

"Ooh Ah. They've moved in."

Dulcie wasn't going to be left out "They've got twins. Twin girls."

Ben turned to face them. "Funny really."

There was a combined "Yes?" from the three.

"Well, you knows 'ow I puts the letters through the box, well it aint like that." Again he stopped as though that was all he had to say.

Janet took the initiative this time. "So where do you put 'em?"

"Ah, they got this metal thing on the wall and I 'as to put the mail in a slot and the box 'as a lock on it so I 'specs they 'as to come outside and unlock it and take the letters out. Seems daft to me."

Nora thought for a moment "But why, when there is a letter box in the door. There is one isn't there?"

"All stuck wi' tape. Can't use it."

Dulcie asked "But what about newspapers, or don't they have any?"

"Ah, there's a slot for them as well."

Sally arrived with Ben's tea and cake and the conversation was confined to the ladies.

Fay had been sitting watching, her head going in the direction of whoever had the floor at the time.

"They are identical, dress the same, everything."

There was silence as all three ladies turned towards her. Nora very deliberately placed her cup on the saucer and said in a rather clipped tone "Tell me why pray, did you not say this before?"

Fay's meek little voice uttered "Well, you were all talking and I didn't want to interrupt."

"Well, we are all listening now dear, what can you tell us?"

Fay looked from one to the other and when they all nodded she continued.

"They went out for a walk last night. I was just going to draw the curtains, not that it was dark but it keeps the room warmer, and I saw them."

"What were they doing?" Janet couldn't wait for her to get to the point.

"Nothing, just walking, but very quickly, arm in arm, in step and both looking straight ahead. I've never seen anything like it before."

After a short pause Janet said "Praps they'd been to the shop." Before Fay could speak Nora said "What time?"

"Um, about six, but they weren't carrying anything."

Wanting to know more Nora asked "So what age do you think they are?"

"Um – it's hard to say, perhaps eleven or twelve, I'm not sure." She started to look harassed and so Nora changed the theme quickly.

"What I'd like to know is what the parents do and come to think of it, why let two young girls out on their own in a strange place to wander about. They don't know what sort of people are living here do they?"

Fay whispered "But people in the village are all right, most of them are very nice."

"We know that Fay," Janet explained "what Nora is saying is that they don't. D'you get it?"

A silence fell over the group as they all considered the facts and were brought to earth when Sally took the empty cups from the table. As if a sign to leave the ladies got up and went away with instructions from Nora to keep their eyes and ears open.

"Ah, that were good Sally, you makes a lovely bit o' cake." Ben picked up his bag and stopped as Sally cleared the table. "Tell you summat"

"What's that Ben?"

"What those biddies were talking about. I just got a feeling some 'ow."

Sally's head went to one side. "What you saying Ben?"

"Dunno yet. But I dunt like that place, that house. Gets a bad feeling from it I does. You'll see. Summat not right there. I aint saying no more yet." With a wave of his hand over his shoulder he left the hall, grabbed his bike and peddled off.

CHAPTER 2

A single soul is thought to inhabit a single living person, so it could be expected that twins would each have a separate soul, triplets three etc. However, it is much more complicated. Twins can be used for many purposes by the good or bad spirit world. They may each house a separate ideal, both being either good or bad, or one may have an experienced ideal monitoring an inexperienced one existing in the other. This is often used to protect a weak spirit in its early stages when it couldn't stand up to the rigours of learning in one being. Sometimes only one very experienced spirit will be in situ with space left for hiding or harbouring one in danger. When one is in control, both twins will appear to act simultaneously, or know if the other is hurt or needs them. In fact they are being controlled by a single angel or demon. When the twins are very independent with their own thoughts and ideas, you know there are two spirits in place.

The dangerous side is when there is a space, say with an angel occupant in the other, a demon can try to enter and take charge, not only of the free space but also of the existing angel resulting in terrible torment in the earthly twins who are unaware of the battles taking place within them. Occasionally, three can try to use the space of two trying to oust the weakest, again resulting in havoc.

So when the new family moved into the village, Ana was alerted to the fact that twins were in the group. Although it may not be a problem, Ana was only too glad to know immediately as she suspected this could be one of Raz's little plans and they had not been put there by accident but very cleverly placed after a period of earth years. This area would therefore have to be very carefully and cleverly monitored. She wouldn't use anyone known to the demon hierarchy, it would have to be a very able spirit drawn from elsewhere so as not to attract attention and she knew just the one for the job, but it would mean seeking the co-operation from another sign as she needed to keep the air sentinels at a safe distance.

The new family would not have welcomed 'Ben the Post' as he was known, as he was a water sign. They were all fire signs and would feed off the air signs for their energy, but water to them was deadly and could drain them if the spirit or earthling was aware of it. Ben didn't bother with such things, but he did get feelings, strong ones sometimes of exceptional good or impending evil. This was what he was picking up when he had entered their territory and couldn't wait to get off their land. He didn't look forward to his next visit, but while post arrived, he would have to deliver it. Strangely all he had handled up to now was junk mail for the previous owners, no letters addressed to the newcomers so he hadn't even learned their names and he couldn't have said, even to save his life, when they actually arrived.

At the risk of sounding foolish, he thought he had better keep his feelings to himself for now and wondered if he should have said what he did to Sally, but she was a nice person and didn't seem to take too much notice. He pushed his bike up the gravel path leading to the little village post office and propping the handle bars against the wall he entered the little hut.

"Ah Ben, that's handy." Molly the post office lady greeted him with a smile.

"Well, I's glad you're pleased to see I." He leaned on the counter. "What you got then?"

Mollie rummaged under the counter and came up a bit red faced from the effort and plonked a small parcel in front of him.

"The delivery van's just been and brought this, it's marked urgent. Reckon you could pop it straight up, it'll go in your basket."

"Ah, give it 'ere, where's it for?"

"Those folk in Bell's old place, didn't know there was anybody in there yet. Don't know what the village is coming to, you never seem to find anything out these days. Not like it was is it?"

If she expected a reply she had a long wait for Ben was staring at the label on the package.

"What is it Ben? You look as if you had seen a ghost" and she laughed but quickly let it die as she said again "Ben, what's the matter?"

Ben looked up slowly and said almost in a whisper "I'll take it, get it out the way," and he picked it up as if it was infectious. As he left Mollie bid him "Goodbye" wondering what has caused such a strange reaction in the man. "Never seen him like that," she thought "p'raps he's not well, getting too much for him I expect." With that she busied about sorting some new display material which had also just arrived and soon put the incident from her mind.

Fay Anders entered her little home and checked the wire basket hanging inside the front door. Two letters today and one was the one she had been expecting. She took off her coat and made her way into the kitchen. Taking a knife from the drawer she sat at the table and carefully slit the

---

envelopes. Ignoring one of them she hurriedly pulled the letter from the other and read

Dear Auntie Fay
Thank you for the information, it was very useful.
I will see you soon, and you will see me.
Bless you.
With kind regards
D

Smiling to herself she returned the letter to the envelope and made her way into the sitting room, as she still called it, opened the bureau and carefully put the envelope in a small drawer which she then locked. Giving it a satisfied pat she went back to the kitchen to read the other mail but it was only wanting her to take out a subscription to something so she disposed of that and sat down to think.

News does have a habit of travelling quite quickly in a small community and it wasn't long before somebody had phoned the Rev. Desmond Conway to tell of the new arrivals, not only trying to be the first with the gossip but hoping to use him to find out as much as possible about these people, but he was used to these tactics and gave little away unless he knew it was already on the grapevine.

As he was going down to Ascott church that evening for choir practice he thought it would be a good opportunity to pay the new people a visit. The congregation could do with a few more in its numbers to say the least. So when the choristers and organist had finished, he got in his car and drove the short distance to the house. It was set back a bit with trees at the front giving the place a rather gloomy look. He pulled the car into the gravel drive and as he got out he shivered thinking to himself that he hadn't realized it was quite this cold. No lights appeared to be on in any part of the house and he was tempted to leave the visit for now and come back in the daylight, although he couldn't imagine why.

He gave himself a shake and thought "Pull yourself together, what's the matter with you?" and strode up to the front door. In the gloom he reached for the knocker with which he was very familiar when he had visited the Bell family. His hand touched the door but the knocker appeared to have been removed. Maybe they had installed a push button bell so he let his hand run down the door jambs but all was smooth. The only thing left was to knock directly on to the door. At first he gave a gentle tap but when that produced no result he tried again, a bit heavier.

He was on the point of leaving when he heard a shuffling noise coming from the inside, followed by bolts being drawn. At least someone was there but he wasn't prepared for the welcome committee that met his gaze. As the door opened he expected to be flooded with light from the house but only a mere glimmer illuminated him. In the doorway were two figures, side by side completely blocking the entrance so he realized he wasn't likely to be asked inside. It took a minute for him to make out a rather small man, not much over about five feet two inches he imagined, wearing a black suit, horn rimmed glasses and his dark hair smoothed back over his head. Desmond wouldn't have even made a guess at his age at this moment and he wasn't surprised that the man didn't offer even the glimmer of a smile. At his side was a woman, possibly his wife who looked as large as the man was small and this unexpected confrontation rather took him aback. Obviously he had to be the first to speak or they would be there all night.

"Good Evening, I am the Reverend Conway, your local vicar and I just wanted to welcome you to......." The sentence was cut short by the man who said "Thank you but we have our own faith so we won't be troubling you" and made as if to close the door.

"I've no wish to intrude" Desmond wasn't put off that easily and was now very curious "I find it very constructive when different faiths communicate and learn about each other."

In the gloom he was starting to make out that the woman was dressed in some long garb with all sorts of things around her neck and markings on her face. Suddenly alarm bells went off in his head. He should have realized but he couldn't see enough until now to tell him that any religion they were practicing was nothing like his own. Also the only light in the house appeared to be coming from candles.

The woman spoke for the first time almost in a chant.

"We do not communicate with other faiths. And we wish to be left alone, we do not welcome strangers." A strange pungent smell was drifting towards him making him very uneasy but before he left he had to ask "Do you include your children in this - um – your religion?"

"It is our calling, our way of life. We are part of a greater family." The woman's voice seemed to be changing as she spoke.

Desmond was edging away from the door "Maybe we can speak again."

"As you have been told, we only communicate with our own calling." And with an unflinching stare from both occupants the door slowly closed until Desmond was left standing in blackness.

He got into his car and drove back to his home in the next village mulling over the encounter but forming the opinion that these folks weren't as sinister as they would have him believe. They may be following some cult or other, but they themselves didn't appear dangerous. He had come across some pretty nasty entities over the years and this just didn't have that feel to it. "They're playing at it" he thought as he parked the car "but the danger is just that. They don't know what they can get into after starting something that began as entertaining."

He made up his mind that in the light of a new day he would approach the matter from the angle that checks must be made to ensure the safety of the children and be satisfied that were in regular school attendance. But that was for tomorrow.

When the vicar had left, the strange pair returned to their back room in silence trying to ignore the interruption and shut out the world outside. Candles were everywhere casting strange shadows as the pair moved across the rays and the smell Desmond had noticed was a strange mixture of many different scented varieties. He had been correct in his assumption that these were 'playing' at whatever it was for the mixture of odours was not very well balanced and far from producing a heady hypnotic effect it was rather objectionable. It could have appeared amusing to the onlooker watching these two fumbling about without a clue as to what they were doing but as he rightly thought they could be opening the doorway to forces which could terrify and eventually hold the novice pair in their power. It would then be too late for them to realize the folly of their ways. Fortunately at this time they did not include the girls in their antics and always dispatched them to their room well in advance of their so called rituals.

The twins needed no second telling and always went upstairs on their parents' bidding. Of their own choice they shared a room which was large enough to be a bedroom and leisure room. They were a bit to old to call it a play area and Fay Anders had been almost correct guessing their age but they were only ten years old and quite tall which gave the appearance of them being that bit older. When they were born, the parents called them their little jewels so when they had to choose names they decided on Topaz and Peridot which they thought were rather unusual and both went well with their surname De'Ath. This unfortunate name was originally spelled 'Death' but over the years most people had inserted the apostrophe and split it into two syllables. It had been written in its original form on the parcel Ben had delivered which was why he stopped in horror when he saw it. The contents of the parcel now lay on the floor in the girls' room.

Frank and Maisie De'Ath realized the girls knew their own minds from a very early age. They had always been obedient, caused no trouble but if they decided they would do something they were so determined that there was no point in trying to advise them otherwise. At first, when they were small the parents had tried to coax them into various interests but it was no use, almost as if the girls were following a route from which they could not deviate. Realizing it was a futile task, they eventually gave up and let the pair go their own way, after all, they thought, they didn't get into any bother or cause annoyance, they didn't even get up to the things young children often do, like climbing a tree or slipping into the brook, if fact they were too good.

The family had often moved house as they didn't seem to fit in with many communities and had sent the children to a private school so as not to have them ridiculed by local youngsters. It didn't end there, often parents would harass the girls trying to find out about them only to be met with stony stares in reply. Some felt it threatening and definitely not natural, so the De'Aths moved on. It was more out of boredom than anything, and wanting to keep to themselves that the parents became religious – for the want of a better word – fanatics.

This village may seem like a new start but they knew it wouldn't be long before the locals would be trying to delve into their business and try to drag them into the fold, but they couldn't let that happen, here or anywhere. They had to protect their girls at all costs.   Frank had a fairly well paid job and with the money Maisie's parents had left them, they just about managed to keep the girls at their school and keep on top of their finances, but the truth was that they couldn't afford another move so this one had to work.

Ana had been updated on the recent movements just in case they had any bearing on past events and decided to converse with the fire angels of her own level as this could be advantageous to both elements. She had often worked in conjunction with fire angel Ignis when he had been in severe conflict with his fire demon equal Lazzan also summoning the assistance of the water angels, which Lazzan didn't forget and was eager to get even with both at some time. He was in no hurry, it didn't matter when, in fact he got a sadistic pleasure in playing the waiting game expecting the kill to be all the more pleasurable. Ana had to keep the safe distance from him which was why the water angels were involved.

Graham was working alongside Kyn, and the two made a force to be reckoned with but Ana did not want to bring them into play at the moment in case it attracted unwanted attention for she knew any interest on her part would be immediately relayed to Raz. So at a safe distance from the earth a meeting took place between Ana, Ignis and Ohley the water angel to form a pact of observation. Each agreed to send reliable but unfamiliar sentinels to the area to monitor anything which appeared unusual or threatening. Ana explained that Shane's whereabouts were still unknown and all caution was to be exercised.

The next morning broke with sunlight streaming everywhere creating a false illusion as to the temperature, for as Dulcie popped her head out of the door to pick the milk from the doorstep, she shuddered in the cool air and was glad to take refuge indoors. As she made her way back to the comfort of the little kitchen the telephone rang and she carefully put the milk bottle on the table before going to answer the call.

"Hello." She glanced at the clock in the hall; 8.30am who could be wanting her at this hour?

"Is that you Dulcie?" The tone was agitated or Dulcie may have been tempted to remind Janet that she was the only one who lived there.

"What's the matter Janet, you sound all of a tiz." She could hear the woman almost gasping for breath.

"I seen 'um."

"Who?"

"THEM." She was almost shouting now as if she expected Dulcie to know what she was talking about. Realizing this was going to take a long time and although bursting with curiosity, she said "Look Janet would it 'elp if I came round then you can sit down quiet like, and tell me what's getting at you."

"Yes, all right, yes, can you come now, I'm all of a tremble."

Dulcie started patting her hair as she said "Only take a minute and I'll be round, how about putting the kettle on and we'll talk over a nice cup of tea?" It looked as though that was the only way she was going to get one at this rate. After replacing the receiver she carefully put the milk in the fridge then checked everything was safe in the kitchen and got her coat from the hall. Picking up her handbag and keys, she remembered the chill from outside and took a warm scarf from the peg. Within minutes she was at Janet's door which was opened immediately and she was almost pulled inside.

They went into the front room and Dulcie was glad to see the tea was already poured out and she gratefully had a sip as she cupped her hands round the hot cup.

"Now then my girl, what on earth is up with you?" As she took stock of her friend she noticed for the first time how pale she seemed and she was still shaking, so she added "Take your time."

Janet sat opposite her, reached out for her cup then changed her mind and almost whispered "I were giving Rover, you know Joe's dog 'is morning walk, like I told you I been doing lately. Well, we was up near the church and I saw those girls coming t'wards us. Like Fay said, arm in arm and in step mind you, going along at a pace and I thought to me self 'What they doing out on their own' like you would, I mean I wouldn't 'ave let mine out at that time, not that age, not nowadays, I mean you could 'ave done when we were small, in fact we used to didn't we, thought nothing going along to Shipton and back but you couldn't these days, It aint safe." She finally took a breath which prompted Dulcie to get her back on track and say "I agree, but what got you in a fluster then?"

"Oh ah, I were coming to that. Well, they gets level with us and Rover set 'em. 'Is head were down, 'is hackles right up and he were growling, staring at 'em. Now you know as well as I do, that dog is the most docile thing that ever cocked a leg up a lamp post, but I'm telling you, 'e were set rigid."

"So what happened?" Although this didn't seem as bad as Dulcie had imagined, she had to admit this was most unusual behaviour for Rover. He had never once been aggressive in any way and being rather old, like his master, he let the world go by not bothering anyone.

"He growled and 'is lips cocked up, showing 'is teeth. And 'he stayed like that until they 'ad passed. When they got by us they stood and stared and Rover got behind my legs as though 'he were afraid. Now that aint 'im. But I'm telling you as sure as eggs is eggs, they freaked that dog and they freaked me. Now you tell me, when 'as that ever 'appened in this village. Well I'll tell you. Never. That's when."

There was a pause, partly as Janet had run out of steam and Dulcie couldn't think of anything to answer such an outburst. Finally she asked "What exactly do you think they did that made you and Rover so – um - uneasy." She avoided the word 'afraid' as didn't want to add to the situation.

"It sounds silly now don't it? Two little girls looking at a dog that growled at'em."

Dulcie sipped her tea. "Well it obviously weren't silly at the time. I thinks we should keep our eyes open where those two are. Wonder what Nora will make of it?"

"Nora!" Janet almost yelled. "I'd forgotten 'er. She'll laugh and say I'm silly. You know what she's like."

"I wouldn't be too sure of that." Dulcie had a half smile creeping across her face. "Give 'er summat to ponder over I shouldn't wonder."

"Ooh ah, you could be right there." And with the tension now eased the two pals finished their tea before Dulcie left to do her daily chores. As she walked the short distance back to her home, something inside her niggled at her that her friend had suffered more of a shock that she thought, but at least she had left her pretty settled for now. Although she had made light of it for Janet's sake, the feeling that lingered was that this was not the end, but the beginning of something which at present they did not understand, and she didn't have a good feeling about it. She made up her mind to say extra prayers that night asking for God's protection for her and her friends. It didn't occur to her to say one now, that wouldn't be in the daily pattern of things.

CHAPTER 3

The Reverend Desmond Conway wasted no time that morning in contacting the authorities regarding the schooling and safety of the two girls. It did cross his mind that up to now he hadn't actually seen them but felt he had sufficient information for the right department to look into it. He would just do his duty in informing them but still approach from the religious side on his next visit which he was determined to make before long, regardless of the rebuff he had received yesterday. After being transferred from one office to another he was finally satisfied that 'the matter would receive attention at their earliest convenience' as they put it. He had added that he did hope so, left his contact details and sat down to think.

Although he knew that Graham had moved on to higher levels, it was at times like this he missed being able to give him a ring to pour out his feelings. He imagined his senior was often in contact but Desmond was not adept enough yet to sleep at will to make communication. So he sat quietly sending out strong thoughts, going through all he knew, little as it was, hoping it would be picked up at some time, if not by Graham but one of his equals. At this time he was still not fully aware that thoughts were like an open telephone line and could be homed in by any spirit on the same wavelength, good or bad and there were usually plenty hovering hoping for such a snippet. He still needed training in this area but that would only come with time and experience.

Fortunately, the school attendance office was visiting local schools as part of his usual checks so when the office rang him on his mobile phone, he appreciated it would save him an additional visit if he covered the case now. He finished the morning calls, and after a quick lunch at a local hostelry, he took out his scribbled note, checked the address and drove to the De'Ath residence.

The first thing he noticed as he got out of his car was that although a sunny day, all the curtains seemed closed and he wondered if he'd come to the right place. He, like Desmond, searched for a knocker or bell and finally knocked quite loudly on the door. After a few moments the door opened slightly and the face of Maisie De'Ath peered round the edge. As she didn't offer to speak the officer introduced himself.

"Good afternoon, I'm David Jenkins, the local school attendance officer. May I have a word?" He felt he couldn't ask to be let in at this stage as the woman appeared terrified but her face softened and she stood back opening the door and beckoning him in.

"Come in please. Please excuse the mess, but we've only just moved in you see." She was in a plain jumper and skirt, very different to her previous apparel and she looked quite dowdy in what light there was. He followed as she led him into the front room and switched on a small table lamp. Clearing some boxes from the settee she indicated for him to sit down.

"I'm sorry about the light but I can't stand the brightness and the sun is very strong at present, so I have to wait until it has gone round. I've always been the same."

David Jenkins could have believed this except for the fact that the sun was already shining on the rear of the house, with the front in shadow but he thought better than to correct her, after all he felt quite an achievement at being in the place.

They certainly hadn't been here long as the room was filled with piles of linen, half emptied boxes and just about anything that could be left somewhere 'for now'.

"I won't keep you long," he tried to put her at ease "but with any new family we just check that any children are registered at the local school. Do you have any children Mrs...... I'm so sorry, I didn't ask your name." This was no mistake on his part. He knew from experience that you confirmed the name of the person you were visiting for obvious reasons, but there were cases, that if you went in asking too much too soon you could hit a brick wall as soon as they 'smelt' authority, so he used the gentle entry, as he called it, then went for the kill when he had their attention.

"Oh, it's Mrs. De'Ath." She must have felt that was all he wanted to know so he slowly took out a form and said "I knew a chap by that name, loved football. What is your Christian name please?"

"Maisie."

Still keeping it casual he said "That's nice, and your husband"

"Frank."

"Thank you. And now, did you say you had any children?"

She smiled for the first time. "Oh yes, twin girls, "and she beamed almost lost in the thought of her daughters. He had to bring her back to reality and asked "I imagine you have given them lovely names too."

"Topaz and Peridot, our jewels."

David had been filling in more boxes than she had realized, and still wanting to keep her confidence he exclaimed "Oh that is nice, you must be very proud of them. Um – how old are they now?"

"Ten, well - they will be eleven early June."

He paused before going for the most important question. "And have you had chance to book them in at the village school Mrs. De'Ath?" This was the bit he had been leading up to and looked her straight in the eye now.

"Oh we don't need to do that, they go to a private school." She nodded to herself as if confirming it.

David Jenkins decided to probe a bit further before asking which one.

"Well at their age, won't they be changing shortly, you know going to a high school or something similar."

"Oh there's no need for that. The school is divided into ages, they will just move from the junior section to the senior. Saves upheavals you see." She stopped suddenly thinking just how many upheavals they had gone through over the girls' short lives with moving house but cleared it from her mind and turned her concentration back to her visitor. This hadn't gone unnoticed by the officer and he wondered what had been going through her mind, but he was patient.

"Well that's all right then Mrs. De'Ath, oh I had better just put down the name of the school, just for the records you understand," then laughingly said, "I get my knuckles rapped if I haven't filled in all the boxes, not than anyone reads them I suppose."

For a moment he thought she was going to close up but he just smiled at her as he started to pack his briefcase, and to his relief she said "St. Anne's Girls Academy."

"My word, that sounds posh." Then after a moment "Isn't it just outside Woodstock?" She nodded. As he got up to go he slipped into the 'good byes' "So they are there now?"

He sensed she now felt as though he was delving further than she wished but said quietly "No, they have let them have a few days extra before the bank holiday for them to get settled here," then added quickly, "but they've gone out for a walk, probably picking flowers."

"Oh that's good. Well thank you again for your time Mrs. De'Ath, you know everything is tied down with paperwork these days."

Before he had reached his car she had gone in and shut the door and he felt that even with his levity she had been most uncomfortable with a stranger being in their home. As he drove away he wondered what the husband looked like and more importantly, the girls. As soon as he had left the village he stopped in a lay by on the top road and got on his phone to the office. In no time they had contacted the school and confirmed that the girls were indeed pupils and were off until after the bank holiday. As far as he was concerned, the story was correct, the girls were in regular and permanent education which satisfied the department he covered so he asked his assistant to give the vicar a call to confirm they were satisfied with the visit. Being a busy man he then turned his attention to the afternoon calls.

The evenings were still turning a little chilly even though the nights were drawing out well. A little group of men sat in the corner of The Swan, the village pub, discussing the weather, their allotments and all the usual chat. Old Tom already had his free pint ready to relate one of his tales. Many had been repeated but no-one every got tired of his rambling and as younger men got to drinking age they too would sit enthralled. Sadly a lot of the local dialect was slipping away as people worked in the towns or cities and became lost in a mixture of sayings and different ways of speaking that it was difficult to isolate some of the tones to one area alone. But Tom would never change.

"Tell the lads about the prayers for a start off Tom," one prompted him. Tom took a slow drink, wiped his hand across his mount and said "Aah well now, you sees one Sunday we 'adn't got a minister in the chapel so old Jake, 'e stands up and 'e says 'I'll do the prayers.' So we says 'all right Jake, you do 'em then'." He took another swig of ale, looked round slowly and continued.

"May Mr. Musty 'ave a good crop of wheeeeeeeat." The last word came out as a sort of squeak which started the young lads laughing and at the right moment Tom stood up and said "Oh Lord, bless I and my wife, our Walt and 'is wife, we four, no more Amen."

Probably the words alone wouldn't have been funny but with Tom performing them in such a broad accent, anyone would have found it difficult to suppress a smile. Quite often visitors would all stop and listen until he had finished, as did two ladies sitting a few seats away from him. They had been well and truly scrutinized by the locals, wondering why two smart females had stopped at their pub.

"So 'he asks were I lives," Tom was off again. "and I says to 'im, well - you know that 'ouse whitewashed yeller (*yellow*), and 'he says 'Aah' I says to 'him 'Well, that bient our'n." At which point the laughter rose again and when the inquisitive ones looked round the two ladies had left.

Ana was in constant communication with fire angel Ignis for they both felt something was brewing in the village. He had found out from one of his trusty sentinels that the parents were harmless in themselves but could be used as tools by fire demons and it looked as though things could possibly be moving slowly in that direction. The twins were another matter for it was thought that one fire demon was in situ in both earthly forms, hence their identical activities. The question was why and for what reason.

"The space is obviously being kept for some purpose. Ignis stated to which Ana added "More importantly by whom, and will it be a fire entity, also will it be there of its own free will?"

"A lot of questions, to which we must find the answers." Ignis assured Ana he would inform her immediately of any change, but not by the direct route as they knew every move would be monitored by all forces. If only they knew just what was in store, but all would be revealed and had they been angels of a lesser power they would soon be wishing they hadn't been so eager to find out.

The two ladies who had lingered at the pub long enough to update on recent cases were now heading their separate ways, the senior of the two social services officers had finished checking on local workers and was on her way home, the problems of the day already going to the back of her mind as she thought of the cosy armchair awaiting her. She did cast her mind to the conversation with the younger woman, and although she felt there would be a simple explanation to the vicar's concern, you could never be sure and had to check out things just in case. Maybe she should have gone with her, but changed her mind as Sharon was a very capable person and had dealt with quite a few difficult cases and she knew she would get a call if there was anything the woman wasn't happy about.

Sharon Forest had chosen the early evening for her visit to the De'Aths as she imagined the girls would be at home and probably in bed. Being the last house in the street she found her destination quite easily and parked on the road outside. As she made her way to the front door, she began to think she had wrongly timed the visit as nobody seemed to be in, but she knocked the door and waited. As she could faintly make out movement from inside she waited and was about to knock again when the door opened and Maisie peered round the edge.

"Hello, I'm Mrs. Forest, from the social services, are you Mrs. De'Ath?"

"We didn't send for anyone."

"No, that's right but we always check these days if anybody moves in to see if they need anything." She knew this should invoke a question or at least a reply but didn't expect another head to pop round the door which was now opened a little wider. Frank looked from his wife to Sharon.

"I understand from my good wife that we've had somebody round, so if you'll excuse us we……"

"Mr. De'Ath?"

"That is correct."

Sharon leaned a little forward as if she was about to impart a secret which made the parents step back a little.

"You see we, that is our department comes under a lot of scrutiny and we have had cases of people needing assistance but not receiving any kind of support, especially in the case of children. Then we are in trouble for not looking into it, so what we do now is, we just check and if all is OK we are in the clear. Do you see what I mean?" She hoped they would swallow this as she was searching her brain for the next step if they didn't.

"So you're nothing to do with the man that came earlier?" Maisie pushed Frank out of the way as she almost filled the doorway.

"Different thing altogether." Sharon decided not to say they all worked in conjunction, as these people might think it was some sort of conspiracy and continued "Do you suppose we could just have a little chat, just so I can say I've been you see."

The couple looked at each other then both nodded and stood aside for her to enter. As experienced by Desmond, Sharon was soon reeling from the mixture of pungent smells and coughed involuntary as she was shown to the front room.

"This can't be healthy" she thought as she sat in the same seat recently occupied by David Jenkins. "Now I just have to put some ticks in boxes, sign of the times I'm afraid," she forced a smile which was only returned with a slight nod. She filled in the information which was obvious, names, the address, ages – Frank was thirty seven but his dear wife forty six. Not a surprise when you looked at them but what an odd couple.

The truth was that Frank had never had any success with women and Maisie was running out of time. Not being the prettiest flower in the bunch to put it kindly, she would have anyone who would have her to settle down and have children. Love hadn't really come into it as he wasn't the loving sort and as she ruled him and the home, he found it easier to just abide by her wishes and opt for the quiet life. They had been overjoyed when the twins were born but having done his duty any intimacy between them seemed to vanish at that point. Maisie would have been happy for their lovemaking to continue as there wasn't anybody else to do it with, but he basically didn't fancy her which in time turned into actual revulsion. Maisie was ready to rule the girls' lives but soon found that wasn't going to be, for from an early age they took on their own will so she had no option but to succumb to a greater power than her own. It was partly out of frustration she had started her phase of 'calling the spirits' as she put it and had roped him in, out of obedience, in the hopes she could get him to perform again, however bad he was at it. Beggars as they say.........

Sharon was flying through the forms until she came to the part relating to children.

"You have children I understand?"

"Yes, two, twin girls. I expect you've got to put their names down." Maisie had taken over the answering.

"Yes that's right."

"Topaz and Peridot."

As she wrote the names Sharon mentioned "How lovely."

"Everyone says that."

"I'm not surprised." She now had to get onto the subject of the girls' whereabouts. "I expect they are in bed now."

"They could be."

This wasn't quite the answer expected. "You're not sure?"

Maisie coughed a little then said, "Well they go to their room you see, and they go to bed when they like. Oh we check on them" she added hastily, picking up the question on the visitors' face, " we make sure they are bedded down by seven thirty but we are giving them a bit of freedom this week due to the move, the upheaval you know."

As Sharon glanced at her watch, and noticing it was 7.45pm she ventured "Any chance of them being up now."

The parents exchanged glances which didn't go unnoticed. They weren't too keen on any sort of meeting which made the officer all the more determined so she tried a new approach.

"It would save me coming back again if I could just have a peep. Clear up all the paperwork in one go, you understand?"

They were interrupted by a movement at the door.

"Why don't you let her come up and see for herself?" All heads shot round as the two girls appeared in the doorway.

"Well, if you don't mind........" if Maisie was going to say anything else, she didn't have change for the girls beckoned Sharon to go with them.

"This is a turn up" she thought as she followed them upstairs through the gloomy house up the uncarpeted stairs and into their bedroom. Immediately she was hit with the difference of this room to the rest of the house. The curtains were drawn back, the evening light penetrating the room, the neatly made beds were draped in beautiful coloured spreads and as she cast her eye around, she wondered how this had become so lived-in in less than a week supposedly. The only explanation was that the parents had concentrated on this place for the girls to settle in and they had left the rest piled with boxes and packages to deal with at their leisure.

"Please sit." One girl spoke as the other pointed to a chair against the wall and they sat on the bed facing it. Sharon was pulled back to reality as her thoughts had taken over since entering this place. Suddenly she felt as though she was the one being scrutinized as they both sat staring at her waiting for her to speak.

"Um – have you always shared one room?"

Together they chorused "Yes, always."

There was a pause as the woman was searching for the next question but settled on a basic enquiry. Not divulging any knowledge passed to her earlier she said "Where do you go to school?"

"Near Woodstock."

"Oh, the one – what's the name now?" The girls didn't offer any help. "St Anne's, that's the one isn't it?" They both nodded.

"Is it boarding, or do you go every day?"

"We go every day. Father takes us then goes to work." One had answered but Sharon wasn't sure which and she didn't want to loose the thread now. "Oh, that's handy. How do you get home though?"

"Dad brings us."

As her mind was piecing all the bits together, Sharon felt she must delve a little deeper and asked "He must work short hours then, is he a teacher?"

"No. They have this system at school that all children who are going to be picked up have a sort of club and we do things for about an hour then our parents come." The other one had answered this time, but had she, they both sounded exactly the same.

"And what do you do, at the club, if you don't mind me asking?"

At this point Sharon thought the interview had been ended but the girls went to the walls looking at paintings which had been hung all round the room. Why hadn't she noticed them before? Probably because the girls had held her attention, but she certainly noticed them now.

"This is what you do?" she almost murmured. They both nodded.

"But these are exquisite, I've never seen colours like this before, where on earth do you get them?

"We mix them." The girls moved to a table where the recently delivered box lay. Father is very good, he sends away for our materials and we work from there.

Sharon was now looking closely at some of the works. "You seem to work in oils, watercolours, pastels and this looks to be charcoal, I tried it once but got in an awful mess, but do you do all these at school?"

"Oh no, we don't show them this kind of work, we just draw mostly." Sharon hardly noticed that the information was now flowing easily, although little realizing she was being fed only what they chose.

"So where do you paint here, have your parents given you a studio in the house?"

"This is our area." Both girls now stood almost joined taking it in turns to speak.

"We like to be where we are comfortable. This room is adequate for our needs."

It was only later that Sharon realized the girls were speaking in terms way beyond their tender years and although well educated they should still have borne the innocents of juniors. The two didn't seem, to marry somehow.

But now she was examining a painting which hung just above where she had been sitting.

"The flowers, I've never seen such hues, you should exhibit you know."

"We couldn't do that?"

"But why not, I'm sure these would sell."

"NO." The two chorused then softened the tone, "we don't sell, but we do give one to people we like now and again."

Sharon stood back to admire this particular work from a distance "I would like to buy this."

"Then take it."

"W-h-a-t ? You said you didn't sell........."

"We don't. We said we give."

The woman sat down harder than she intended. This wasn't at all what she had expected on her way here. These two were obviously prodigies their talents hidden from the outside world, but was it by their parents or by themselves? And they were hardly old enough to decide, but then they were capable of producing such masterpieces, unless they were two little liars and were playing with her. As these thoughts pulsated through her brain she realized the painting had been removed from the wall and was being carefully wrapped in tissue. They both approached her and together placed the parcel in her hands and with a smile opened the door to indicate the meeting had ended.

As she made her way back down the gloomy stairs, the parents met her at the door and saw her out.

"They very kindly gave me a painting," she turned and smiled.

Maisie, as though it was an everyday occurrence said quietly without emotion, "They do that." Frank stood motionless until the door was closed again to the outside world.

CHAPTER 4

Miss Fay Anders, sat in her comfy armchair, her eyes closed and her mind floating back some sixty three years. Then a mere nineteen, her mother encouraged her to get a job in Oxford to learn the tailoring trade which she said would not only give her a living for as long as she wished, but would save her a lot of money if she could make her own clothes. She would also be following in her footsteps and as young Fay didn't have much idea of what she wanted to do for a living she drifted into the job, much to her mothers' pleasure.

As she travelled back and forth on the train each day, she found herself sitting next to a rather attractive young man who got off at Charlbury, the stop before hers. Gradually they exchanged a quick 'Hello', he introduced himself as Samuel and soon they were sharing little conversations until they realized they were looking for each other. If the train happened to be rather crowded they preferred to stand together rather than be separated if there was only the odd spare seat. They found they both had bicycles and arranged to meet half way between the villages and go out for a ride. This soon grew into him coming to call for her and was well liked by her parents and even better liked by the other girls of a similar age. Fay started to feel a few pangs of jealousy when she thought some of them were trying to get his attention but she needn't have worried, for although he found it flattering, his heart was already hers. She in turn visited his family and was warmly accepted and it was obvious to all that an announcement would be made after a reasonable period of time.

Unfortunately it didn't go quite to plan, as Fay found she was expecting. The word pregnant was not used much then. In those days, this situation brought shame on the family if word got about, so as happened in many cases, her father threw her out. Her mother couldn't bear his harshness and arranged for Fay to go and live with her married sister in a nearby village until 'it was all over' as she put it and then she could come back. But her father said 'out' meant 'out' and that was the end of it. Fay loved her mother dearly, but her father had upset her so much she decided she never wanted to set foot in their house again.

She didn't know whether to tell Samuel at first but broke down when they were out for a cycle ride and he was excited at first but also dismayed that they must be parted. He also knew that his parents would have none of it so the lovers had no choice but go their separate ways.

Life drifted along but he was getting more and more depressed and was determined to contact Fay through her sister. At first there was some reluctance but as he was so determined, the two met at regular intervals relieved at the chance to express the love that had been buried. But the happiness was short lived, for as he was cycling home one evening, his front wheel must have hit a loose stone in the road and he was catapulted down a slope, landing in the river. As he was unconscious, he was unable to crawl out and his lifeless body was found the following day by a farmer who noticed the hole in the hedge he had made during the fall.

It took a while for the news to filter through and it was only because someone knew of their attachment, that Fay learned as soon as she did. She was inconsolable at first, but being of strong spiritual beliefs she lost herself in the fact that he would be with her in spirit and knew that she would never want or love anyone else.

When the baby was born, her sister who could not have any children, offered to adopt the boy and it was agreed that they would never let him know who his real mother was. At Fay's choice he was christened Digby but would of course have to take her sister's married name. It hurt for a while but in those days an unmarried mother would be shunned and Digby would bear the stigma of being a bastard. So she had no option but to carry the secret for ever and just be his Auntie Fay.

She found a small place near her sister and started to take in sewing until she felt like looking for another job. But word of her work soon got round the village and before long people were bringing her garments for alteration, clothes to be cut down for the children to get the last bit of wear out of them, new clothes to be made to measure and it then extended to neighbouring villages. Her mother was so proud especially when she was told that Fay had been asked to make a wedding dress complete with bridesmaids dresses. Without realizing it, Fay had become her own boss and self supporting.

All seemed to be going well until she learned that the true parents' names had been put on Digby's birth certificate and it was only when he was getting married and needed it, the truth came out. At first he was shocked but when told the whole story, he felt such a feeling of sadness for his parents who were so very much in love that he wanted to know all about them.

Fay was told gently, and after many emotional tears was able to hold her son after all those years, but they agreed for the sake of her decency he would still call her Auntie Fay. He asked to visit his father's grave and as they stood side by side he said "I would like to take his surname." Fay was overcome and could only whisper "Yes, yes."

Before they left he stood with his head high and said proudly   "Hello Samuel De'Ath, I am your son Digby De'Ath, and I will always make sure mother is alright."

Fay snapped back to the present. The letter from her son, thanking her for letting him know there was a house for sale in her little village, for that was the meaning behind the few words, was in her hand. He always wrote so that no-one who may find any letter would know what he meant, but a mother always would. He knew his son had to move again, and he knew why. She brought the envelope to her lips, kissed it gently and smiled as she thought of the prospect of seeing Digby soon.

Sharon was only half way home when she felt a slight shudder from the front of her car, seemingly to come from the wheels. After a moment it stopped and she put it down to tiredness. She had put the wrapped picture on the front passenger seat and a slight movement caught her attention. The tissue paper had blown back exposing half the painting and she noticed something odd about one of the flowers. She glanced back at the road and then looked quickly at the painting. It was there, a face was looking out of the flower and it was smiling. She was tempted to pull over and look again but this was a lonely road and she felt the urge to get home. She was approaching a rather nasty corner well known for accidents and she tried to slow down but the car kept going at the same speed. Trying to touch the grass verge to slow the car she somehow managed to get round the bend and as soon as she was on the straight again the car started to slow down. She pushed the accelerator harder but still the card slowed. A flutter from the seat made her glance again and the full painting was now on view, and there wasn't one face but several and they were all grinning at her.

Frantically she turned the picture over and tried to get the car to increase speed. Slowly she felt she had control again but was visibly shaken as she pulled into her drive. She sat for a few moments trying to compose herself when her husband appeared at the side of the car. She jumped.

"What on earth's the matter?" he looked concerned and opened the door for her.

"The car didn't seem to do – I mean it wasn't right - and I nearly........." she was crying now.

"Ok, enough, let's get you inside and you can tell me what happened."

After she had sipped the tea he made, he said "Right, slowly, I want to know, because this isn't like you."
Although she tried to recount the terrifying journey, sitting there in her lounge with his arm round her made it all sound stupid. She then remembered the painting and told him about how it seemed to have unwrapped and then looked at her.

"Now you know I'm crazy." She was almost sobbing again. He got up and left the room and a few moments later returned with the offending article in his hand.

"You mean this, - but it's beautiful." He held it at arms length admiring the colouring and brushwork.

"I don't know, I don't know."

"Tell you what," he sat beside her, I'll have the car checked out thoroughly tomorrow, put both our minds at rest, and I think you are getting over tired. You have been working all hours God sends."

"Yes. You're right as always."
He put the picture on the side table and said "We'll find a good place to hang that, needs good light."

And so the work of art was in its new home.

There was much consternation among the higher levels of angel elements. Ana, Ohley and Ignis were all brought together with the announcement "I know who we are dealing with." Ignis had succeeded with help from his watchers, to learn that the fire demon occupying the twins was none other than Daku, an underling of Lazzan

"So it is something big?" Ana had dreaded this.

"Not necessarily," Ignis was aware of the danger but wanted to be sure of his facts. "You know he is of the calibre of Fica in your air element Ana, full of his own importance. Could be trying to gain favour with his almighty for some reason. Lazzan doesn't have to be behind it."

"Wish we could be sure" Ohley thought, then to Ana "You said you had someone in mind to oversee?"

"I did, and they are already observing." There was a pause then she said "It's fair that you should know Ohley for they are water angels.

"They?" Ohley queried, we thought there would only be one and from the air like you."

"Yes, there are two and they always work together, one is in earthly form and the other has been in spirit for many years. They have done some fine work but have been kept at a distance since their last triumph."

"Oh, I know who you mean." Ohley brightened "but why not.........?"

"Tell you" Ana finished for her, "because you could not hold the thought for the slightest moment, or the fire demons may have homed in on it so it was safer."

Ignis was showing his approval "Very canny move Ana, but with this level of demon, we have to be. Now, the next move."

"Shouldn't we watch for a while?" Ohley was afraid to disturb the hosts, namely the twins as their true occupants would be put in placement as soon as they could get the intruder out and she was worried about them being so young. One false move could jeopardize the whole operation

"Can't." Ignis was blunt. So Ana explained. "The longer the girls are out of their host bodies, the more difficult it will be for them to......" she paused for a moment "I was going to say adjust, but am I right Ignis that Daku took them whist still in formation?"

"Correct. He took over while they were still in the womb, almost at the moment of conception, so the two ideals who were being placed are still in waiting."

"Oh I see," Ohley was piecing everything together, "so speed is important?"

"Very." Ignis was gratified he had made his point and that all would be done to close this incident as soon as possible.

"One question Ignis?" this had been niggling at Ana. "The two who should have been placed, are they fire signs?"

After a slight pause, Ignis imparted, "No Ana, they were only taken over by a fire demon, they are both of the air, and like you are angels."

"So that is the reason for the haste." Ohley's thought was more to herself, but felt the warmth of agreement of her companions sweep over her ideal.

This was going to be a delicate operation with many angels involved which would undoubtedly draw unwanted attention from all sources. Also the two in waiting must be held at a safe distance for protection, but as soon as Daku could be removed, the space must be filled, even temporarily or another unwanted 'squatter' would be in.

Definitely a task for experienced ideals from all elements. So the three arch angels set about forming a plan for the removal of Daku.

Desmond looked at his watch, yawned and thought it time to retire for the evening. He had been wondering how the visits by the authorities had gone and expecting they wouldn't hurry themselves due to the usual high workload they were supposed to be staggering under. It may not have been a very charitable thought, but he wished they sometimes had the situations to cope with that he had, when you couldn't go back and discuss it with a colleague, in fact you couldn't discuss it with anyone, except Him. Oh well, maybe he would get some feedback in the morning.

He made his usual checks round the house, windows, doors etc and was just bolting the front door when he imagined he heard a slight rustle from the step outside.

"It'll be that ginger cat again," he smiled to himself. Ginger often visited him and he had taken to leaving a saucer of milk or scraps out, all which had disappeared by morning. He pulled the bolt back and opened the door ready to give the cat its usual greeting, but no cat. Instead a small parcel was propped against the door frame. He carefully picked it up, looked out into the darkness but there seemed to be no-one about, no movement, nothing.

He closed the door and re-bolted it and took the small package into the sitting room, and sat down to see what some kind soul had left for him. Written on the brown paper in large letters was simply "To The Reverent". He was forced to smile. "I've never been called that before." Slowly he undid the paper to expose a small painting in a simple frame. He had mixed thoughts as the questions raced around his mind. Who had brought it, or sent it? Why had he been given it? Was it for a church sale and not for him? Ah that would be it, it was a donation for a future fund raising. He looked again at the paper. Well perhaps they had just put his name because he represented the church, but wait! All the locals knew him as 'Vicar', 'Reverend Conway', and some even 'The Reverend Desmond' and his close friends just used his Christian name. He could almost understand 'The Reverend' but the churchgoers would not have spelled it incorrectly.

His attention was now drawn to the painting itself. At first he thought there must be some mistake as it was obviously a work of art. The colours seemed to move before his eyes and he had to stop and rub them before continuing. The flowers were such as he had never seen before but between two of the blooms there seemed to be a face with hands over the mouth. Thinking this was a new theme on the three wise monkeys, he cast his gaze over the rest of the picture. At the foot of the tree, another face was slowly emerging with something else. A hand was positioned under the chin with the forefinger pointing, and he was in no doubt it was pointing at him. As he watched, this image faded and he was drawn to letters which were falling like leaves Y - O – U. The painting was turning from a thing of beauty to something with a very bad feeling emitting from it. He started to pray and felt his aura strengthening in protection and chanting aloud he grabbed the picture and wrapping, instructing what ever was surrounding it to leave and never return. As he got to the front door he could feel a tremendous burning in his hand, but he struggled to draw the bolt and unlock the door and threw everything into the darkness, still ordering it to be gone from this place and go where it could harm no-one. Desmond was not alone for Graham had been at his side until now, when he suddenly rushed passed him still ordering the entity to go. As the picture landed on the ground it burst into flames almost with a manic scream because this time it had been beaten by good forces stronger than itself.

Graham accompanied Desmond back inside and placing a calming wave over him, guided him to a chair where he induced him to sleep. The two met on a higher level and discussed the events. Ana had been waiting for something to show itself and had brought Graham back temporarily to help his friend but it had to be a short visit as he was still being kept a safe distance from the earth. However Graham had brought other air angels to give added protection while Desmond slept this night. He returned him to his waken state safe in the knowledge the thing would not return, but had to report the outcome to Ana as she would then know the fire demon was showing its hand. It was no longer dormant.

CHAPTER 5

It was the Friday morning leading into the late spring bank holiday and although several villagers were preparing for a long week end away, Sally still opened up the 'Coffee Break' as it had become a main little centre for a bit of company for the elderly. Also the village school children were encouraged to visit with little works of art thereby narrowing the age gap and teaching the little ones to have thought for older people who may need a bit of help sometimes, but also showing the elderly that the young of today were not all thoughtless and only up to mischief. Sally wished this community spirit could extend to other villages, and also towns and cities as it promoted care and consideration.

Of course there were some, and she didn't have to look too far, who would always enjoy moaning, but that was nothing to do with age, they had probably always been the same.

"What's up with your face?" Nora's demand to know could be heard all over the small hall. Dulcie nudged Janet and said "Tell her."

"Tell who what?" Nora looked from one lady to the other, not only impatient to know what was going on, but a bit indignant that she could have been left out of it and seemed to be the last to know. When nothing was forthcoming she turned her attack on Fay.

"I suppose you know as well?"

Fay shook her head, "I've no idea what any of you are up to" and seeming detached from the group continued to sip her tea. This situation always brought the worst out in Nora and her façade slipped for a moment.

"Well, I wants to know." She was so intent on finding out, the faux pas went unnoticed by all except Fay who smiled to herself.

"Janet had a funny turn." Dulcie offered, at which Janet looked a little relieved, hoping she wouldn't have to relate the recent scare with Rover. Nora was back to normal now that something seemed to be emerging.

"You ill then? What sort of turn? Have you been checked out lately, could be your heart you know at your age."

"Oh give her a chance to speak Nora, you're just bombarding her." Dulcie felt annoyed knowing what her friend had been through.

Janet almost whispered, "You say Dulcie, tell them what I told you, but I'm sure I'm only being silly."

Nora wasn't going to let that chance go by and cut in "Well you probably are, as usual I expect, but let's hear it then, from somebody." The last two words held the frustration she felt.

"Well," Dulcie was speaking but looking at Janet all the time, "she were walking Rover, Joe's dog, you know 'cos of 'is leg," she paused and cast a glance at Nora who was tapping her fingers on the table and realized she didn't want the saga of Joe's leg again so she hurriedly went on "and she got near the church." Slowly she related the tale of the girls and Rover's reaction, probably elaborating where she thought necessary so that Nora wouldn't think it too much like imagination. Fay sat quietly taking it all in, but looking very thoughtful, after all they didn't realize they were discussing her great granddaughters.

When the tale had finished there was a silence. Even Nora seemed stuck for words, but she was never quiet for long and said "Well, I don't know I'm sure," took a drink of tea and continued "it's obviously shaken you up, but I should forget all about it if I were you."

"But I can't." Janet was almost in tears so Nora changed her tactic.

"It must be the dog, bet he's going funny in his old age, they can you know." All three ladies were looking at her making her feel very uncomfortable, forcing her to make the next move.

"Perhaps it's his time - you know."

Both Janet and Dulcie chorused "No." They were animal lovers, Nora was not and that made a difference.

"He could be poorly." Fay's little voice broke in. "Perhaps the vet should see him."

Janet had found new strength at the thought of the dog being put down when she had witnessed his reaction at the girls but was perfectly calm on the way home.

"I know what I saw, and there's nothing the matter with Rover. It was them, they freaked him out. If anyone needs putting down it's you." And she stabbed the air at Nora before bursting into tears.

"Now look what you've done Nora." Dulcie had left her chair and was consoling her friend.

This little scene hadn't gone unnoticed by other visitors, especially 'Ben the Post' who had arrived in the middle of the outburst.

"I told you" he whispered to Sally "summat aint right wi' that new lot."

"Yes, I remember you saying Ben. What d'you reckon it is then?"

"Still can't put me finger on it. But who has a name like Death, I asks you?" Sally pushed his mug of tea towards him. "That can't be right. I never heard of a name like that."

"It's right I tells you, saw it on a parcel – Death – that's what it said, as clear as I's standing 'ere."

Sally was at a bit of a loss for words and whispered "Well you just be careful now Ben."

As he took his tea to a table Sally's eyes went to the four ladies. She had never seen them so subdued in all the time she'd known them. "Something strange going on here" she thought to herself.

For some reason, children can be very unkind to one another, but tell them about it later in life and they probably won't even remember it. If one of their own has some sort of disability they can be quite protective but let them see one on its own, or a stranger doing something unusual, they will be the first to mock and poke fun at it. Sometimes this experience can follow the child into adult life and they will never forget it.

So it goes without saying that when the village children encountered the De'Ath twins they had a situation just made for their enjoyment. It started when four of the lads were hanging about on the village green and the two girls appeared, usual gait, arm in arm. If one head turned so did the other. The group watched them as they neared the green, the twins almost unaware of their presence, but when they had passed the kids fell into step behind them a few yards back and started to imitate every movement. This caused giggles as one child laughed at another and so on until they were so convulsed they almost fell over with mirth not realizing the two girls had stopped suddenly and they almost careered into them, landing in a heap in the road.

Slowly the twins turned, and without a word just stared at the heaving mass. One by one the lads nudged each other and stood facing them. Not one of them could move, as if they had been stuck to the ground where they stood and a feeling of utter terror started to creep over them. They began to feel hot, very hot, their mouths parched, eyes burning in the sockets, their clothes clinging to their bodies as if they were trying to rip the flesh from the bones. As quickly as the feeling had started, it released them and when they had regained their ability to move, looked at each other in horror of the experience. The two younger ones were crying and shaking but as they all looked towards the girls, they had gone.

As the lads made their way home, they were still fairly quiet, but one said "What you going to tell your mum?" After a pause one said "They won't believe us."
Another almost whispered "My dad'll leather me, he'll say I been telling lies."
"He can't do that, he's not supposed to" the eldest cut in but was just given a look by the younger. So they decided that as they had no marks, and everything seemed to be back to normal, they had better keep it to themselves for now, as it would just be their word against the girls. But this experience would haunt their sleeping hours for a long time.

Daku was enjoying his use of the two bodies, a step up from the last poor specimen he had occupied but he soon left that one as it gave him little satisfaction and the greater powers had been an annoyance as he put it. If fact, he had been exorcised by priests experienced in such things, and his ego didn't accept they had made him leave but that he had chosen to go. But this placement, ha, it would take powers greater than a little vicar to move him, for he reckoned he was here to stay for a while, until of course it bored him and he wanted more. More power, larger territory, but why stop there, he could have the whole of this meager little bit of rock if he wished, after all, what was this scrap in comparison to the whole universe. But little did he reckon on the whiles of the arch angels who would try and use this jumped up egoist to produce his own downfall and self destruct his own ideal.

Plans were already forming around him, with the hierarchy holding well away leaving the sentinels, which were changing at irregular intervals, feeding back all the important information. Ana was pushing thoughts away so as not to attract unwanted entities but the one thought she was having the most difficulty suppressing was the question of who was about to enter the spaces. Logically it could not be Shane as he now had to rest, wherever he was, until his normal life span had elapsed and that could be for another fifty or sixty years as he was only on his second earth life. Short stays are only usually at the end of the seven visits when the student has already learned the requirements in the previous six, and merely makes a short appearance as they are bound to be born but are not required to stay. This is little comfort for parents not of a spiritual understanding who don't know why their precious gift has been taken.
But sometimes, things do not always go to plan of things, and an earthbound that has been snatched before the right time, has been known to re-appear in another young form with the knowledge taken with them at passing.

The two ideals then occupy the one body until the 'visitor' is ready to move on, leaving the host to live out his or her life alone. As in this case there were two spaces. Could it just be possible that an experienced ideal returning for the last time would be caring for an insecure one, protecting it until it was ready to rest?

Dulcie saw Janet home, knowing the encounter with Nora had done her little good and wanting to make sure she would settle as soon as she was back in her familiar surroundings. As they pottered up to the front door, Janet exclaimed "What's that? I'm not expecting anything."
Dulcie bent down and picked up the small package.
"It's just got your name on it, not been posted look."
They went inside and sat at the table where Janet started to unwrap the parcel. She stopped "What do you think it is?"
"We'll know when you've got it open." Dulcie tried not to be harsh but the answer was rather obvious.
"Oh, look, it's lovely." Janet held the little painting at arms length. "But it doesn't say who sent it. Perhaps it isn't for me."
"Of course it's for you girl, got your name on 'asn't it?" She put out her hand to take the picture but between them it slipped, breaking the glass causing small cuts in both ladies' hands. The shock made them both shout but Janet was near to tears again. Dulcie went to the kitchen, found some paper towels, put them under the cold table and hurried back to put them on the wounds.
"I can't take any more, first the dog, now this, I can't... I can't..."
"Just hold still and let me get this on, don't bother about the spots on the cloth, they'll wash." Dulcie was trying to cover her own cuts at the same time and realized they needed some help.
"Can I use your phone?" She was already making her way to the sideboard.
"What are you going to do?" Janet seemed to be weakening, not from the loss of blood, but from the shock.
Ignoring her Dulcie rang the local doctor and quickly explained what had happened and tried to convey that her friend needed attention in other ways. Fortunately the receptionist asked if she with the lady and soon gleaned that it wasn't easy for her to be precise. She quickly took down the details, double checking she had everything correct.
"The doctor is out on his calls at present, but I'll page him and get him to call. Will you be staying with your friend?"

"Oh yes, that's very good of you, thank you." She replaced the receiver and sat beside Janet who now seemed lost to the world.

The picture lay among the glass on the table. The idyllic scene which had been so much admired when they first saw it, now had an image in the grass of the meadow. An image of a creature with a black head, its teeth snarling and long flames surging from its jaws. But from where the ladies innocently sat, they were unaware of the horrific artwork.

It seemed ages before the doctor arrived, but the sight of a middle aged man with his medical bag brought comfort to Dulcie as she opened the door.

"Hello, I'm Dr.Day, the locum for this area, I understand you have a problem. May I come in?"

Dulcie stood back "Oh yes please doctor, this is my friend's house, she's in there," indicating the door to the sitting room.

This man was very astute and had taken in the toweling clutched in Dulcie's hand, also her agitated manner which she was doing her best to hide. He was soon at Janet's side speaking in low very soothing tones. She turned her head slightly as he introduced himself to her and whispered "I'm not going mad doctor, really I'm not."

Ignoring the remark he turned her attention to the cuts. "Now what on earth have you done here young lady?. His tone was putting her at ease very quickly and she started to tell him about the picture being dropped. He turned to Dulcie and said quite cheerily "Better have a look at your hand too in a minute then."

He slipped a small light onto his forehead and said "Right, let's see what we have here," and peered closely at the small cuts.

"They don't seem very deep, but I just want to check there are no fragments of glass still in there so hold still for me please." Dulcie watched as he took out a magnifier stand from his case. She paled a little as she thought "This is going to be me in a minute."

After a few moments the doctor removed the glass and switched off his light. "That seems all right Mrs. Mercer, the cuts are long but not deep, they should heal in no time." Janet smiled for the first time as he turned his attention to Dulcie. It didn't take long for him to come to the same conclusion, her cuts were not deep, but he praised her for her actions in keeping them both protected until he got there, which relaxed her.

Now he had reassured the ladies over their wounds, he wanted to know what was really behind the panic, for he sensed there was much more to this than they were telling him. He turned his attention to the picture on the table.

"Is this the offending object?" He poked the glass away with the end of his pen. They nodded but were fascinated when he reached into his bag and took out a pair of tweezers which he then used to lift the picture from the shards. For a second, he held it to his face then just as quickly put it back on the table.

"What's the matter Doctor?" Dulcie being nearest to him saw the sudden change in his manner.

Ignoring her, Dr Day turned to Janet and said "May I take this away for you?"

"But why, somebody has sent it to me?" Janet could still only see the pretty landscape as there was no sign of the creature which, had she been aware of its image, she would have begged someone to take it away and destroy it. The doctor had to think quickly.

"Well, you see I suspect this has been painted in a certain substance that we have come across quite a bit lately, and can cause irritation, in fact we are trying to stop it being used at all. For your sakes let me dispose of it for you, and at the same time, I'll clear up all this glass."

They seem to have accepted his explanation and Janet nodded as she said, "If you think its best, I do, don't you Dulcie?"

The other lady nodded but added "It's strange now we come to think of it, that it doesn't say who sent it, I mean if you're going to give somebody something, you think you'd let them know, wouldn't you?"

"I quite agree," Dr Day made the statement as if to seal a bargain indicating that it was settled and he would take the picture, glass and packing out of this house.

Making sure everything was securely deposited in a strong bag he always kept in his car, he returned to the house and said "Can I just ask ladies, has anything else happened to either of you recently, something you can't explain?" He looked enquiringly from one to the other sensing something was there that he should know about.

"If you promise you won't tell, only it sounds silly."

"I promise you I won't tell a living soul." There was much more to this reply than the ladies would ever imagine, because he didn't promise he wouldn't tell a spiritual soul.

Dr Day, although in bodily form, was one of Ana's key sentinels working right under the nose of Daku without him even realizing it. The demon was so full of his own devious ways that he, like Fica was not always open to the obvious. When the doctor had received the call from his receptionist, alarm bells went off in his head for this could be what they had all been waiting for, some sign of communication from Daku to people he thought were a threat or who could get in his way.

The arch angels of all elements had been alerted when the Rev.Conway had received his parcel and it looked as though the demon could be playing right into their hands. At least he could remove it from the current targets until greater entities could destroy it.

His attention was now on Janet who seemed to want to say something but was still hesitant. So he said quietly "You know, anything you say, although you might think it strange, may not be to me, let's say, I may have heard it before. Some one else may have had the same - how shall we say - feelings."

The ladies exchanged glances and Dulcie nodded for Janet to relate her experience. When she had finished he said very quietly "I can assure you Mrs. Mercer that you certainly are not going mad or anything of the sort. Her face brightened for the first time since Rover had freaked.

"You mean it? But what happened then?"

He looked from one to the other and said very slowly not wishing to frighten them any more "I have heard of this sort of thing, but I want you both to do something for me." They looked at each other, then him and both nodded.

"Sometimes animals sense things, they are very clever, especially dogs, but then I'm biased as I love them," he smiled in reassurance "and sometimes they can detect illnesses, or sometimes they are just protecting us from someone they don't particularly like. No reason, but I always listen to them, as I call it." He stopped to let that sink in.

Both ladies were fascinated and seeing the half smiles of relief on both faces he went on "give you an example, I had a lovely dog once, Jimmy, friends with everyone, lovely nature, then one day I stopped and spoke to a new person in the village where I lived then, and my dog slowly put himself in between us and started pushing me back. When the chap put out his hand to pet him, Jimmy did what you've just told me Rover did. Now I never knew why mine did that, there was nothing bad about the man but you see, we don't always sense what they do."

The ladies were really taken up with this and all fear had just about left them when he added almost as an afterthought "Now, I asked you to do something for me if you remember?"

"Oh yes, we'd forgotten".

"I don't want you to tell anyone about this at the moment."

Janet's face dropped. "Oh dear. We told Nora."

"Nora?"

"Yes," Dulcie joined in now, and she said the dog should put down, but he doesn't have to be does he, not with what you've said?"

Dr. Day jumped straight onto this angle, "That's why I am asking you to play this down now, for the dog's sake. We don't want people pointing the finger, which they will, and Joe would be heartbroken."

"You're saying that because you are an animal lover." Janet was very relaxed now.

"Hmm, but also because I've just been to see him - and his leg!" He laughed and was glad they saw the joke and joined in. "And," he added "I would say there is nothing wrong with the dog, he is just very aware."

"Oh what a relief Doctor, I don't mind saying I was feeling a bit off, just as an excuse like." Janet was almost enjoying the thought that Nora wouldn't be included in something for once.

"As long as you do feel all right?"

"Oh yes, Doctor, what a weight you've taken off my shoulders."

"And mine" Dulcie chipped in, "she were worrying me."

When the doctor had left, the two friends decided it was time for another cup of tea, the atmosphere very relaxed, which was just the opposite in the car as the smile faded from the doctor's face as he knew he had to dispose safely of the dangerous package now in the boot. He drew on added protection from waiting sentinels who had been alerted to the fact this meeting could achieve a positive result. He therefore used every ounce of concentration as he drove, for the slightest lapse was all that was needed to bring this earthly visit to a tragic end.

CHAPTER 6

Daku was not feeling as triumphant as he had hoped. He had expected his initial attacks to have caused some consternation in the area but he felt as though a force was already working against him, long before they should have even given it attention. Maybe he should have let the family settle a little longer, or could it be he had used the wrong targets, but he, Daku couldn't make that kind of mistake, he was perfect, that is, by his own standards.

He knew the picture to the vicar had been destroyed by angels of some element or other, and he was now aware that the one sent to the old lady had been removed. The one was still in situ at the social worker's home but it was time to up the heat and really show who was the cleverest force amongst all elements. This is where he would have to use the parents more, they had been satisfactory in delivering the pictures, but he would now pull on Maisie's dabbling with the spirit world to really shake things.

He planted the thought in her head that this evening would be a good time to hold one of her little rituals, that way he would pull on more forces, not to perform his tasks for him, but to add strength to the feeling of terror he was trying to impose on the village and surrounding area. His own force alone had worked in other areas, why not here. This was a bad start but he felt he was better and stronger than anything which opposed him and so he was about to charge headlong into the next phase.

The two girls were out walking, mainly on his order to meet as many people as possible for this was how he selected his prey, he had to have some sort of visual or bodily contact with them, which is why David Jenkins had escaped his share but the vicar had been observed from an upper window through a chink in the blinds. Daku was determined the girls would meet the postman, for he could be trouble, and they had already been observed by some little old lady, although he was unaware of the family connection and it must be time for a visit to the village shop. The school was breaking up for the bank holiday, so they would have to be positioned near the gates for the mums and dads to collect their offspring. That should add to the pile quite a bit and he could pick them off, selecting the easiest and most vulnerable.

While he was thus engrossed, Maisie was following his order to deliver a small package to the old lady at a certain house in the street, and soon a picture was on the doorstep of Miss Fay Anders.

Ana and Ohley were planning their meeting with the two water angels who were to play a big part in removing Daku from his position.

"I know why you chose them now Ana." Ohley was fitting the pieces of the jig saw together."

"I wondered at first if it was right, but in the circumstances it can't be any other way, and they would want, even beg to do this."

"When do we confer?"

"Tonight, in their sleep hours, Ignis will be in attendance also and we will go over the plans in detail. The slightest slip....."

"I know" Ohley was quick to understand "could be terrible, not only for the two in waiting but for others he is trying to destroy. For he is isn't he?"

"Oh yes," Ana was adamant now, he has only been playing but he will go for the kill wherever he can, regardless of who it is. Just for the sheer delight of it."

The interchange between the two had taken but a few seconds in their time and they parted knowing there was much to arrange before the earth night, with every angel from each element knowing their part in the plan.

Maisie had returned home, her quest complete and she turned her thought to the evening. What a good idea of hers to have a little 'do'. The girls would be in their room, and Frank would do as he was bid. He often objected but found it easier to fall in with her plans for a quiet life, and that was just what he would do tonight. But she always hoped that one of her little chants, combined with a cocktail of various drinks and the scented candles would sway him to perform like a proper husband again. If she was that intent on capturing his bodily attention, she should have studied her aromas and herbal teas a little better, for when she once tried to give him something to relax and calm him, he ended up downing a stimulant which had the opposite result to what she had hoped and he had stormed out of the door in temper.

So that he could not use the old excuse of being too tired, not inclined, not expecting it etc. she rang him at work to warn him what was in store, although she wrapped it up a little so as not to put him off altogether, and made the excuse she needed something bringing from one of the shops in Woodstock.

He hated her ringing him at work, finished the call abruptly, and scribbled a note to remind him of the things she wanted. It was always busy in his office and he tried to put her from his mind. She took over their home life and the only time he felt he could think for himself away from work, was on the drive home or sitting locked in the toilet.

It was obvious she was planning a 'candle thing' and it was always on his mind as to how to get her to stop these silly antics and do something useful. Little did he realize he wasn't only fighting her but a power waiting to be unleashed in his very home.

Doctor Day, with the protection of the water sentinels around him drove carefully to a planned spot; a lonely bridge over a fast running stream. Messages had gone to higher levels that they now were sure of the identity of the perpetrator although he was using a different method to those he had used in different earth areas. Slowly, the doctor let the car come to a halt, switched of the engine and got out. He carefully lifted the entire bag containing the damaged items taken from Janet's house, and at a given signal the whole lot was dropped over the bridge and into the water. The stream wasn't deep at any place but the water angels rose and encompassed the bag with as much fluid as possible until it was dashed to the stream bed where it dissolved into dust, useless and without any evil force governing it.

As the message was relayed to those above, the sentinels knew that somehow it would be intercepted by a watchful fire demon and be relayed to source.

The experienced ideal of the doctor knew that there was no need to take a further look at the picture for it would be blank. Daku had such a powerful hypnotic talent, he could make anyone see just what they thought they were seeing. So the subject matter was well chosen for each individual, flowers for the social worker in the colours she had been wearing, flowers and trees for the vicar as he loved nature, and the meadow scene for the one who had blamed the girls for upsetting the dog. Adding a beast to that one seemed very apt but he didn't realize they had never seen it. Such was the danger of his power, for little could be proven afterwards as the young lads had already experienced.

Not knowing Fay's history, Daku wished her to see a beautiful little cottage, maybe one she had dreamed about, with geraniums near the front door. This is what she would find on her doorstep any minute -   now.

Thinking she had seen someone crossing her window, she was about to make her way to the door when her telephone rang.

"Digby, how lovely to hear your voice. When are you coming down?"

"Soon I hope Mu......Auntie" he corrected. "I know this seems very silly, but I just wondered if you are all right?"

"I am very well thank you Digby, but why do you ask?" she sensed a tone on concern in his voice.

"Don't know, I sometimes just get these feelings, but it's me, don't worry, only Auntie..."

"Yes?"

"I don't know why I am saying this, but just be careful will you. Only I've learned to listen to these sort of – oh it sounds daft when I say it, almost premonitions."

"Digby, it doesn't sound daft to me. And you listen to them. Sounds like you take after your father."

"Why, did he get them?" Digby was excited to think he might have inherited such a gift.

"Not exactly, but he was a very deep person." She couldn't even start to explain, especially over the phone that they met almost every time she went to sleep, and he was indeed spiritual for he had no earthly body, and it was possible he was trying to warn her of something through Digby. She made up her mind to have a little nap and find out.

Promising to be extra vigilant, she exchanged farewells with her son and sat down. She remembered that she had been on her way to the front door, and as she was about to open it she stopped, and slowly returning to her seat, she decided this was a good time to communicate with Samuel before doing anything else, just in case. Seconds after she had relaxed in her chair, her ideal had sped to distant realms and she was merging with Samuel.

"You got my warning, "he imparted.

"So it was you, I thought so. What is it?"

"He is moving in on you but we don't think he knows the connection yet. Seems you are just another target at present."

Fay's love for Samuel acted as a protective barrier and they often communicated for longer than most, keeping their thoughts safe from passing threats.

"In what way?"

"There is a picture on your doorstep."

"So that's what it was I saw, who came with it?"

Samuel strengthened his love bond and said "one of his servants, the twins' mother."

Fay seemed dismayed. "He's not using Maisie and Frank again?"

"Seems the obvious thing. But don't touch the parcel, we'll see to it."

Fay offered "I could do it, there's plenty of water in the butt."

"Thanks but no. Don't you see, that would expose you, and it's vital you stay undetected a bit longer."

"Of course, what was I thinking?"

He started to separate their ideals "Until later then." And with one final love surge between them, she returned to her armchair and Samuel to his duties.

Nora couldn't keep her nose out of anything for long, and she sat at home wondering what was the matter with Janet. Dulcie obviously knew which made it all the more mysterious and she was determined to dig until she found out. No good asking the mouse, referring to Fay, as she seemed to be in her own little world most of the time, and they often wondered if anything actually went in. She got up with a very determined attitude and made her way towards Janet's home. A car was just leaving as she got to the front gate and she watched it depart wondering who it was as she didn't know that one, and she liked to know everything.

"Who was that, and what are you doing here?" she demanded of Dulcie who opened the door, and Nora almost pushed her aside as she marched into the room. Janet was feeling altogether better, and the thought of 'putting one over' on Nora had added to her confidence.

"Dulcie was worried and called the doctor, because I was very pale." Janet shot a glance at Dulcie who managed to hide the smile as Nora had her back to her.

"I told you to get sorted. I knew it, it's her heart isn't it?" and she swung round to Dulcie who just managed to straighten her face, but giving Janet the chance for a controlled smirk. At that point Nora noticed for the first time, the bandages and plasters on the hands of the other two.

"What on earth has happened? That's not caused by heart trouble."

Janet grabbed a hanky and sniffed into it to hide her face, and muttered "You will say it's silly, but um – we had a bit of a mishap, didn't we Dulcie?"

"Yes - yes, we both went to pick up a glass and between us we dropped it and – um- and it broke."

Nora looked around. "And where is the offending glass now?"

"We threw it away." Dulcie took over, "while the doctor was examining Janet, I got rid of it. And he looked at our hands and said they were all right but to be more careful."

"Hmm." Nora seemed to take it in but just to be sure Janet added "You were right to get me to see somebody Nora, it must be my age."

The little bit of praise carried more weight than either of them could have hoped and they both breathed a sigh of relief when she changed the subject to a bit of gossip she had picked up. It was only later they realized how easily the little fibs had slipped off their tongues, and it gave them fuel for future times when she was being nosey and they didn't want to tell her things. Dr.Day would have been proud, but relieved had he seen their performance.

Sharon Forest had gone into work as it was the last day before the mini break, although she still felt shaken after her ordeal. Her husband had got the local man to check out her car and all seemed fine, but told her to be aware of anything shaking or knocking and let him know so that he could have another look. Putting the images in the picture down to tiredness she didn't pay much heed to the painting as she left.

It was mid afternoon and she had filed all her reports to date and was just about to make a well earned cup of tea when the office phone rang. A colleague answered and handed the receiver to her "It's your husband."

"I expect he wants to know if I'm getting away early." She smiled and said laughingly into the mouthpiece "Hello, yes I'm still here." But her smile faded as she listened. "I'll come home now, I've finished all the reports. Don't do anything 'til I get there."

"What on earth's the matter?" the other girl asked.

"No sure, something's caught fire, I must go, explain to 'madam' when she gets back will you?"

"Of course, you get off, and I hope everything's OK."

Sharon probably drove quicker than she ought, but her husband hadn't been very specific and only keep saying "fire" and "it's awful" and such phrases that she was dreading what sight might meet her. The fire engine was still outside as she pulled up. Jumping out of the car she slammed the door behind her and pushed her way through the small crowd that had gathered.

"You can't go in their m'dear." Strong arms stopped her as she dashed to the front door. The fireman almost lifted her from the ground.

"But it's my home, where's my husband?"

"Ok, Ok, just a moment, your husband's not badly hurt, but you'll have to stay out here until we know it's safe."

"What happened, I want to see him." She was hysterical now.

"Just listen to me one moment, Sharon is it?" she nodded "well I'll tell you then you can see him."

"I want to see him first." She didn't know who might hear her, all she wanted was to see he was safe.

"He's in the back garden, but you can't get round until we've cleared the equipment, he's just had a bit of a burn trying to put out the fire, but he will be all right."

Slightly relieved she calmed a little but her mind was churning. What had caught fire? How much of a burn? Any damage didn't seem to matter until she could see for herself that he was really not badly hurt.

The chief fire officer came over, checked who she was and introduced himself.

"Sorry to do this, it must be a shock to come home and find this but I just have to ask you a few questions."

"Questions? What sort of questions?" Sharon felt it should be she who was asking questions.

"Do you have any sort of lamps around the place, not electric if you know what I mean?"

Sharon thought this a strange question and said "No, nothing like that, I don't even think candles are safe, I don't have that sort of thing. Why?"

"And you and your husband don't smoke I understand."

"That's right."

He paused and looked at her for a moments before saying "On your sideboard, what do you keep on there?"

"The sideboard - photos, a couple of ornaments, the post usually gets dumped there, that sort of thing." She was still trying to fathom out where this was leading.

"Is there a plug nearby, I mean would you have had anything charging on there, like a phone, or a game, anything of that nature."

Sharon took a deep breath. "There is no plug near enough for that, and anything I charge up is done in the kitchen, on the flat surface, I'm a very careful person."

"Yes, I thought so, that's what so strange you see."

She looked at him for more explanation.

"The fire seems to have started on the right hand side of the sideboard and scorched the wall, and I'm afraid has rather damaged the surface of that piece of furniture. Lucky it didn't catch the curtains. There was nothing there to suggest what could have caused it, I was rather hoping you could shed some light on it."

It hit her like a bolt. The only thing that was different on the sideboard was the picture. They had put it there until a good place could be found for it. But she thought that couldn't catch fire, until the horrible images came flooding back and she knew that something evil was responsible. Immediately her mind flew back to her encounter with the girls, but it was impossible to connect them to it.

A movement made her turn and her husband was escorted into the street by a paramedic who said he would like to have him checked out at the local hospital where they could dress the wound better. She was relieved to see it was only his hand that was covered and he seemed physically sound, but the poor thing looked so shaken, that she still felt there had been more to this than it appeared to anyone else.

Fearing they would be ridiculed, she decided not to mention anything to do with the picture and hoped that all vestige of it had been destroyed.

The fire service wanted to do some investigation to find the cause, and so it was decided that they would both go to her mother's until it was all right to return. At that moment she wasn't sure she ever wanted to. Daku was working well.

Molly had had a busy Friday morning in the post office and was looking forward to having the Monday off. It was just after lunch and she was waiting for Ben to call in case any parcels had come by the van and must be delivered. She glanced at her watch and thought there was plenty of time yet and as there was only a small one for the school teacher, she could always drop it in herself, so she put her mind to other things.

Ben had gone home for his mid day snack. As he had got older he liked to have a little break and read the paper with his meal to set him up for the afternoon. There wasn't always a lot to do, but being a small community, if anything arrived he like to get it out straight away in case it was important. This is how he had always been and he wouldn't change now. It was often mentioned that when he retired the village wouldn't be so well cared for, probably just one delivery per day and anything arriving late would wait until the next day. He had built up great respect over the years although he didn't realize it.

As he leant his cycle against the wall he saw a small parcel on the step. He thought that was funny as he was the postie and he knew all the parcels round here. He picked it up and noticed it had been delivered by hand and just bore his name 'BEN' in bold letters on the paper wrapping. Bemused he took it inside and after putting the kettle on, he sat down to open the bundle, wondering who had left him something. Carefully, he undid the wrapping and there in front of his eyes was the most accurate painting of a cricketer he had ever seen.

"Oooh," he said aloud, and again "Oooh." His mind was whirling, partly because of the fine work in his hands, but also for the fact that somebody had thought of his love of the game and bothered to get it for him. So taken was he, that the noise of the kettle switching off made him jump for a moment. Carefully, he put the painting in its cardboard frame on the table and busied about getting his tea and a sandwich, glancing back at the picture constantly. Even while eating his lunch, his gaze barely left the object.

He finished the snack, wiped his mouth on the back of his hand and took the crockery to the sink. He almost dropped the things into the bowl as he again was drawn to the picture. He put his beaker and plate down safely and returned to the table. Why hadn't he noticed before? The face was that of himself as a much younger man, reminiscent of his days when he used to play for the village team, and look, there was the little mascot he always wore. This was more than a coincidence, this was a complete copy of him, the stance, the smile, everything. But why?

Maybe he should have felt honoured, but a feeling was creeping over him that could only be described as unpleasant, so he went to his fireside chair and sat for a while, trying to work out just what wasn't right.

The arch angels from all elements were in conference. Time was getting near to the operation to remove Daku and replace the twins' bodies with their proper inhabitants. The two in waiting were being drilled in the lives of the girls to date so that they were aware of school mates, where they had lived etc. Fortunately, due to Daku keeping them apart from society as much as possible, it would be easier for them to come out of their shells gradually, and take their proper place in the world. Checks were being done with various important players in this game, but far away from the earth and its surroundings so that the element of surprise would not be ruined. Therefore, anything planned near the earth would soon be picked up by one demon force or another which was all part of the strategy.

The twins would be eleven on June 8th, just over a week away and that date was set for the operation to be completed, but the sooner the better. Word had got to Ana that the De'Aths were planning one of their rituals for this evening, or rather Maisie was planning it, and Daku would no doubt be hovering waiting for any pickings of wandering spirits which may be attracted by her chants. As they needed his attention elsewhere for the transition, it was decided to let him play for now but put sentinels around just to monitor his actions. However, the rest of the plan could start to take shape. The two water angels were due to start playing their part this earth night, and the arch angels were moving nearer to earth for their plot with the exception of Ignis who was now almost in the earth's area but concentrating on a different country. So everything was set for the downfall and evacuation of Daku.

As the operation has been so carefully planned, Daku was unaware of the net closing in on him, in fact he was now beginning to gloat as his contacts were suffering more each time, but the next would be something to stop everyone in their tracks. This would be a beauty. He was aware of the forthcoming evening's entertainment, as he put it, so knew the two girls would be confined to their room for the entire evening, not that he really cared. This sadistic demon had ruined the first years of their lives, so what if they got pulled into more sinister activities, it didn't bother him. He would enjoy whatever this amateur event could produce, but was planning his next attack.

It was late afternoon and Topaz and Peridot were in their room just fiddling with the pastels in the box. They had never used them of course, but Daku had made them break them and rub them down a bit to make it look as if they had been. He despised the parents for not checking further into their daughters' activities, for even the slightest examination would have shown that these girls had never created a painting in their little lives. At school the best they could do was splash some paint on the paper but the teacher thought they just hadn't got the talent for art. At the after school club they merely doodled on the paper, but the teacher was happy enough that they were safe until the father came. You didn't question the De'Aths somehow.

Topaz went into the en suite bathroom to wash her hands and as she looked into the mirror saw a reflection she didn't recognize. Staring at the image she called Peridot but she was already at her side. Together they saw two little girls smiling back at them, but it wasn't them. Gradually the illusion faded and as Topaz dried her hands she asked quietly "You saw them?"

"Yes, I wonder who they are."

The two returned to the room and sat together on the bed, a feeling of love sweeping over them, which they had never experienced before. As the warm glow slowly diminished they again took on the glazed cold look with which they had become familiar. The first phase had worked.

Rev.Desmond Conway popped his head round the door of the post office. "Hello Molly, Ben all right?"

"Well it's funny you should say that Reverend, I been worried about 'im. Not turned up this afternoon, you see. But what made you ask?"

"Probably nothing," Desmond smiled "it's just I've come passed his house and his bike's there, not like him to be home this early."

"I tried ringing 'im, but no answer." Molly looked really worried now.

"I did wonder if there wasn't much mail, just before the holiday," Desmond suggested.

"You joking me?" Molly laughed, "I been that busy this morning."

"Well, I'll go and knock on his door if you like. He could be in the back" he said to reassure her, "that's why he didn't answer when you rang."

"He'd 'ave been down for any parcels, I got one by the way."

"Should I take it?" Desmond was keen to help and had a gut feeling that somehow they wouldn't be seeing Ben that afternoon.

"That's really kind of you Reverend but as you're not employed by the Mail, you know."

"Oh yes, sorry. Well I'll go and see if I can find the chap." As he left, the thought was racing through his mind about his own picture and wondering against hope that poor old Ben hadn't had one that had upset him.

He was soon at Ben's front door and sure enough his bike was still where he had left it. Desmond tapped gently at first not wanting to make the man jump if he was asleep. Silence. He opened the letter box and tried to peer through but was met with an unusual smell. It was at times like these he was glad he had been persuaded to carry his mobile phone with him at all times, and was soon talking to the local policeman who said he would be there in a few minutes and would break in.

True to his word the constable arrived, got out of his car and approached the door.

"What we got, d'you reckon vicar?"

Desmond held his nose "Not sure, but he is always out in the afternoon, postman you see."

"Well risk of danger to life, or worse, so here we go." And he went to the boot of the car and pulled out a piece of equipment for the job. In no time the two men were in the room, but the constable held his arm out to stop Desmond going any further for the sight before them was something neither of them had ever seen before.

CHAPTER 7

As the evening draw near, many players were in readiness for the enfolding drama. Maisie and Frank would be holding their ritual, with Daku in close proximity, Ana, Ohley and very experienced ideals would be within the earth's boundaries where they knew their thought vibrations would be monitored by any tuned in demons, and Ignis was causing a distraction of his own, supported by fire angels occupying the Europe continent. The two special water angels were well away from earth at present going over their part in minute detail.

Frank had returned home with the purchases, not looking forward one bit to the evening's events. Why couldn't they live like a normal family. It was the Bank Holiday week end. Most of his colleagues were heading off somewhere with the children in tow for a well earned break. He appreciated they had just moved, again, and should welcome the time to get a bit more settled. The house looked a mess, apart from the girls' room. You couldn't say the back room, really a dining room had been sorted, as there was so much mess with the draped material, images and candle wax that it looked as though it could do with a good clearing out and cleaning. And they'd only been there a few days. What was going through his wife's head was anybody's guess. She never used to be like this, and much as he would like to fight her on it, she always seemed to get her way somehow, but he was getting to the end of his tether and he was seriously wondering what he could do. He had considered talking to his father, but they had never been really close, and although he had helped him to get this place knowing the problems that had dogged them since the birth of the twins, he didn't want to involve him in his marital problems. Auntie Fay was out of the question as they were virtually strangers and he wasn't too happy with the fact she lived in this village, but he had not been in a position to be too choosy. So for now he must turn his attention to this evening, and hope it would not be too much of an ordeal.

The Reverend and the constable stood in shock horror. They had both heard of this strange occurrence but neither had ever seen it first hand, only in pictures. From where they had stopped suddenly, they could see Ben's feet still with the boots on but just above the ankles there was nothing, that is apart from ash where he had touched the chair.

"Spontaneous combustion." The policeman whispered "there'll be nothing more left of him."

"Look at the walls," Desmond was casting his gaze around the room where a yellowish substance seemed to be sticking to the wallpaper "body fat."

The other man, still whispering said "You read about these things but when you see it, ugh it's different."

Desmond said "I know we have to leave it all untouched and I won't go any further but may I just offer up a prayer for the safe transit of his soul?"

"Please do vicar." And the two bent their heads as they prayed with 'Amen' in unison bringing to an end all they could do there.

"Well, better get the forensic lot in here, they will want to go over it." The constable replaced his cap which he had removed out of respect and said "I know I don't have to ask vicar, but can you keep this, I mean the details quiet for now?"

"Of course, you can't have this sort of thing going about, bad enough when it has to come out." The two exchanged contact details and Desmond was assured they would be in touch with him, whereby the officer moved the bicycle into the hallway as he couldn't get access to the back of the house and he didn't want to alert the neighbours. This would stop inquisitive passers by asking awkward questions. He would have to mention it in his report and also state the point at which he and the vicar had halted.

Both men departed with similar thoughts. These cases were rare, with the known ones documented but with theories as to the cause. It wasn't something most people would ever have to encounter.

One description was that the body burns from inside like a candle leaving the body fat to melt, this is what was adorning the walls in Ben's house. Nothing else ever seemed to ignite surrounding the body, and as the two men had guessed the part of the chair where Ben's body had touched had ash deposits. His feet and the lower legs, the only parts left intact, finished abruptly. This house would take some cleaning after the tests and it would take professionals, experienced in such cases to tackle the job. Something else it would be hard to keep from the village.

The constable knew that within a short time the 'men in overalls' as he called them, would have a protective tent erected covering the entrance to the house and hide from view most of their activities. This was going to be something this quiet little village had never seen before, and hopefully never would again.

Ana was concerned it seemed, there was great unrest in France with fires springing up all over the place. None of them had caused damage to property or life yet but it was something to be watched. Ignis had done his homework, and covered a great area with these little pyrotechnics, but had been equally sure that nobody got hurt, even the animal kingdom.

It wouldn't take long for this to filter through, and some of the fire sentinels were sending positive vibrations back so that attention was growing already. The arch angels knew that Daku must be torn between his own activities and those going on just out of reach for he dare not travel in spirit to view the scene and leave the twins unprotected even for a moment. He had a few yards leeway which gave him freedom in the house to cover the girls and the parents but beyond it would be too dangerous to attempt anything further afield and ruin all his good work up to now. He must therefore call upon a lesser demon to act as feedback for him. That would not be difficult for there was always a little creeper who would jump at the chance, thinking it would stand them in good stead with Daku later. How little they knew him, for as soon as they had fulfilled the task he would rid himself of them, despising them for their weakness.

The messages were flowing fast, many false ones, but that was the plan to cause disruption, distrust and panic among the fire demons that something big was being hatched without their knowledge. Soon demons were rushing everywhere, going from one venue to another, fighting each other to be first like a load of paparazzi. The more that arrived, the more Ignis spread the fires. But he was also a master of illusion, for among the real flames were virtual ones creating a scene of utter havoc. He had considered just using the power of thought but knew the demons would soon realize his game and that would be the end of the whole distraction, so he combined the two including the smoke and heat with such amazing results, even he felt gratified with the end product.

This was just the overture, for Daku must only have his appetite whetted for now until they drew the enticement nearer home and he would be overcome with temptation to leave the girls for long enough to investigate. So when word filtered back that the scenes were under control, he turned his attention to the matters of the evening.

Nora was still a little bit 'niggled' as she liked to put it. She didn't like to be left out of things and had definitely got the feeling that the two were holding something back, or planning something without her knowledge. Sitting alone at home, her mind wandered back to the earlier events. Could it be that Janet had something more serious and they didn't want to upset her? No, it couldn't be that because they would have been more subdued, and if anything they were almost elated. The thought that they weren't good actresses came to the fore and she knew that if anything juicy cropped up they wouldn't be able to keep it to themselves and would fall over being the first to report it. Little did she know the charade they had acted out for her benefit, and would continue to play for some time.

Loneliness took over and she picked up the phone. First she rang Janet to enquire as to her health and noticed a bubbly attitude which was something quite new.

"What pills are you on?" she demanded in her usual tone.

"I don't know." Janet giggled.

"You must know, silly girl. It is dangerous not to know what you are taking, What if you took an overdose?"

Janet felt like telling her not to be so dramatic but settled for "Oh the name's on the bottle, but I can't say it."

"Well they seem to be doing something to you. I wouldn't take any alcohol if I were you, not while you're on them." Nora just had to give an order, it never came out like advice. "And how's the hand while we're on the subject?"

"I didn't know we was, I thought you was talking about my heart." Janet was enjoying this new wave of humour, with Nora as the butt of the joke.

"Well I think those pills are sending you funny. And of course if you don't want to tell me, after all these years."

"Oh Nora, my 'ands fine, only scratches. Be better in no time."

As this was not the intelligent conversation she wanted, added to the fact she had found out nothing of any importance, Nora hung up arranging to see the ladies in the morning.

Next she tried Dulcie, but was met with as much sense as the previous call. Yes, her hand was perfectly all right, and she thought Janet looked better than she had done in years. So Nora patted herself on the back, as it was she who had prompted Janet to see the doctor. Where would they be without her?

It crossed her mind to ring Fay, but one question would lead to about six more to come back to the answer she wanted in the first place and the woman was clearly feeling the passing of time. She probably only tagged along for the company, didn't contribute much but you never knew if she had seen things and not said. Nora remembered the conversation about the new family and it had taken all that time for Fay to say she had seen the girls. Now a normal thinking woman would have said straight out, not sat on it like an egg waiting to hatch.

"Think she's going senile." She thought as she made a cup of tea.
It was fortunate she didn't ring Fay as there would have been no response, for the elderly lady was having an early night with her attention far away from the earth.

"Is that all?" Frank finished the small dinner, and noticing there were no spoons for dessert wondered what his wife was up to now. He wasn't in the best frame of mind with the imminent 'candle thing' looming.

"Now, now dear, you don't want to go stuffing yourself with things that are bad for you do you?" Maisie busied about clearing the table and even the girls looked rather bemused at the abrupt finish to the meal. Ignoring her husband she almost whispered to the twins "I've got some of your favourite cake and there's some juice for you to have while you're watching the television in your room. Don't be too late out of bed though, there's good girls."
Frank snorted under his breath. The twins may keep to their own ways and be a bit different from other children but there was no need to pat them like good dogs, for that was what her manner was implying. He wondered if the woman had eventually flipped for good, and made up his mind to stop her in her tracks before she could get going on whatever it was she had planned for tonight.

As the girls disappeared to the comfort of their room, Daku hovered over the dining table for it would be here that the silly woman would make her base. She may refer to it as an altar but she would be alone in that illusion, but this time even he was wrong. As Frank started to talk she brushed passed him, dumping the remains of the meal in the kitchen adding to the mess in that room. He tried to keep up with her as she tried to convert the room into her love nest, folding down the table and pushing it to the wall, where she made space even though there didn't appear to be one, and starting to pull a rather tatty sofa to the middle of the floor.

"For Christ's sake woman, will you stop and listen to me, for just one moment."
Maisie stopped in her tracks shocked at the outburst from this normally timid streak of rainwater. His face was red, and with hands clenched until the knuckles whitened, he seethed inches from her face "Stop it. You've got to stop it. Now – do - you – hear - me?" The last five words were shouted individually and though he was hammering a nail in with each blow.

For the first time since he could remember, his wife trembled and seemed close to tears.

"F-f-frank, what has come over you? I've never seen you like this."

"Then it's about time you did." He still did not feel calm, even at the sight of his wife obviously terrified, cowering in front of him. She had fallen backwards onto the sofa which ironically was what she had been planning, but not this way. The sad woman was still searching her brain for a way to turn this to her satisfaction, hoping the evening would still have a passionate ending, but Frank was still trying to knock some sense into her and lovemaking was the last thing on his mind.

Daku, had he been in earthly form would have been clapping his hands for this was more entertaining than the sad little acts they had been producing up to now. This, he could build on for the air was now rife with antagonism and almost hatred on the man's part, and Daku wondered just how much it would take, with a gentle nudge, for him to kill his wife. Unfortunately, he knew the ripples would soon filter out and attract more evil demons hungry for entertainment, and that was the last thing Daku wanted, for this was his, he had arranged the setting, and he certainly wasn't going to share it with some upstarts.

As Daku's attention was thus occupied, the twins were, in a way, half free of his possession and the air angels were quick to home in on this again. As Topaz spoke, Peridot turned and gasped, for her sister's face had a different look, just like the one in the mirror earlier. Topaz also was shocked but in a warm way and they flew to each other embracing as they had never done before. They were so lost in the loving wave sweeping over them, they were oblivious to the argument downstairs, and the air angels would keep it that way for as long as possible but diligence was paramount, as Daku would soon sense the intrusion.

But this evil demon was not alone, for Lazzan was overseeing the area and was attracted to the fracas, and not wanting to miss out on the possibility of it turning into something worthwhile, he hovered at the side of the underling.

"Is this of your doing Daku?" the question was full of contempt, "not up to the standard required of one who wishes to rise on the ladder of control."

This made Daku furious. He didn't welcome the intrusion from any source, but to have one of the hierarchy criticizing him added fuel to the fire especially at this moment when he hadn't had chance to inflict his power on the scene. But he knew that to vent his thoughts on such a one would be disastrous and could even result in him being removed and that couldn't happen, not now. Thankfully Lazzan appeared to shrug it off, and before Daku could reply, the elder left with the retort "Well have your fun, but don't mess it up this time." And he was gone.

This put the spark back into Daku's determination. The event had got to be good and he wasn't going to let a mere mortal spoil it, and he could not loose face among his own kind, so with that he turned his attention to the sad couple in front of him.

"I didn't know I was that bad, "Maisie was sniveling, hoping this new approach might work, "I know I've never been attractive but I've never looked at anybody else, and I've been a good wife to you haven't I?"

"Yes, yes, "Frank had calmed a bit but was still determined to get her to stop these silly rituals. "I just want us to be normal, not doing these dangerous antics, you don't know what you might stir up."

She had to think quickly. "Well how about if I promise never to do them again, but can I just have one last one tonight, I've so looked forward to it, then that's the end of it, I promise you."

Frank would rather she stopped it there and then, but at least she was listening, or so he thought, so he said "If you promise, and keep to it, and then get rid of all this stinking stuff, and lets clear the house up to livable standard."

She started to throw her arms around him, but he wasn't quite ready for that, so he held her at arms length and said "A promise is a promise, no more."

Maisie would have signed anything or agreed to anything at that moment, for if she got her way, one night of passion would be worth any sacrifice. Little did she know that's just what it may be.

CHAPTER 8

Graham was paying a quick visit to the Reverend Conway, knowing he would get all the information he needed through this man and was grateful to see that Desmond was snoozing in the chair. Instantly they conversed on a higher level and Graham was now piecing the jigsaw together but still trying to estimate what Daku's agenda could be. Knowing this demon, he was aware of his delaying tactics hoping no higher authority would work out his little schemes and up to now he had merely attacked anyone who had even annoyed him, but that wouldn't be enough. The assault on Ben had sent shock waves through all entities, the evil ones enjoying it but the angels saw something else.

Daku had made another mistake. A wiser spirit would have done their homework and found that Ben, a water element had reached his present and last earth span and was of a much higher status than the fire upstart. His passing had taken place just before the spontaneous combustion, and when he had sat down feeling strange, he had died of a heart attack there and then.

But he was now free and being used to full advantage to down this fiend for a long time, or so it was hoped. The air and water angels also knew that if they could get Daku to loose face amongst his own kind, it would be more of a tribulation than they could hope for.

Ana was very concerned, as news had just filtered through that the evil demon had occupied the two girls with little fuss until now, this special time of their lives, puberty. This was where he was going to have his fun. The knowledge made all the good elements shudder as this was their most hated crime, the ones against children. Time was even more important, they must rid the girls' bodies of this evil thing which was threatening to ruin them for ever, also anyone who was later placed in them for he would make sure that every last memory would be stored, hopefully making them into future perpetrators in the sordid field of child abuse. The ultimate sin. So the fire antics were just a temporary amusement, and he was about to go in for the kill.

Maisie drew the curtains slowly and started to light the various candles around the room. As she reached one particular large one, Frank cut in "No, not that one" and with an afterthought "please."

His wife stopped and turned slowly so he said gently "I think it was that one made me feel rather ill before."

Satisfied she left it unlit and went to the sideboard and cleared a small space. She opened one of the doors in the cabinet and took out two glasses, a bottle and a small package which she placed in the gap she had made. There was no semblance of an altar or anything strange so Frank began to relax a little, thinking that at last she had seen some sense.

With her back to him, Maisie undid the small package which revealed a few white tablets with markings she didn't recognize. She had brought these with her from their previous home and kept them in readiness for such an occasion as this, when things needed a kick start. The person who had sold them to her had assured her they would achieve all the results she needed as they were so good that even an ugly old witch could appear to be a beautiful goddess.

Frank was expecting her to start one of her meaningless chants and was surprised when she came over to him with a drink in her hand.

"You start yours, I just want to go and get into my favourite kaftan" she breathed, "then I can enjoy mine." He took a sniff. "Alcohol" he thought, "now that's an improvement on the muck she's been dishing up."

As he sat there waiting for her return, he sipped the drink which for the first time in ages was quite enjoyable and was considering whether to help himself to another when his wife returned in all her glory.

"Are you doing something different tonight, as it's the last one?" he enquired hopefully.

"Maybe." she was quick to pick up on his change of mood and didn't want to spoil it. "but it might be nice to relax and talk for a while first don't you think?"

"If you like." He was hoping that the idea of a ritual might slip from her mind, especially if he could get her to down more wine, or whatever it was he was drinking. He cast a glance to the sideboard. Only one bottle, well they wouldn't get very merry on that, but it still was better than anything she had made him go through up to now. He had slumped in the sagging settee so that he was almost lying with his legs outstretched across the floor, and hadn't seen that Maisie had moved behind him and was holding a candle in one hand and her glass in the other, whispering under her breath calling on help from the other side, begging them to make her husband enter her temple tonight and claim her as his possession.

Daku was enjoying this, at last he could watch as this simpering excuse of a man was overcome by firstly, earthly substances, and later by powers beyond his control.

The whispers had turned into prayer like pleadings, calling on all who where near to come forth and share the pleasure which was about to ensue. Frank's eyes were almost closed as his body wasn't used to the mixture he had consumed, but through the slits he could see spirits floating around in the air and they were lovely, beckoning him with open arms until he too was floating with them, Maisie forgotten.

Her chants hadn't gone unnoticed, for gradually the room was filled with evil entities which had been hovering waiting for the call. Some were fighting to take over her body to receive the treasures she was hungry for, others were tantalizing Frank, playing with his hidden sexual desires threatening to erupt them like a volcano.

Daku observed with a slight apprehension as he only wanted a few demons to pick off for his own needs, not the invasion this was turning out to be. He would have to halt the flow, but the opening was growing by the second and more and more arrived giving Maisie the illusion her powers were at last achieving the success she had long for. Her chants rose as her arms plucked the air, welcoming more and more to her.

Lazzan was at Daku's side again. "Very good" he imparted sarcastically, "and just how are you going to sort out this little lot?" The next second he was gone.

Maisie had moved round to Frank and with a few quick moves had stripped him, amazed but elated to see he was fully aroused. As he didn't seem to be able to respond in any other way, and not willing to lose the moment, she stripped off her kaftan, beads and anything that would get in the way and lowered herself on to him. There was great amusement amongst the evil onlookers, as due to the woman's proportions, little could be seen of her husband beneath the heaving blubber.

What she hadn't noticed was that Daku had made the flames on all the candles rise gradually until the room was well illuminated. The ones near the curtains were dangerously licking at the hems, and as Maisie had thrown her kaftan down without noticing where it had fallen, Daku tipped a candle near so that it soon ignited.

The demons were shrieking with delight fanning the flames until the whole room was ablaze. Maisie in her stupor desperately tried to crawl to the door and Frank was now too far gone to do anything. Daku picked off a couple of likely helpers and instructed the rest to depart immediately and find other dabblers to annoy.

The De'Ath's neighbours fortunately noticed the fire at the back of the house and called the fire brigade which had to come six miles from the nearest small town. Other villagers tried to help with buckets of water but to no avail.

"The children," one woman screamed, "the girls are in there." At which one brave man tried to get in by breaking one of the front room windows but was driven back by the heat and flames which now seemed to be taking over the ground floor.

"They could be upstairs, look for them at one of the windows."
As more people arrived, they tried to get a view of all the upstairs windows but there were no lights, and no faces peeping out. Before long the fire engine arrived and the firemen moved everyone back while they tackled the blaze. Even with breathing apparatus they dare not venture in as far as the stairs as they weren't sure how safe they would be by now so ladders were put up outside, and upstairs windows broken to gain access. The fire was up the stair well which meant they would have to enter each room on the upper floor via its own window praying all the doors were shut. All the rooms were empty. Sadly the chief could only surmise at this point that the whole family must have been together downstairs, but only the fire investigation officers could determine that.

One person missing from the crowd was Fay, but she and Samuel were soon informed and knew they must find out if the bodies awaiting placement had in fact been destroyed. This would change the well laid plans, for these two lovers were the water angels being held until ready to play their part in the final move to put their great grandchildren in the spaces of which they had been robbed. If the children had been killed in the blaze, Daku would be doubly responsible, firstly for taking over their bodies at the initial stage, and now destroying them so that the proper spirits could not have their correct earth life. A parents' love is great, but so is that of the great grandparents hence their personal interest, and the reason for them being selected for the task.

Fay had been forced to return to her earth body, as the commotion was so great, and not that far from her home, so that when Digby would eventually be informed of his son's family's demise, she would be the first one to be contacted, and it would seem very strange if she was not available. As she awoke, the first thought that flittered through her mind was Digby's obvious intuition that something was threatening and apart from the parcel, it may be that he had been picking up vibes of this greater horror. She had just pulled on a dressing gown when the phone rang.

"What on earth is going on at your end?" It was Nora.

"I'm not sure, Nora, people are running about and shouting and there are flames from the house up the road and now the fire engine is there, and the police."

Nora's first instinct was to put the feeble woman's mind in order. Most people would have been excited and said 'There's a house on fire' but not this one. Trying to be civil she asked more questions but couldn't glean any more. Just her luck to have the doziest person living the nearest to the event. She also rang the other two ladies, but they could tell her no more.

Fay's one regret was that Digby had chosen never to tell anyone else about the true relationship, so Frank and family had always thought she was just Auntie Fay. Well, now, they would find out the truth. As she replaced the receiver from Nora's call, she rang her son, telling him as briefly as possible to expect the worst.

Frank's passing had been overseen by fire angels who swooped and took him before Daku could even think about it, not that he was really bothered about that scrap of nothingness. He much preferred someone with more spirit and had considered grabbing Maisie to pander to his beck and call, but even she had bored him by now so the fire angels had no obstructions when seeing her over just behind her husband.

As neither of them was very high in the spiritual ranks, they would have to be carefully nursed for a while, as the shock of their passing would have a traumatic effect for some time. But before they were removed by helpers, Ana requested confirmation as to the girls' whereabouts at the onset of the fire. The sentinels knew they were in their room earlier but were not certain if they had stayed there and not wandered downstairs out of curiosity. This was of the utmost importance and demanded urgency.

A small village usually has little excitement, but the recent known happenings were causing a stir. The Rev.Conway had not divulged receiving his picture, and the two ladies had almost forgotten their incident, so amused were they with dangling Nora on a string, and nobody had heard of Sharon's fire, so the main news which had shocked the place was that Ben had died suddenly. But immediately to be followed by a house fire seemed very strange until one onlooker passed the comment that it had been the girls' doing. This prompted added views and opinions about them being strange but to start a fire, in their own home didn't seem likely even for them and some were told in no uncertain terms to keep unsavoury thoughts to themselves. One mother reminded them that the children appeared to have perished in the fire and to have come compassion. The Reverend was at the scene and agreed they should pray for everyone in the house until they knew anymore, at which a group lowered their heads in prayer. Some were crying now and the realization that a whole family had been burned to death. No one knew that Fay was even 'Auntie Fay' so nobody went to tell her. But she was away ahead of them, awaiting news from the air or water angels of the girls' present state.

A main problem faced the good spirits of all elements at this point. If the girls' bodies had been occupied by the proper souls and had perished in the fire, helpers would have witnessed the release of their ideals. If they had not died, no ideal would have left, thus proving one way or another whether the girls' were, in earthly terms, dead. But, because Daku had been in situ, and the girls had died, there would have been nothing to leave the bodies as he was permanently in spirit. Therefore more proof was needed urgently, so sentinels were posted to track Daku and hopefully lead them to the girls'. One thought transferred between Ana and Ohley that he could have abandoned them and they would now be free to receive their own spirits. This in turn would present danger as any passing entity could take them over and would also need to be removed.

It wasn't long before the message came in that Daku was hovering just outside the village and as he only had a short radius from their bodies there was a possibility they were still nearby. The arch angels decided it was time to take chances so Graham and Kyn were sent straight to Daku. Within seconds Graham had located the two girls huddled together in a small copse and satisfied they were still alive approached Daku from each side.

"Oh, I am honoured. Running out of tactics are we?" The sarcasm, penetrated the late evening air. The two angels did not fuel his satisfaction but started to circle him increasing the speed until even he was getting confused as to the method they were using. He tried to summon his underlings but they were bounced off the whirling atmosphere, and realizing they were up against something much more powerful than their new master, soon disappeared into the gloom.

Daku was still holding on to the power he had over the girls' bodies and gradually sinking back in to take full possession for he guessed the angels were trying to extract him. But at this precise moment it was the last thing they wanted, for as Ana had pointed out, the two in waiting must preferably be placed in a less aggressive setting so they could slide in peacefully. Just let him think he had won for the moment and his guard might drop. In assuming he had guessed the plans correctly, Daku had made another mistake. As quickly as Kyn and Graham had appeared, they left, leaving him with a feeling of bewilderment. For the first time he didn't feel in charge and this bothered him. He would have to plot his next move, as he wasn't about to relinquish these two bodies just when they were getting interesting.

Digby went straight to the scene of the fire but was blocked by the fireman. He managed to get them to listen to the fact that it was his son and his family so he was kept at a safe distance sitting in police car and away from the main onlookers.

"How did you know about it then?" The officer had already got his name and address and knew he didn't live in the village.

"My Aunt lives down the road, elderly lady, wouldn't want to come out when it's late, you understand, well she rang me and said there was a bad fire, looked as though it was coming from my son's so I came straight over." Then with an afterthought added, "I really should go and tell her what's happened, she must be worried sick."

"Perhaps in a minute sir, or my fellow officer could go."

"Oh I think that would scare her, I'd rather do it, tell her I mean."

As the family are often the first suspects, until proven otherwise, the officer wasn't that keen to let this man out of sight, so he came up with a compromise.

"Tell you what, you go down with my partner here, and then perhaps you can get a friend to sit with her, then you come back here."

It was more of a statement of permission and was better than nothing so Digby agreed and was soon heading off down the street. He was rather grateful for the constable's presence as he was bombarded with questions from the crowd and his escort made a path pushing them away for him to get through. Although he wasn't known by many, he had only been there to view the property and oversee the sale, the word soon spread that he was related to the weird family and also they were related to Miss Anders.

"Well, she certainly kept that quiet." One gossip monger was first to cast the first stone.

"Think I would with a family like that. I wouldn't brag about it."

This fuelled a general input.

"Not all families get on you know, I don't with some of mine."

"I wonder why?"

"And just what is that supposed to mean?"

"Oh nothing. If the cap fits."

"I said they was peculiar, didn't I say to you May, that they was peculiar."

"Oh yes, you did, I remember you saying."

Desmond decided it was time to slow the pace before somebody was guilty of something they didn't do.

"Ladies, ladies, please let us think of the poor family here, and if Miss Anders is a relative she deserves our support, not condemnation. Everyone's business is their own, hers, yours. Right?"

That quietened the mood somewhat and one or two guilty looks were exchanged.

"Ok everybody, you might as well all go to your homes now, nothing more to see." The fire chief had been in conference with the older policeman and agreed to disperse the crowd, willingly or otherwise. Reluctantly they made their way down the street, all slowing as they passed Fay's house but Desmond had foreseen this and persuaded them to go and leave the lady to her grief.

Fay couldn't divulge her spiritual position even to Digby, so she went through the actions suitable to hearing the news. She assured him that the last thing she wanted was for Nora or anyone to come round, and as he would be staying there overnight there was no need. The officer was satisfied with that, and accompanied him back to the scene.

What Fay really needed was to sleep again, so that she could return to Samuel and the plans for the removal of Daku, but she would have to wait until her son returned.

Desmond informed Nora, Janet and Dulcie so that they knew the facts regarding the relationship before the nosey parkers had a chance to elaborate. He also made it perfectly clear that she wasn't to be disturbed and she was in good hands as her nephew would be taking care of things.

One can only imagine how indignant Nora must have felt at that point at not being the first to know but it would have confirmed her suspicions, the old dear had 'lost it', probably forgotten she had any family at all.

CHAPTER 9

Just after nine o'clock the next morning old Tom, the story teller, shuffled his way down to the post office. Molly the post lady had kindly offered to get some flowers for him to put on his late wife's grave, and as she opened in the mornings on a Saturday, he thought he'd get down and get them out of her way. These little kindnesses were what had made the village a happy little community for many years, but sadly it was dying out with the changes to modern living.

"What's the matter, my girl?" Tom was just opening the door and saw the lady wiping her eyes which were very red. She shook her head so he closed the door behind him and went to the small counter.

"Well, there's got to be summat. Can't you say?"

She sniffed, wiped her nose and almost in a whisper said "It's Ben, he's dead."

"What, Ben the post, No!" Then after a moment, "What 'appened to 'im?"

"Don't know Tom, the police came round yesterday to say they'd found him. I was upset, I can tell you, but the Reverend came and helped me make sure everything was locked up, because I didn't know where my mind was, you know?"

"When were it?"

"I can't say exactly, 'cos I was all over the place when I heard, afternoon I think."

Tom stood leaning on the counter deep in thought. "What's that tent thing up near 'his house?"

Molly started sobbing "That's just it Tom, it's those forensic people or something, I mean why would they want them here?"

Tom shook his head. "I doesn't understand it. Never 'ad anything like that."

"I'm surprised you hadn't heard Tom, I bet it's gone all round the village, but you haven't got a phone have you?"

He shook his head. "Nah, don't need one."

After a few minutes in thought, Molly said "I got those flowers for you Tom," and she lifted a pretty bunch of blooms from behind the counter. After he paid her for them he slowly made his way into the little churchyard and up to his wife's grave. As he took out the old flowers, changed the water and placed the fresh bunch by the headstone, he stood talking to her, which he did every time he came. As he started to relate what Molly had told him, his eyes were drawn across to Ben's house which was quite near to the edge of the church boundary. A van had pulled up outside Ben's and immediately two people came out through the tent which covered not only the door but the front window. Tom's mouth dropped open. They wore white suits with hoods and gloves and even white foot coverings. He'd never seen anything like this and couldn't take his eyes from them. As some stopped, he saw that they had masks and eye goggles so that they were completely covered.

"This aint no ordinary dying missus." He spoke towards the grave but kept his eyes fixed as they carried out Ben's bicycle covered in plastic and put it in the back of the van. The driver hadn't got out which Tom thought was rather odd, so thought it was because he hadn't got this strange stuff on. Everything was racing through his mind until suddenly a small box was brought out and carefully laid in the back of the van, and the doors closed. One of the men gave two bangs on the back door and the van was driven away.

It wasn't the usual practice to open up the 'Coffee Break' on a Saturday, but this being Bank Holiday weekend, and with all that had gone on, Sally decided to give it a try in case anyone needed somewhere to congregate and 'Just be together' as she put it. So she put out the advertising board saying it would be open from 10am – noon. She had spoken to Desmond who thought it a wonderful idea, and told her that her kindness was much appreciated and he for one would come down in case people were upset and wanted to talk. He knew she would miss Ben and guessed that it was she who may need a shoulder to cry on.

At ten o'clock sharp, Nora was on the doorstep and virtually pushed her way in and plonked herself at the table nearest to the serving hatch.

"I'll have a tea while I'm waiting for the others."

Sally wasn't really in the mood to be given orders and added 'please' under her breath but said aloud "It's just brewing Nora, won't be a minute, didn't expect anyone in just yet." Again to herself 'but might have known you'd be the first'. Many would have said, like the vicar, how nice it was of her to bother at all but Nora would always be Nora. So the only reply she got was a "Hm."

As promised, Desmond arrived and placed a kindly hand on Sally's shoulder at which her lip started to tremble.

"I really loved Ben vicar."

"I know you did, and I'll tell you something, he loved his moments of respite in here."

She was pouring the tea as she said, "You'll think I'm wicked."

He gave a little laugh and said "I doubt it very much." Noticing Nora's ear seemed to be stretching towards the hatch at a rate of knots he said "When you've done that, why not come and sit down for a minute and tell me why." He indicated to the table furthest away from nosey Nora. His manner made her smile and she nodded, and took Nora's tea to her table.

"The other two will be here in a minute, so don't go far."
Sally knew it was no use waiting for a 'thank you' and thought better of getting drawn into any exchange at the moment so let the silence speak for her. She took two cups of tea over to Desmond and sat opposite him with her back to Nora.

"Now, what have you done that is so wicked?" Again he smiled to put her at her ease.

"Nothing that I've done, its just that when you know someone, and you don't know others, - what I'm trying to say is – I will miss Ben so much, but that other family – and that was awful – and......"

".........and you feel guilty because of what they went through and you can't feel the same compassion?" he finished for her almost expecting this was what was her concern.

"That's it, but that's wrong isn't it? We should feel sorry for them, and......" she indicated over her shoulder towards Nora "what about Miss Anders poor lady?"
Not wishing to give any comments Desmond said "That's why you have such a kind heart Sally, never change. It's sad everyone doesn't share your tenderness." She didn't have to turn to know which way his attention was directed but he had to be diplomatic in his position, and so an answer to her question was not forthcoming.

One or two villagers started to drift in, followed by some who had never been before as they were at work all week, and although they looked a little uneasy at first, Sally soon put them at ease and before long people weren't confining their conversations to themselves but discussions were going round all the tables. Janet and Dulcie arrived together and were immediately admonished by Nora for their tardiness to which Janet looked at her watch, gave a little sniff and sat down. Neither was in the mood for this woman, or her domineering this morning.

When the room was full, Desmond stood up and thanked Sally for providing this much needed haven. He explained this was not a planned meeting but as so many had come, he would like to say a few words.

"Much has gone on in our parish over the last twenty four hours and it will in some way, affect all of us, some more than others. What I want to stress is that in the case of Ben, and the De'Ath family, little is known of the true facts yet and we must not speculate. It is a very sad time, and it will cause further hurt to people if rumours are spread when we don't know the facts. We may, or may never know all we would like, but we must accept that. So we are here to share the sadness as a community but please keep your hearts open."

Everyone was silent as the vicar said a short prayer for those departed and those left in grief. A few were dabbing their eyes and there was a loud "Amen" by all in the room, even Nora who felt this would impede her thirst for knowledge, or rather, gossip.

The hum in the room made it impossible for her to grill the other two about Fay, and any remark was answered with "We don't know any more than you do."

Digby had made a cup of tea and taken it up to Fay's room. He tapped gently on the door, and on getting no reply slowly pushed the door open and quietly made his way to the bed. She was still in a deep sleep and breathing quietly and he thought how peaceful she looked and how sad it would be when she awoke and had to face the awful truth about the family. He put the cup and saucer on the bedside locker and thought it better to leave her for the time being. Little did he imagine the work that lay in front of her as she and Samuel were about to execute the final part in the plan.

Daku knew the girls would have to be found soon which didn't bother him unduly, for as long as he still had control of their young bodies he felt he was still in charge. The fiend had called them from their room before the fire had taken hold, and emulating Maisie's voice, had told them to get out and she would follow. He had then held them within control distance until he could leave the blazing room and willed them to run away as far as possible, letting them think their parents would be following. It was only when they found themselves in the copse and Daku had full control, they realized they were very alone. But it didn't take him long to pull them back to doing his will without question. As he spread himself over their bodies, enjoying the feeling of caressing a flower which was about to burst open, he realized this was not the right time for such indulgence. He would savour the wait until it was the moment to pick the blossoms, so after a suitable time he led them, very bedraggled, from the copse and down the lane leading to the charred remains of their recent home.

"There they are." A neighbour ran out of her house, followed by others. "Get the police, I'll take them in and keep them warm."
There was a mad scramble as more people appeared.

"May the Lord be praised, poor little things." A lady put her hands together then said, "I'll call the vicar."

"I saw him going out," a lad offered, "p'raps he's gone to the hall, they've got a coffee thing on.

"I'll ring him on his mobile then," and she dashed into her home to get the number.

Digby heard the frantic knocking on Fay's front door and ran to open it.

"They've got the girls, they're alright, isn't it wonderful, thought you should know straight away. Can you tell your aunt please?" The neighbour hadn't paused for breath yet but as soon as Digby could speak he said "Of course. Where are they?"

"At the lady across the road from their house." Then after a pause, "We've rung the police, I hope that was alright."

"Of course, thank you all very much. I'll come up as soon as I've told Aunt Fay."

The police soon arrived along with the fire investigation officers. It was suggested, although not really requested that the girls be taken to the local hospital and be checked over, in any case they needed proper care after the traumatic experience and Digby wasn't able to provide it being on his own, and Fay certainly wasn't capable. The police also wanted to be able to carefully interrogate them to find out as much as possible about what had happened. They agreed he could accompany them for support but wouldn't be able to remain there. He went back to Fay's house, checked she was still asleep and left a little note by the untouched tea explaining the girls were safe and that he would be back as soon as he could.

It was still assumed by all at this point that the parents had perished, but until full examinations had been carried out, no-one was certain of anything.

There was a large conference of upper level angels of all elements. It was time for the move. As luck would have it, the hospital was the best place for the transition, as, if the girls appeared dazed or seemed to have a slight loss of knowledge of things past, it would all be put down to recent events, and any care could only help the proper occupants adapt to their new surroundings.

Kyn and Graham of the air were to escort and place the two ideals in the twins' bodies. Ignis the fire angel was to draw Daku's attention far enough away to release his hold at which point Ohley the water angel would bring in Fay and Samuel for their part, hence the need for Fay to be asleep at this point. As an added insurance, a third air sign was due to accompany Kyn and Graham, and would, for a period remain in with the twins until they had acclimatized. Ana had given much thought to this selection, as this caretaker had to be of a high level to combat any possible attacks, but after consultation with Ohley they agreed it would have more effect if a water sign was used in case of a fire demon trying to take over, and there were several fit for the job. All senior angels were now hoping that Daku would assume that all attention would be on the bodies, or their remains being found in the house, and with the girls being safe, it would give them all plenty to occupy their thoughts for a long time. Another of Daku's faults – he assumed - and this hopefully would be his downfall.

Desmond had arrived in time to see the girls briefly before the ambulance came. He was struck with the lack of warmth in their eyes, and the hostile stare he got when he prayed for their recovery, little knowing whose eyes were looking back at him with contempt. He told Digby he would call in on his aunt later at a convenient time then returned to the hall to spread the good news about the girls. To save having to answer any questions he made it clear he knew nothing important until enquiries had been made and when Nora made to open her mouth he held up his hand to silence her and left.

"Well, that was short and sweet." Nora sniffed.

"What else could he say," Janet was ready for her, "he said, he knows nothing."

Dulcie added quietly, "Makes you feel sorry for 'em, them girls I me."

"You mark my words, there's more to this, you'll see." Nora nodded knowingly.

"What about Fay, I mean it aint nice for her is it?" Dulcie looked very sad now.

"I'll go round." Nora was about to get up from the table.

"You can't, you know what the vicar said last night. Nobody's to go, not just now." Janet was emphatic and added. "And that includes you Nora."

"Well – I - I " Nora stuttered.

The other two took that as a good time to get up and leave, not giving her chance to even finish the sentence.

It was about lunch time and the skies over Banbury hospital were getting darker by the minute.

"Looks as though we are in for a storm." A young nurse had just arrived for duty.

"Oh?"

"Yes, the sky's really black, and there's that lull in the air."

"You don't see much from in here, it could be snowing for all we'd know." The two laughed and went about their tasks.

But the skies were dark for a reason, the plan was underway with the first part targeting the hospital. Suddenly there was a flash of blinding lightening followed immediately by a deafening clap of thunder which seemed to shake the foundations of the building. People shouted in shock and nurses tried to comfort patients who were afraid of thunderstorms. Another flash – another clap – followed by a shout that a tree had been hit by lightening. Daku left the twins just far enough to observe the strike but his attention was taken by a building in the distance which appeared to have caught the full impact and the dark sky showed the flames licking higher. As he watched, drawn with a burning desire to find out more, another lightening fork went to ground and another cracked as it split a tree from top to bottom.

Daku hadn't realized that he had strayed just beyond his hold on the girls and while Ignis created his terrific illusion to draw him away, Fay and Samuel opened the heavens and the water fell in torrents blocking his return. When Kyn and Graham were certain the bodies were completed uninhabited, they placed the correct Topaz and Peridot in their proper vehicles along with the water angel to protect them.

There was mayhem all around the hospital, everywhere was flooded, drains blocked but fortunately the building hadn't been hit, the angels had seen to that. They almost sent an apologetic thought for what they had incurred but knew the outcome was worth more than a soaking which would soon be gone.

Daku had tried to return but felt the force against him, which was so much stronger than anything he could have ever mustered, for the fire, air and water angels were not working alone but had seconded an army of sentinels to help at the precise moment, so no demon could have worked out the enormity of the attack.

The twins were resting in a side room. Their new ideals had no knowledge of the transition, but the grooming they had undergone recently put the memories of their earth life into place so they could gradually pick up the pieces and start their lives eleven years late. Their water angel guardian would remain with them as protection for as long as needed but this meant she would have to relinquish her present earthly life which was almost complete. Fay had begged Ohley to let her take this task to make up for the family time lost during her life, to which Ohley agreed, knowing there could be no better guard than this great grandmother. Of course she would never again wake up as Fay Anders.

CHAPTER 10

Nora wasn't one for being told what to do, and with her curiosity burning away inside, she waited for her two companions to be well out of sight then changed her direction and was soon approaching Fay's house. She could see the activity going on near the De'Ath's and noticing Digby's car wasn't outside his aunt's she quickly slipped round to the back door, out of sight of passers by. She knocked quietly at first but after a moment gave quite a loud knock which anyone in the place should have heard. Still she was met with silence, so she tried to peer under the gap at the bottom of the net curtain but there was no movement in the small sitting room. It crossed her mind that Digby must have taken his aunt with him and she stood in thought for a moment, trying to recount what the vicar had said. The girls had been found safe, but where and who had found them? And where were they now? She came to the conclusion they must have been taken somewhere, perhaps to a doctor or hospital and Digby must have taken Fay with him.
If she had lost her mind a bit, she wouldn't be safe to be left, not with the upset and everything.

So Nora's mind rolled on but coming to no conclusion, she had no option but to return to her home determined to be one of the first to see Fay when she returned. Little did she guess that the lifeless body lay upstairs while its previous owner now had a very important task ahead protecting her descendents.

Digby had been speaking to the doctors about the future care of his grandchildren but in view of the current situation they decided his main concern at present was to establish what had happened to his son and daughter-in-law. It seemed fairly obvious that the girls were going to have to be told of their parents' death at some stage and he would be there to do it. But for now he would return to his aunt, and would have to be available while investigations were being carried out at the house. Being assured that they would be safe and cared for he went into their room to say that he would be back as soon as he could.

He almost gasped at the sight which met him. The two girls smiled as soon as he entered, something he had rarely seen, and Topaz reached out her

171

hand and said "Grandad" very softly. They were both relaxing on the same bed and as he went to sit down they moved for him to sit between them. Amazed, he looked from one to the other. Never had he seen such warmth and affection from either of them in their short lives, and they were both smiling at him. He felt the tears burning the back of his eyes and he held out both arms and pulled them to him. As they cuddled in he realized just how much he had missed over the years and knew he must tell his mother when he returned. He was brought back to reality at the thought of having left her asleep, and he knew he should get back to her as soon as possible.

"I have to go now, I've left your --" he paused as he wanted to say great grandmother and instead whispered "...your aunt, and she will be worried."

"Will you bring her to see us?" Peridot looked up at him with the most appealing eyes and it struck him how pretty these girls were.

"Just as soon as I can." And he gave them a kiss on the forehead and stood up to leave.

Fay's ideal reached out to touch his hand and thought "There is so much time to make up, and if this is the only way, at least Samuel and I will be part of it." Then she settled back to enjoy being so close to these little relatives of hers.

As Digby drove back to Ascott, he felt a heaviness at how short a time his son's family had spent in their new home which was to have been the last chance of a fresh start they were likely to have. His mind raced with unanswered questions. How had the fire started? How had the girls got out, but mostly had his son and Maisie perished?

He had never been that close to his son but had helped him whenever possible and would have been there for the family no matter what. It hadn't been easy since the birth of the twins, who had never been as normal children. Something in his instincts warned him to be wary and not cross them but he never knew why. So what he had witnessed at the hospital was what he felt they should have been like from the start. There had always been trouble surrounding them and it was this that had caused his wife to leave. She had had enough of the constant moving about, there was always trouble concerning them although nothing could ever be proved, and the children didn't like her.

Digby felt it was only right for her to be informed of what had happened, but how could he? She had made it perfectly clear that she wanted nothing to do with any of them ever again, and after the divorce had moved away with no forwarding address or telephone number with strict instructions to her solicitor that any communication was not welcome.

He turned into the road and pulled up against the house noticing the bedroom curtains were still closed.

"Ah just the person I wanted to see." The detective appeared from round the back and made Digby jump a little.

"I've just got back from the hospital, I need to check on my aunt."

"Must be a shock for her." The officer identified himself as he walked with him.

"Yes, could you excuse me for a minute, only she was still asleep when I left and she doesn't seem to be up yet."

"No, you go ahead sir, I'll just wait if I may."

Digby unlocked the door and indicated for the man to sit in the room while he went upstairs. He knocked on the bedroom door but his hand was already on the handle and he quietly looked round the door. Fay appeared to be asleep, a slight smile on her face.

"Mum" he whispered, aware the policeman was in the house. He touched her shoulder and realized she wasn't breathing. Sadness filled him as he wished he had never left her and thoughts raced wondering if the shock had been too much for her frail body.

"Is everything alright sir?" The voice called up the stairs.

"No. Would you come up please?" Digby knew that sooner or later the police would have to be informed, so he might as well use the man that was here.

"She's died, and I wasn't here." His voice trembled now partly due to all the events of the last hours.

The detective took over and told him not to touch anything for the moment, then noticed the tea and note at the side of the bed.

"Did you put them there?"

"Yes, I brought the tea but she was asleep so I left it."

He asked what time that was then said "And the note?"

"I came back up and left that when the girls had been found and I went to the hospital with them. Didn't want to disturb her."

There was a pause as the officer was making notes but the next statement hit Digby like a bullet.

"So, it seems you were the last person to see her alive then sir?"

"What?"

"Just getting the facts, we'll get the doc out, examine her you know."

"Oh this is too much." Digby felt quite weak as they both went downstairs and into the sitting room where he almost fell into the armchair. The officer let him settle for a moment then said "I'm sorry to have to tell you this, but you know I came here to see you, before .." and he indicated upstairs.

"Oh, did you, I'm sorry, there's been so much going on."

The detective seemed to be accepting that Digby was having to cope with more than most could handle and said quietly "At first inspection of your son's house, it appears there are the remains of two people."

Digby put his face in his hands as the truth was confirmed. He had lost his son and his wife, and now his mother all in the last twenty four hours.

It was all too much and he wept out of grief and tiredness. How long he stayed like that he didn't know, but when he wiped his eyes the officer had made them both a cup of tea which sat in front of him.

"I'm sorry to have been the one to break the news." The tone was softer now.

"I was hoping that somehow it wouldn't be, but it seemed inevitable didn't it?" He took a sip of tea then asked "Do we know what happened?"

"Not yet, early days." The man took his time before he said "You'll be staying here will you sir?"

"For a while, but I will have to go home to see everything's alright. They've got my details."

After another pause, "The doctor will be down soon, I'll stay until he's been, just to do all the paperwork, you know how it is."

They spoke about the twins and made general conversation, and whereas at first Digby had felt he was under scrutiny, he now felt glad of the man's company as someone strong to lean on, and someone who would keep others at bay.

The next hours were hard to cope with but suddenly Digby felt a strength returning and he wondered for a moment if his mother was somehow supporting him. He wasn't far wrong, for his guardian angel was none other than his father Samuel.

Frank and Maisie had been taken care of by helpers who would assist them to acclimatize to their new state. In time they may learn the truth about the Fay's relationship but for now they had to go through a period of adjustment due to their sudden wrench from their earthly bodies and there was no rush for them to learn the secret. They would be taken far away so would have no contact with Fay or Samuel until such time was deemed correct, if ever.

The laughter ripped through every realm. Daku couldn't appear in any area without ridicule, Lazzan had seen to that.

"These jumped up little demons think they own the show, they know nothing!" Lazzan's sarcasm and contempt was felt through all elements.

To be overcome so easily proved to the hierarchy that his guard could be dropped at the most vital moment and he was no good for important tasks. To be mocked by the other elements was bad enough, but your own kind, as Fica had learned.

Ana and the air angels, along with Ohley and Ignis felt certain elation but experience had taught them not to be blinded by the fall of a lowly spirit for that was often when the higher levels were plotting to jump in and catch them unawares, so they were satisfied their present task had been successful but had already moved on with their diligence in all fields.

The doctor was very kind to Digby, but gently told him that Fay would have to undergo a post mortem as she hadn't been to the doctors for some time. Hard as it was, he knew this would have to be done and after all it couldn't hurt her now, also they would know he had nothing to do with it, for that thought after the police questions was still in his mind.

When she had been taken away, Desmond came to sit with Digby and before long he was picking up a strong spiritual feeling from him, very similar to one he always felt when he had been in conversation with Fay. So he put it down to the fact they were related, but knew this was a good man. His mind slipped to the twins and when he raised the subject he noticed a change come over Digby. It was almost as if a weight had been lifted and he felt the grandfather wanted to tell him something. Feeling a bit silly, Digby ventured to explain the difference he had noticed at the hospital. He was amazed when the vicar clasped his hands together, looked upwards and seemed to be praying.

"What have I said vicar?"

"I need to see them, is that possible?

Digby thought then said, "Of course, you can get in anytime, but why?"

"Can't say just now, let me be sure, but I think we have something to celebrate out of all this."

Digby looked quite bewildered but smiled "Anything good would be nice." He had a feeling the vicar knew something about the change in the girls which could only mean that they hadn't been their true selves up to now, which in turn would explain their demeanour from birth. This reaction from Desmond gave Digby a thread of hope for the future.

The village was very quiet. The recent events seemed to touch everyone in some way for although the new family hadn't exactly made a very good impression, people couldn't help but feel sadness at the tragedy. There were the odd few who ventured to say that some people got what they deserved but they were soon put in their place by the more tender hearted. Most wondered as to the fate of the girls as they had only seen the strange side of them up to now and the general feeling was that they wouldn't be likely to be living anywhere nearby again. Ben was known to all due his job, and although people like Molly would miss him greatly, most were very sad at his sudden passing, but curiosity about the activity surrounding it seemed to have diminished for a while. Fay had always kept to herself, just passing the time of day with villagers and was known as being a very gentile lady. Even in her contact with Nora's group, she tended to not contribute to the gossip, but sat quietly observing the others. Nobody knew just how alert she was, and they would have been amazed to learn of her recent role, and the bodies she was now guarding.

For a bank holiday week end there seemed little to celebrate but one or two families had made plans for the following couple of days, partly for the sake of their children, and also as a bit of respite from the events. Digby had a few days to settle his emotions, for although he would have to arrange his aunts' funeral after all the official side had been taken care of, there was nothing he could do until all the necessary offices opened again after the break.

It was the middle of the afternoon, and he toyed with the idea of going back to his own house, but knowing he would be returning to the hospital soon, thought he would save the running about and stay where he was. The little house seemed to be closing in on him and he needed some fresh air, so he decided a little stroll down to the river would be refreshing, and he wouldn't be likely to bump into any one there. He certainly didn't feel like making polite conversation, not just now.

His steps took him past the little green, and he realized as he saw the edge of the churchyard, that this is where his aunt would be laid to rest, and he felt drawn to see where it would be. He slowly opened the gate and turned up the small path leading to the front porch of the church. Again, he felt pushed forward and he was compelled to approach the entrance as though he was meant to go inside, but suddenly the feeling left him as he noticed a man with his head lowered, standing in front of a headstone in front of which a small rose tree was in bloom. Suddenly the man turned and looked at him, his face etched with grief. Something held the two men for several minutes until Digby looked at the name on the stone and asked, almost in a whisper "Your son?"
He was answered with a nod, but the man noticed Digby's lip trembling and asked "The fire, was that......?"

"Yes." Digby managed to say before he felt another surge of tears welling up.

"Come on let's sit for a minute," and he took his arm saying "I'm Tony."

"Digby."

The church was locked but the two men sat in the porch until both regained their composure, apologizing for their display of grief.

"This is too public. Would you like to come back to my home for a drink?" Tony couldn't understand why he was making the invitation, but knew only too well what this person must be going through. His son may have been much older than his, but a father's loss is the same, regardless of age.

"I was going for a walk, but that would be very kind, thank you."

There wasn't too great a gap between their ages, and although the circumstances were very different, both felt a support from the other.

Graham pulled back, having drawn these two sad lonely men together, he knew they would seek solace in someone with similar circumstances who would understand without having to be told every detail, and knowing it is sometimes easier to talk to a stranger than someone who is too close.

"This is it," Tony indicated.

"I didn't know you lived so close," Digby followed him to the door "but then I haven't exactly been here to socialize."

They went into the living room and Tony asked "Tea, coffee, or something a bit stronger?"

"No, coffee's fine thank you, white no sugar."

"Sit down, won't you, won't take a minute."

Digby sat on the settee, his attention drawn to the framed picture of Shane which seemed to be staring at him. He was still transfixed when Tony returned with the drinks.

"Good looking boy wasn't he?" He said as he put the cups on the coffee table near to the photo.

"Very. A bit of a lad though." Digby smiled remembering when Frank was that age.

"Oh yes, but no trouble really."

Digby sipped his coffee then asked "If you don't mind my asking, how old would he have been now?"

"Would have been coming up to twenty one and no, I don't mind, in fact to be honest, this is the first time I've felt like speaking about it." He thought for a moment. "Do you know, this is really strange, you're the first person I've sat with like this, apart from the councilors who say they are helping but don't do anything. I mean they just let you talk, only I couldn't you see."

The two men talked at length, Tony pouring out all he could remember, the initial facts still wiped from his mind, but Digby soon realized the torture this man had been through, and was still going through. Obviously, there was little Digby could offer relating to the fire but he talked about his 'aunt' so lovingly that Tony soon realized there had been a special bond between them and to loose so many from his family at once seemed to make his own grief seem less harsh.

"Oh I must be going, I have to get back to the hospital, to the twins." Digby looked at his watch and almost jumped up. Tony rose instantly "Look, I don't want to intrude or anything but can we keep in touch, while you're here."

"I would appreciate that very much, thank you Tony. And I don't have to say that all this is between ourselves. I'm not one for chat."

"Taken as read."

They said their good byes and Digby returned to Fay's house to prepare for his next visit to his grand children.

Tony bent to pick up the cups, his eyes resting upon his son. He looked again. Was it his imagination or were the eyes softer and the lips smiling more than before? Tony smiled to himself, as for the first time in over ten years, the face looking back at him appeared peaceful and happy.

"Is this what you wanted Shane? A companion for me?" He held the photo close to his heart but through the smile he felt the tears of emotion still threatening to overtake his control. But from the picture a warmth reached out and caressed his entire body until he felt lifted in spirit, surrounded by a beautiful blue hue and he was being drawn upwards in a feeling of tremendous love and care. He had not experienced anything like this since the episode at the hospital and it was a feeling he didn't want to end.

The air angels gently floated his spirit back to earth, leaving him refreshed and with a new strength he couldn't understand, but he knew that this was a new beginning and he was ready to grasp it with both hands.

CHAPTER 11

As could be expected, such a chapter of events in a small community filtered through to the local press, followed by reporters from the national papers and before long, an assortment of vans were parked around the village. Strangely enough, one was outside Nora's, and she just happened to be in her Sunday best when she was interviewed on camera.

"Trust her," one of the locals remarked as small groups appeared wherever filming happened to be taking place. But while some couldn't wait for their moment of fame, others dreaded the invasion, knowing their privacy was at risk at a time when they wanted to escape into their shells and come to terms with the happenings. But with Nora in the foreground, that peace was threatened, for she quickly pointed the finger in any direction, as long as she was the one to be the first with information. It never occurred to her that this could come back on her if words were twisted or misquoted. People would believe what they read if it was juicy enough.

So it wasn't long before cameras were aimed on the charred remains of the De'Ath residence, followed by intrusive attention on Fay's house, much to Digby's annoyance as he wanted to get to the hospital but was afraid to leave his Mum's home unattended. Fortunately, the press were drawn away to Ben's place for the protective tent was still in situ keeping out any onlookers and some reporters felt that story must have more interest than an old dear who had died from shock.

An eager young reporter from a county paper stood chatting with some of the villagers near the churchyard. He had no pad and pencil, no recorder on view and just appeared to be interested, and posing no threat.

"How sad for you all, had he been ill?" He asked nobody in particular and only turned his head when old Tom said "Fittest bloke around."

"'e was the postman," another added "there won't be another like 'im."

A slight murmur of agreement went round the group with heads nodding slowly. Waiting for the right timing the reporter said "Where did they take him, do you know?" He was met with silence, so he quietly said "I think there is only one undertaker round here, I expect he has gone there then."

"He ain't gone if you ask me?" Tom said very precisely.

"What do you mean?"

Tom sniffed and looked round at some of the people who lived at nearby houses. "I ain't saying."

The young man looked from one to another, and as his gaze fell on each they turned their heads as though no-one wanted to be the one to say.

"Well, they wouldn't have left him until now I shouldn't think." They knew something and weren't saying, but he would get it out of them. A bit of whispering filtered through to him and he turned to face one of the ladies who ventured "I live over there and there's been no hearse, no coffin coming out, nothing." At this offering more joined in explaining that if an undertaker had been in the daytime or evening one of them would have seen them as their windows overlooked Ben's. As it was always very quiet at night, any vehicle attracted their attention. He did think that maybe it would be their only source of interest but pushed the unkind thought away as they explained that if Ben had been taken away in the night the movements would have awoken somebody at least. One lady said she was a very light sleeper, and with the awful news that he had departed, she couldn't sleep anyway.

"How did you hear he had died?" He tried a new approach.

"The vicar told some and then they passed it on, but we knew there was something wrong with all this stuff covering the front."

Knowing he would get no further information from this source, and he wouldn't be allowed anywhere near by the police, he knew his next frontline attack would be the vicar. Casually asking where he might be found, he left the bemused little group for the 'horse's mouth'.

The nurses welcomed Digby as he greeted the girls. He didn't relish the task ahead and had accepted the offer of one of the senior staff to be there when he explained about their parents. As it turned out they were not needed as trained police officers were in constant attendance hoping to learn about the events leading up to the fire. The girls had been rather vague but seemed to know they had been called away just before but couldn't say by whom.

As he sat on the bed the girls took up their positions either side of him and he gently put an arm around each.

"I have something rather sad to tell you both. Do you feel strong enough?" His voice was already trembling but Topaz spoke almost immediately.

"You've come to tell us about Mum and Dad haven't you?"

He nodded. "Yes, I'm so sorry, but..."

Peridot squeezed his arm. "We know they died."

He looked from one to another then to the police officers. The girls looked sad but there were no tears and they seemed to be comforting him.

"It was the fire you see," he wasn't really sure of what to say next but added "you don't know how happy I am that you two are alright."
Peridot said quietly "It must be sad for you because Dad was your son, but he is in heaven now isn't he?" Digby nodded. This wasn't what he expected at all, but Fay was in charge and controlling the girls through this sad exchange.
"Yes they are both in heaven, and nothing can hurt them any more."
Topaz's face took on a very strange expression as she said "I don't feel we knew them very well, do you Peri?"
Her sister replied "No at all really, I don't think we understood each other."

Everyone sat in silence for a while. The officers had taken everything in but not sure they understood it completely. They could only think that children were very resilient and bounced back quickly, but not usually this quickly.
The grandfather and the twins stayed locked in a group hug as though somehow they knew they had to make up for eleven years of lost time. But it was Fay who was cementing the bond between her family and she and Samuel would make certain it could never be broken.

As he sat there, Digby knew he had also got to tell the girls about 'Aunt Fay' but as they never really saw her much, it may not upset them too badly. But his own feelings were so near the surface, he knew he hadn't the composure to do it now, it would have to wait until he felt strong enough.

One of the police officers slipped from the room, hardly noticed by the family, leaving the woman detective to stay and hopefully get some of the information they needed by just listening in. Immediately a nurse popped her head round the door and asked "Cup of tea anyone?"

"Oh, do you know I could just use one of those," Digby would normally have had coffee but at the moment tea would be very comforting. The officer shook her head almost wishing the nurse hadn't drawn attention to her as she was trying to merge into the background.
As the girls beamed up at the nurse she smiled as she said "I know ladies, you would like pop." And she disappeared wagged her finger at them playfully.

The atmosphere was relaxing by the minute and Fay's ideal was gratified to realize it was progressing without her nudging it along, so she withdraw slightly to observe, from the outside, the love which was growing around her. A tap on the door made them all jump for a moment but the girls chorused "Come in" and Desmond's head appeared round the door.

"Any room for another one?" He couldn't believe, but was overjoyed at the transformation in the girls' expression from the ones he had witnessed earlier.

"Oh do come in Reverend," Digby politely got up and shook his hand as he indicated to a chair. "You might be lucky enough to get a cup of tea, they're just fetching one."

Desmond shook Digby's hand firmly and saw, under the smiling façade, the pain which this brave man must be enduring, but hoped the girls would be a crutch for him to lean on, and give him something to fight for in his recovery.

When the drinks had been delivered and the nurse had left, Desmond stood facing the detective.

"I wish to speak with the family alone please. Would you mind leaving us for a moment?"

The woman's face showed no emotion which the vicar felt should have been there when dealing with a case of this nature. Her reply was curt.

"Sorry, can't do that."

Desmond fixed her with a stare "Oh? And why not?"

"Rules. They're not to be left, that's why there are two of us, one stays here all the time."

There was a very poignant pause before Desmond moved a little closer until he was staring her in the eye. "Are they under arrest?"

"Of course not." She was becoming very uncomfortable under his gaze, which was not improving her temper. She rose to her feet so that he was not towering over her and faced him.

He was unflinching as he said in very precise clipped tones "Correct me if I'm wrong young lady, but are they not here to be, in what is in yours and my terminology 'a place of safety'."

"Why ask if you know?" she snapped.

"And your roll is to protect that safety, is it not?"

She gave a very insolent sigh knowing he was stating the obvious and guessing where it was going, but she was determined to carry out her orders.

"So," he was giving one of his smiles reserved for such situations, "we are both here for the same reason. The church is considered a sanctuary, and I represent the church. What higher authority do you need?"

"But........." she started to argue but he was already escorting her to the door.

Desmond spoke directly into her ear as she passed "And just to keep your records straight, you can tell your superior that the vicar is conducting private prayers with the family at this sad time. Thank you." And the door was closed with her on the outside.

The girls were almost whooping with delight but he put his finger to his lips indicating for them to be quieter, and even Digby was smiling broadly for the first time.

"Well, that's that settled," Desmond sat down and took a closer look at the family. "We will say a prayer before I leave, but I wonder if I could just have a chat with you first, and I'm not interrogating you, you've probably had enough of that.

Topaz was still smiling "The police asked us questions about the fire but we couldn't tell them much could we Peri?"

"No, we said that we heard mother telling us to get out and she would follow, but we can't remember any more, honestly we can't."

"That's fine my dear," he said kindly, don't you worry too much." And he cast a smile towards Digby which the man found reassuring, knowing the vicar was happy with what he was seeing.

"Can I ask, do you know who I am?"

The twins looked at each other surprised at the question which didn't seem intrusive like their previous questioning sessions they had already undergone before the vicar arrived.

"Of course." They both laughed and Peridot said   "You are the vicar of the village where we live now.

"That's right, but do you know my full name?"

Again they laughed. "You are the Reverend Conway." Fay was prompting the information which had been previously fed to them.

He smiled at Digby again before he said "Now, this is going to sound a very odd thing for me to ask but would you try and help me, I'm getting old you see and my memory isn't what it was."

"Of course we will." Topaz was clapping her hands and Peridot added "This is fun isn't it, not like those others."

"You're very kind." Desmond took a breath. "Can you remember when you last saw me?"

"Oh you are funny," Peridot started but her sister grabbed her hand, "That's rude, he said that he........." and her voice trailed off as she didn't think it polite to remind the other girl of the vicar's supposedly short memory. But then they looked at each other and went into a little discussion about when it was. Nothing was very clear now. They had a vague recollection of seeing him a day or so before in the street and they felt they had seen him that day but they weren't sure where. Fay was not helping them for she knew the good man was nearing the truth and just wanted enough to satisfy himself of what had possibly happened in the girl's existence.

Desmond smiled, "Don't you worry your heads about it, it doesn't matter anyway, I must be getting too old eh?"

"No, you're not." They were both laughing and he had his answers.

Before he said prayers he checked discreetly with Digby as to how much the girls knew, and Digby made it clear that he had only told them about the parents. Desmond just said "Would you like me to take on that extra task?" to which the man nodded fighting back the tears he must only shed alone.

They sat quietly as Desmond explained about how old their aunt was and the news had been too much for her so she would be in heaven now with their parents. Fay appreciated the kindness but thought "If you only knew how near I am, and how far away they are."

The girls took it very well but said they felt sad for Grandad, at which point Desmond took the attention away from Digby as they lowered their heads and prayed for the departed family, and also for the love of the people in this room.

As the "Amen" came from all their lips, the door opened. Desmond guessed who the intruder might be so kept them all with their heads lowered for some time before he said "May the Lord comfort you and keep you all safe."

He purposely shook hands with each of them, making everyone else wait until he was ready then slowly turned to face the two officers.

"Thank you, I'm finished here, for now." Then to the family "I'll see you again soon. I'd like a word with you before you leave please Digby."

"Of course."

The smile on Desmond's face was in contrast to the expressions on the faces of the detectives, the senior of which was now following him down the corridor, while the woman resumed her seat in the room.

"A word vicar, if you don't mind." The male officer caught up with him.

"Of course, what can I do for you my son?"

The more experienced officer knew better than antagonize a man of the cloth so tried a subtle approach.

"You did put us in a sticky position then you know?"

"Oh, why was that?"

"As my colleague told you, the girls have to be watched at all times. Look, we don't know much about the fire and if somebody was, how shall I say, well, got it in for the family, the girls could be in danger."

"Yes I do realize that" he stopped walking and smiled directly at the man "and I also know that you need to get all the information you can while you're about it." He gave a very knowing and searching look which didn't go unnoticed.

The detective now came in for the kill. "I know it's not strictly right to ask but I don't suppose they gave you any indication of what might have happened."

Desmond started walking again "No it wouldn't be right, anything told to a priest is strictly confidential, but I will say one thing."

"Oh yes." The officer would have anything.

Again Desmond stopped to get full impact. "Speaking in my capacity, I am pretty sure that you have heard all you are going to hear, and they are not aware of anything more they can help you with. So they must be allowed to adjust after this ordeal as carefully as possible, without any undue stress, if you understand me."

The policeman was deflated, he had hoped for a moment that this man would cast a gleam of light on the business, but he should have known better from his handling of the situation from the start.

"Well, if you do think you can help us at all vicar, perhaps you would be so good as to give me a ring." He couldn't help including a little sarcasm as he handed Desmond a card.

Digby joined him in the car park, and knowing this wasn't the right place to discuss his findings they agreed to meet back at Fay's house on their return to the village.

Old Tom was in his usual seat in the local pub. He'd come down a bit earlier as, having seen the village teeming with strangers, and guessing they would want some refreshment, he should be in for a good few pints from strangers who hadn't heard his tales before.

"There y'are Tom," Jim the landlord put a half before him "that's yer starter to wet yer whistle. On the 'ouse"

"Very kind o' ya Jim."

"Hope yer in good voice, could be busy."

"Ahh, could give some o' the old tales an airing."

Jim never minded giving the old boy a drink as the entertainment brought in more custom and Tom was the last of his breed. It would be a sad day when he departed.

Before long the place was quite busy and word soon got round that Tom was a bit of a character. The young reporter had arrived, disappointed that he hadn't managed to track down the elusive vicar, but knew the public house in any settlement was usual the hob of information.

"Hello again, can I get you a drink?" He sat down opposite Tom and indicated to his glass.

"Well, that's kind of yer." Tom always looked surprised but the locals knew this was all part of his act. When they were both settled with drinks, the reporter started pumping Tom about anything he may have seen around Ben's after he had left.

"That's just it, "Tom had a noisy slurp of ale, "there b'aint nothing to see."

"Ah," the young man was not averse to shady tactics when it came to getting information, and if Tom didn't know, he would probably be the best one to root it out of someone else, "only there was a rumour that all was not as it seemed."

Tom leaned forward. "Oh ahh? In what way like?"

"There is talk that he was helped on his way, I don't suppose you've heard…"and he started to shake his head slowly from side to side eyeing the old chap inquisitively as he did.

"No. Not Ben. Not a chance. Too well liked round 'ere. What made you say a thing like that?"

"No no, not me. I'm only saying what I was told, you see" and he beckoned him nearer, "they don't bring in the forensic team for a sudden death, only murder."

"Get out." Tom sat musing for a minute. "You know, I were telling the wife, God rest 'er soul, that this weren't no ordinary dying."

"You see, you knew – I mean – instinct told you this wasn't normal."

"Ahh lad, 'specs yer right." And Tom downed the last of his drink knowing it wouldn't be too long before the next offer came.

"TOM, there you are." A couple of locals knew the drill and always got Tom going on his tales and songs, but the reporter didn't welcome the intrusion as he felt he could have squeezed a bit more out of this gent. If he had guessed that something wasn't right, then it probably wasn't, as these country folk had a knack of knowing by gut feeling, just as they could tell you what tomorrow's weather would be just by looking at the skies the night before.

The young man moved back from the table to let others get near to Tom, and he slipped into the background his ears strained for any leads possible.

"Come on Tom, you 'aven't done The Blackbird for a long time. 'Ow about it?" Then to the group which had gathered they explained "You've probable 'eard it sung by one o' those folk groups but old Tom 'ere says it was always recited. Go on Tom, let 'em 'ave it."

Making sure that he had enough lubrication in front of him, Tom related.

> *"Where be that blackbird to,*
> *Us knows where he be.*

He be in yon turmut field
And us be ah'ter 'e. (after he)
Now 'he sees I, and I sees 'e
And 'e knows I be ah'ter 'e."

The place erupted in applause and Tom wasted no time in following up with the prayers including Mr. Musty and his wheat.

The reporter mused on the fact that hours earlier the village had almost been in mourning and now you wouldn't think a thing had happened. What were these people made of? Now that would be a good angle for his report, but he couldn't leave without something more concrete.

When quite a lot of ale had been consumed, and Tom was singing the words to the country dance 'The Merry Merry Milkmaids', the young man left and headed towards Ben's house. His timing was perfect for he noticed two people coming through the tent to a small van. They were still suited in white outfits and carefully put some small boxes in the back of the van, shut the doors, banged on the roof and the van was driven away. The reporter was at the tent before they had chance to re-enter.

"Excuse me".

They turned suddenly but still trying to return to the house.

"Can you tell me what happened?" and he waved his media identification as he spoke.

"Sorry sir, everyone will know in good time. Good night."

"But we've heard it could have been murder, can you confirm that?"

One man had already gone back inside but the second a man of very burly build turned and said very slowly "I repeat sir, everyone, and that includes you, will know in good time. Now is there any of that you have a problem with?"

Knowing this was futile but being reassured that something serious was going on here he just shook his head and mumbled "Thank you."

He waited for the man to disappear and stood looking round the area. So many of these little dwellings had windows overlooking this place, so if he could only persuade one of the occupants to give him some digs for a day or two, after all who would refuse an extra bit of cash, maybe, just maybe he could be on hand when things began to take shape. But that would have to wait until tomorrow, as these gentile folk wouldn't welcome him banging on their doors at this hour.

Desmond had been talking to Digby for some time as they sat in Fay's house. Now and again they would sit quietly musing over the revelation that the vicar was now sure was the answer to many questions. They had shared a small meal and now sat with the remains of the coffee in front of them.

"I know this must seem very hurtful to you Digby, with it being so close in your family." Desmond broke the silence.

"Yes, it is, but do you know, in a way it is a relief. I never gave it a thought that someone – thing, could have taken them over, but it does explain a lot."

"Let's just clarify that, not taken them, that is themselves over, just their bodies. It's not the same as being possessed you see." He was able to speak with some certainly for Graham had been feeding him the facts in his sleeping moments, and although he knew he hadn't a shred of proof, Desmond, after his tutoring when the older man was alive, knew that by instinct he was right.

"It's hard to think that they weren't in their bodies. How does that work?" Digby's head was still in a turmoil.

"Well, as far as I can say, in cases like this, they are often somewhere else." There was silence for a moment. Then Digby, still looking bemused asked "Where?"

"Ah, that is not for the likes of us to know, we just have to accept. But remember, it hasn't affected them much has it?"

Digby brightened. "No, that's what I can't understand. They are, well seem so happy, not what you'd expect after going through..." he paused for a moment, "but what you're saying is they didn't did they, because they weren't there, in their own bodies." He shook his head "I'm afraid it's all a bit beyond me."

Desmond smiled. "A lot of what goes on around us would be incomprehensible to many, that is if we only knew about it. I'm no expert, and I'm learning a lot all the time, but I can tell you one thing." He paused to make sure he had Digby's attention. "There is so much that we do not have the power to understand in this life. As we move on, a lot becomes clearer. If we were told too much now, we would never we able to comprehend. Does that make sense?"

"Do you know, it does in some strange way."

"You look very thoughtful," Desmond smiled, "there's something you want to say isn't there?"

Digby looked amazed. "Well, it will sound silly."

"I doubt it."

"It's just what you said about knowing things, I have had – how can I describe it, feelings, and I think my aunt did too. She never said but I felt it. And do you know, I felt her presence so strongly when I was at the hospital."

Desmond was beaming now. "You don't know how pleased I am to hear you say that. She was there wasn't she?"

"You felt it too!" Digby almost leaped from the chair.

"Oh yes, I think she is protecting the girls, getting them acclimatized so to speak."

"Well she would want to protect her........." Digby stopped suddenly.

"Go on, protecting her what Digby?" Desmond studied the man in front of him who was now close to tears.

"I can't – can't say." The voice trembled as Digby fought to keep Fay's secret, even after her death, her dignity was important.

After a moment Desmond said "Let's see, they would be her great grandchildren. Does that make it easier for you?"

Digby's mouth opened but closed again and he nodded slightly.

"Don't ask me how I know, there was just something in the way you reacted, and I noticed the resemblance, but please be assured no-one will ever know from me. Let's keep her little secret, and yours, for her sake."

"I don't know how to thank you. It wouldn't have been proper you see, you know what people are like. But I loved her so much."

"Then that's all that matters. And can I say, I am sure she is of a high level in the spirit world, you can feel the power when you are in her vicinity."

"Yes, that's what I noticed many times. She appeared to be this little meek and mild spinster, but underneath she was a very strong person, don't you agree Desmond?"

"I certainly do, and I hope this comforts you, knowing she is near."

They both seemed to look at the clock together, and realizing how long they had been talking Desmond rose. "I'm sorry, but I will have to take my leave of you now Digby, but please contact me if you feel the need." He said a small prayer and left, leaving the bereaved man in a calmer but still thoughtful state of mind.

CHAPTER 12

Nora was the first at church for the 8 o'clock Communion the following morning, wearing her 'holier than thou' look. As she took her usual seat and waited for her two companions to arrive, she gave the Reverend Conway several searching looks, hoping for the slightest indication that he would confide with her some sort of information as to the events.

This proved how misguided the poor woman was, for not only was she the last person to whom he would have divulged anything, she was, after all, in God's house to receive communion, not exchange gossip, but that didn't seem to register with her.

Her head turned as each member of the congregation arrived, but when the time came to start the service, she was still sitting alone. Most people would have been rather concerned as to the welfare of their friends, but this was Nora, and she sat feeling indignant that they hadn't had the decency to bother to turn up, today of all days. If there had been a problem, they could have rung her, but to her that was only to satisfy her curiosity as to their absence.

With indecent haste she almost rushed from her seat at the end, and realizing she would get no information from these few, she hurried home and picked up the telephone.

"Hello? Is that you Janet?" Her tone was curt, demanding an explanation.

"Of course it is." Janet was equally short in return which took the caller aback for a moment.

"Well, where were you and Dulcie this morning, you weren't at church."

Janet thought "I know that, what you really are asking is why wasn't we at church." She drew in her breath and said very precisely "Some of us are still rather shocked and didn't feel like mixing with other people just now, can you understand that Nora?"

Nora spluttered, appalled at the retort, but was not going to let that go without a lecture.

"I would have thought Janet Mercer, that, as a Christian, you would have found solace in being close to the Lord. I was on my own, totally."

"Ah, there we 'ave it Nora. You, a Christian, didn't like sitting on your own. You, a Christian couldn't find out any sordid details about anything that 'as 'appened. Did you say a prayer for those poor souls that perished in the fire, did you say a prayer for poor old Ben, did you shed a tear for one of our friends, in fact, did Fay even cross your mind?"

Nora had never heard anything like this before and could do no more than slam down the phone. She had considered ringing Dulcie, but in her own mind knew she would get the same response. Her temper slowly turned to tears, as for the first time, she felt completely alone. Janet's words were still ringing in her ears as her thoughts turned to Fay, and she wondered how many times the spinster had faced the same solitude in her life. She dropped to her knees, and with genuine repentance asked God to forgive her for not seeing beyond herself. Maybe she could have extended the hand of friendship in a different way, but it was too late now, and her tears were of grief and loss. Her protective angel looked down and stroked her head sending the message, "It is never too late to be sorry."

The Bank Holiday slipped by with little activity in the village, and as soon as he could, Digby got to grips with registering the deaths. Everything seemed to take ages, waiting for the fire officers' report, waiting for the coroner, waiting, waiting. Fay's was the easiest to sort as the doctor wasted no time giving him the result of the post mortem. He could have carried on with his mother's arrangements but wanted all three to go together if possible so he would have to be patient and let the system take its course.

One bit of good news did cheer him considerably. He was on one of his visits to the hospital to see the twins and a social worker had arranged to meet him there.

"I think we have something positive for you," she smiled.

"You have found somewhere for the girls?" He was eager to know how near it would be for he wasn't about to loose contact with them now.

"Better than that. We have a foster mother who lives in Charlbury not far from you, and she has no children in at present, and prefers long term stays, rather than lots of short ones."

"And she will take them?" Digby looked hopeful.

"She knows about the fire and due to their ages would take on the challenge of seeing them through the biggest change of their lives, puberty."

Digby thought for a moment then asked "And I'd be able to see them, regularly I mean?"

"That's why we were keen on this placement. You could see them, almost as often as you like, but the girls do need a woman's care. She is a widow by the way, so there would only be the three of them in the house. You wouldn't have to worry about their upbringing, but still enjoy having family near."

"When can they go, I mean it would be easier to have them nearer."
The officer said "Well, the hospital say they are perfectly fit and don't need to be in here, but we just have to do all the right paperwork, you know how it is, but as soon as that is in place, off we go, so to speak."

"I can't thank you enough." Digby shook her hand. "I'm staying at my aunt's for now, but I could just as easily sort everything from my home." He thought to himself "and the police know where I am so I don't see any problem."

He and the social worker made their way to tell the girls the news, hoping they would be as excited as he was, but he needn't have worried for they jumped up and down then danced round the room.

"Well I didn't expect you to be that happy," he smiled "but things will only get better from now on."

After a few weeks much had taken place. The police were satisfied that Digby had no involvement in any of the deaths and the funerals had taken place. Fay's house was up for sale and the girl's were settling into their new surroundings. They had been booked into a different school which had proved a wise move, as they now had their own characters which would have taken some explaining at their previous one. Digby's own house, on the edge of Charlbury was only a few minutes walk from their new home which meant they were in touch but not living on top of each other. He had built up quite a friendship with Tony, both finding an understanding listener in the other, and they would visit one another on no particular arrangement, but felt there was always someone on the end of the phone should the need arise.

The air and water angels were happy with the peace which seemed to have fallen on the area and Ignis the fire angel felt the demons had now had their fun and would look for pastures new. All higher elements knew they still had to keep up their guard, for that was when demons from all areas could slip in almost undetected.

Daku was lying low in the outer reaches of the earth waiting for the last episode to die down when he planned to take his vengeance and prove to Lazzan that he was better than this higher power. Thinking he was alone, he was surprised to find an air demon in his vicinity.

"Out of your area aren't you?" he shot the thought at it.

"I'd have thought you needed allies at the moment." The demon almost hissed at him.

"Oh, why?"

The air demon's sarcastic laugh echoed through him. "You think we don't know?"

"Just what do you want?" He was curious but distrusting. The demon was sexless, showing no definite form making him uneasy.

"More a case of what do you want. My help for instance."

"Your help!" He was astonished at the cheek of this being. "I don't need anybody's help."

"Oh I think you do."

"You are of the air, I can destroy you. We don't work together."

The demon was circling his ideal, confusing him. "We have the same purpose, revenge."

He had had enough, "Well you go and take yours, and leave me to take mine. I don't need you, your help, nothing."

"You say you don't need me, but when you are using your fire, what feeds it? Together we can show them."

For the first time he started to take a slight interest and his silence spurred the air demon on.

"I already have someone I am using. I flit in and out. I've been watching you make a hash of things." The jibes came like needles and he knew this one had something planned which included him, but he was also realizing this thing couldn't do it alone, it needed him, so it wasn't all that strong without support. Maybe the ball was now in his court.

"So just where are you planning this – this - assault of yours?"

"Where do you think?"

"Not there."

The air demon was still now, positioned in front of him. "After all your hard work, wouldn't you like to finish it?"

"Why are you so interested?"

"I also have unfinished business. We could work together, then they wouldn't laugh at us."

"Aha." The truth dawned on him. "I know who you are."

The demon was circling again "Then you know I won't be put down for long."

The temptation was too great, the carrot had been dangled and taken and a pact was formed between two of the most dangerous entities of the lower levels. Daku and Fica were working in coalition, but for how long?

Tony was driving along the top road leading to Charlbury feeling better than he had done for some years. The knowledge that others had traumatic experiences, even worse than his own had helped him to realize he wasn't the only one with problems. The 'helper spirits' had been working to give him the strength and will power to carry on with his life but of course he hadn't attributed anything to them, not being aware of their existence, but there were times when he would pause and wonder what was going on in the pattern of things. This was when the angels exercised their strongest power and they knew he was tuned in to their thoughts but not quite grasping the reason.

The weather had been very pleasant as summer made its mark on the temperature, and Digby had invited his friend to help him with a job in the garden that needed two people. It would also give them a chance to share a meal instead of always both eating alone.

As Tony reached a certain part of the road, he felt the urge to pull over although he didn't know why. He stopped the car and got out onto the grass verge. This was such a pretty place, known to the locals as 'Bluebell Wood' because of the magnificent carpet of these flowers which appeared every year. The trees offered shade, and a gentle breeze brushed his face as he soaked up the peace and tranquility of the surroundings.

Without warning, he felt his feet being drawn to the earth until he was rooted to the ground. But it wasn't unpleasant, in fact he felt the strong urge to go with it and submit himself to the pull on his being. Suddenly Shane's face appeared in his mind and he could hear "Dad, Dad" being shouted in his ear. He wanted to go to the voice, to hold his son for he knew he was close to him at this moment, but over this euphoria came another command "Go, leave now."

"Need any help friend?" The human voice brought him out of his trance and he noticed for the first time the young reporter had stopped his car and was standing at the side of him.

Tony jumped. "No, thank you, I'm sorry I didn't see you there."

The reporter paused for a moment. "Wondered if you'd broken down?"

"No, no, it's just so pretty here, peaceful, you know, and I like to stand and admire nature sometimes." This wasn't strictly the truth but Tony didn't know this man, he had only seen him nosing about the village and was wary of reporters.

"Well, if you're sure......? The young man was making his way back to his car with a half smile on his face.

"Yes, I am - thank you," and Tony got into his car and drove away before the man changed his mind and came back to him.

"YES! I've got it." Fica was ecstatic. "That's where they have been keeping him, in the deep earth under the wood. That's why the silly father was drawn here, the child has rested and is trying to get back." Satisfied with herself that she had been patient in lying low, but had now located Shane's ideal, she knew it would only be a matter of time before she could crow over Raz and prove herself to be the greatest demon yet. She preened herself on selecting such a useful host as the unknown reporter, but now she had no further need of him.

The air angels knew Fica's ego and had played it well. Sadly they had been forced to use Tony for a moment to draw the little demon to a false trail, letting her believe she could now track down her quarry. Tony would soon forget the moment, he had endured many since Shane's death and had learned to shake them off, blaming his mind for playing tricks. But at least the air angels could keep Fica occupied to keep her away from other areas where there was important work to be done.

Daku, equally full of his own importance had targeted Digby as his temporary home. What better place to keep an eye on his little treasures, and being situated in a family member of the opposite sex to them, he hopefully could fulfill his wicked dream of defiling their bodies. But he hadn't realized who their guardian was, nor did he expect the battle which would undoubtedly ensue.

Ana and Kyn of the air angels were hovering over Jane Bryant together with two helpers. Jane had unknowingly been housing her son since he had been snatched from the river area. Little Billy had stayed in presence as a guardian and due to his high level, he could switch off any thought patterns and remain undetected for great lengths of time. To the outside world, the poor mother was in another realm with no recognition of those around her, not communicating and apparently with her mind far away. She wasn't actually aware of the two ideals within her which was why she had been chosen, for she could not relay any thought waves to passing sentinels from any element, hence the message had not got back to anyone, either demon or angel.

Even Ana had not been aware and had only just been informed as Jane appeared to be sinking, and therefore Shane would either have to be moved, or progress on his own if he had rested long enough, with Billy keeping him under watch if needed. But Jane's ideal would have to be seen over during transitions which is why the helpers were ready. Knowing the attention this activity would attract, was the reason that Ana sent angels to create the illusion that Shane was in deep earth.

Ana surveyed the scene. It seemed that Jane would not last beyond another twenty four hours, but that was too long to wait so having made herself familiar with the lad's current state, she decided he was more than ready to move on under Billy's care. In seconds the two had left for another area leaving Jane to slowly slip away at her own speed.

Digby and Tony had been working for some time in the garden clearing an area to convert into a place for the girls to call their own.

"There're a bit big now for a Wendy house," Digby laughed, "but I guess they will welcome somewhere to relax and read and such like."

"What are you going to put up for them?" Tony was well into this change of activity.

"Thought I'd ask them, let them choose." Then after a minute he said "D'you think they'd like one of the swing things, you know the kind of thing, like a sofa only with a cover over."

Tony actually laughed. "Well that's a vague description but I think I know the kind you mean. Then they could curl up and talk about the things girls talk about."

Digby stopped. "I think I'd better stick to asking them, but they can have what they want. First chance I've had to do anything for them." Then glancing at his watch he said, "Hey look at the time, we should be having a meal."

They tidied up, put he tools away and went indoors for a wash before settling down to some well earned refreshment. They were relaxing over a coffee and Tony was just thinking he ought to be getting home, when his phone ringing made them both jump. As he took the call, Digby cleared away the coffee things and went into the kitchen to give his friend privacy which his way, but when he returned he was amazed to see Tony sitting with his head in his hands.

"What is it, what's wrong?"

Tony wasn't crying but looked very upset. "That was the nursing home, they don't think Jane will last, she's gone right down suddenly. They think I should be there."

"Of course. But let me drive you there." Digby didn't know where it was but that didn't matter.

"I couldn't ask you to."

"You didn't, I offered, now do you mind my knowing, only I know you said........."

"That's alright, "Tony cut in, "that was only for the nosey lot, but it doesn't matter now anyway does it."

Digby shook his head. "Do you have to go home first?"

"No, it's good I brought those old clothes to work in. As a matter of fact I'm nearly half way there already. It's a few miles outside Woodstock."

"There you go then. Come on, you can pick your car up on the way back."

Never had Tony been so grateful for having a friend. Since Shane's death he had shut himself off, always hoping Jane would recover, after all, she wasn't that old, but life had meant nothing to her. He would have had to cope with today alone and that terrified him, but as he sat in silence for the duration of the journey, he felt a relief that she would be free of mental torment soon, but mixed in with these feelings it felt so final that she would not be there to visit any more. Also the two most precious people in his life would have been taken away.

Daku hovered over the newly cleared garden with sadistic satisfaction seeping out of his ideal. The spider was ready to draw the two little flies into his web, and he would be using this man to achieve his disgusting goal. Fica pulled him away to the home where the girls now lived, taunting him with their beauty and innocence, knowing that by him occupying Digby, she had a first hand contact with Shane's father.

The fire demon was getting more frustrated by the moment and as he rose from the scene, his pent up power released and in the heat of the day a small barn in the area erupted in flames. Nobody heard the roar from Daku as he ascended above the village, but he knew he must have what he had nearly lost, and it must be now.

Shane had rested well, and as he rose with Billy, Graham escorted them to his new waiting area, well away from the earth as he knew it. His form had lost the unsightly arm, and he emerged untroubled and trusting his guardian, ready to stay in waiting until his next placement.

Topaz and Peridot were happily settled, but blissfully unaware of the tussle concerning their wellbeing, both physically and spiritually, and having no knowledge of the important part they would be playing regarding the final outcome.

End of Part Two

PART THREE - AMEN

CHAPTER 1

"What on earth possessed you to do something as stupid as that?" Peridot looked at her sister in horror. Topaz just shrugged and admired her new look in the mirror.

"Grandad will go spare, and what about Auntie Perkins," as they lovingly called their foster mother, "what do you think she will say?"

"Nothing to do with her, in fact it's got nothing to do with anyone."

Topaz and Peridot, now sixteen bore little resemblance to the two innocent girls taken into care five years before. Although still sharing almost identical features, their taste in clothes, people, in fact almost everything seemed to be heading in opposite directions. Fay had remained as guardian for the first two years, but satisfied that they were now in a stable environment, and in constant touch with Digby, she had to undertake tasks further afield. Samuel paid regular visits to his son, but also had other duties demanded by his high spiritual status. There were always sentinels to oversee the family but they could only report back any unusual activity and not intervene.

Peridot had kept her sweet nature and was a very 'girly' person, helping Auntie Perkins in the kitchen and taking on bits of ironing to help. Although she liked to keep up with the latest trends, she always dressed in an attractive manner and had the appearance of someone who had just stepped out of the shower.

As the years had gone by, Topaz seemed to be leaning towards the untidy, sloppy style. She had caused great annoyance to all when she appeared with her nose pierced and when Digby had asked where she had obtained the money to pay for it, she upset him by saying it was from money Auntie Perkins had given her for Christmas.

Now as Peri looked at her sister preening herself in front of the dressing table, she wondered what was going on in her mind. The once beautiful head of hair had been shorn to about an inch and was coloured the most hideous shade of pink imaginable.

"And who paid for that?" Peri was almost in tears.

"Who do you think? I did, so none of you can start going on about it. I earned it, I can do as I like." Seeing the look on the other girls' face, she swung round "Now don't go getting all soppy again. Get up to date, you're so behind the times."

Peri collected herself before she asked "How could you earn enough from that Saturday job, it doesn't pay enough? And another thing."

"Yes, go on" Topaz sighed loudly for effect.

"What Grandad is going to ask is who did it for you, without knowing if it was all right with your family." If she expected a logical answer, she would be disappointed for her sister jumped up until she was looking her straight in the face.

"You sound just like Grandad, and the teachers. Just get off my back Peri, if you don't like it, don't look at it, because I do. This is me."

Much against her will, Peri started crying and ran downstairs to seek solace in Auntie Perkins who, after a moments consolation marched upstairs to see for herself what had caused such an upheaval. As she approached the room Topaz came storming out almost knocking the woman over.

"And you needn't start, I don't need any more lectures thank you."

"Just one moment young lady," Mrs. Perkins called down the stairs, "just where do you think you are going?"

"Out." And the door slammed behind the girl. Peri was crying even more now and it was only moments before the foster mother was on the phone to Digby who said he would be there immediately. The door was open ready for him to walk in and after thanking Mrs. Perkins as he entered, he made straight for Peri and cradled her in his arms.

"What's happening Grandad, she was never like this?"

"I know my dear, it's worrying all of us." Still holding his granddaughter, he looked up at Mrs. Perkins. "I'm so sorry, after all you've done."

She brushed the remark aside. "Don't you worry about that, had much worse I can tell you. No, I'm just upset for this poor girl here."

Digby got the full picture of the latest in Topaz's antics then said quietly "You know, perhaps we are reacting just how she wants."

Mrs. Perkins thought for a moment then almost whispered "The attention seeking. That's it isn't it? She will grow out of it, if we let her get on with it. Isn't that what you are saying?"

"More or less, but I also feel I have to still keep her under control, almost without her knowing it."
Peri looked at him, "This is very confusing Grandad."

"I know it is, sweetheart, but you just keep doing what you are doing, that's right isn't it Mrs. Perkins?"

"Indeed it is. Don't you change a thing, you are a lovely girl. We just need to sort your sister out."

After a few more words of consolation, Auntie Perkins stroked the girl's hair lovingly and said "Cup of tea I think."

"That would be welcome." Digby said hesitating slightly.

"Don't you worry, you'll have your coffee."
The mood lightened a little as the lady busied around making the drinks and opening a new packet of biscuits. Peri was helping as usual and said "Would it be alright if I took mine upstairs, only I should be doing that course work I was working on?"

"You do whatever you want my dear, and take some of those biscuits with you."
Peri gave her a loving peck on the cheek, "I don't know what I'd do without you Auntie," and grabbing her drink and a few of her favourite cream biscuits she headed off to her room, planting a kiss on the top of Digby's head as she passed.

"Oh she's a lovely girl." Doris Perkins smiled towards the stairs as she sat down.

"Now come on Mr. De'Ath, help yourself."
Digby smiled as he reached for his coffee. "You know Mrs. Perkins, I know we are both of the old school, but I would be very happy if you would call me Digby, especially after taking my granddaughters on the way you did, just when they needed some stability in their lives."
Doris almost blushed "Well, that's very kind of you, yes that would be nice. My name's Doris, never liked it that much, but what's a name?"

"It's a lovely name, and it makes it less formal doesn't it?"
She smiled back at him and after a moment said "What do you think about the other one?" She didn't have to explain the lack of names as Digby was ahead of her.

"I was hoping to talk to you about that. In your experience Mrs... sorry......
Doris, have you ever come across a similar situation?"

"Never had twins, had siblings, some of them could be a handful make no mistake, but............."

"Yes do go on, I want to know what you think."

She paused for a moment deep in thought "Well I don't want to cause any offence, but – well Peri she's no problem at all if you know what I mean, but well – Topaz now, she's different. Can't put my finger on it though, almost as though she's someone else from when I took them in."

She was amazed at the look of relief with was spreading over Digby's face.

"You don't know how glad I am to hear you say that, and thank you for being so honest." He finished his coffee before adding. "I thought it was my imagination at first, I think it was about three years ago when I began to wonder."

"You're right, it was soon after their thirteenth birthday party and Topaz threw that tantrum and I said it was because she was a teenager, and you laughed and said you didn't think it happened overnight. Do you remember?"

"I certainly do."

They both sat musing in silence for several minutes then Digby rose to his feet. "I had better be off now, can I just call up to Peridot, wouldn't want her to think I'd gone without saying 'Bye Bye' to her?"

"Of course you can...."she was cut short by the appearance of the girl in the room. "Oh Peridot, your Grandad's going, he wanted to say 'TaTa', I'll just get rid of these. Bye Digby." And she gathered up the tray and disappeared into the kitchen to give the pair a moment in case they wanted to discuss the other girl.

"Grandad, she called you Digby!" Peri was beaming.

Digby was amused but pleased to see her looking so happy. "Well, that is my name."

"But she never has before." Peri was almost nodding as if she was going to learn a romantic titbit.

"Then it was high time, in this day and age that we got up to date, don't you think, you little monkey."

They talked briefly about Topaz but Digby assured her that things would sort themselves out, and that her sister was just going through a funny phase.

Digby couldn't wait to get home for there was someone he needed to speak to urgently and in minutes he sat alone in his lounge dialing the number of the Reverend Desmond Conway.

Daku and Fica, both not wanting to loose face again were riding on each others backs in the hope that if things did not go according to plan, the blame would fall on the other one. Each felt they were so clever that no entity would suspect them and they could slip away undetected. The higher levels wondered just how long it would take them to learn the folly of their ways, but with such self assurance that would probably be never.

As soon as Fica learned of Tony's association with Digby, she knew it would only be a matter of time before she located Shane's whereabouts, and although she was being led on a series of false trails by the air angels, she knew that with patience his true location would become apparent. She would also use Daku as a source of information, thus keeping her presence unobtrusive.

This should have been apparent to Daku had he not been so full of proving himself to be the supreme power which was beyond his grasp. He would keep this pest in tow while it suited him but hopefully in awkward situations, such as mortals interfering with his plans, he would make sure he had baited her to be present while he made his departure. The hierarchy would then not associate him with the events.

His plan to occupy Digby when it suited him had been quashed by the presence of Samuel. A demon with more patience would have learned that Samuel was only protecting on a permanent basis for approximately two years, and had Daku waited, he might have had a clear run. However he was dealing with arch angel powers and Samuel knew that this fire underling had already given up on his son. With the sentinels in attendance he would learn immediately if Daku made even the slightest approach.

So Daku turned his attentions to other sources and found one ready made for him; one where he could ogle his prey at close range without anyone suspecting. For the last three years he had been using the body of Topaz, flitting in and out at irregular intervals so that the watchers could not estimate his moves. The messages had got back to Fay that there was an interloper, but every time she was in presence, he had gone. He didn't need to be around for long at a time, the girl wasn't going anywhere, and when he was there he had the perfect view of Peridot who believed she was only undressing and showering in front of her twin sister.

Unfortunately, this plan was not going as smoothly as he had hoped, but he only had himself to blame. For, while turning the sister into her present unpleasant self, he was pushing Peri away. Of course she still loved Topaz, but the warmth wasn't there and he knew the closeness they shared when he first took possession was slipping away.

Something had to be done, and quickly before he lost her altogether.

Billy had taken Shane to a holding area to let Jane pass quietly with the helpers guarding her. As soon as she had left her earthly trappings her spirit started searching for her son but the helpers assured her that after a moment's resting time to let her adjust, they would take her to be reunited with him. Although she was impatient, she knew in her soul, this was better than trying to find him not knowing where he was. Little did she guess how many had already been in that situation.

Before too long, she was guided to the area of Europa, one of Jupiter's moons, and with Billy and the entourage covering them with a powerful cloak of aura protection, they enjoyed an overwhelming spiritual reunion which was for them alone.

CHAPTER 2

Topaz almost crept back into the house. Daku was not in presence and her arrogance had been taken over by her normal calmer nature. She knew Auntie Perkins would hit the roof when she saw her, and she was beginning to feel rather silly. The overwhelming urge to take out her body piercings, scrape the overdone make up off and put something on her head to cover up this awful hair was making her very confused, and as she pushed the front door open, she was trying to understand what had made her be so stupid. She didn't expect the welcome that met her.

"Topaz, what a beautiful colour. Why didn't you show me before?" Doris was an old hand at coping with the funny stages youth often went through, and she knew by being antagonistic with the girl, would only push her further away and not resolve the matter.

"But - - I thought - ," Topaz was at a loss for words.

Doris looked up from the table "What did you think dear?" but carried on not waiting for a reply. "I was just asking Peridot what we should have for dinner this evening, but she doesn't seem to know."

Topaz put her bag on the sideboard and hovered, looking as though she wanted to speak, but nothing was forthcoming.

"You're back, we wondered where you had gone." Peridot appeared from the stairs a broad smile on her face. Doris had groomed her into keeping the atmosphere calm in the hope that things would sort themselves out.

"I was just walking, wanted to clear my head." Topaz was looking at the floor as she spoke, almost ashamed to face the other two.

"Oh, I used to do that a lot when I was younger. Bit of fresh air's always the best medicine my old aunt used to say." Doris carried on tidying up as if she was on her own. "Course, I can't walk as far now, not with the old bones as they are."

"What old bones?" Peridot laughed, "Can you hear her Topaz, you'd think she was an old crock."

Even Topaz was forced to smile at this exchange and raised her head to take in this strange approach.

"Think I'll just go up for a while," she indicated to the stairs.

Doris nodded hiding the smile which was threatening to appear, while Peridot followed her sister up to their room. She flopped down on her own bed saying "Look, I'm sorry for getting so up tight earlier."

"Forget it, I have." Topaz flung her bag on the floor and lay on her back on her bed.

"Only when Auntie saw me upset she said that people have to live their own lives in their own way and we can't expect people to do what we want, they have the right to their own choices."

"Then she is a wise old owl." Topaz was looking at her sister's body relaxed on the covers, her gaze travelling the full length of her curves. Daku had returned.

Reverend Desmond Conway pulled up in Digby's drive, and before he could get out of the car, Digby was already coming out of his front door.

"It's so good of you to come over this quickly," he welcomed him.

"It isn't far, and I thought it best we speak in person, I don't like phones sometimes."

They went into the house and after settling down in the lounge, Desmond opened the conversation by asking Digby to voice all his worries regarding the girls, or one girl in particular.

"I'm remembering our conversation when you came back from the hospital and feeling that the girls were settled, with any bad entity having left them." Desmond had listened carefully to what the man had said and realized that one of the girls was being invaded, but not wanting to worry him too much until he was sure.

"What are you saying, that they are not themselves again?" Digby was ahead of him.

"Let us not rush into any sort of conjecture at this stage. The good thing is that Peridot is obviously alright, she is herself as she has been since – um – since she was eleven."

"It's just Topaz then, but why?"

The vicar realized that he would have to be up front with this man as he knew he had the same tuning as his mother, and was probably picking up vibrations or even messages without actually being aware of it.

"Can I just say that it is possible the girl is doing what many teenagers do, going through a phase which is opposite to what you would wish?" He paused for a moment noticing Digby's look of disagreement.

"On the contrary, there could be an unsavoury power at work who has targeted something in her makeup it is playing with, or........." this time a longer pause "it could be the original occupant."
As the truth sank in, Digby whispered "But how do we get rid of it?"

"We don't." The reply sounded curt but Desmond explained that it would take powers higher than his to oust the evil thing.

Having gained all the information he could, Desmond said he must see the girls before going further, meaning he would have to be in touch with Graham as soon as possible. The telephone interrupted them and as Desmond made to leave, Digby held up his hand for him to wait as he guessed it would be Doris telling him the wanderer had returned.

"Good timing," Desmond smiled, "I often pop in if as I'm passing although it's not my parish, but Doris likes to know how her previous charges are doing. Be the perfect opportunity."
Digby looked towards the sky "Somebody might be helping us."

"How true that could be." Desmond also looked heavenwards but added a prayer for the protection of them all.

A few miles away in Ascott, Tony sat facing the photograph of Shane which had occupied the same place on the same table since his death. The tears still flowed easily but the years had softened any memories of the last moments of the lad's life that Tony could recall, and he now seemed to be filled with a feeling of closeness and protection which had increased since Jane's passing. As he relaxed, he tried to pull them both close to his spiritual being, but something seemed to be blocking his attempts and after a time he gave up with a sense of defeat.

His present guardians had strict instructions to protect him from any sort of contact, and although Shane and Jane were at a safe distance, the pull of Tony's combined love for them may just be enough for them to home in and try to be reunited with him. The air angels were playing a delicate game, for they had to provide enough cover to keep the family safe from unwanted intrusion, but at the same time not deploy too many sentinels or suspicion would be aroused by any observant demon.

As a chill ran over him, Tony realized how cold the days were getting and he reached out to switch on the electric fire. He always tried to put off using the central heating as long as possible as it forecast the coming of winter and he always felt more depressed during the dark days leading up to Christmas. He stood for a moment, an uneasy feeling creeping up the back of his neck and as he spun round he felt he would see someone or something there in the room with him, but as he faced the area the feeling left and the warmth of the fire took over the atmosphere of the room.

He shook himself, putting the sensation down to nerves of loneliness and made straight for the telephone. He would ring Digby, the two men had an agreement that if either felt unable to cope alone, they would meet and help whichever one needed support at that moment. This had worked on many occasions and now seemed as good as any. Little did he know that an evil demon messenger who had been ordered to the area hoping to trace any communication with Shane had left, sensing the block which had left it frustrated knowing it would have to report back a negative result and risk the wrath of Fica.

Tony sensed the tension in Digby's voice immediately and after a brief exchange agreed that Tony would go straight away so that they could talk whilst sharing each other's company. As he drove, his mind was uneasy. Something must be wrong for Digby had been quite a tower of strength recently, but his voice had a distinct tremble in it. Common sense made Tony drive with care and keep his mind on the road and he concentrated every thought to the short journey but was surprised as he pulled into Digby's drive, to see the man eagerly waiting for him.

"What's the matter?" Tony got out, locked the door and was following his friend indoors. Digby pointed to one of the armchairs.

"Sorry to burden you, but I needed to talk."

Tony sat opposite him and, not being too sure of what he would hear kept his reply as neutral as possible.

"Of course, that's what we agreed."

Digby took a deep breath and said "Before I start, I must ask, what was it that you rang me about?"

Tony was slightly taken aback, expecting the man to pour out whatever was troubling him. "Oh it seems silly now, just nerves I expect."

Again Digby paused. "Could it have been anything strange, I mean a feeling of some sort, let's say something you didn't understand, or like?"

Tony's mouth fell open in shock for a moment. "Well, yes...that is......" he stuttered. "But what made you ask?" Then it hit him. "Is that what you wanted to talk about, something you felt?"

Digby almost smiled in relief. "It will just make it easier that's all if you have experienced, shall we say, strange things. I would never have burdened you, only........."

"No, no that's all right, please go on." Tony cut in, eager now to hear what he had to say.

Digby took his time and, holding nothing back, related the circumstances surrounding the twins, his chats with Desmond and the current worry that the evil ones were still at work. There was a silence for a moment then Tony said "My God, you have been through the mill. It makes mine seem insignificant, at least Shane wasn't like that, his was just a virus that............" his voice trailed off little knowing the torment his son had endured. Then after a moment "What are you going to do?"

"Watch and wait for now." Digby managed a faint smile. "But I have a lot on my side. Desmond is aware of all of this and he is making a visit right now." He looked at his watch. "Well probably a short time ago, didn't realize how long I'd been going on."

"So he's been in on all this?"

"Yes. Helped me to realize I wasn't going completely mad, which was a bit of a relief."

Tony was still mulling everything over. "What beats me is just how long you've had to cope with this. And of course there was the fire, your son." He didn't want to elaborate as he knew this would only add more painful memories but Digby was only too pleased to talk.

"Yes, I think that's when it came to a head, but I thought things would get better after that, and they did, but now. I don't know if I've got the fight. I'm sixty eight Tony, I feel drained."

"But you're not alone. You aren't fighting this by yourself and I will support you, it must all help." Tony was leaning towards his friend, finding a new strength rush through his body.

"You're right, in more ways than you know. You see I feel my Mo..I mean my aunt is also looking after me, possibly my father too." He realized the slip and as soon as he included Samuel, knew Tony had sensed the truth. There was a long pause before Tony asked "Want to get it off your chest. I won't repeat it."

"Might as well. You know the rest and it would make life a lot easier not to have to keep going round the truth."

As Tony listened, his face softened as his mind drifted to Jane and the love they had felt. With a smile he almost whispered "That's a beautiful love story isn't it? Use that love to give you the strength, and if they are working for you, I don't think you could have a better little army on your side. Parent's love and all that."

Digby stood up. "You've made me feel so much better." And making his way to the kitchen called "Coffee?"

"Please." Tony replied, but as he sat alone he wondered if anything of what he had just heard could have something to do with the feelings he had experienced when looking at Shane's picture, or was that just his imagination and the effects of grief.

Graham had watched this scene, glad that Digby had confided in Tony but he knew some caution was needed. Together they would certainly add to the power needed to overcome Daku, but there was also the ongoing matter of Shane and his whereabouts and the kind of attention Daku could attract was the last thing the angels needed for some time yet.

Billy had Shane constantly under his watch. The lad's trauma during the abrupt ending of his second earth life had left its mark on his ideal, and although fairly well rested, he was becoming increasingly disturbed. The effect of his Mother's state of mind had only fuelled his wish to get even with the perpetrator of the virus, which he believed to be Fica. Although Billy explained it had come from a higher source, Shane believed that he and his parents had been robbed of their life together, and although not allowed to visit his Father, he could only imagine the loneliness and grief he must be enduring. Therefore, as Fica had been the one who had been taunting him, he knew he would never be at peace until he had brought about her downfall. Somebody had to pay, so why not her?

With his high level of experience, Billy was concerned at this goal Shane had set, and knew that he must use all his own cunning to continue to protect him. Another angel would watch Jane so that she could not be pulled into any danger Shane may attract. So Billy began piecing together his plan of action.

Daku knew he had taken the wrong path by occupying Topaz, but would be the last one to admit such a slip. He and Fica were floating a few miles from the village appearing to discuss their individual progress, but both hiding the fact that neither was having much success at the moment. Fica was trying to give the impression she was rather tired of these 'silly games' and was needed elsewhere, but her arrogance finished the statement with "but they can wait, I go when I please."

Not to be outdone, Daku added that he was in no rush, and beholden to no entity, and he only hung around this area because it suited him. Due to their own inflated egos, neither probably realized the others' shortcomings, and it was only when Fica added "If that lad had still been alive, he would probably be married by now, or courting at least." As she departed in an instant, Daku rose high above the surrounding countryside.

"Of course" he almost exploded "I should have thought of that before, she needs a boyfriend, one who could really get close." As he slowly floated down he pondered. "But which twin?"

Apart from Billy being able to change his appearance instantly at will, he also had the power to change that of anyone in his charge or in his vicinity, but it was only generally used in worthy cases and not wasted irresponsibly, which was why he had attained a high level of spiritual awareness. He also had the unique ability to work equally efficiently in any element, so he could move from air to water or ice, or even fire and earth with ease, a talent only assumed by few of the hierarchy. His trick was to appear as a young spirit whom nobody would take very seriously, but as in the case of the rescue of Shane's ideal, demons should have realized he was a major force to be reckoned with. However his secret weapon was speed, so few had ever guessed the part he had played in many such operations.

He decided to pay Tony a quick visit, and quickly locating him, gleaned the current situation regarding the friendship with Digby. He also was aware of the two troublesome demons lurking in the area but was gone before either of them could catch on to him being in presence. It also came to his notice with the vibrations emitting from Digby that there was a connection with the twins and in an instant noticed Fay departing having made a quick check on her family.

Fay had been alerted to the recent changes in Topaz, but Ana the air angel advised her not to stay for too along in case it alerted demon watchers, so Fay often made short visits around her other duties. Samuel also had been called in as a guardian for Digby, again not staying for long intervals, so quite a powerful little contingent was observing the happenings at all levels.

CHAPTER 3

"Getting a bit parky these mornings." Doris busied about making coffee as Digby settled himself in an armchair.

"Very autumnal indeed." He called over his shoulder.

"Here we are, this will warm your cockles." Doris smiled warmly as she handed her friend the cup. "Are you sure you won't have a drop of something in it?"

Digby's hand paused over the drink, "Oh No, thank you, this is good as it is."

After a few moments of settling down, Digby slowly opened the conversation regarding his visit.

"Doris, we said we would have a word about the girls. You've been very good keeping them on after their sixteenth birthday the way you have, you didn't have to…………" he was cut short.

"Now, don't you say another word about it. We have a good arrangement, I mean you see me all right for their board, and you couldn't have taken on two lively teenagers by yourself now could you?"

Digby thought for a second before saying "Well, no I admit it isn't something easy for an old man to take on, but with the problems Topaz seems to be having lately, it seems to be putting too much on your shoulders."

Doris looked at him quizzically. "Just what is going through your mind?"

"Oh, I'm not sure I know myself, but I don't want you to have problems, and I feel I should be doing more to help." Digby's mind was not on what had already gone on with the change in Topaz, but what was likely to be forthcoming in the future, whatever it may be. He just didn't know and was rather wary of the unknown.

"There's something you're not saying Digby, and I don't feel comfortable with it. If there's something I should know about, I'd rather you came out with it, not being all mysterious like."

"Well," Digby coughed uneasily, "I wondered if we should, um, maybe, um, well, live under one roof, so to speak."

Doris looked almost relieved. She had wondered what her friend was going to say, half expecting it to be something unpleasant about the girls, or at least one in particular. She smiled and almost whispered

"You mean, we all live together," then after a moment "in what way exactly?"

"I'm afraid I haven't quite thought this through properly, but I have three bedrooms, or perhaps we could put a flat extension on for you, if you would like your privacy."

Doris laughed. "Oh Digby, I see now, I thought you were ......"she cut off not wishing to embarrass the man further by saying 'proposing'. Then quietly she said "I think we need to talk this through Digby. I love those girls like my own now, and I'm not taking any more on, I've told the authorities that, and I'd be lost if you took them to live with you, but let me just think a minute. This is my own little house, been here years as you know, and I'd be sad to leave it but sometimes changes have to be made." There was a moment of silence then she said

"Never thought of it before, but it makes quite a bit of sense."

The smile on Digby's face held more relief than anything. "We'd obviously have to sort everything out, I mean, you wouldn't be doing all the work or anything like that, I've got used to living alone so I can clean and cook, but those girls do need a mother figure don't they, and they do look up to you."

Doris gathered up the cups saying with a little laugh "I think we need another drink." Digby followed her into the small kitchen.

"I think it would answer both our situations. You would still have the girls to keep in order, I would have companionship and neither of us would have to go to the other in case of, um well, any minor crisis." He was very careful to keep off the real reason of the girls' possible possession which he felt was being slightly deceitful. On conjecture he reasoned that if they were left with Doris alone, it may be putting more problems at her door so in a way he was doing her a favour.

When they had returned with recharged cups of coffee, Doris almost jumped "Oh I forgot, meant to tell you the minute you came in, but we got talking."

"What's that?" Digby hoped it was nothing untoward.

"Peri has said this lad has asked her out. Wants to take her to the pictures this weekend, only they don't call it that now do they, anyway I said it would be nice if we saw him first but she gave me a funny look."

"Why what's the matter with him?"

"Probably nothing, but I wouldn't feel right just letting her go when I don't know who he is."

Digby assumed an almost 'master of the house' pose. "And quite right too, especially nowadays. I think we should see him. How is she getting there, and where is it they are going?"

"Well, he is picking her up, got a little car she says, and they are going to Woodstock Saturday night."

"Do we know how old he is?"

Doris thought for a minute. "Eighteen I think. Or he's just had his nineteenth birthday."

Digby looked quite serious. "Well I think it proves our point of sharing the responsibility Doris. The twins are at an age when decisions as to their welfare have to be made, and it isn't fair on you to have to make them all."

"I must admit it bothered me a bit when she said last night, and I was glad you were coming round so I could tell you."

Giving a little cough Digby said, "Well, we will have a look at him when he calls for her, and make a stipulation as to when you expect her home."

Doris nodded feeling somewhat relieved, and after Digby had left set her mind to the possibility of leaving her home for good.

Jane, having rested was gradually being made aware of her present state. Caring helpers were slowly adjusting her ideal to the fact she was free from the earthly trappings, but aware the strain of her torment from her last years on earth was something that had to be handled with patience and understanding. Her controlled meetings with her son had helped her to overcome some of the trauma, but as she realized his own strong self-will was driving him on his own accord, she turned her attention to her husband. She asked repeatedly how long it had been since they were together, and her entire being reached out to the lonely man she knew she had left.

As she pieced things together, she asked if she could return to comfort him, as the thought of him having lost the two people most dear must have been tearing him apart. If only she hadn't failed him by letting the grief take over. He had needed her and she hadn't been there for him. Another thought flashed by. Was he still alone, or even still in the physical? If he too had died, where was he? Had he been searching for her and Shane, and for how long?

Eventually this new torment permeated every crevice of her being and she begged her guardians to let her make contact. It was agreed that she may visit for a short time at first but under the very strict control of an experienced guide. She would have agreed to anything at this stage and as her strength was returning rapidly knew she was able to cope with it.

Ana the air angel had been kept fully updated about the progress of the two family members, and while she wasn't too worried about the mother, she was becoming rather concerned about the restless spirit of the son. Even letting them be together did not dampen his urge for justice, however misguided. So the matter would have to be treated as two very separate tasks. Firstly she called Kyn to her area, requesting him to oversea Jane's visit to the earth, but advising him to send another angel to guard her closely whilst he kept a safe distance. The fact of observation by unwanted sources was still uppermost, so no chance, however innocent, could be risked.

After consultation with Graham and other highly advanced air angels, Ana realized they would probably have a difficult job to monitor Shane at all unless of course he attracted unwelcome attention by his actions. For this reason they knew that Billy's part was vital. Not only had he already changed the lad's image but he would have to be in constant attendance to change it further if necessary. They knew Fica's whereabouts, as she saw no reason to be furtive. She came and went between menial tasks set her by her superiors, and if anything, would liked to have been the centre of more attention, but hoping that someday soon she would redeem herself, for once she was prepared to sit back and wait, as long as it didn't take too long.

Topaz fairly bounced through the front door. Doris and Peri looked up slightly startled at the sudden intrusion but soon smiled at the happy teenager now standing in front of them.

"Well, you look like the cat that got the cream young lady." Doris was pleased to see this welcome change in the girl. The hardness had left her face and the old warmth seemed to spread across the room. Smiling at them both Topaz said "We've done it Peri, that bit of course work that was clagging us, we sorted it. You can copy mine if you like."

Doris looked at Peri's half open mouth, and smiling said "Slow down a bit my girl, I'm not up to these modern expressions, and I'm not sure if your sister is taking this in."

"I'm not sure who the 'we' is yet Topaz." Peri still looked a bit stunned as she didn't know the girl was going out to see anyone.

"I like to be called Taz now," Topaz started "you know Peri, Dizzy, Dizzy Palmer."

"I know of her" Peri still looked confused, "but I didn't know you had anything to do with her."

"Well, she happened to say her dad was good at maths and he sorted it out for us, oh by the way" she turned to Doris who had been eyeing her with rather a quizzical look "OK if I go out Saturday night? Only Dizzy's dad will take us to

Chippy, the local term for Chipping Norton, to see a movie and bring us back. Should be a blast."

"Now just slow down one minute Topaz," Doris started.

"Taz, I like to be called Taz."

"You can call yourself what you like, you will always be called Topaz by me, now listen, it will probably be alright but your grandfather must have the final say in where you go, like he has with Peri here."

Topaz flung herself down beside her sister. "What does she mean? You don't go out."

"Well, I'm going out too, on Saturday." Peri was a little confused not knowing of Digby's stipulation on her movements.

"Who with? One of the girls from our class?" "Why didn't you say something?"

Doris intervened. "Now then Topaz, which question do you want her to answer first?" and glancing at Peri she thought it better if she explained. "Some lad has asked her out and, well, um of course I had to mention it to your grandfather, it's only right after all, and he just wants to know who you both go out with. That's it really."

Topaz gave a rather sarcastic laugh. "So he's keeping tabs on us eh?"

"No it isn't that at all. But he loves you both, and he is being a bit protective. Isn't that better than not caring?"

"Yes, I don't mind." Peri said softly.

"Hey, time out, come back." Topaz realized they were getting away from her questions. "You haven't said where you are going, and I still don't know who with."

Doris smiled "Best tell her, or she won't sleep tonight."

Peri covered her mouth as she spoke and the answer came out like " mmmn asked me to go to see the latest 'Planet Probe' movie on Saturday."

Getting rather frustrated Topaz turned to Doris as asked "Who is she talking about?"

"Don't ask me, I don't know his name."

Peri took a deep breath. "His name is Ben."

"Ben. Ben who?" Topaz was staring directly at the other girl waiting for some sensible reply.

"Thomas." Was all she got.

Topaz sat staring for a moment then almost jumped up in the air.

"You don't mean Ben Cooper-Thomas?" One look at Peri's face told her she had hit the nail. "Oh Auntie, you know who he is don't you?"

"I'm afraid I haven't the faintest idea." Doris shook her head.

"He's only from one of the wealthiest families locally. Is he fetching you in his sports car? Oh my God, how did you hook him?"

Both Doris and Peri had to smile at this sudden enthusiasm and perhaps a little jealousy emitting from the other twin.

Peri gave a short account of how they had met when the school had done a charity fund raising project, and he had represented his mother who just happened to be the president of the foundation.

After a few moments Doris turned the conversation back to Topaz.

"Now your turn."

"What do you mean?"

"We've heard all about hers, now yours."

"But she's not a boy friend, she's just a girl in our class and we hit it off."

Peri turned to Doris, "She's quite new, but not very popular, think she's a bit of a swat."

"Doesn't sound like your sort, you usually like the ones with a bit of go." Doris eyed her again not too certain of what was going on.

"Look, she said she could help with the work, think she was looking for company. And you don't have to worry about us going to Chippy, because her dad isn't only taking us, he's staying with us so we'll be quite safe." She put a condescending accent on the last two words as she gave the others a satisfied grin.

"If you want to know what I think," Peri almost wished she hadn't started the sentence and paused.

"Yes, we'd all like to know what you think." Topaz wasn't going to let her get away with it.

"Um – it's just - well, I think you got behind with your work, and you are buying her friendship to catch up."

"WHAT!"

Doris drew a deep breath feeling there was more to this innocent one than she imagined.

"Well, you've got your work done for you, and no I don't want to copy it thank you, and you get taken to the film, free I expect, but you don't want her, you don't even like her."

There, she had said it and in some way felt a lot better for it. Doris would like to have added "Good for you" but thought it better to turn the conversation back to Digby.

"Anyway, your grandad is taking an interest and as long as he knows you are going out with decent people, and…" she paused for effect "he knows what time I am to expect you home, I can't see there will be any problem."

"We won't let either of you down Auntie Perkins." Peri beamed at her, then turning to her sister said quite firmly "will we?"

"Course." was all she got in reply.

Tony was taking advantage of his unused holiday entitlement and spending a few days tidying up the garden and making a pile of rubbish which would be collected later for the local bonfire and fireworks party in November. He still didn't have too much enthusiasm, but felt it would be a good thing to keep his mind occupied and the bit of physical exercise wouldn't do any harm. The lawn had had its final cut, so he needn't bother with that and turned his attention to cutting off the last heads of the hydrangea. He picked up the clippers and tried to position the waste bag at his feet, when he felt a slight tug threatening to pull it out of his hand. He jumped back in amazement. Not because of the strange occurrence but because that is what Jane used to do in their early days of marriage and it had carried on into a ritual when ever they did this kind of job. Afraid it was his nerves playing tricks, he again bent to grab the bag and again it was pulled away, this time with more force.

His emotions jumped between excitement but also fear that he was loosing his nerve completely.

"Jane." He whispered softly then stood motionless, his head turning to catch a reply or another movement but all was still. He felt the tears welling up but forced them back, and grabbing the clippers willed himself to do the job in hand. There was no further interference and after a while he had regained his composure, and although he would put it down to imagination, at the same time he knew he would share it with Digby the next time they met.

"Get her out, now." The order came from Kyn to the guardian to pull Jane back, even though she was struggling to embrace her husband, her whole being straining to be part of him. Fortunately, the upper angels of any element would foresee this natural desire which is why Kyn was in charge and dare not leave her in the area a moment longer.

A couple of young demons hovering around the school area had been observing this activity and instead of one remaining on guard, they both flew to be the first to report to Fica. Having admonished them for both having left the scene, she secretly now gloated as she felt her web pulling in her prey. For where there was a mother and father, there had to be a son.

When Kyn reported to Ana that demons were lurking and had obviously picked up Jane's presence, he was surprised at her pleasure.

"Good. Let's hope Fica will now concentrate on them. We must let Jane go back, on short visits only because if we are too blatant it could look suspicious. Let's look as if we don't realize they are on to us."

"Is that good then?" Kyn was still a bit bemused. He thought the last thing that was wanted was for the upstart to be concentrating on this specific space.

"Perfect. She wants Shane, and only him."

"That's why I can't understand your satisfaction in letting him near, because he will come."

"But he isn't with Jane." Ana reminded him. "He has pulled away and I don't think he will want to bring any further distress upon his mother, so wherever she is, he won't be."

Kyn took in the thought but added "But Fica is his objective, he is out for the kill and he won't rest until he has achieved it. He's not the little lad she was chasing remember." he reminded Ana.

"Don't forget who his protector is." She let the thought sink in and knew Kyn could have no further argument.

Fica was hovering over Tony's cottage in an instant, not expecting anything interesting at present for she guessed Jane would have already left but felt she had to be there to glean for herself any recent activity. She passed from the garden where Tony was gathering together the remains of his work, floated herself into the kitchen and was about to move to the stairs when she caught a movement ahead of her. Thinking Jane had returned she slowly move forward not wanting to displace any spirit at present, and was about to reach the landing when she realized what she had observed was Shane. There was no mistaking the boyish figure, his left arm hanging at his side, and as he turned for an instant she recognized the same doubtful expression she had encountered before. She was so shocked, that it took a moment for her to take in the fact her prize was in front of her, but in that mini second of delay he had gone.

She had a mixture of delight at the sighting but frustration that he had been snatched from her grasp. So wrapped up was she from the experience she didn't notice the speed at which he had left, leaving no wake in the surrounding air to give any clue as to his route. It should have alerted her that she was dealing with a power much greater than that of the young spirit.

Fay and Samuel had been called to high levels to assess the current situation with their family. No-one could quite estimate Daku's objective, and while he was being a nuisance in many ways, they knew he was looking for an outlet to prove himself. But hovering round the twins and Digby hardly justified any rise to fame, so what was the fire demon up to. He would be monitored on a shift basis so that he didn't realize he was under close scrutiny and hopefully soon he would show his hand but with the least distress to the family. Then they could rid him from the area and hopefully have him banished by his own kind to a distant space area. Little did they guess how he planned to crush anyone who got in his way from now on.

Daku was surveying the cards before him. He had three new players. Ben, Peri's new boy friend, Dizzy, Topaz's so called girl friend, and not forgetting Dizzy's father who could prove to be a very useful pawn in the game. But he was bored at present and needed a little entertainment for the time being. He was positioned behind Doris who was busily preparing the evening meal. She was on her own and he moved in front of her and let his ideal brush against the back of her left hand.

"OUCH." She let out the involuntary cry as the burning sensation hit her skin. Quickly she ran to the sink and let the cold water run over the painful area. Slightly shocked, she tried to work out what had happened. She wasn't near the cooker, she was only chopping vegetables at the table, so what had caused it? The back of her hand was quite red and she grabbed a clean towel to wrap around it to keep the air away and thus reduce the pain. As she sat on the chair at the table, the shock took over and she started to cry a little, cross with herself for giving in to such a silly thing. A sudden knock at the door made her jump. Holding her hand against her chest she slowly went to the door.

"Oh Digby, come in." She was so relieved it was him and not somebody trying to sell her something. In an instance he took in the scene and guided her to a comfy chair and asked her what had happened. When she had finished he said quietly "May I use your phone please Doris? I'm not good with these mobile things."

"Who will you ring? I don't want a fuss, it's so silly."

"Just someone who may know what caused it." Was all he would offer, and quickly dialed Desmond's number. The vicar answered almost immediately, and said he would be there straight away.

As he replaced the receiver, Desmond made sure he had certain items in his bag and left for Charlbury. Many questions were flooding his mind as he drove. Why Doris? He had only seen a couple of cases of 'burning' but it was felt that it had been some sort of retaliation, that some evil entity had been angered and had burnt someone in revenge. He hoped Graham had homed in on this and could advise him later, but for now he must give what comfort he could to the innocent woman.

Billy was more than satisfied with the result of the meeting with Fica. He had left Shane under the guard of one of his equals while he homed in on the demon and returned almost immediately. Shane had hardly been aware of his absence and was becoming more restless by the minute but Billy now had a new angle to play. Ana wasn't too certain if he was following the right path when he stated his game plan, but she knew he was of such high standard as to be able to pull it off successfully. He would take Shane into his confidence, to a certain point, but enough for the lad to believe he would get his satisfactory revenge, but Billy emphasized that, for it to work, he had to follow the rules to the letter, and not branch off on his own when he thought fit. At first Shane was a little uncertain, but when reminded of some of the events just after his passing, he conceded it was better to have an ally of this calibre than risk failure and be forever trying to hunt the demon down. And so the plotting began.

Desmond paused outside Doris's front door and said a short prayer before entering requesting any malevolent spirit to leave the place. Digby opened the door and led him inside to where Doris sat pale and shaken. Drawing up a stool he sat at her side and in a very gentle voice said "Hello Doris, I understand you've had a bit of scare."
"Y –Yes vicar, so silly, I don't know what happened."
Digby felt that Desmond would like to speak to her alone so he whispered "A cup of tea?" and left the room. Grateful for the thoughtfulness, Desmond nodded then leaned forward until he was looking into Doris's eyes.
"Firstly, Mrs Perkins, do you need to have your hand looked at?"
She took the towel away and said "Oh no, it'll be all right, I have burnt myself before."
Desmond was able to have a good look at the area before saying,
"Better cover it up again, but I think the doctor should see it, it does look very sore."
"Well if you say so vicar."
Guessing Digby was keeping out of the way, Desmond called to him and he appeared immediately.
"I'd like her to see the doctor at his evening surgery, could you arrange that please, I just want to have another word with Mrs Perkins before I go."
Desmond hesitated as he looked towards the phone.

"I'd like you to show me just where it was, if you don't mind Mrs Perkins." Desmond was helping her up and leading her to the kitchen and as he left he indicated over his shoulder towards the phone. Digby nodded, and as the two disappeared he rang the doctor.

"Now, I know this all seems a bit strange, but could you tell me, very slowly, exactly how this all came about."

Doris was relaxing under his very soft voice and was soon going through her movements. The partly cut vegetables and knife were still on the table and Desmond stood back eyeing up the layout and trying to remember every detail. From his little experience in this field he was pretty sure this was a 'burning' from an outside source. Firstly she was too far from the cooker which was off anyway, and there was no means of heat on the table so there was no way this burn had come from anything in this room. Her voice suddenly drew him back.

"One thing I don't understand vicar."

"Oh yes, what's that?"

"Well, I may not be the brightest in the bunch, but why did Digby, I mean Mr De'Ath fetch you, just for a burn I mean?"

Desmond thought before he answered, not wishing to alarm the woman who by now didn't seem to be accepting the accident as natural.

"Well, I'd like to think we are friends, we've all known each other for such a long time, and the vicar is supposed to be there for all kinds of things, not just preaching on a Sunday."

She eyed him thoughtfully, her head tilted slightly back.

"Hmm, you also have to be a politician don't you?"

He laughed now. "How's that?"

"Never giving a straight answer to a question." She smiled guessing she wasn't going to learn any more but feeling better by his manner and presence although she guessed there was more to this than he was going to say.

Daku was gloating in the satisfaction the annoyance this simple feat had produced. He was fire, and fire burned but to achieve his status he couldn't waste his talents on the puerile little fires he had played with until now. No, he must really excel, think big. The idea came to him as he crossed the open fields and small villages, coming to a halt over a large city. He surveyed the amount of electricity being used in one space on the earth. Electricity caused fire. As his thoughts tumbled around he hit it. The Earth. What good was this bit of rock zooming around on its orbit, it was only another space area that happened to have some substance to it. Many holding areas were simple space, nothing more. Who would miss this sphere? He circled around the city, musing until he ascended straight up with the answer bursting from his very being.

"They teach about the earth being flooded, with an ark full of animals floating about on the waters. Well, bow down to me, for I will destroy this earth with fire!" And in an instant he had gone.

CHAPTER 4

Graham had been in situ when Desmond visited Doris and knew immediately the cause of the burning, he knew the tricks of the evil fiends and knew this had to be stopped before further cases emerged. Having consulted with Ana, they decided to hold a conference with the water angels, and as Ohley was in the space area at present she was only too pleased to be involved. In such cases they had found, that with pre warning, if they could get to the object early enough, they could prevent the burn, rather than try to ease the poor soul afterwards. Sadly Doris had been the brunt of this attack and they would do all they could to cool the area but they must be ready for any new targets. The obvious question was who was responsible for the burning, and when Daku's name came up, for he had already been observed, the angels relaxed a little. He may be a terrible nuisance, but he was hardly a threat of high order and a bit of intervention should be all that was needed.

The doctor had told Doris she was wise to take the advice given and had the nurse dress her arm. Thankfully, the burn was only on the surface and hadn't gone deep, so she should make a full recovery very soon. Making arrangements to be checked again in a day or so, she gladly let Digby take her back to her cottage.

Ohley made sure a water angel was on duty to reduce the heat in the limb until Doris was feeling better, but also to be on guard against the return of Daku, or any other wandering troublemakers. So Doris was much more protected than she knew which was partly why she was able to relax with a peaceful aura about her.

The weekend was upon them before they knew, but to the twins it had seemed to take forever. They were both dressing to go on their separate dates, Topaz in leggings and denim shorts and some sort of skimpy top that didn't look big enough to keep a flea warm, while Peri had the modern look of jeans topped with a short dress. She also had the sense to add a little warm fleecy jacket, especially if she was going to travel in an open top sports car.

"Won't you be cold?" Peri, combing her sleek hair, watched the reflection of her sister in the mirror.

"Nah." Was all she got in reply.

"Auntie will worry, and she's had a lot to put up with this week." Peri was concerned for Doris since her mishap.

"I don't suppose I'll get any peace." Topaz was in a good mood and laughed as she grabbed a large scarf and said "OK I'll take this, it looks more than it is and I can always leave it in the car."

"Better than nothing."

Both busied about and making sure they had everything in their bags they were giggling as they went down for Auntie's approval.

"Let me look at you both," she said getting up "well, I've said it before and I expect I shall say it again, but I can never understand what you gals wear these days. But you both look very nice I'm sure." They both gave her a hug as she added "Now are you sure you'll be warm enough?"

"Yes auntie, we will." they chorused and were relieved to hear a sharp knock on the door.

"That's for me!" Both jumped up together and went to fly to the door then slowed at the last minute, not wanted to look too eager. Doris smiled for she knew the knock only too well.

"Well, look at you glamour pussies." Digby beamed as he entered. "What about them Doris, they get more grown up every day."

Both girls were a little taken aback as they hadn't expected him to be there this early and instantly guessed he had come to see who was picking them up, which was just about the truth.

"Well we are sixteen Grandad." Topaz was first to find the words.

"We didn't expect to see you." Peri was looking from Digby to Doris.

Doris coughed and said, "Well you are both going out and we are on our own so it seemed sensible to watch a film or something – together."

Peri gave her a saucy grin and laughed "You don't have to explain Auntie, just be good."

How the conversation would have progressed one can only guess for at that moment a gentle tap was heard on the front door. Before either of the girls could move, Digby turned and said "I'll get it." He wasn't sure what he was expecting but the shock on his face must have been apparent for he stood there speechless for a moment. Before him stood a tall well groomed young man, dressed in casual but very smart attire. A smile was already on his face as he introduced himself with outstretched right hand.

"Good evening sir, I am Ben Cooper-Thomas and I have called for Peridot. You must be Mr. De'Ath."

"Um yes, that's right," Digby shook the offered hand "won't you come in?"

"Thank you." As he followed him into the room, Ben first greeted Doris then the twins who all seemed to have their mouths open in surprise, even Peri who was impressed with his entrance.

Doris was the first to find words "Well, it's very nice to see you Ben, I hope you both enjoy the film." She was at a bit of a loss and felt afterwards that she could have said something a little less bland.

"I'm sure we will. I should have her home by ten thirty and I will make sure she is inside before I drive off."

Peri kissed Doris lightly on the cheek and said "See you later Auntie," but whispered, "you be good now!"

"Get off with you, you naughty little monkey." Doris was laughing partly at the girl's cheekiness, but mainly from relief at the sight of this responsible and very handsome young gentleman who would be her companion for the evening.

Topaz was getting a little edgy and the older ones were wondering if she thought her lift would actually arrive. In fact her mind was on the young man sharing Peri's company. Added to that, she had hoped that she and Dizzy would be left at the cinema where they may just get to know any tasty lads that may be also on the look out. The thought of the dad staying there rather dampened the night out and she couldn't help envy the prospects of her sister having all the fun.

A very soft tap at the door woke her from her reverie. Digby rose but Topaz was there before him.

"Hello Dizzy, come in."

A timid voice was just about audible.

"My dad sent me to get you, so I'd better not."

Digby had moved to the doorway behind Topaz and noticed a car a few yards up the road with the engine idling. He gave Doris a knowing look and said "I'll just have a word with him, so as we know what time to expect her back."

"Good idea" was the reply.

Digby didn't feel comfortable with the situation. He would never have expected a parent or guardian to let a young person out not checking who she or he was with. He bent down and looked into the car.

"Good evening."

The driver turned slowly and watched the girls climb into the back seat before giving Digby a slight nod.

"What time can I expect my granddaughter home?"

The man shrugged. "After the film's finished. Why?"

"Because we like to know who the girls are with, and when they will be back. That's reasonable I think."

The car was being revved up in an obvious sign that they were leaving.

"She'll be safe with me" was all he got before the car sped away leaving him feeling the opposite to the departure of the other girl.

Doris looked up expectantly, but immediately noticed the worried expression of Digby's face.

"You wish she hadn't gone, don't you?"

"Oh I don't know, we can't keep them in cages, they've got to go out into the world sometime, but I'll be glad when they are both home, safe and sound."

Although she picked up the apprehension, Doris tried to stop the man from sitting there worrying all evening.

"I suppose it was the same in our day. Our parents laid down all the rules and my dad used to be standing at the window when I came home, even if I'd only been for a bike ride."

Digby sighed "Do the younger ones, I mean parents, do they have the same worries do you suppose?"

She smiled. "Who can say? Some do I expect, then there's those who don't bother. Know which I'd rather be."

Digby sat deep in thought then almost in a whisper said "I wonder just how good their parents would have been."

"What?"

"I'm sorry to say it, but I don't know how much attention the twins would have got from them."

Doris stood up "Now you just put those sort of thoughts from your mind, or you're drive yourself silly, sure enough you will. Let's just see what happens, after all it is the first time either of them have been out alone, if you know what I mean."

"I even find that strange," he sighed "must be something to do with them being twins."

"Enough," Doris moved to the kitchen, "time for a drink, and I've got some nice home made scones, and you never say no to those."

So they settled down for the evening, their thoughts in different directions, waiting for the hours to pass.

Desmond had made an impromptu visit to Tony and soon the men were chatting about usual things men talk about until the vicar turned his attention to Shane. He noticed the father's lip tighten.

"Still hurts, doesn't it?"

Tony nodded but before he could reply Desmond went on "I don't want to open old wounds, but I do need to ask you something."

"Oh? Anything, what is it?"

Knowing he had to handle this very carefully Desmond said "I just wondered if you had felt him near to you lately? You see when there is a close bond, people do often sense that their loved ones are keeping a watchful eye on them, as could Jane be also." He let the thought sink in but was carefully watching the man's reaction.

Thanks to Graham alerting Desmond that a possible visitation of Shane could be imminent, both wanted a good presence to permeate the building as they knew evil spirits would be watching, one in particular so the vicar was spreading good vibrations around the room hopefully acting as a shield for the man in front of him.

"I do get feelings, but I put them down to my imagination." Tony was almost talking to himself.

"Anything specific?"

After a moment, Tony related the garden incident saying it could only have been Jane as that was a little game that was theirs and only theirs.

"No more?" Desmond waited.

"Oh I want to reach out and touch them, but it doesn't seem to work."

"That's understandable, but I'm going to ask a favour of you?"

Tony looked bemused now. "What kind of favour? I don't understand."

"I'm not asking you to. Let me say that in this calling, we come across many things, but some are not always what they seem."

"Now you've really got me baffled." Tony was fidgeting in his chair.

Desmond smiled and held up a hand to emphasize what he was going to say.

"I know you personally haven't done this, but sometimes when people are grief stricken, they visit so called mediums who say they can contact the other side. And lo and behold, they get messages from loved ones, or so they think."

"Are you trying to say that wasn't Jane?"

"Not at all, I would like to think it was, and there was no third party involved, so very possibly, it could have been her."

Tony shook his head then asked "So what are you trying to tell me about Shane?"

"I just want you to be on your guard. I know you pick up feelings, probably warnings without realizing it, I can tell from the chats we've had, but you see Shane could be trying to reach you, or someone wants you to think that."

"But why would anyone try to do that?"

This wasn't going quite as well as Desmond had hoped so he thought he had better tone down the warning.

"Tony, there are many things we have yet to understand, but please trust me, in my profession we perhaps learn a little more than many people, and there are various entities, some good, some not so good and some just plain playful who occupy our space. Now some of these playful things like to torment people by thinking they are in contact with passed loved ones. They pick up your thoughts and use them, in other words you are giving them all the information they need."

There was silence for a moment then Tony looked straight at the vicar and said "One thing I have picked up over the years is that you don't say anything without reason. The fact we are having this conversation tells me you know something, or think something like this is going on. Am I right?"

"I won't insult your intelligence Tony. All I can say is there may be. We can't be sure. But what I want you to do for now, is not reach out to Jane or your son just in case."

"Oh put a mental block on you mean?"

"Exactly. That would be a great help."

Tony smiled a little "Well, I'm not saying I understand but it can't hurt, and if you think it necessary, well OK then."

Just as Desmond thought he had closed the matter successfully, the other man surprised him with a sudden outburst.

"Hang on a minute. The lady that looks after Digby's girls, she got burnt recently didn't she, and they don't know why. It was a mystery. Has it got something to do with that?"

Feeling he was in a bit of a spot Desmond kept the answer as simple as possible.

"Who knows, could be something quite different, but maybe there is a lot of activity in the area, and I want to keep you out of it."

"All right. I think I see what you're getting at. In general terms of course."

"Of course." And Desmond rose to say a prayer to keep Tony and the home safe. The guardian angel on duty took the vibrations and spread them over the dwelling like a cloak of protection leaving peaceful calming rhythms reaching every corner.

Fica approached Daku saying he could, in passing, keep a look out for someone she would like to contact. There was no way she would ask his assistance or give him any idea how important it was to her, for she didn't trust this demon and knew he would take great delight in either keeping her quarry at bay, or stirring up trouble once they had reunited, also he may even guess there was more to this than first appeared.

He seemed to nonchalantly take in what she was communicating without much interest until he asked how he would know the ideal. She passed a thought image of Shane's appearance just after he had died, and Daku asked what was so important.

"Oh nothing really, just that we worked together and I understand he is in the area. Got on really well, wonder what his task is." She let the casual thoughts ride over him, but the distrust between the two could be felt, even by a passing spirit.

"You can return the favour, if I find him." The reply surprised her and she wondered what he was scheming now.

"Go on."

"I'm doing a world sweep. In your travels you could always pass it on if you find any new volcanic eruptions."

She wondered if she had understood him correctly. What was he up to?

"Am I likely to know more?"

He shrugged of the question. "Don't know myself at present, just an idea, but if you aren't bothered, leave it."

"No, I will keep a look out." She didn't want to risk Daku finding Shane and not informing her, also her curiosity was eating away wondering what he had planned, for she guessed he knew exactly what he was doing, and if it was disruptive she wouldn't mind a part in it. It amused her to think that he could be taking on more than he could manage, for when the molten lava was pouring out it was actually coming from the deep earth which was another territory altogether, a boundary of several elements. So she decided it would be a good idea to keep him in very close observation, anticipating great entertainment at his expense.

CHAPTER 5

The placing of ideals in newly born earth bodies is by no means a casual affair. All are carefully planned and arranged, sometimes for specific geographical or spiritual reasons, although to the families involved it may not always be apparent.

The two selected for the twins were of very different spiritual experience. Peridot was to house a very young innocent spirit on its first earth life, a very vulnerable position and often a target for unwanted undesirables. Therefore Ana had selected a knowledgeable mentor on her last visit as a guardian who would occupy Topaz. When Daku had taken possession, the Topaz spirit could easily have ousted him from her bodily form, but he would have taken sole use of Peridot and refused to leave, so the arch angels decided to keep the two back until such time as they could occupy together, thus not leaving the Peridot spirit alone at any time.

Therefore the differences between the two over the last years were down to them housing their own individual ideals. Topaz was not only of a high level, but of a very strong capable character who seemed to get her own way. When Daku had used her body for the purposes of ogling Peridot, she soon realised his game and allowed him to stay for short periods while the hierarchy monitored his movements. As soon as possible she would rid herself of him by controlling his will and giving him the sense of frustration and boredom, letting him think he had left of his own accord.

Her skills had often left her unpopular with her current earthly families, but she knew this was a tough game and if it achieved the present goal, it had to be done. Fay and Samuel were glad at her placement for she could send instant messages to warn ahead of possible trouble. The guardians and sentinels had been kept in place, not that she needed them but it would have been a warning light to passing demons that there was a high power in presence, and for now she was a hidden secret weapon. Fay had been there while she became accustomed to her placing for normally she would have had another ten years to acclimatise, but now when Fay visited on her checks, they were a combined force to be reckoned with.

Of course, Digby and Doris had no knowledge of this; to them they were just the twins. Desmond also had not been made aware, so no one in the physical form knew what latent power lay before them.

Just after half past ten, the door opened and Peridot came in beaming followed by Ben. Digby was on his feet to greet them.

"Had a good time?" he smiled.

"Wonderful Grandad." And Peridot threw her arms around his neck then made her way to Doris and gave her a hug.

"Would you like a drink Ben?" Digby indicated for him to sit down as he spoke.

"That's very kind of you sir, but I have to get home now thank you."

He shook Doris's hand, then Digby's and made for the door, his mind partly on the fact he had parked the car almost blocking the little pavement. He stopped just outside, having checked it was all right then turning he said "Is it all right if I take her again next week-end? Only I don't like to cut into nights when course work has to be done. Had a lot of that myself, and my father was very strict on it."

Digby was more impressed by the minute.

"That will be fine" then smiled "of course, that's if she doesn't mind."

Both laughed and said their 'Good Nights' and it was a very contented man that returned to the room.

Peridot was fairly bubbling to Doris, telling her what a gentleman Ben was and how he opened the car door for her."

"Well, he's certainly got breeding that one."

"I'm so glad you like him Auntie."

Doris rose, patted her lovingly on the head and said "Well, I'm going to have a cup of cocoa, how about you?"

"I'll make it" Peri was buzzing and felt she needed to be busy, "you sit down" and as she gently pushed her back into the chair whispered "then you can tell me all about what you've been doing."

Doris grabbed a little cushion and playfully threw it at the girl "I've told you young lady........." and they both laughed as Peri dashed for the kitchen.

Digby sat down but the smile soon disappeared.

"I only hope the other one comes home in such high spirits but somehow I doubt it, I doubt it very much" he sighed.

"Wait and see" Doris said in an undertone, "don't spoil her enjoyment" and she nodded towards the kitchen.

Soon Peri was back with three cups of cocoa and a little plate of biscuits which she put on the table, and they all sat back to await the arrival of Topaz.

It was getting on for midnight, Peri was nearly falling asleep and the two elder people were glancing at the clock continually. Digby's voice stirred Peri and she looked up, glanced at the clock, then their two worried expression and said "Right, I'm ringing her." She dived into her bag and brought out her mobile phone. Listening intently while it rang out, she too was beginning to feel apprehension when there was no reply.

"It's ringing out so it's not switched off," she was almost talking to herself. "I'm surprised the messaging hasn't cut in."
Doris and Digby looked at each other, not too sure what she was saying but hoping something positive would come of it. As she finished trying Peri said "I'd ring the girl she's gone with, but I don't know her number, come to think of it I don't even know if she has a phone, but she must have, everyone does." She was babbling a little as she too was now becoming concerned. Another ten minutes went by and they were just deciding what action they could take when the door burst open and a flustered Topaz burst in.

"Bleeding hell fire!" she exploded.
The mixture of relief at her being safe and the horror of her outburst stunned all three. After a moment Doris, who always wanted to calm the waters said "I think we had all better sit down and hear what Topaz has to say."
Digby looked towards to the door. "You did come back in the car? Only I didn't hear an engine."

"Dropped me a couple of doors back."

"What?" the chorus of disbelief echoed round the room.
Doris held up her hand "Before we go any further, are you hurt Topaz?" When the girl shook her head, she said "Now would you like a hot drink to calm you down a bit before you tell us – whatever it is."
Topaz nodded "Please Auntie, and I'm sorry for that."
Peri left the room and soon returned with a cocoa which her sister accepted gratefully. After a few sips she said "I might as well tell you now and done with it."
Digby shuffled uneasily, "It's not something you would rather talk about yourselves, what I'm trying to say is………"

"No, no Grandad, you may as well hear it from me, but you might be a bit cross."

"Well, let's be having it then."
Topaz looked round them all, took a deep breath and began.

"We went to the cinema and Dizzy hurried in the seats so I followed her, then her dad sat next to me. I don't know, but I wished he had been the other side, you know, next to Dizzy."

"What did he do?" Digby was on the alert now.

"Well nothing at first but I kept feeling he was staring at me, put me off the film. Anyway when it was the interval he gave us some money to go and get some ice cream and he went off to the loo."

Digby shuffled at this point, rather wishing she would get on with whatever had happened, but after a glance from Doris he kept quiet.

"We got back with the ice cream expecting to see him there but he seemed to be ages. I tried asking Dizzy if she would swap with me but the silly thing just cowered and shook her head. Now, what was funny was that just before the lights went down again, her dad came back and I could have sworn one of the men on the staff had followed him but at a distance."

Peri cut in "Are you sure you weren't just imagining it Topaz, only sometimes you do seem to read into things, more than is there, you know?"

"Ok. Maybe. Forget that. Well I was still on edge. Then after a bit his hand crept onto my leg. I can tell you I'm glad I'd got these leggings on."

Digby had heard enough. "I may be an old man, but I've learned enough in my life to know what sort of person he is. Tell me Topaz, honestly, what else did he do?" He hoped that in the cinema the man wouldn't have had much chance for anything personal, but his mind was already racing to the journey home and why they had been so late.

Topaz chucked and looked at her sister.

"Nothing, I gave him a dead leg." At which both girls screamed in laughter.

Doris ventured "I can't see what is so funny, he doesn't seem very nice, and what about that daughter of his, I reckon she's been on the end of his antics if you ask me."

They all quietened a bit at that then Topaz continued.

"Don't worry about me Auntie, I brought my knuckle down on his thigh, like this," and she clenched her hand making the movement in the air, "girl at school taught us that one, didn't she Peri?"

Digby wanted to get the full picture regarding his own kin before they gave any thought to the daughter.

"Before we get off track, tell us why you were so late getting home, did he try anything else?"

"What? After that, not likely." Topaz took a big gulp of her drink. "But he said we had to make a detour because one of the side roads was blocked. We both wondered about that one. Then when we were on the road from Chippy he stopped the car and said he had to take a pee. Well, it was lonely and we couldn't see a light anywhere but we thought he couldn't be long and at least we were together in the back seat so we held hands."

"He left you two alone!" Digby almost exploded.

"Oh, think about it Digby, he couldn't take them with him could he? Now I would have worried about that." If it hadn't been such a serious matter, Doris's remark would have seemed quite comical.

"But it doesn't take that long to get from there to here." Turning to Topaz he asked as kindly as he could "Was that the only time he stopped?"

"Yes, but he had been gone longer than we expected. After that he seemed to be going out of his way and I wasn't sure exactly which lane we were on. Anyway we finally ended up here, but I wish you could have seen Dizzy when I left her. She was holding on to me so tightly, as if she didn't want to be on her own with him. No wonder she's such a timid little bird, I wouldn't want him as my father."

"I rang you" Peri cut in because we were worried."

Topaz grabbed her mobile "Damn, I'd left it on silent. Sorry everyone."

Digby looked at Doris and said "Well at least she's safe and unharmed" then to Topaz "I don't need to ask if you'll be going again."

"No way." Then after a pause "He's molesting her isn't he?"

"That's something for tomorrow I think. Look at the time." Doris knew this wasn't the time to speak rationally about something which they may never be able to prove, but which needed to be addressed by the right people.

Peri lay in bed smiling happily as Topaz returned from the bathroom.

"That'll teach the filthy bastard to try and get into my knickers." Topaz had such a comical delivery but all Peri could think was "I wonder how I would feel if Ben wanted to get into mine." Feeling half ashamed as the thought ran fleetingly through her innocent mind, something inside her knew that she would be rather happy to find out.

Ignis, the fire arch angel had been kept informed of Daku's fumbling attempts to create havoc, not giving any of his antics too much attention, but when he had a report that the under demon was concentrating on the subterranean lava flows and hovering in the areas of both active and dormant volcanoes a warning bell rang. This demon, not through his talent but his meddling could actually cause some major damage to the planet he was inhabiting at present. Such was his concern, that Ignis held a conference with the higher ranks of other elements and the combination of knowledge made them agree this was a matter for serious observation. Fay and Samuel knew Daku had not been paying so much attention to the twins, but always seemed to return to that area, so care had to be taken that he didn't get a foothold. He could be closely monitored by the Topaz spirit even to the extent of letting him enter the physical body for a while so that she knew of his whereabouts, but caution was of the utmost importance so that her true identity could be kept secret.

Ana shared her concern regarding the so called partnership between the fire demon and Fica, knowing that her target Shane, was also seeking her for revenge.

A delicate balance was needed, but attention in any area must not drop for a second or the identity of the Topaz spirit would be exposed.

Fica was at present trying to enter Tony's abode, but the protective screen put in place by Desmond and maintained by the air sentinels was preventing her. At first her anger flared, but after a second thought she knew there must be a solid reason for this action, therefore she would keep the place under close scrutiny. As she hovered she was aware of a young female spirit skipping over the garden.

"Be off" she ordered the child "this is not your area, go somewhere else."
The spirit ignored her demand and carried on in her playful pursuit, rising up to the trees one moment than darting along the ground the next. Fica was getting angry. She did not want to be distracted by some young thing that could be equally occupied in someone else's garden, not this one.

"You don't belong here, this is not your area. Go!" The air was disturbed as the ripples extended over the village. The child spirit knew she had Fica's full attention as she rose and fell in every part of the garden, taunting with her playful laughter.

"I can remove you." Fica was getting angry but as she moved towards the spirit, it disappeared in an instant but the laughter was still echoing around the demon. Fica then realised the thing had not gone but was on the roof looking down on her. As she was about to try and attack it again, an older spirit, appearing to be the child's mother, came and led her away.

Disgruntled but satisfied this meddlesome thing had been removed she sat back to consider her next move. After a moment she knew she was being watched, the feeling coming from the fields just beyond the houses on the other side of the road. Again a small girl spirit was staring at her, smiling knowingly, then behind her a larger girl appeared and the small one faded into the background. As her image went a larger girl appeared behind the second one and as she took over the position. This repeated itself until the image in front of Fica was the height of a three storey building, but the appearance had returned to that of the young spirit.

Although not always being too quick on the uptake, Fica recognised she was being played with and decided it was time to go as this entity was of a much greater power than she. Making a slow side movement she gently floated down the street, across the village green and was just about to take on some speed when she was faced with a line of these children, all identical, who started circling around until she was pushed up the hill leading from the village and out into the open fields. She hadn't had time to feel anger at being manoeuvred in this way and just as she was contemplating her next move, they disappeared from her mental view, but she could still feel the presence closing in on her.

Billy surveyed the scene with a certain satisfaction but wariness. Shane had performed well along with the little band of air angels assigned to help him but he was always afraid the lack of experience would be the lad's downfall should Fica summon demons in a counter attack once she realised the plot against her. Plus the fact that Shane was not playing but still wanted revenge and all this little game had been was a practice run for the real thing. But Billy had his orders and was keeping a safe distance, or he could have brought the air demon down already with no problem.

Shane was feeling self confident, driven by his desire for revenge. Unfortunately without Billy's strong guidance he could end up similar to Daku and Fica, forever trying to prove himself, but in his case, with one precise target and this would be a never ending battle which he most probably would not win. However, he was now planning the next move, but still keeping an image unrecognisable as the young lad Fica sought.

Being a fire demon, one would think such an entity could play with it and remain unscathed, but that sense of false security was going to be Daku's downfall. He was careful not to remain in one area for long as he guessed he would be drawing attention to himself, but he was becoming obsessed with the power of the molten rock, soaking up the intense heat and planning just how he could use this to best advantage in his plan to destroy the earth and achieve his status. Then every entity would look up to him, he would rule. He would disappear frequently using the body of Topaz and her stupid friend to remain undetected, in fact he could also use the father, or flit between all three. He had tried out the father body at the cinema but felt the man was drawing to much attention to himself in general to be there on a longer basis. He sensed he was dealing with an unsavoury character, which normally would have given him untold pleasure, but this time he needed a safe haven. If he had only known, the Topaz spirit and Fay were awaiting his move so he wasn't quite as safe as he would have liked to believe.

Tony was soon to return to work after his few days holiday and had arranged to spend the day with Digby who said he had something very pleasant to tell him. When they had settled down after the usual early day chat, Digby explained that Doris was prepared to move into his home, not as anything personal as he put it politely but to keep an eye on the girls and for companionship. She would have her own room but not her own flat. As the house had only three bedrooms, he had thought about having to have an extra room built on, but the girls said they had always shared and were happy to carry on doing so; therefore he would not have that expense. Also he was happy to move into the small room and let Doris have the larger one, but they had to arrange that sort of thing.

"Well, I think that's champion." Tony was pleased his friend was happy with the change. "And it will be good for the girls, they love Doris very much you say."

"Oh yes, they would miss her, she has a wonderful way with them."
Tony smiled. "And when is all this going to happen?"

"Well, not in five minutes of course. She has to sell her little house. She could move in before it's sold but you don't want places getting damp, and the weather's pulling in a bit now."

"Yes there's always a lot to do. If I can be of any help, you will say won't you?"

"Thank you, of course I will. Might be glad of another man's view, with three women to contend with." Digby laughed but continued very seriously "You realise that we will go on the same as now."

"I appreciate that with all the changes, but don't forget you are always welcome at my place."
They sat for a moment then Tony asked "I take it the girls are all in favour, you did that bit of garden as an area for them, you'll probably be glad you did even more now."

"Yes, but they are growing up fast, wouldn't be surprised if I don't see a lot of them. Started going out on their own now you know." Digby noticed the change in his friend and realised he would be thinking that Shane would also be going out or even be married, so he added "That's where the companionship will come in nicely."

"Oh yes, it all makes sense." Tony had returned to normal and in an attempt to shrug off his melancholy, he asked about the girls and any possible boy friends they may have. Digby was happy to relate the events of the Saturday night and agreed that obviously Topaz could take care of herself more than they thought, but from a man's point of view, discussed Dizzy's father from a totally different manner than Digby could ever have done with Doris.

CHAPTER 6

Daku was using the local villages more as a homing base than for the means of creating any disturbance. The new surge of desire to destroy the planet was taking over at an alarmingly increasing speed, with his sole being intent on the glory which he believed lay ahead of him. Nothing must get in the way or ruin his chance of supremacy. He had been examining the earth in detail until he knew every inch of the crust, especially any weakness or fissure through which he could send added eruptions. He knew all the volcanic sites but needed to be aware of the slightest thing which he could use to his advantage, for, properly fed and nurtured, the smallest flame, even from a match could be turned into an inferno in his hands.

For a short period he returned to the villages, in case his plans were being observed, and out of curiosity floated over Doris's home. The twins were not to be found, so he idly wandered around until he settled near Digby's. Homing in on the wavelengths remaining from the sorrow Tony had emitted when thinking of Shane, Daku remembered the air demon was searching for some youngster. Although it was unlikely this could be the one, it would do to offer her as fodder in case he needed a favour from her. As soon as he homed in on the name, Daku left and headed for the area where he normally teamed up with Fica.

She had been somewhat deflated after her encounter with the children but would never have let it show, especially to Daku. She idly wandered over the little woods, and when she realised he was already in presence, slowed her pace so that she appeared to have come upon him casually. He let her approach and casually passed the thought to her "That youngster you were interested in, I may have found him." Not wanting to appear grateful or surprised she returned "Youngster? Can't remember one."
Daku was aware of her devious ways and replied "Oh, if you're not bothered then, it doesn't matter."

"I suppose if you have found one, I may as well know. Might come to me later what I wanted it for." She purposely kept off the sex of the child hoping to show even less interest.

"Shane I think, or was it Wayne?" Daku was playing her on a string now for he had picked up the slight movement of her interest. As she had been under the impression that she had already encountered the child a mixture of feelings ran through her. On one hand, if Shane was near, Daku had taken his time finding out and telling her, on the other, it only proved that he was around which was good news indeed.

After a moment, Daku asked Fica if she had noticed anything ready to erupt to which she give a string of locations, all which he already knew. Whilst not wanting to relinquish any of the glory to come, he felt he should involve her enough at this point just in case of slip ups and keep her handy for any retribution from higher sources.

"So where did you see this –um - this child?" Fica was on the point of departing.

"There." Daku indicated to Digby's place. It was untrue but that didn't matter to him, and he wasn't totally certain that this was the one she sought. Before they parted, he indicated for her to meet him near the Canary Islands, as he would value her advice. As the communication ended, both knew of insincerity between them, but neither could take the risk of not going along with the other for now.

Fica guessed that Daku had picked something up from the area, but knew it was unlikely that Shane would frequent a house where he had never lived. But the connection with Tony and Digby must have some bearing, and it was too much of a coincidence that Daku had mentioned him without cause as he couldn't have got the presence from any other source, there would be no need. With these thoughts teasing at her, Fica hovered around the place for a while but nothing was forthcoming, so feeling agitated with frustration, she made her way back down the valley to Ascott. Slowly she approached the little green, and noticed a small boy standing in the middle of the grass looking towards her. The last encounter with children still niggling at her being, she slowed until she was barely moving forward.

Without realising, her attention became focused on the boy's left arm which seemed to be growing and changing its form rapidly. Visions of Shane flitted through her thought, but this was not Shane. Now there were two boys, same age and height but of very different descriptions, but both had an unsightly arm. The arms lifted together and pointed at her, all three, now four, they kept on increasing in numbers until again she was surrounded, but now with a circle of boys all of different nationalities, all with an arm resembling Shane's just before his death.

She was conscious of a vibration, not a chant or a hum, but an energy being directed at her, from all round, above, below, she was held in a bubble aware only of all the limbs pointing, poking invading. Had she been in bodily form, any pain or discomfort could not compare with the virtual mental torture she was now undergoing. Her spirit screamed to be released, unheard by the earthly neighbourhood, but echoing far into space. When she felt she could stand no more, an image of Shane's face just before the virus attacked him was thrust upon her, and held as she was, she had to endure the vision of all the changes he went through until his end.

"You did this, you did this." was beating its way through her until she felt torn apart from every angle.

"Not me. It wasn't me. I was not responsible." She tried to retaliate but she was more than overpowered.

Fica could never have estimated how long her ordeal lasted, for it had such an effect on her existence that she appeared to loose awareness of everything for some time. When she took stock, her ideal was stretched over the green abandoned and she had to literally pull herself into one area before she could depart. Everywhere had a strange stillness over it and for the first time in her whole being, she felt totally alone in the entire universe.

Doris was making stew and dumplings for the twins and Digby. He had most of his evening meals with her now as they agreed it made sense to do one lot of cooking. Her hand had healed very well, and although it gave her no trouble, she was still careful to cover it when it was near heat or steam. She hummed happily as she pottered about, and almost jumped when the front door opened and the girls arrived from school.

"Hello Auntie." They chorused before dashing upstairs to drop their bags.

"Don't you two do anything slowly?" she laughed, although neither was near enough by now to hear. After a few minutes they came tumbling down again. Topaz sniffing the aroma said "Oo, can do with that today Auntie, it's getting much colder now."

"I was only saying to Dig...... your Grandad that I shouldn't be surprised if we have a frost any time now."

Peri pouted a little. "Oh don't say that, it's too early."

Topaz laughed "You're only saying that because you'll be too cold in that sports car."

"Get out." Peri picked up the nearest thing in an attempt to throw it at her sister."

"Now just a minute, don't you go throwing my things about. Haven't you got any homework to do until dinner?"

"Is that what you used to call it Auntie?" Topaz grinned.

"It's course work." Peri smiled.

"Well what ever it is, haven't you got any?" Doris made a play of shooing them away.

"But we're starving." Both said between them.

"Then take a biscuit with you. I don't know I'm sure." She bent to take an apple pie from the oven, and by the time it was on the table the two had disappeared with a few biscuits each.

When they got to the privacy of their room, they started to unpack their books and Topaz asked "So, are you going tomorrow?"

"Of course."

"Don't look so coy."

"I'm not." But Peri was blushing a deep shade of pink.

"Where's he taking you, film again?"

"No. I don't think he is."

Topaz eyed her up and knew she would have to extract this information.

"But you do know where you are going, I can tell."

"Maybe."

"Then that's a Yes, deffo." Topaz meant 'definitely' and Peri knew that but used it to try and throw the questions off.

"That's a horrible word, Topaz, and you know Auntie doesn't like it."

It didn't work. "Don't change the subject. Where are you going?"

"Well, he did ask if I could go to his house, instead of going out."

"Tight fisted plonker." Topaz's first reaction soon changed. "Are his parents in, are you going to meet them?"

Peri's lip trembled slightly. "Um, I don't think so, possibly not."

Topaz opened her mouth to speak but Peri jumped in "Don't tell Grandad or Auntie Perkins because I don't think they'd let me go."

"Too right." But after a moment "How are you going to work it?"

"Well, Ben will pick me up as he did before and say he will have me back about the same time, so if nobody asks, he doesn't have to lie about it."

"And just suppose they do, ask I mean, then what will you say?"

Peri was getting a bit flustered now, she wasn't used to this sort of thing and didn't want to tell any untruths to the elder people.

"I know," Topaz beamed "I'll come with you."

"But...but..you can't."

"Ha! Just as I thought, he wants to get it on with you."

Peri was blushing now. "Oh No. It's nothing like that, anyway I wouldn't."

"Then he is going to be disappointed." Topaz flung herself back on the bed smiling across to her twin. "Should be interesting," and she picked up her history studies and left the other girl to ponder on her forthcoming date.

Ana had learned that Billy and Shane's episode had certainly achieved a satisfactory effect upon Fica, and she suggested that the lad should now be satisfied with the results and resume his wait for another earthly visit. Not his true third earth life, but one which would complete the one snatched from him. The longer he sought revenge, the longer it would take to get him a placement, added to which he was only making future existence in any form all the more difficult for the demons would not forget his actions. Kyn, who was also in conference pointed out that Shane must learn that he cannot achieve these effects without help, and left to his own powers he would soon by crushed suffering even more mental torture. The time had come to let go and leave things to those in greater power.

Billy would not leave the lad for a moment, knowing he would take the opportunity to go, so the angels placed themselves in a communicating distance to converse with him directly, and not use sentinels as messengers. Holding Shane on a mental lead, Billy reported that unfortunately the revenge was now becoming a drug to the young spirit, the more results he got, the more he wanted, until nothing was enough. The main question was 'Where would it end?' In human form, a period of rehabilitation would have been recommended, and the same method could be used spiritually. In other words, his self will had to be cleaned, dried out, until he had reached a safe level to be allowed to wander alone. It was not practical for Billy to be concentrating on one particular soul for this length of time as, due to his high status he was needed in many other areas.

But one factor was on their side, time itself. Much has been written of time travel, time warps etc. but obviously only from living man's perception and investigation, but man has much to learn. Only so much information can be fed to the physical brain at a time as it does not have the comprehension to absorb the vast extent of knowledge of the various forms of existence. For example, people talk about two worlds, earthly existence and the spirit world. Is there life after death? But there are many more forms of energy, and when sometimes a trickle of the unknown filters through, there is much speculation from all sides as to a logical explanation. To those who know, it can be quite amusing watching the various theories being bandied about. You only have to mention crop circles or UFOs to start a serious debate with opposing ideas.

It has already been suggested that time 'on the other side' is completely different from what we know. So if a relative had died months or even years ago, to them it may only seem like minutes, but their remaining families could have been grieving all that time, as Jane did, although her poor mind was so sick. And it doesn't have to move at the same speed for each extra terrestrial entity. So while Shane had experienced the entire periods of tormenting Fica, Billy had only used a mere few seconds, whilst to Fica herself it had lasted indefinitely. To some extent this change of speed is experienced in earth time, for when you are enjoying yourself the time seems to speed up, but stand in the cold waiting for someone to join you, it slows. Imagine that feeling as being a mere pinprick compared with the entire surface of the earth and you have some idea of the vastness of things beyond the two dimensions.

Using these factors to advantage, the upper hierarchy of angels and demons are in a constant tussle not only using our living space but reaching far out beyond man's mapping of the heavens.

Billy being one of high power could twist and turn time to suit his current need. He could speed it, reverse it and even let it run parallel to itself creating a sense of Déjà Vu to anything caught up in the effect. He had many more tricks, but mostly they were not divulged, again for the reason that even the supremacy of most elements would have difficulty understanding them. So when the angels had visited him, he could have told them there was no need, but he knew it wasn't for them to know yet. He could keep Shane under his power and the lad would not dare move as he was under such a close watch, but Billy could also have part of his being many light years away, and another part light years in the opposite direction, thus gathering facts in mini seconds and returning to his host being. Whilst he still had to have part of himself near enough to Shane to keep control, it only had to be a very small part, but of course whoever he had hold of at any time never guessed just how much they were being deceived. In a world where few had this talent, he could almost control his surroundings, but imagine the effect of an area filled with such beings. The speed at which they would operate would be phenomenal and the energy produced would only fuel further speed until the human eye or telescope would not make out any movement whatsoever. And this is only the next step up the ladder of what is beyond our belief.

So to have Billy working for him was certainly a better option for Shane than to have him opposing him. The next scene concerning the boy was being set but the plans were not going to be divulged to any source.

Jane spent most of her time with Tony now. In one way she wished he wasn't so lonely, but was secretly glad he hadn't let another woman into his life. If she had seen him being intimate with somebody else, it would have torn her apart so for herself she kept as close to him as possible. She was glad he had Digby as a friend but was aware of some of the visitations the man received and a feeling of apprehension would run through her, hoping her husband wouldn't be drawn into anything that didn't concern him for she wanted him to have a peaceful life until they could be reunited properly. She was aware of unstable vibrations at times but didn't know what they were and was afraid because she didn't know what she was facing. This new existence of having contact with the earthly and spiritual worlds was taking some getting used to, but she took comfort that she was with Tony and Shane was never far away. Although she hadn't made contact with him recently, she had received thought messages that he was nearby but had a job to do.

She sat now in the chair opposite, watching Tony flick through a newspaper, then flick through the television channels with the remote control, finally giving up and resting his head back in his chair. She floated over and started caressing his head, letting her form slide down over his body until she was lying covering him from head to toe. She felt him relax, a half smile creeping over his face, but then noticed he wasn't quite so relaxed in places. The frustration of her not being in physical form was rewarded with the fact she was with him alone and he must be feeling her presence judging by the reaction in his lower body. He was breathing differently now, almost arching his back as he was giving himself to her almost knowing they were sharing something long forgotten. After his few gasps of relief, she rose above him, pleasure warming her spirit as she knew he would have one big surprise when he came to his senses. This was the best moment she could remember for a long time, but knew this was only the beginning. From now on he was her husband again, in every sense.

Kyn had posted a trusty guardian over the place so this precious moment would not be viewed by prankster demons who would take a great delight in a session of voyeurism and maybe do all they could to spoil it. But it hadn't escaped one of Fica's little snoopers who couldn't wait to report back.

"And?" she snapped at the demon. "Is that all?"

"I thought you'd want to know, you said to tell you everything."

Fica was livid. "If you want a job doing…" she let the rest trail off before facing her underling.

"You were kept out?"

"Yes. Nobody could get inside."

"NOBODY." The air trembled with her wrath. "Well somebody did."

"No, nobody, there was a shield up."

"Exactly. Do I have to explain everything?"

The lesser demon was shrinking, struggling to find the answer her limitations failed to produce.

"Try and take it in." Fica hissed. "You were kept out along with any other stupid onlookers. But why? Because there was someone of their sort in there. Someone they didn't want you to find out about. Now do you get it?"

"Ooh. Who do you think it was?"

If Fica could have sighed she would. "The child was there of course."

"Oh I didn't see a child."

Exasperation took over and Fica dismissed the idiot, furious that she had missed the opportunity of grasping the lad when he must have been unguarded. A ripple of sadistic laughter settled around her and she knew that demon Raz had already learned of her latest failure, little realising the false conclusion to which she had leapt.

Desmond had kept in touch with Digby under the guise of just being a friend at first, not wishing to alarm him of any possible danger concerning the twins, himself or Doris, and with Tony being in his parish, he had no need for an excuse to visit him spontaneously. But now they all seemed more than just sheep in the flock, their welfare was becoming of prime importance. The vicar had become very aware of changes in vibrations recently as his spiritual side had been nurtured by Graham. He knew immediately he entered one of the dwellings if the atmosphere was safe or threatened.

Graham had alerted him to the current situation regarding the pursuit of Shane and to the fact that none of the hierarchy were sure of Daku's scheming and were still keeping the twins and their immediate family in close scrutiny. Desmond had been requested to report the slightest indication of change in surrounding temperature or 'ripples' as they called the disturbance caused by passing threats.

The vicar often felt quite inadequate for he knew there was far more involved than his novice status was aware of. The knowledge would only come with time and experience but he prayed relentlessly, asking for the strength and ability to be able to be of use in combating the forces against him.

He was approaching Doris's little house on his way to see Digby, when some instinct made him slow the car to a halt. Sitting for a moment to sort out just what this strange feeling was, his attention was taken by a sports car pulling off just a few doors away, and in seconds had sped out of sight. He was tempted to knock on Doris's door just to check, but it seemed too insignificant, so he started up the car and continued to Digby's.

"You look thoughtful today." His host smiled as he offered him a cup of tea.

"Oh thank you, yes." Desmond didn't really want to sound dramatic but felt he may learn something, knowing Digby's ability to sense things.

"I'm sure I'm being over sensitive," he started "but we've said before, you can get a sort of feeling, but you don't know why."

Digby laughed "Oh you're talking to the right one here, I've realised over the last few years, there's more going on that we'll ever know." Then after a pause "Want to talk about it?"

"This is just a friends' chat, all right?"

"Of course, I don't discuss private matters, only with those they concern."

Desmond sipped his tea. "You said one of the twins had a boyfriend, well to do sort."

"That's right. Grand lad he is too. Very well mannered. I don't know if it's serious, but he's one you wouldn't mind her ending up with. But she's a bit young yet. Bit too soon to read much into it." Then he said "but why did you ask?"

Desmond was feeling more uncomfortable by the minute, wishing he'd never mentioned it.

"Oh forget it, I probably read it wrong."

"No go on, you must have had some sort of instinct. You might as well get it off your chest then we can forget it."

After a moment Desmond said "I was just coming past Mrs Perkins house and I got a strange feeling of apprehension so I stopped with the intention of checking up to see if she was all right."

"And was she? "Digby look a little worried.

"I didn't ask, you see my focus was on this sports car just up from her place and, oh I don't know, it went off at speed and I wondered if the man had come to arrange to take one of the girls out and – you see its nothing."

"But the feeling was strong enough to bother you though." Digby's words were almost comforting to him until the man added "But wait a minute, they are at school and he wouldn't come to arrange anything with Doris. Just up the road you say?"

"Yes, a good three or four doors up. But the parking isn't too good there so maybe he chose a suitable safe spot." Desmond looked at Digby and both their brains were churning.

After a moment, Digby looked straight at his friend and said "Do you know Desmond, I'm just going to keep my eye on things, in light of how you felt. Don't know why, but I'd feel better about it."

"Well, that can't do any harm, and thank you for not scoffing at it."

Knowing of the attention being given to anything concerning the twins, he was rather relieved now that this grandad would keep a very watchful eye on procedures on a physical level and that couldn't be a bad thing.

After the vicar had left, Digby rang Doris and after a general chat about what time he was to arrive for his dinner, he casually asked if the twins had dates this week end. Doris gave her view that Topaz had had enough after the last experience to seem to be bothering with anyone at the moment and perhaps was waiting for a suitable young man to come along, and she though Peri had said something about 'same as before' so she would be going to the pictures with that nice young man.

Digby didn't push the point as he knew if anyone had called, Doris would certainly have made a point of saying, even by ringing him to tell him, so he left it there and agreed to see her soon.

The air around the twins was calm, for Daku was becoming impatient and wanted to get his operation under way. But anything as massively destructive as he was attempting should have had endless planning right down to the last detail, and timing would be of the utmost importance. Even the fire demons of a much higher status would have had more cunning than to charge in without backup plans, and would not have merely relied on their own sense of power. But meddlers can cause as much if not more harm by their own folly.

He flitted around the earth, checking the weak spots, and reactivating the dormant volcanoes. He was angry that he could not check enough possible underwater earthquakes, but he was not of that element and could not encourage any water demons to work with him, so he would have to rely on his estimations. Because of this, he would have to let the operation take the form of one large eruption hoping that would give enough force to overcome the unknown underwater factor. Then this precious bit of rock would be blown to pieces, and then he would reign.

If it had occurred to him that the neighbouring planets would feel the effect from such a holocaust, he wouldn't have given it a second consideration. For one thing, he did not have the understanding to know that the spiritual world of each galaxy is balanced with the pattern of the planets, their moons and everything occupying that space for that time. Already in one small area, the effect of Earth's moon moving slowly away will eventually not hold the earth on its present rotation, so the knock on effect of Daku's devastating action would change the format of all as it is. This would in turn affect the spiritual level and the vast levels beyond that affecting the afterlife as people believe it.

CHAPTER 7

Saturday evening had arrived and the girls were both in the bedroom as Peri got ready for her evening out.

"Have you thought what film is showing this week, just in case they ask? Topaz raised her forehead as she watched her sister fumbling with her necklace.

"Yes, I know what it is."

After a few moments, Topaz whispered "Why do this if you are such a bag of nerves?"

"I don't know. I've said I'll go now."

"Well don't."

"What do you mean, I have too."

Topaz sniffed and grabbed a girly mag. "You don't have to do anything, you have a mind of your own don't you?"

"But I like him so much, and he is so nice, but I'm surprised he asked me so soon, to go to his place alone I mean."

"Soon! You're a late starter by some standards."

"What?" Peri looked shocked.

"Most expect you to do it on the first date, and some don't really even have a date, they just do it."

If it hadn't been so serious it would have been comical. Peri's jaw was hanging open, her eyes wide in innocent astonishment that Topaz had to suppress a giggle.

"You mean you think he really will want me to............."

"He'll be damned disappointed if you don't." Topaz finished for her.

There was a silence.

"No, I think we will just kiss."

Topaz spluttered now. "Don't you ever listen to the girls at school? Most of them are on the pill."

Peri smiled "Oh I never believe them, I think it's just said to keep up with everybody else, well not everybody, because we don't, but you know, they don't want to loose face. And I don't mind telling them I'm a virgin." She blushed at the last word.

"That's why they laugh at you," thought Topaz but didn't upset the other girl by voicing it aloud.

Doris's voice called up the stairs, "Peridot, are you nearly ready, he'll be here in a minute."

"Coming Auntie," then to Topaz, "I don't want to go down too soon in case she asks anything."

"If you go on the way you are, she'll guess, she's a wise old bird." With that she got up, thrust Peri's bag into her hand and said "Come on, I'll be there, I'll put her off if anything's said."

It wasn't long before Ben had called for Peri and with the promise of "about the same time" they left.

A rather flustered Digby arrived some moments later.

"Oh have they gone" he appeared disappointed "was hoping to see them off."

"Grandad, we're not little girls any more, she'll be fine. They'll be back same time as usual." And Topaz gave him a peck on the cheek. He appeared to still be in thought and continued "Phone went, just as I was coming out."

Doris didn't miss the anxiety in his voice but passed it off by saying

"Good job we had dinner at dinner time today or she would have been gobbling hers down and then got hiccups I expect.

"You not going anywhere?" he addressed Topaz.

"No, I'm going to stay here and pester you pair," she laughed.

Digby was quiet for a moment then said "What film is it this week then?"

"Oh don't ask me," then to Doris "Ok if I go up and watch my telly?"

"Course dear. Could you make us a cuppa first?"

With a nod, Topaz disappeared into the kitchen. When she returned with the tea, she grabbed her beaker off the tray and was out of the door before they could speak.

"These youngsters do everything at break neck speed these days," Doris nodded at the closed door "we'd have been told to slow down, do you remember?"

"Um - oh yes."

"All right, let's have it, what's on your mind?"

Digby took Doris's hand. "Ignore me, I'm just being silly."

She smiled. "You worry about those two, I know you do, so don't say you don't."

"More Peri really. We don't know anything about who she's with, or if she's safe."

"Safe? Of course she's safe." Look, you've got to let got the reins some time you know. And I know this might sound strange, but I'm glad when either of them walks back in that door."

"You're right." He relaxed a little and reached for his tea. After all, there had been nothing more than Desmond seeing a sports car drive off. It could have been another car, or the lad may have had business with somebody else. But he would have been more settled if he had known, or so he thought.

Billy was holding Shane a distance from the earth in order to gain his full attention. The young spirit had been more than satisfied with the effect the latest encounter had inflicted on Fica, even though he now understood she was not the original cause of the virus. But he was not prepared to let her go that easily and was almost begging Billy to tell him when they could go in again and cause even greater havoc until she knew she was up against a force against which she had no chance of overcoming. His mentor let him exhaust his pleas before placing himself before him, holding him in that position while he imparted what was going to be the most important lesson Shane might ever receive from one so highly placed.

"Shane, you have probably realised by now, although you do not wish to admit it, the power used to goad your adversary was not yours. You would not have lasted a second in earth time, before she would have had you in her power, for eternity." He paused to let that thought sink in.

"Before you add any comments of your own, you will hear me to the end. Listen well, for this not only affects you but the general plan of things."

Whether it was the way Billy was imparting his lecture or whether something had hooked the lad's interest, it had the effect of almost hypnotising him into submission and he gave his total being to absorbing the power which was now surrounding him.

"There are greater plans for you than seeking revenge from a lowly air demon, you do not need to waste your spiritual time, things are always in balance, when a factor upsets it, the balance will be restored, without help from any source. Therefore, if you take your revenge to put the record straight in your eyes, that also has then to be redressed" A pause. "Yes your second earth time was cut short, but we are allowing you to return to use up that earth time instead of having to wait the required time until your third life when you would have not gained the amount of knowledge required. This would have made you appear as an idiot which is not as planned." Again a pause. The only way we can get you back to catch up, is for you to relinquish this desire for revenge."

This time the pause was quite lengthy, almost as if Billy was awaiting Shane's reply but none came.

"While you are in earthly form, you will have no knowledge of your previous short stay, as you also had no knowledge of your first visit. But this will correct the balance and you will be able to progress at the required rate."

Shane appeared to be coming out of the grip that had been holding him and he communicated slowly at first.

"If I agree, when would I go back?"

"In earth terms, we have a placement about one year from now, but to you that will seem much shorter."

"Will I be near my father?"

"Would you know him if you were?"

"Suppose not."

Billy was amused for a moment, but at least his charge had taken in the truth of the situation, to him it would be a completely new start.

"Then shall we say you are prepared to accept the terms?"

"I think so."

"Do you have any questions?"

Shane felt his freedom returning slightly, but knew Billy would not let him stray from his grasp.

"There is one thing I don't understand"

"Which is?"

Shane paused as though he was piecing together his thoughts before he asked the question.

"You are of a very high level aren't you?"

"Pretty high." Was all Billy was prepared to divulge.

"Then why are you so bothered about me? Haven't you got more important things to do?"

"Do you think you are so unimportant?"

"No, but I can't work that one out. It's almost, what did you say about the plan of things or something, don't we all do what we want?"

"To an extent, you have free will, but how you use it can make drastic differences to so many other people or events."

It was obvious that Shane did not understand quite what Billy was trying to impart but wanted to know, so it was right that enough time should be given to explain it to him.

"Ever heard of The Horseshoe Nail?"

"No."

"Been going around the earth for many decades."

For the want of the nail the shoe was lost
For the want of the shoe the horse was lost
For the want of the horse the battle was lost
For the want of the battle the kingdom was lost
And all for the want of a horseshoe nail.

"There are many plays on the words but the meaning is the same."

"Are you saying I am like the nail?"

Billy moved nearer to him. "Do you remember in your last life you had a little construction set, and you couldn't find a little tiny piece that joined two bigger pieces together?"

"Yes, and it meant I couldn't make the digger."

"And what did you do with the digger?"

Shane was ashamed as he replied "Threw it away. Dad wanted to get another bit made but I was so angry I smashed it and chucked it in the bin."

"And what do you think the outcome would have been if you hadn't."

"It would have been complete."

Billy said slowly "And maybe it would still be there for your dad to remember you by, and maybe your parents wouldn't have been upset at your behaviour. And when you were a dad, you may have wanted to show it to your son. But none of that is possible because of........."

"A tiny bit of plastic." Shane knew he was beaten. He tried to get his thinking into place. "So you have to get me to do things properly?"

"Because............ finish it off Shane"

"Somehow, in a way I don't know, I fit into a bigger picture, and how I act could affect something more important." He almost gabbled the last words as the truth hit him.

"Well done. Now you see the trouble I've been having with you." The mood was lighter now.

"But why didn't you let me know this before?"

"I had to let a lot of the anger come out of you or it could have had the wrong effect later."

"Now I'm getting confused again, what about later. Where do I fit in?"

"You probably won't even know. I've tried to explain the 'knock on' effect to you. Think of dominoes. The first one falls knocking the whole pattern over, but the one at the front doesn't really have any contact with the last, except by the falling of the others."

"Oh now I think I've got it. Will you be staying with me until I go back?"

"Possibly."

Shane was now liking this new challenge but couldn't resist asking.

"Billy's not your real name is it?"

"What's a name?" was all he got in reply.

Very few knew his true identity. The angels and demons of all elements had heard of him but had never had contact with him, or so they thought. It was almost a joke every time he returned to his ultra high realm and he was usually greeted with "And what name did you use this time?" Only there did he answer to his real name Veloce, one of the highest powers in the galaxy. He knew Shane had to be rescued and replaced or major future plans could be jeopardised, which was why he had intervened so that he could put the boy's spirit back in placement. At this point only the extreme high powers were aware of the reason which was for now, many earth years away.

If Tony had been aware of Jane's presence he may have been overjoyed at first, but if he had realised be was becoming an obsession to her he may have felt quite differently about it. Her last visit had given her a new purpose. It could be thought that a parent would want to concentrate on her child, in whatever form, but she had felt rejected when her son had chosen to take the path of revenge in preference to wanting to stay with her. Some of the sick mind had taken its toll on her spiritual being and she was still showing signs of the trauma which had been the original cause and she would have been unrecognisable as the mother who had begged Shane to stop scratching his arm. She was now tunnel visioned, her whole purpose to be with Tony, constantly, never to leave his side. Although she had been pleased at his friendship with Digby, this was now getting in the way of her freedom with him, and she would try and pull him home to get him alone with her. The thought of him going back to work shook her, and she was determined to engineer that in some way as to make him leave his job, or at worse, be dismissed, just so that she could have him with her. She was in bed with him, in the shower, helping the food into his mouth, watching the television, every where he went, everything he did, she was part of it, trying to control.

In spite of what he had endured, Tony fortunately had a fairly strong will, and there were many times when he felt the urge to do something, but then changed his mind. This began to anger Jane as she knew she hadn't full control of him, but she would eventually, he would see. After a few minor incidents, he decided to have a word with Desmond, and possibly Digby, as both had an understanding ear and would not scoff. They may also have experienced similar feelings and it would be good to talk. He found this often cleared his mind and stopped him dwelling on such things when he was alone. The incident of the garden rubbish had dimmed as he now felt there was a presence but it was interfering. Jane wouldn't have done that, so he wondered if it could be from another source.

He was washing up from his evening meal and thinking he would get his clothes sorted for work the next day when he was aware of the closeness at the back of him. This was not unusual these days but this time it was very strong. He stiffened a little as he felt the arms slide round his back until the hands came to rest upon his stomach, gently massaging, soothing. He tried to turn round to face, whatever it was, but was held in a powerful warm loving feeling.

"Is that you?" His voice was barely a whisper. Silence followed but he felt a breath float across his cheek.

"Jane, is that you Jane?" His instinct told him that if it wasn't her, he would be repulsed at such an intrusion from another source, but if it was her, all he wanted was to succumb to her as he knew he had before. The pressure of the hands had moved down to his groin and his head was spinning now. He couldn't push this away, it had to be Jane, it was her, and he gave all he had to this feeling of euphoria until he slumped over the sink almost crying with emotion knowing he could never share this experience with anyone. This he would have to keep to himself, Jane would want that. As the decision was absorbed by his wife, she drew back a little, satisfied that she was achieving her goal so easily.

Doris had enjoyed the film and said to Digby "Shall we swap over and watch that one about gardens, you like that."

"That would be nice."

The reply was rather bland and Doris felt she had to mention it.

"You've been looking at your watch all evening. Stop worrying, she'll be all right."

Before there was time for an answer, the front door opened and there was a sound of footsteps hurrying up the stairs. They gave each other a questioning look and Doris said "I'll go and see what's up." As Digby made to join her, she held up her hand "Better see if it's women's trouble first I think." He accepted that and returned to his chair.

As she approached the bedroom door, Doris could hear sobbing with Topaz trying to calm the situation and get some words of sense out of her sister.

"Can I come in dear?" Doris's voice had to be loud enough to be heard and Topaz opened the door immediately and beckoned her in. Peri was curled up on the bed crying uncontrollably, her make up smeared over her face, but what Doris saw first was her torn clothing and general dishevelled appearance.

"Oh Dear Lord No." was her first whisper as she looked from one sister to the other.

"Can't get anything out of her yet Auntie." Topaz looked distraught at the sight.

Doris was an old hand at some things and she knew that people had to run out of steam eventually if the fire was not fuelled, like someone in a temper, so she sat on the chair and indicated Topaz to sit on her own bed. This was rather confusing but the elderly lady knew what she was doing. Sure enough, after a few moments Peri's sobs were reduced to sniffles and as she hunted for tissues, Doris calmly handed her a box.

"When you are ready Peridot, you can tell us."

"Where's Grandad?" Peri sniffed.

"Oh he's downstairs, time enough to drag men into things unless you have to."

Peri seemed a little easier and began to notice her clothing.

"Now don't you worry about that for now dear, you just tell us what's been bothering you." She had a way of making a situation sound more trivial than it was, but from her past experience knew that if the girl had been assaulted, or worse, she would have to be kept exactly as she was, no shower, no nothing until examined, but she certainly was not going to voice that at present until she knew what had happened.

"I don't know what to say?" Peri felt she was under pressure now and didn't want to admit she had gone to Ben's parent's house when she should have been at the cinema.

Before Doris could ask a delicate question to ease her into divulging how she had got in this state Topaz in her usual manner came right out and asked "Did he shag you?"

"Topaz." Doris was more than horrified but realised this had achieved what it may have taken her much longer.

Peri was shaking her head vigorously. "No I wouldn't let him, and he got cross."

"Well, thank goodness for something." Topaz was in again. "At least she's not been raped Auntie."

"No, I gathered that." Doris was still a little shocked. "I'll just go and assure your Grandad that you are not hurt, but he may want a word later." She left the room with some relief, but wondered just what she was going to say.

When she walked back into the bedroom she said "He's glad you are all right but obviously would like to know what went on. It is his right after all, and he cares about you very much. So where do you want to start?"

Peri looked from her sister to her aunt. Topaz suggested it was better to get it all off her chest and done with it, so slowly she hedged round not going to the pictures as if it was only decided that night, which was half the truth, and waited for the repercussions. When none came she related how Ben had given her a drink, some sort of lemonade she thought and they sat relaxing in the lounge. Then he said her bra strap was twisted and he would put it straight for her which meant putting his hand under her top.

Topaz's eyes shot heavenwards "Give me strength" she muttered more to herself than anything. "Then what happened?"

"Well, that's how it got torn you see, because I pulled away."

Both Doris and Topaz were feeling that this was going to take a long time but knew they had to get to the bottom of what had happened. Slowly, as far as they could tell, Ben had then tried to get her jeans undone, rather forcefully which had frightened her and they ended up fighting, or rather scuffling, it wasn't actually fighting. She had got upset because he had said that that's what she knew would happen and that was why she went, and was just as much a slapper as the next girl. But he had thought she may be a virgin and that appealed to him as something different but she was a right disappointment.

"So did he bring you home then?" Doris was hoping this was a narrow escape. The phone was ringing but Digby called up asking should he take it.

"If you would please. Call me if it's urgent."

Peri was ready to assure them that he had driven her home but because she was so upset he just dropped her off. And she did tell him to get out of her sight and never speak to her again.

Doris wanted to be absolutely sure that nothing else more serious had happened.

"So he didn't touch you anywhere?" and turning to Topaz added "just keep your descriptions to yourself for now please". The girl's mouth opened and shut with an expression on her face s much as to say "What, me?"

Peri shook her head. "No Auntie."

"And he didn't get you to do anything to him?

"No Auntie."

Again Topaz was itching to summarise the situation in her own inimitable way but another glance from aunt made her think better of it for now.

They were interrupted by Digby calling from the bottom of the stairs. As Doris went to join him she said loud enough for the girls to hear, "She's all right now, just going to have a wash and brush up and then I'll make them some cocoa."

As she joined the man out of earshot of the twins he said "That was young Ben on the phone. Didn't want to disturb you, and he wanted to talk to me anyway."

"Well, I'd have had a few words to say to him if I'd had the chance." Doris's back was up, feeling deprived of protecting 'her girls'.

"Now, I don't know what's been said to you, but just listen a minute, then we'll see."

"Go on then." Doris flopped down in a chair.

"He took the trouble to ring to explain why he hadn't brought Peridot to the front door as he normally would. It seems she was hysterical and his presence seemed to make it worse. In fact he had a job getting her in the car to get her home she was in such a state, tore the pocket of her jeans on the door handle."

"Ah but did he tell you why she was hysterical. I'd like to hear that."

"To start with he explained that he knew he was in the wrong, because they didn't go to the pictures after all but went to his parent's place. I told him I didn't approve. She's not a worldly wise girl that one. Anyway I got the idea that they must have started something which went too far for her liking and she objected."

"That's putting it mildly." Doris snorted.

"You mean she said he had..........."

"No No, it didn't get that far, in fact I don't think it got very far at all, but she didn't like what he said."

Digby look bemused "Said. What was it that he said?"

"Oh look it's finished now, no point in picking over the crumbs."

"No I want to know."

Doris sighed "Let's just put it down to experience, for her I mean, as long as she doesn't want to see him again, let's leave it at that."

"Well I told him I appreciated his calling, not a lot would do that so he must have some decency in him, but I did say I thought it best if he didn't take her out again."

Doris waited a moment. "And?"

"And he agreed."

"Well thank goodness for small mercies. I really though she had been interfered with at first." Doris looked a little more relaxed.

Digby smirked a little.

"Now what?" Doris got up to head for the kitchen.

"Was just wondering how it would have turned out if it had been Topaz, bet he wouldn't have rung me then."

With some of Topaz's recent vocabulary still ringing in her ears, Doris could only imagine.

Upstairs Topaz persuaded her sister to have a good soak and forget all about it.

"Could have been worse," she joked "you could have come back pregnant!"

"Don't say that, I'm saving myself." Peri answered adamantly.

"Now that's more what I like to hear." Topaz threw her a towel, Oh not the saving yourself bit exactly, more because that's the real you. Didn't like you coming home like that, so........."and she wagged finger inches from Peri's nose "don't do it again." Then after a second "Take me with you, I'll fix the sod." As she clenched her hand in a very unladylike way, Peri was reduced to laughter.

"I will, that way I'm sure of entertainment."

Doris was delighted in the change in the girl as she brought their drinks up to the bedroom and had to admit Topaz certainly had a way with her. Puffing slightly she pushed open the door to have the mugs taken from her and found herself being pushed gently into the chair.

"Now, we've been thinking" Topaz had the floor again. "There are going to have to be changes round here, and when we get to grandads."

"Yes, we've decided," Peri took over, "You've been running about for us long enough. No more waiting on us, Oh we know you love it, but it's time for us to fetch our own drinks, and run around for you more."

Both nodded to each other, shook hands, faced Auntie Perkins and said "Well that's that settled then. Good Night."

After the evening's upset, the relief was apparent over Doris's flushed face.

"Do I have a say in it."

"No."

"Well, what more can I say?" and she held out her arms as they both charged towards her in a three way hug. The tears in her eyes were a mixture of relief and happiness. What would she do without these lovely girls?

CHAPTER 8

Fica was angry. She knew she was being thwarted at every opportunity. So let them play their little games, if they tried to draw her to a specific area, she would not go, and soon they would give up thinking she had lost interest for good. At first she had been annoyed that she felt she had Shane in her grasp, but later wasn't sure of what she had experienced, and what she thought was his image was possibly only an illusion created for one of two things. It could either have been to draw her off the scent because he was somewhere hereabouts, or some playful entities had homed into her thoughts and had been having a game with her all along. In her deliberations, it didn't cross her reckoning that these couldn't have been just mere meddlesome spirits, because the total effect had to be produced by something greater, therefore Shane was important. So for now she was feeling lost and to occupy her time while she planned her next move she might as well home in on Daku for the want of a bit of entertainment.

Daku had reached the position of being almost ready to explode the earth and at this point he had no further need of this air demon. She would only be in his way now and could only be detrimental to the outcome. She could even take the credit for what he had perpetrated if it went according to plan and that was the last thing he needed or all his achievements would rate as nothing and he would again be ridiculed for his failure, never to rise again.

He tried to anticipate her presence, leaving the area just before she got there, and the fact she was tailing him proved to him that her own plans were not coming to fruition. Therefore there was no more time to be lost, he had to act now, and set off on his final check of the spots for simultaneous eruption.

The angels and also demons of the deep earth had been aware of an intermittent presence hovering over the underground lava flows. At first they gave it little attention, but when it became more frequent they began to show interest. They were always aware of tests being carried out from the mortal zone, not only concentrating on the flows but the cracks and weaknesses, but man's thirst for knowledge had it's own mark on it and was not disruptive. The observations being made by this entity was not for the benefit of man, it was like an army scouting out the opposition before making its attack. The only factor which seemed to point against this was that it was not being carried out in force, and a mere single foe could not achieve a major disaster. Had it been one of the demon hierarchies, other high levels would have identified it immediately, so what was a lower form up to? All this was being deliberated by the high angels of the deep earth and extra sentinels were positioned to monitor the activities.

There seemed to be no set plan, no route, so to try and get in position before the demon was, at this point, not possible. It was allocated to Eeron of the deep earth to guard an area in the Atlantic Ocean just off the coast of Africa covering the Canary Islands, an archipelago produced by volcanic eruptions. On Tenerife, Mount Teide which is one of the largest volcanoes in the world had been visited more than usual of late and this with many other specific sites were chosen for close watch. Sentinels were posted all over the globe, and at the first indication of any change, messages were sent to the high angels for them to try and organise a way to halt any attempt at disruption.

The deep earth demons were also trying to determine the source, for if anything was to threaten the structure of the planet, it would also affect their present home and surroundings, and although not known for working in conjunction with the angels, they were fearful of any change which would be perilous so whilst letting the good forces do most of the work, they also posted their own little watchers. If Daku had only known the attention he was attracting, he would probably have been delighted in one way, but he must not be identified until it was all over. So he flitted at speed, hiding in the heat and flames, darting about so as not to be traced.

The constant trailing of Fica was getting in the way of his movements and he was afraid she would be also becoming noticeable. He tried sending her off on wide goose chases on the pretence that the lad was in a certain area, but she had become immune to his lies and was beginning to cling to him, knowing he was planning something and not wanting to miss it. He tried telling her that she could be in charge of a certain area, well away from him, but she wasn't falling for that either. This was not what he expected or needed and he was becoming afraid that the diligence required to monitor her was getting in the way of his project. He must try and deal with her once and for all, but in their world you can't just kill off a spirit because they are annoying you. He would pause a moment to take stock, and then he must find some way of escaping her clutches. It only took a few seconds for him to form his plot. He now knew what he must do.

The twins had bought a present for Auntie Perkins' forthcoming birthday and were making their way upstairs to wrap it and sign her card. Their spirits were high as they dumped their bags on the beds and Topaz almost flopped onto hers, her back leaning against the wall. She had been feeling a bit peculiar today but didn't want to say anything as Peri had seemed so good these days, the incident with Ben long forgotten. Life had been good. Grandad and Auntie were making plans for the move and it would be a new start for them all.

"Oh I forgot the sticky tape," Peri was already going back out of the door and called over her shoulder "don't start until I get back."

Taking advantage of the twin being on her own, Fay came and took the ideal of Topaz in her arms and gently lifted her from the body. The girl was always pleased when she was in presence but sensed this was different.

"You have done well," Fay breathed into her soul, "but your job is finished here."

Topaz felt her being tense slightly. "How do you mean, done?" She looked down at her form slumped on the bed, her back resting against the wall and her head dropped forward. The truth was dawning on her.

"No, you can't, I was never told this."

"Your original allotted time is up." The thought was gentle but one part alerted Topaz.

"What do you mean, original?"

"You have completed your task for which you were sent, you have made Peri capable of fending for herself, which she wouldn't have done, had she been sent here alone."

"But I can't go yet."

Fay indicated to the bed. "We have further need of you, another situation has arisen which will give you a bit more time."

"What situation, and how long?"

Fay imparted very calmly, "All will be revealed at the right time, you know how it works. You will be given guidance as and when you need it."

"But what is happening to me now?" Topaz was becoming upset at her supposedly lifeless form beneath her.

"You aren't ill at present, but your body will develop a sickness in due course."

"Is this the way you plan things? It's barbaric."

Fay caressed the girls' spirit and said "Time to go back now?"

"What do I say to Peri?"

"Nothing, you will remember none of this, just take it as it comes."

"But what task?"

"You will find out, soon." And with that she lowered Topaz back to her form.

What may have seemed to take minutes during this communication was in fact no more than about five seconds in earth time and as her sister came rushing back into the room, Topaz was still unconscious. A slight scream brought Doris up the stairs.

"What is it? What's happened?" She appeared in the room wondering what she would find, and the sight of Topaz out cold made her gasp.

"What's happened Auntie?" Peri was leaning over the bed. "She was fine a minute ago."

A slight stir made them give a sigh of relief but their attention was on bringing the girl round from her faint.

Peri was almost crying "Look how pale she is."

"I'm ringing the doctor," Doris said firmly as she went to go down stairs, "just keep your eye on her."

Topaz tried to reach out her hand "No, I don't need a doctor, I just passed out that's all." But Doris was already downstairs.

"What happened?" Peri was stroking her hand, "you don't normally pass out like that."

"Don't know. One minute you were going to fetch the tape and that's all I know."

"Can I get you anything, drink of water?"

"Just a sip, I feel a bit sicky."

Peri was almost in tears feeling very useless and trying her utmost to do something to help. She was just helping her twin to a drink when Doris came back.

"Doctor's coming out, he won't be long, says to keep you quiet and leave you where you are, and not to give you anything."

"Oh." Peri almost snatched the cup away.

"Don't worry, I only had a sip." Topaz assured her, then turning to Doris said, "Sorry about this."

"Now don't you go apologising, it's not your fault." But something in her expression could have been interpreted as a knowing look.

Digby had been told and was round at the house in minutes. Doris kept him downstairs and said that the girl was feeling a bit rough and best left alone until the doctor had been. Her sister was with her and that was enough, but assured him she knew he was there.

"But what could have caused it?" he asked "I don't know much about these things but isn't she past that funny age, you know what I mean?"

"Oh there's more to the female side than you'll ever need to know my man, so let's just leave it to the doctor shall we?"

A knock on the door sent Doris hurrying to open it.

"Oh Good Evening doctor, it was good of you to come." She beckoned him to follow her upstairs and it was soon obvious that they would not all fit into the room comfortably.

Quickly he said "I'd like to have a word with the young lady with maybe just one of you here if that's all right."

Topaz said that perhaps Doris might be better, aware that Peri was a bit over emotional now.

"Would you go and sit with Grandad and tell him I'm OK?" She indicated to Peri that she had made up her mind and would like her to get on with it. Reluctantly she went downstairs but as soon as she reached the room she burst into tears and Digby had to console her, trying to assure her that Topaz would be all right soon and perhaps it was something she ate."

The doctor asked a few questions and left a small sample bottle which he instructed should be filled in the morning and taken to the surgery. He was pretty sure he knew what the results would be but had to do the usual tests, which in turn would only confirm Doris' earlier suspicions.

Tony was becoming very confused with the recent change in his feelings. It did occur to him at one point that he may be loosing his mind and would end up like Jane but he pushed the thoughts away. One thing he did notice was that everything went along smoothly as long as he made no contact with the outside world. If he visited Digby, he had an overwhelming urge to return home and found himself looking at his watch continually. When the vicar had called to see him, Jane had overtaken his will and kept him in the bedroom until the visitor had gone. She wanted him to have no-one but her and it was very unsettling. He didn't know for sure she was behind this change but he could find no other explanation and he knew that he needed help of some kind, either spiritual or medical.

His hand went out to the telephone and he found difficulty pressing the buttons to dial Desmond's number. The receiver although very light was becoming extremely heavy and as he heard "Hello, Reverend Conway speaking" the instrument was snatched from his hand and flung to the floor. He picked it up calling into it but all he heard was a crackling noise which obliterated any voice on the other end. It was his intention to redial but as he sat there composing himself the phone rang, it was Desmond.

"Hello Tony, is everything all right?"

"Yes… yes thank you, I just rang you."

"I know, I did a 'last number called' and saw it was you. Are you sure nothing is the matter?" At that point Desmond heard a distinct whisper over Tony's voice.

"Leave him alone. He doesn't need you."

Desmond realised he was up against something which needed to be removed and hoped Graham was in presence to pick up on it immediately. Not wanting to aggravate whatever or whoever it was he just said "OK talk to you later" and put the phone down.

This was more for Tony's safety than anything. He suspected the presence was Jane, but would not form a definite opinion until higher sources could confirm it. If it was the wife, at least Tony should be safe as all she wanted was to be with him. He had heard of such cases, but when born of a sick mind or spirit the love turns into possession and has to be removed, permanently. But that was a job for one more experienced in that field than he. Making up his mind to visit the man as soon as possible, he tidied his desk and saying a prayer for the immediate safety of all concerned he took his bag and set off.

The angels in presence to guard the husband had long since alerted the higher levels and plans were already in place for Jane to be removed to a safe area well away from the earth until such time that Tony would join her in the natural course of things. She had not become totally earthbound yet so now was the time to act. A small group of six spirits surrounded her, calming her spiritual being into submission before they carefully lifted her away from the cottage, far up from the earth and positioned her in a safe caring holding area where she would stay in a peaceful state for as long as required. Had she taken a firm hold, it may have been impossible to remove her and her effects on Tony would have made his life a living hell.

As Desmond reached Tony's place he felt the absence of any unwanted force and was glad when Tony greeted almost immediately.

"I'm so glad to see you, do come in." He opened the door wide and beckoned the Reverend inside.

Without any small talk Desmond said "Things have changed, everything is at peace in here."

"How can you tell?"

"When I came before, there was a feeling of being pushed away, and you didn't answer the door but you were in."

Shamefaced Tony admitted that had happened but Desmond said "Don't feel bad about it. There are some pretty powerful forces around, but you are free, I can feel it."

When they sat talking, Tony admitted he had wanted to speak to him or Digby but later felt he couldn't, and then he didn't want to confide in anyone. Desmond wasn't going to alarm Tony with his thoughts on the matter, especially if it was all over, so he continued "We do get these strange things sometimes, especially in older places," then almost as an afterthought "ever considered maybe moving to a newer place?"

Tony smiled. "You know, that may not be such a bad idea. New outlook, lay some of the sadder memories to rest."

The atmosphere in the cottage was the best he could remember for a long time, in fact when he thought about it, possibly the best since Shane's death. The vicar had been right, he would look for somewhere else and make a fresh start. He touched Shane's picture.

"What do you think son?" The look on the lad's face was the nearest one could get to a smile.

CHAPTER 9

There was an unusual stillness in the living room. Doris was deep in thought and the twins looked from one to another than back at her, then to Digby whose face was still in shock. Peri broke the silence with almost a whisper.

"Pregnant? You can't possibly be pregnant."

Topaz shrugged and nodded, still keeping her attention on the two older people.

"Well," Doris slapped her hands onto her knees and said "what's done's done, no use weeping over it. We will just have to cope that's all."

"Auntie! You don't mean that?" Peri was flabbergasted. "I would have thought you would have been cross."

"Well, I can't say I'm pleased about it but things have changed. In my young day she'd have been thrown out and had to go and get married and live in another village to save us from the shame of it." Then turning to Digby she said "It's your great grandchild after all, your flesh and blood, we've got to make sure it's all right, especially after what these two went through. Got to give it a starting chance."

Digby spoke for the first time "We haven't heard much from you young lady. What have you got to say for yourself?"

Again Topaz shrugged, but looking at Doris asked "You knew didn't you?"

The shock showed on the faces of the other two.

"Well why didn't you say something Auntie?" Peri was going from one moment of disbelief to another.

"Of course I didn't actually know, I just guessed that's all." And not wanting to be the butt of the enquiry said "But that's not getting us anywhere."

"What I would like to know is who the father is." Digby's words were very slow and precise.

"Doesn't matter." Topaz was looking down now, not wanting to meet anyone's direct gaze.

"Excuse me, it does very much matter."

"Look Grandad, it's not going to make any difference."

"Oh, and why not may I ask?"

"It just isn't that's all there is to it." And Topaz curled herself up in as tight a ball as possible and hid her face.

Peri, although still shocked felt she had to offer something.

"Topaz, if Auntie and Grandad are standing by you, shouldn't you at least tell them. It's only fair after all."

If she expected her sister to sit there and divulge all, she was disappointed for the girl jumped to her feet and ran out of the room, her face covered with her hands.

"Oh just leave her for a bit," Doris knew better than to try to extract information when a young person was in that state, "just give her a while. This hasn't been easy for her."

"And you think it is easy for us?" Digby waved his hand around the three of them in a useless gesture.

"Of course I don't, I'm sure we're all as upset as you are and she gave Peri a nod which was asking for her agreement.

"We are Grandad, but we will all stick together, won't we Auntie?"

"Of course we will." She turned her full attention to Peri "Give her a little while then you could just go and sit with her, might not be so embarrassing if there's just you."

When Peri had gone upstairs, Digby took Doris's hand as she sat beside him.

"There's not many folk would do what you do for these girls, and I do appreciate it."

"Oh get on with you now, and she gave his hand a playful slap, they've become like my own. And I wouldn't turn her out then would I?"

"All the same, I've been thinking."

Doris noticed a slightly more relaxed man and said "Now you be careful."

Digby managed a smile but looked serious.

"All this has made me take stock. They're growing up, got their own lives to lead soon. What about us?"

"What *about* us?"

Digby coughed uneasily now. "Well, you will be moving over to my place and we aren't letting the babby go anywhere, so......"

Doris felt this needed a push. ""And?"

"Well, there are only three bedrooms, and the twins wanted to share, and the little room could be made into a nursery and........." Digby was going all round to get to his question.

Again Doris tried to lighten the tone. "And you want me to go and sleep in the garage!"

"No, for heavens sake!" Then he saw her smile, plucked up his courage and said "We could always have the room I'm in now, only sort of, well we could get married, then it would all be right and decent."

She laughed now. "Well, I never thought I would be proposed to so I didn't have to sleep rough."

He was beginning to see the humour and his smile was warm when he said

"I've grown very fond of you Doris, I think you know that, and we get on well."

"It will be nice to have such a gentlemanly companion in my later years, and I've been fond of you too, for a very long time."

Now it was his turn to sit with his mouth dropped open. "You never said."

"Wouldn't have been the thing to do. But I knew that in time if you felt the same, well, I hoped that's all."

It was a good job the twins didn't see the kiss that followed.

The girls had been talking quietly for some moments, but the subject of the father kept coming to the fore.

"But you know and you won't say." Peri was getting impatient. "What difference does it make now? Oh does he know?"

Topaz shook her head.

"Well he ought to help pay for it, the upkeep I mean. It's not fair that Auntie and Grandad should fork out."

"Look let's just leave it."

Peri suddenly had a brainwave. "You'll have to put it on the birth certificate."

"Why? I'll just say father unknown."

"Oh great. Then everyone will think you've had so many you don't know which one it was. Wonderful!" This was sarcastic for Peri, but she was having to grow up fast.

"Trust me, you wouldn't like it."

This was a new twist, and Peri stopped fiddling with her hair and looked Topaz straight in the eye."

"You can't say that without telling me now. Because I won't stop pestering you until you do. And, I will tell Auntie."

"Oh stop sounding like an infant." Then mockingly "I'm telling on you da da da da da da."

Peri was in a huff now and sat on her bed with her arms folded. Topaz said "Look, if Grandad knew he would know the family could well afford to pay and he would make sure they did. But the son would deny it."

"But it can be proven with DNA tests, you know that, so why are you stalling. Hey, wait a minute! Well off did you say?" Then after a pause "Please Topaz, tell me I'm wrong."

"Don't have to. I wondered how long it would take you."

Peri was close to tears "Not him, how could you?"

"How could I what?"

"Go with him, you knew I liked him."

Topaz sighed then said "If you will listen a minute, I'll explain it."

There were some loud sniffs, possibly for effect, then a sullen Peri said "Go on then, I might as well hear all the dirt."

"It was before you went out with him, I'd found out what he was like and I did try to put you off, but you thought I was jealous. I knew you would have to grow up and find out for yourself, but I was pretty sure you could take care of yourself, which you did."

"But he phoned and explained."

"Oh yes, he's good at charming the family, that's why he gets away with so much, nobody believes anything against him."

Peri was musing now. "You know, when some of the girls reckoned they had been with him, I thought they were just kidding, doing it to look good. Did they all do it with him then?"

Topaz gave one of her laughs "Ha. Some, but some only said it, as you say, because they didn't want the others to think they hadn't been asked or he just didn't fancy them. After all he is tasty, until you get to know him."

After another moments' deliberation Peri ventured "What I can't understand is when you did it. You never went out with him.

"Oh Peri. The opportunity is always there if you make it."

"Was it just the once?"

"You'll be asking me to draw you a diagram next."

"But was it?"

"No! OK?"

There was a silence for a while whilst both gathered their wits. So much seemed to be changed in such a short time. Peri was shocked to learn so much about her twin she didn't know but Topaz was cross with herself at her slip up, little knowing this was in the greater plan of things.

Daku had to act now or his chance would be gone for ever. He had noticed how much he was being observed and knew that a plan must be in place for his demise, so this was it, zero hour, good bye Earth.

To try and throw his watchers off the scent of his next move, he had selected several random points to trigger all over the globe to avoid a pre-emptive attack. He was about to start the effect when Fica appeared at his side.

"Go. You are out of your territory." He ordered her.

"And you think this is yours?"

"It is fire controlled, you are not wanted here."

She suspected he had something big arranged and wasn't about to leave at the exciting part.

"So this has been your little game has it? I knew you were meddling in something."

He was now becoming side tracked. He hadn't bargained on this intrusion at the vital moment, he had to loose her and fast, for how could he take the glory if she was there, and worse still, what if she ruined it all just for her own self praise.

They were positioned over Mount Teide and he made the snap decision to descend into the mountain thus leaving her in the air sector, but she followed him like a missile. His plan was to drop into the flames he was about to cause and she would have to escape and return to the air above. Faster he went until he was riding the lava flow beneath the surface. This gave him the satisfaction that her ideal could not remain in this environment, surely she must have departed by now.

The commotion was just what Eeron of the deep earth was waiting for. This was his chance to right the wrong which had been haunting him since snatching Shane from the hands of the demons. Now he had the chance to be the one to crush the meddlesome fire demon and make amends for his unforgivable error. He didn't seek the glory or any recognition; it would put his own soul at rest knowing he had done his bit to save the planet from possible explosion.

Daku was still descending at such a pace to rid himself of the air demon, he failed to notice the powers of the deep earth surrounding them. Fica was struggling now, trying to return to the surface as she was in a hostile environment, even Daku sensed this was not as easy as he had hoped. Although the heat aided him, the effect of the earth's crust was slowing him down to a crawl. Hideous screams echoed around the entire area as the two felt themselves being overcome by the earth forces, hating and blaming each other for being in this predicament.

Slowly the powers of the deep earth dragged the unwilling souls lower and lower until the pressure started to fragment each one. Their ideals were no longer in tact, but spread far and wide across the barriers of this unknown realm holding them apart. How much they were aware of, or which part of them held any reasoning can only be surmised.

They would both be held for an unknown time in this state, but if the theory that 'matter can neither be created nor destroyed, it only changes its form' is correct, the same could be applied to the next dimension, so the two entities are still in existence in some state which can be reformed at another point in time. A likeness can be drawn with mercury. It will run round a sample dish in one piece, but spit it up and it will run round in little balls. When it meets, it rejoins and it is not possible to see where one little ball starts or ends. So it will be with Daku and Fica. When all the minute pieces come together, the spirit will reform, but whether or not the pieces are in the previous place is doubtful, so the question is, what kind of entity it will produce. The other question is all a matter of time.

If the star of this galaxy, the sun has an expected remaining life of approximately five billion years, will the earth have that long a life which means they could both be trapped until then? Again, with the moon moving away, the Earth will become unstable, and while this could have a drastic effect on the surface, it is unlikely the deep earth will give up its souls then.

For now, everything was at peace in the various earth areas, the balance of things had equalled and the sentinels reported that calm reigned. The volcanoes had been returned to their natural function, the earth dwellers had all found a way of dealing with their own problems and the spirits in situ were ever watchful for the smallest threat to the area from whatever angle.

Tony had found a small bungalow which just suited his needs, Digby and Doris had married and all were living happily under one roof. Peri had become more able to stand on her own two feet and enjoyed fussing over Topaz who was now nearing the birth of her child which she had been told was a girl. Jane was far from the earth and being rehabilitated in readiness for Tony's arrival which was several earth years away, but time was nothing in that existence. The Reverend Desmond Conway went about his duties relieved that the happenings had seemed to have dispersed, but always aware that nothing stays stable for long between the worlds.

Shane was waiting patiently, for he knew his chance was imminent and nothing must get in the way to spoil it. A guiding arm slipped around his ideal.

"Time to go now Shania."

THE END

UKBookland gives you the opportunity to purchase all of the books published by UKUnpublished.

Do you want to find out a bit more about your favourite UKUnpublished Author?

Find other books they have written?

PLUS – UKBookland offers all the books at Excellent Discounts to the Recommended Retail Price!

You can find UKBookland at www.ukbookland.co.uk

Find out more about **Tabbie Browne** and her books.

Are you an Author?

Do you want to see your book in print?

Please look at the UKUnpublished website:
www.ukunpublished.co.uk

Let the World Share Your Imagination

Lightning Source UK Ltd.
Milton Keynes UK
UKOW05f1911290414

230812UK00001B/4/P